MURDER ON THE INTERSTELLAR EXPRESS

BELL BEGRUDGINGLY SOLVES IT

MURDER ON THE INTERSTELLAR EXPRESS

GREGORY D. LITTLE

Cursed Dragon Ship Publishing, LLC

6046 FM 2920 Rd, #231, Spring, TX 77379

captwyvern@curseddragonship.com

Cover art © 2024 by Tithi Luadthong

Cover design © 2024 by Lena Shore

Developmental Edit by Kelly Lynn Colby

Copy Edit by S.G. George

ISBN 978-1-951445-74-4

ISBN 978-1-951445-75-1 (ebook)

For Debbie, who for years has been telling me to "write a funny book." This was the result.

CONTENTS

CHAPTER 1
SHOOTING THE MESSENGER

THE SUN WAS AS ETERNALLY bright as always, the sky was rusty orange, and Bell was on her way to court to be arraigned for crimes against humanity.

They were not *real* crimes against humanity. Hers were, Bell's lawyer kept insisting, the kind of crimes against humanity people only trotted out to make a political point. You pled guilty, then they self-importantly fired you from your cushy public service job. Then you'd wrangle with the courts for a few months or years until you got your pension restored, after the press had forgotten about everything.

Since this was the outcome Bell viewed as most favorable to her current life goals, she wasn't too fussed about a little fuss upfront. So, she walked to her court date with more of a spring in her step than her circumstances—or even Anaranjado's relatively low gravity—could really account for. It was fine. She had the plea-deal in place and everything. Today would just make it official.

"I see her!" Bell's cluster of audio processing units picked a recognizable voice out from the general hubbub. For all but the very wealthiest of residents, to be alive on Anaranjado was to be at least partly cybernetic, and Bell was a more extreme example of that than basically anyone, which had both advantages and disadvantages in times like these.

"Oh, fuck." Bell had never had much of an opinion on paparazzi until very recently. Now she ranked them with organized religion and Harmony as the very worst concepts the colonists had brought with them from Earth. This was her particular group of five, and they did their best to follow her everywhere.

It was her hair they cued in on every damn time. She'd meant to bring a hat to try and gather up the white, dandelion-seed mess sprouting from her head in every direction. Then she'd walked right out her door without it, probably because deep down she'd resented the notion of having to disguise herself just to walk along the fucking street.

"This is fine," she said to herself. She sped up as much as the crowd let her. At two-point-five-ish meters, she was above average for an Anaranjadan, but not so much so that she could just force her way through a crowd fighting like hell to get to work for some reason.

At least she wasn't having to negotiate the teeming throngs with bulky broadcasting equipment.

"Why don't you vultures wait an hour and then you can report on my case being dismissed?" she shouted back over her shoulder. That was dumb. Fucking stupid. It would come back to bite her. Cockiness in the face of these kinds of charges generally tended to. The case wasn't *going* to be dismissed. But they were awful garbage-people who deserved to be fucked with. If not her, who?

"Ms. Beauregard! Do you have a statement?"

"Bell, Bell! Talk to us. We want to hear your side."

"We can't debunk rumors if you won't answer our questions."

"Are you worried you've drawn Judge Heller?"

"What did the aliens say, Bell? What did you talk about with them?"

"I told them," Bell called back, finally getting downright rude in her attempts to gain ground through the crowd, "that if they were going to eat us, they should start with you all. I gave them all your contact information." The Fuckhead Five—as she liked to think of them—had made a real mistake when they'd provided Bell with every last bit of their contact info in exchange for her promising to *think* about giving an interview. They'd all fallen for it. She'd made good use of it. "Then I looked up all your parents and faked a message to each of them this morning telling them they were going to be grandparents. You should be hearing from them soon!"

The aliens-eating-them thing wasn't true. But the grandparents thing was.

"You *what*?" Louise exclaimed from the crowd. She didn't shout the next bit, but Bell was still able to parse it. "Oh no, thirty-seven messages."

Laughing maniacally, Bell waded further through the crowd.

The court complex occupied a sizable block of the governmental portion of the Meridian Cities. Three domed-over engine nozzles of mind-deleting size erupted like three giant warts—the universe's worst STI—from the massive rift valley which dominated one side of the tiny planet from equator to middle latitudes. The human colonists had found the structures already in place when they'd arrived from Earth, and rumor had it that if all three were fired, it was enough to alter the planet's orbit, though they were very nonfunctional now.

Satisfied that doing so wouldn't send their previously owned planet spiraling inward into its parent star and desiring very much not to die, the colonists had co-opted all three structures, ultimately designating the northernmost one for government works, but governmental types were not as valued as the rich, Equatorian fat cats in the central structure sitting squarely on the equator, so the atmospheric dome surrounding the northern unit didn't do anything fancy beyond keep air in and block out the most lethal portion of the sun's light and radiation.

Not that Bell was concerned as far as air and sieverts were concerned. She'd traded a heart and lungs for power cells years back, and skin for protective scales even earlier.

This high up, the fact that the engine sat upon the planet's terminator—the permanent and unchanging band of twilight separating Sunnyside from Shadyside—didn't matter. A monstrous wedge of the colony's angry, orange parent star, Naranja, could be seen over the horizon at all times of day or night, however much the latter word applied here—the joys of tidally locked planets knew no bounds.

Bell preferred her rift valley–shaded apartment lower down to Naranja's permanent temper tantrum. The people around her were a sea of thermal-regulation upgrades. Clothing wasn't enough. The dome wasn't enough. Nobody poor enough to have exposure to the light or heat of Naranja, even occasionally, had baseline human skin. The central of the three engine-cities, the one reserved for ultra-rich assholes who ran the planet, got extra protections their lowly lessers did not.

It sucked balls.

Still, the thought of never having to go to work again kept Bell's laughter going. The truth was she had been meaning to quit her job since her second day, which had been . . . ten years ago? That couldn't be right. But her computational module did the math without being asked, because it was rude like that. Bell did her best to starve it of numbers as a matter of principle, so it was always bored and cranky.

Ten years, it insisted. The number flashed red in her HUD in a way that felt more like a taunt than was strictly necessary. Ten years almost to the day. It even pulled data from the city net down and forced her to look at horrifying photos of work functions in which a gradually more cybernetic Bell always lurked uncomfortably in the background, her shock of pure white hair marking her out no matter how much she tried to go unnoticed.

A decade on the job. This fact appalled her. Under other circumstances Bell would have chided herself that she really should have been getting on with that whole "quitting" thing. However, given that she was even now approaching the court building, self-loathing hardly seemed worth the effort. She should have done her job properly and been accused of crimes against humanity as a result years ago.

Instead, Bell resolved to punish her computational module's impertinence by finding a grammar textbook to read just as soon as she wrapped up this whole trial thing. It would be for one of the really dumb, counterintuitive languages, like English. She'd read it slowly, savoring it with her actual eyes. It would take months, with not a number or logical rule in sight. She could almost feel the module quailing in dread. Delicious.

At last Bell fought free of the crowd. She crossed through the faux-imposing courthouse double doors, done up in some eye-rolling gothic style to inspire a sense of awe and majesty and oh dog, she couldn't even finish the mental analysis.

Instead she noticed that the air screens hovering in front of every wall of the atrium broadcasted nonstop coverage of the arrival of the New Calgarians. Under normal circumstances, that would have made her happy. The only reason she had five reporters dogging her heels instead of five hundred was because of the refugee crisis / invasion. But she'd already caught a glimpse of her own image as well. Superimposed over her face was the question on everyone's mind.

BELLEROPHONA BEAUREGARD: CASSANDRA OR COLLABORATOR?

Cassandra, obviously, fuckwads. Bell was way past used to being the smartest one in the room, and yes, sometimes that meant knowing something bad was going to happen and being cursed with too many idiots surrounding her to be believed like some figure out of Greek myth. Bad enough the alliteration was cheesy as hell, but what was with that picture? Apparently they'd caught her mid-sneeze. She told herself she was imagining the gaze of every other person in the atrium following her as she walked. But both she and the reporters had been pretty loud.

The air screen went on, listing casualty numbers in the Ashrock skirmish and analyzing the nature of the planet's invaders, or at least whatever drabs the Equatorian richies let slip. Reacting to Bell's recent net searches, her algorithms tried to force the news to the front of her awareness. Bell restricted their access, hastily erecting mental keyword blocks in an attempt to tune it out.

Heh, *erecting*.

The information stream pivoted instantly in response to her restrictions. It now brought her updates and images of the colony ship *Ultima Thule,* addressing some kind of rumors that had begun swirling about it in the past few days. Bell angrily nixed those keywords as well, because the rumors inevitably circled back to the sort-of invasion that was so inconveniencing her entire world. Meaning her name was destined to resurface.

She made a disgusted noise. If everyone on Anaranjado was intent on blaming her for this flaming shit-heap clusterfuck, there was nothing she could do about that. Nothing but cash out and disappear into a long-desired and almost-deserved early retirement—ideally into as deep a hole as she could find.

Well, not *too* deep. That would mean the Shadyside tunnels, and her final upgrades—the ones that were the most questionable in terms of legality—had come from down there. And the parties responsible for procuring and installing those upgrades might not be best pleased to see her again.

Excuse me for trying to help you, asshats. She meant it both for the weirdo cultists who had done her upgrades and the colony's population at large. *Ungrateful planet full of bleating sheep waiting to be bled dry for mutton.*

Bell forced herself back to calm. Harmony—source of the sheepery she so despised—wasn't technically the colonists' fault. She had to remind herself of that daily.

The doors into Courtroom One were nearly as imposing as the exterior doors had tried to be. Only, for some reason, it worked a little better on Bell this time.

That's just the news getting to you.

Rather than recessing into the walls like sensible doors, these swung open on silent hinges at her approach. Her lawyer had worked hard to impress upon Bell the importance of decorum within the confines of the courtroom. Bell had, in turn, told him to go sit on a cactus, one of the really big ones they grew in domed greenhouses. They had agreed to disagree.

Fuck it. I'm doing the dance. She'd prepared it specially for him, an extremely undignified little jig to perform in the courtroom, just to see if she could shine his scales a little. It wasn't as if she was making him work for this case.

But when she turned her gaze on their seats, wearing her best shit-eating grin, the expression died on her face. Bell was only just on time

—which was a minor miracle, as anyone who knew her could attest—but of Anthony Maldonado, Esq. there was no sign.

Recovering clumsily into a face of fragile solemnity, Bell made her way quickly to her seat, hoping that none of the flashes going off in the periphery of her vision had caught her gob-smacked expression.

Their shared table wasn't totally empty. Where Anthony should have been was a flattened disc she recognized as a holoprojector. Bell ground her teeth. She knew she hadn't given him much to do, but the idea he wasn't even going to attend her arraignment in person set her teeth on edge. She briefly considered taking her frustration out on the device, when it sprang to life the instant she sat down.

"Hiya, kid. Ready to be done with this thing yet?"

CHAPTER 2
OUT OF THE SOLAR SYSTEM

BELL HAD LIKED Anthony Maldonado the moment she'd met him. Mainly that had been due to his rumpled nature, with poorly fitting clothes and hair nearly as un-styled as Bell's own, which was a lot. He was also covered in protective scales, a testament to his working-class background.

It all lent Anthony a kind of earnest authenticity. Here was a man so focused on the well-being of his clients that he could barely take care of himself. Bell was very well versed in barely taking care of herself and being amazing in all other aspects of her life—her job excluded on a technicality—so she could appreciate this quality of the man.

These early impressions of Anthony were why the three-dimensional image projected before her now shook her so badly. The holo-projector was good. It almost looked like Anthony was sitting beside her, *the way he really should have been.* Wherever he actually was, Anthony Maldonado's suit was no longer a rumpled, hanging thing, but crisp and white, and the scales of his skin were polished to a fine sheen in a way that made Bell's, so in need of a buff, seem less like an indictment of the fashion and beauty industries and more like an indictment of Bell's capacity to function as an adult.

And she was already dealing with a rather more serious indictment.

Regardless, Bell had never seen Anthony so put together. But of course, that only stood to reason. Surely if he were going to go all-out on his appearance in only one place, it would be in the courtroom. Likely he only had one really nice suit, and this was what he saved it for. But part of her couldn't shake the unsettling notion he'd become a different person since the last time they'd met.

"Relax, kid," he said, misreading Bell's anxiety. "Just like we practiced, and it will all be over." And he at least behaved like the man she'd gotten to know over the past two weeks, so maybe there was nothing to worry about.

She didn't have time to respond, though, because the bailiff, a man nearly as tall as Bell, intoned for the benefit of the murmuring crowd. "All rise. This court is now in session. The Honorable Judge Halford Heller presiding."

Bell did as bidden, forgetting in her sudden bout of nerves to act like she didn't care. All the sense of languid ease she wished she could muster was possessed by Judge Heller as he entered from the back of the courtroom.

He was tall, if not quite as tall as the bailiff. His lean face made Bell think of a fox, a creature no one alive on this world had ever seen except as pictures and videos left over from Earth. Heller was infamous in his reputation as a stern administrator of justice, yet he managed to stay popular among the citizenry even though he'd sent more than his fair share to Defective labor camps. Bell suspected this was because of his appearance.

Unlike most of the Equatorians, the skin of Judge Heller's face was as swathed in protective scales as Anaranjadans who stood far below him on the social ladder. Whether it was affectation or the uncorrected result of a youth of more modest means—online records about his history were spotty at best—it leant him a strange credibility with ordinary people that the baseline human skin most Equatorians sported didn't.

Heller's eyes, an arresting turquoise, scanned the crowded courtroom as though looking for familiar faces. They did not linger on Bell any longer than they did any other face, and yet she felt unaccountably *seen* by them. She had to suppress a shiver, but that might have been because Heller's entry into the courtroom had marked the severing of Bell's connection to the wider city net—and that of everyone else in the courtroom—cut off as dampers were activated to signal the start of session.

Anthony had warned Bell this would happen, yet she still found it unsettling. It was like being lobotomized. Not that she had experience with that. Although, technically, she did. She'd had parts of her brain scooped out lots of times when she was under the care of the Shadyside Weirdos. They'd just always immediately been replaced by cybernetic modules replicating the lost functions before she'd even wakened.

Best not to dwell on that little violation of law, however. She was in enough trouble as it was.

The only good thing about the cutoff was it signaled a respite from the constant attempts to intrude upon her brain by malware. That was how she thought of the constant pleas for charity or other acts of generosity the citizens of Anaranjado were bombarded with on a minute-by-minute basis. She relaxed a degree almost without realizing it as the encrypted portions of her thoughts and memories were, for this brief window, unmolested by overeager do-goodery. Bell always forgot the little thread of stress those constant external attacks kept alive in her, like a fire that just would not stop smoldering.

"Be seated," Judge Heller said. Bell had researched him as thoroughly as her short attention span and predilection toward boredom would allow, so his vocal tics didn't surprise her. She still found the strangely formal, almost archaic sound of his voice comforting to her on some brain-stem level. Perhaps that was another part of his popular appeal. His accent was rooted firmly in the southern parts of the ancient United States of America, deep and resonant, and it had held up far better than most accents she heard this many generations removed from Earth. It was usually child's play for Bell to listen to a person talk and process their regional ancestry based on the particular mishmash of dialects making up the stew of their voice, but with Heller, she didn't even have to try.

The courtroom seated with some shuffling and clicking of footwear, then fell silent. Bell expected some amount of pre-plead ceremonial bullshittery. Nobody liked pomp more than the courts. But in this she was disappointed.

"Bellerophona Beauregard," Judge Heller said, finally directing his gaze firmly upon Bell and not missing a beat with her full name, which was a feat unto itself. "You stand accused of crimes against the good people of this world in the form of sending a message to entities of extraterrestrial origin, an absolutely forbidden action under any circumstances as stipulated by Colony Charter and a list of subsequent laws, regulations, and strictures so numerous I would have had to begin yesterday to cite them all and keep us on schedule."

The courtroom erupted in titters. Bell mentally added "thinks he's a comedian" to her internal picture of Heller.

Bell opened her mouth to say that it wasn't *extraterrestrial*, that the message had come from another of Earth's colony worlds and had been clearly labeled as such by the computer algorithms to one who knew how to recognize such things. She started at a strange tingling on her forearm and looked over to see the Anthony-gram reaching out as if to restrain her, the image vanishing as it contacted her arm.

"You have something to say, Ms. Beauregard?" Judge Heller asked, one eyebrow raised and the beginnings of a smile on his face. "I haven't yet gotten to the part where your reply is required, but if you are eager to speak, I will indulge you."

It took every ounce of Bell's self-control, plus some borrowed from the future at exorbitant interest rates, not to blurt out a heated defense of her actions. But at Anthony's pleading look, she fought the urge to a bitter stalemate.

"No, Your Honor." Bell considered it a victory she'd managed to un-grit her teeth before getting the words out.

"I see. Well, this is a very grave charge. Very grave indeed, particularly given our colony's current situation stemming from that regrettable act of first contact."

"None of that was my fault!" Bell blurted out heatedly. Oh well. "They knew we were here. They knew exactly where to send the message. They used *Bridge* technology for dog's sake. Instantaneous transit. That's old Earth tech. *Plus* they'd have needed our exact coordinates and orbital information to manage that. Even if none of the other identifying factors held up, those two things alone would be enough to identify them as colonial in origin. I had no way of knowing they were—"

She cut off at the frantic tingles of the Anthony-gram slapping at her, his image vanishing wherever it made contact, his holo-face exasperated.

"I must say, Ms. Beauregard, this is both not how I expected this proceeding to go and *exactly* how I expected it to go." Far from being annoyed at her outburst, the judge was decidedly unruffled—even amused! Bell supposed she should be thankful, however much it annoyed her when contrasted against her own behavior. Mostly she just wanted to deck him. "But since you insist on experiencing these proceedings out of order—and yes, I mean that in more than one sense—in your own statement, you recognized that signal was both an automated one and was spoken in a voice that was 'trying hard to sound like a human yet definitely wasn't a human. It was really creepy.'"

After another round of titters that wrapped the courtroom's gallery, Bell found she wished Heller had refrained from quoting her directly.

"And yet, despite knowing these things right away, you elected to actively respond, to demonstrate to them that we were, in fact, here and listening. And I'm sure you remember what happened next."

Bell did. Even coma patients knew by now. Unconsciously avoiding Heller's gaze, Bell caught a glimpse of the prosecutor, a haughty woman who looked only a jumbo-sized bucket of popcorn shy of having a grand old time watching her favorite movie. She didn't have to do jack-shit today. Not with Halford-fucking-Heller running things.

"That's right," Heller said, as though Bell had responded. "Just two standard weeks later, these 'creepy, definitely not humans' opened up a Bridge portal between our two worlds for a second time. This one, however, was a full portal, one capable of transmitting matter, and they arrived in force. And given that this was just a few days ago, I would think that memory would be quite fresh in your mind. Does that sum up the sequence of events?" Heller spoke as though Bell were the only other one in the room and the room was the principal's office and he was the principal.

Bell glanced at Anthony-gram, whose exasperation had reached god-tier.

"Don't look at me. You have to answer him now," he whispered.

"I was afraid by what I heard," Bell said, already dreading she'd ruined her plea deal, that she'd tripped over her own damned foot on the way to the best future she could hope for and was about to face-plant her way into a Defective labor camp. Even without her communications fuckup, there was ample justification for locking her away in one of *those*—if anyone knew more than they should. Now here she was, not even having entered a plea and being cross-examined by the fucking judge. "So I told them in no uncertain terms not to come here."

Heller only nodded, as though this made perfect sense. He waved one hand, and an air screen sprang to life from nowhere, showing a paused vid.

"So you admit to responding actively to a communication attempt."

"No." She wasn't even certain her response had gotten through. The carrier wave had terminated the instant she'd replied, the portal snapping shut.

"To what have since been clearly identified as alien life forms of some undetermined origin."

"That's not—" But the vid had started playing, and the associated audio drowned out Bell's attempt at a response. It showed two distinct forms of alien horribleness that seemed only vaguely related to one another. One was like a giant, mutant insect nightmare, all shining-black carapace with a red undertone. The other was like a green-black worm with articulated bony spears for legs. Both were advancing on a cowering group of Anaranjadans.

The audio was all screams and horrible, squelching sounds.

Reflexively, Bell tried to will away the images by restricting keywords, but that didn't work for her eyes. With a wave, Heller froze the image, somehow finding the most horrible spot, with both creatures leaping forward, mouths agape.

"Well then, since it seems you are finished arguing, on the charge of crimes against this colony in the form of illegally contacting an alien civilization, how do you plead?"

Bell looked again to Anthony-gram, who gestured her on.

"Deal's still the deal," he whispered. "But please, no more freestyling," he added with a hiss.

"Guilty, Your Honor," Bell said, throwing her trust behind the man to give her the strength to speak the words, the very act of which felt like being bent over a barrel.

The crowd gasped in a way that would have made Bell's stomach twist up into a knot if she'd still had one.

"So be it," Judge Heller said, his formality returned. He waved the image away, as though banishing it were a reward for Bell being a good girl. "You've spared us the expense and waste of time of a trial, for which this court is grateful, so let's not waste any further time than necessary. In terms of your sentence, I've heard rumors bandied about of some kind of plea-deal, and I'd have thought our friends in the press would know me better than that."

"What?" Bell got the word out, but Heller just kept right on talking.

"This would be a grave crime even in any normal moment in our colony's life. This community, perhaps above any other human community in history, does not place the individual above the collective good. Ever. In this particular moment, considering the state we now find ourselves in as a colony, as a nation, its gravity is beyond description. Indeed, it's impossible to overstate the seriousness of what you've done, young lady."

She couldn't be hearing this. Something must be wrong with her auditory module. "They already—"

"On a world as starved for resources as ours, the prescribed punishment for a violation of this magnitude is death."

For the first time in Bell's entire life, words failed her utterly. She turned to Anthony, fighting panic, but he merely stared up at Heller, his expression expectant.

"But I am not without mercy," Heller said. "And despite some of the ravings of our friends in the press, I don't believe you acted with malicious intent."

Bell let out a gust of breath. She didn't have to breathe to live, but in one of the colony's more morbid discoveries as it had worked to ruggedize the human race, it turned out not being able to breathe made a person feel like they were drowning forever, so the ability remained to her. In fact, false-drowning was a sensation not entirely unlike what she'd just experienced emotionally.

Grandstanding. That was all the old fart was doing. Grandstanding and being publicly tough on crime at Bell's expense. *I hope he sentences me to free psychotherapy*. That had been a pretty heinous thirty seconds.

"Avoiding punishment entirely is quite impossible, of course," he said, sending Bell's metaphorical heart plunging once again. "But there is a kinder way forward. A less wasteful one. Exile."

The word hung in the air, and Bell's mind was, for a moment, utterly blank. Then the implications of that word began to rain down, and she found a strange feeling blossoming in her chest. Hope. Excitement.

All her life, what she'd wanted more than anything was to do the one thing most forbidden to Anaranjadans: to go off-world, to travel and meet the alien civilizations they all knew were just a neighborhood over, cosmically speaking. And all her life, she'd hated living in this stifling society full of forced smiles and false unity. Heller seemed to be excising her from both that and, crucially, the rules that bound it. Because if she wasn't allowed on-planet anymore, they couldn't enforce their rules, could they?

However much they might want to.

Another hint of a smile quirked Heller's mouth as he regarded the epic poem of expressions that must be playing across her face. This wasn't the deal she'd discussed with Anthony at all. It was *better*. She had no idea what was happening here, but she was going to get a chance to meet aliens. *Real* aliens. And not the kind that were invading her planet and eating her people. The civilized kind. Some of them might even be hot, might even want to b—

"You will be held in isolated custody until the scheduled launch of the *Ultima Thule*, aboard which you will journey as a member of the crew. You are hereby sentenced to spend the rest of your life in indentured servitude to first the ship and then the new colony the great people of Anaranjado seek to found."

The great architecture of hope Bell had constructed in mere moments using the dreams of her entire life as building blocks came crashing down around her into a pile of diarrhea—like a house of cards, if the cards were also dirty diapers.

"What?"

Heller's smile was like that of a predator when the prey had just realized it could not escape the closing jaws.

"Do not think it has escaped us, Ms. Beauregard, that you are guilty of far more than that to which you confessed today. Now, I don't know how the court system worked back in the days of Earth, but here on Anaranjado we take a dim view of people who have tampered with the physical structure of their brains, seeking to circumvent your duty to the sense of the collective good that every citizen of Anaranjado shares. Such an action might even put the Harmony symbiont in your head at physical risk." And, just as Bell thought this could get no worse, he went on. "Or it might, rather, if you even possessed the Harmony symbiont. *Which you do not. And never have.* And, Ms. Beauregard, this court takes an even dimmer view of that."

You could have heard a gnat shit in the courtroom.

"There are other ways to punish you for these things, Ms. Beauregard, including forcibly rewiring your *completely synthetic* thoughts until they mimic all the ways Harmony would steer you to behave. But that's not really a punishment, is it? Because once the changes take hold, you'd agree with us that it's the best way. No, I feel this punishment is *far* more suitable."

His smile was in full bloom now, the teeth closed and locked up tight.

"This is about fucking *Harmony*?" Bell said. "What kind of bait and switch is this?"

"The kind where you get to keep on living, Ms. Beauregard. As yourself. In truth, you should feel fortunate. You get to go with those lucky few who are set to pioneer a new world. Those of us who remain will face a harsh present and an uncertain future. This is a gift. But I'm afraid it's not the kind of gift you can refuse. You will go with the colony ship." He paused for dramatic emphasis. "And for once in your life actually contribute to your society."

"The fuck I will." Unfair. Unfair! She'd meant that retort for the part about going with the colony ship, then his grandstanding pause had ruined the timing of her response. Though, to be fair, it probably applied to both. "I'm not going to be some galley slave on your *SS Indentured Servitude*. Which is a shitty fake name, I know, but there's no way I can top the perfectly fascist undertones of a name like *Ultima Thule*, anyway. Either you people don't know your history or you really, *really* do."

She was babbling to stifle her panic. Desperate for any straw to grasp, Bell turned to her one and only ally. Hologram or no, Anthony would get her out of—

Anthony was gone. The projector had gone dark, powered itself down.

His absence from the courtroom. His fancy clothes. His fancy, expensive, *probably brand-fucking-new* clothes. And now, in the crucial moment, his abandonment of her.

I've been set up.

In that moment of sublime clarity and panic, Bell decided she was going to fight her way out of this courtroom. Actually, it was not so much a decision as it was her limbic simulation module sending command override codes to the rest of her brain architecture. She was running before she was consciously aware of it.

"Bailiff!" Heller's voice boomed across a courtroom thrown into turmoil by Bell's outburst. But the big man was already behind her, and monolithic as he was, Bell was willing to bet she could outrun him. She pushed her legs to their design specification limits then beyond. If she was set on becoming a fugitive, there was no sense half-assing it.

Then a uniformed figure stepped confidently out to block her path to the exit. He was, if anything, even wider than his colleague in pursuit. Worse than his breadth, though, was the light switch gun he drew smoothly from its clip on his belt.

Bell had no chance to dodge at this range. She ran through an array of amazingly defiant things to cry out, things that would immortalize her in story and song. Then she saw the amber light on the light switch gun go green and the man's trigger finger squeeze.

"Having two bailiffs is no fair," she shouted as everything went black.

CHAPTER 3
LATE TO HER OWN GOING-AWAY PARTY

THE FIRST THOUGHT Bell had was that she was asleep. "Sleep" was kind of a nebulous concept for her all-synthetic brain, but she wasn't conscious when she slept. Even Stranger still was how cold it was. Not even Shadyside-underground cold, where she'd spent all that time getting her brain replaced. This was Shadyside-*surface* cold, where nobody lived because living was impossible.

Eventually the confusion and resulting irritation were enough to snap her eyes open. Scratch that. Upon further review, they were enough to let her eyelids ooze open as though held together by tar.

What the ever-loving fuck-a-duck is wrong with me? This was like a full reboot of all her systems, something she never did unless things got *really* hinky.

The ability to focus, either on thoughts or her visual field, returned begrudgingly. But gradually Bell became aware that she was staring up at a blue-white glaze of material, within which she could see a faint reflection of her own drunk-ass-looking face.

It was one of many times she regretted telling the cultists who had carved up her brain that she still wanted to think and physically behave in nearly all the same ways she had when she'd been made of meat.

Ice, one of her modules whispered. Pattern-matching. Intuition. She couldn't tell which. *Frost,* it amended.

Cryosleep.

Oh, fuck, Bell thought. "Oh, fuck!" she shouted. The words echoed painfully inside the close confines of, what she now realized was, a cryopod. "Shit me, fuck! I'm on board the—"

"Good morning." said a painfully chipper, electronic voice. It presented as male, though at the falsetto end of that spectrum, and sounded as if it was inside the cryopod with her. "Actually, the concept of morning lacks objective meaning aboard ship. And even taking into consideration the subjective shipboard schedule, it is not, in fact, morning by *any* definition. But my conditioning suggests that wishing 'good morning' to a crew member who is just coming out of cryo-stasis is the politest way to begin a working relationship."

She was nearly as freaked out by the disembodied voice as by the fact that she was apparently *already aboard the ship*. It wasn't supposed to launch for months, if not years. She realized some part of her had been sure she'd have time to weasel her way out of the situation, find herself a new lawyer, and start an appeal.

"Who is speaking right now?" Bell asked. The voice wasn't generated by human vocal cords. That much was obvious to her linguist's ear. But it was also way too advanced for the dumb computer interfaces she was used to dealing with.

"I am the ship's brain."

Even though it was half what she'd expected to hear, the confirmation brought Bell up short.

"Anaranjado doesn't do Artificial Intelligence."

It wasn't quite a law, but a custom as strong as. Cybernetic augmentation and replacement of human body parts were both permitted and encouraged because, on a planet where growing food was next door to impossible, anything the citizenry could do to reduce overall caloric needs was preferable. Power cells were cheap to charge with access to infinite solar energy, but apples didn't like to grow in oppressive heat, abyssal cold, or a lack of surface atmosphere.

But all replacement of meat stopped at the blood-brain barrier. Harmony, the ubiquitous parasitic organism that kept people from killing each other, if you believed the brochure, needed a meat brain to live and make its puppets dance—plus some source of oxygen and nutrients for said brain.

All of which meant synthetic intelligence was more than frowned upon, lest somebody get the idea to do exactly what Bell had already done.

"I am not artificial. In fact, I am an organic brain grown for the express purpose of piloting and maintaining the ship, its passengers, and its crew."

Oh. Well, never mind all that previous stuff.

"That being said, I should warn you that the accelerated launch schedule resulted in the truncation of my conditioning period. In the interest of full disclosure, though I am organic in nature, I am currently suffering from numerous quirks which you might equate to bugs and potential exploits were I a synthetic panda bear onion grass."

"Was . . . that one of the bugs?"

"Was what one of the bugs? Did I say something nonsensical? If you would please fill out an error report, I can—"

"You know what? Never mind. I appreciate the warning. It's all very alarming. But can I get out of this pod now?" Bell's teeth were beginning to chatter. Perceiving and reacting to cold was a holdover from her meat-sack days, but some of her systems must still be in a reboot diagnostic because she was having trouble remembering how to turn off temperature sensation.

"Of course. Your cryopod diagnostics have completed, and you are operating within normal parameters. This is welcome news. You were the only member of the crew who was already unconscious when brought aboard and put into cryo-stasis, and unpredictable interactions in such scenarios have been known to—"

"Just open the pod, please!"

The pod door sprang open as if its hinge was spring-loaded.

Moving joints that shrieked with pain-simulating feedback, Bell rose, unable to stop a series of groans as she forced herself first to bend enough to climb free then to straighten again. It didn't seem fair that both actions hurt.

Finishing its boot cycle at last, her HUD began attempting to establish connections with any local network, but all it returned were errors and troubleshooting queries. There was not even a local chronometer as far as she could tell, and the bailiff's weapon had left Bell's blinking 12:00. The damage didn't seem to be permanent, but she needed something external to sync back to if she didn't want to do it manually. Which she emphatically did *not*, because in all humanity's great expanse into the stars, they had still never invented a digital clock that was anything but a pain in the ass to set.

But that was for later. Now, she had more pressing concerns. Bell spun up the bullshitometer. This wasn't an actual module in her overall brain-o-plex—though not for lack of trying—but it might as well have been. The more she thought about the ship-brain's self-admitted limitations, the more hopeful she felt. With any luck, she could talk herself off the ship then secure a berth on one of the alien trade vessels that routinely came and went from the orbital platforms—a local, friendly-ish one, not the weird invaders currently eating her colony.

Citizens of Anaranjado were forbidden direct contact with any of the aliens, even though the Equatorians were happy to make money off the goods only such beings could provide. But persistent rumors held that plenty of citizens managed to break that rule. And Bell wasn't even a citizen any longer.

The one certainty was that she could never go planet-side again, which was perfectly fine by her. Let the aliens choke on it and both groups die in the result, like a shitty alligator being eaten by a slightly less shitty python.

"So, listen, er, brain. There's been a terrible mistake, and it's critically important to the, um, war effort that I disembark *before* the ship breaks orbit. How long was I out, anyway?"

Bell tried to keep an air of urgency but spoiled it by cracking a wide yawn. It was so irritating. She was entirely synthetic, brain and all, yet nothing seemed capable of weeding the urge to yawn out of the species. But she wasn't that worried about the answer. She had internal fail-safes to prevent her from being unconscious for too long, whatever the cause. Heller's bailiff's little stun gun hadn't done any real damage, as far as she could tell, which meant—

"You were unconscious for approximately twenty-two point seven years."

All thought of aches and pains fled as Bell tried to process this statement.

"Not possible." Her voice was firm as she repeated her own previous thought aloud. "I have fail safes to keep me from being unconscious for that . . ." She trailed off, a nauseating thought occurring to her.

"Yes, indeed," said the brain. "Fail safes which can be rendered inactive by extreme cold. That's why we had to put you in cryosleep despite your being at the extreme end of synthetic physiology."

"Fuuuuuuuuck." For the first time, Bell noticed the hum of the ship around her, a noticeable vibration that she felt throughout her body. She'd never been aboard an interstellar ship before—or any kind of ship—but it seemed strange that a stationary one with its primary drive powered down would vibrate. It was not a particularly even vibration either.

But she couldn't let it go. "That—that's another one of the tics you mentioned, right? Your internal clock is off?" *It can't be. We can't have left already. I can't have lost twenty-three years.*

"Negative! I am pleased to report that my chronometer is functioning perfectly. No degradation to its performance has been observed for the entirety of the journey. We are approximately 99.94 percent of the way to our destination."

"I don't understand. The ship wasn't supposed to depart for months. Did they put me in cryo as soon as they hauled me out of the courtroom? Just how accelerated was this launch sched—oh. Oh, those *fuckers*." She didn't need the explanation anymore, but the ship's brain was going to give her one anyway.

"We departed approximately one day after your court appearance. It was determined that with the clear and present threat the alien incursion represented, the ship needed to break orbit at once."

"And let me guess," Bell said. "All the richest and most powerful assholes in the colony are the passengers." It had to be the case. There had been talks of a lottery for others to join the passenger list, but there hadn't been time for that. The colony's shit-heel elite had just cut and run.

"I'm afraid I'm not permitted to discuss passenger manifest details at this time. Or any time! And now, if you'll join me in the crew ready room, Staff Sergeant Dietrick Horváth, it's time for your orientation."

"Um, what?"

CHAPTER 4
ORIENTATION

"I'M SORRY," Bell continued, brought up so short by the AI's statement that she momentarily forgot to despair. "*What* did you just call me?" There was something familiar, and unpleasant, about that name, though Bell couldn't quite put her finger on it.

A series of audible clicks and hisses emerged from whatever concealed speakers the brain used. "It is on me to apologize," it said at last, still sounding cheery rather than contrite. "Despite the physical partitioning of my brain enabling me to split my attention, one of the errors I have noticed is that when speaking to more than one of the crew at once, sometimes I can get the messages mixed up. You will meet the staff sergeant shortly, at the orientation!"

The way it said *orientation* sounded as though it was simply pulling from the same canned audio file every time. Still, its words gave Bell some small hope.

Bullshitometer, don't fail me now.

"I think maybe the error goes deeper than a mix-up," she said as earnestly as she could. "You see, I'm not supposed to be here at all. This is all a case of mistaken identity."

The pause went on just long enough to tease her with hope.

"Ha. Ha. Ha. That is an excellent joke, Ms. Beauregard. But my scanners are perfectly calibrated, and I have positive identification of you through your internal power cell's residual bleed signature. You are Bellerophona Beauregard, self-admittedly guilty of crimes against humanity, sentenced to a lifetime of indentured servitude to the ship and, ultimately, the resulting colony!"

"Just Bell will do," Bell said leadenly.

"Just Bell, of course. One particular stipulation of my crew interaction conditioning is to only refer to each crew member by their preferred name, even across species lines."

"Species?" she asked, not daring to hope. "Do you mean there are actual aliens aboard the ship?"

"Yes, indeed, Bell. If meeting one is your wish, you are in luck. Please follow the sound of my voice." The brain projected its words from progressively further down the corridor between rows of pods. "And you'll get to meet several of them."

Seeing no other choice, at least until she could assess her odds of escape, Bell did as she was asked. The darkened catwalk she strode down was full of pods like hers, with matching catwalks above and below, each with their own double-rows. She kept fighting bouts of dissociation. She had just been in the courtroom, getting told off by Judge Hump-and-Dump Heller and telling him off in return. The memory pressed on her like an unpleasant weight.

She considered stuffing the whole episode past her event horizon, the discrete module in her brain she kept specifically as a kind of one-way storage bin for memories she didn't want to think about anymore. That hadn't been the module's original purpose, but it suited Bell just fine in this new role. But it seemed like a bad idea to discard any information about her situation when more information was what she desperately needed.

Still, it all left her feeling snappish.

"Why am I awake, anyway?" she demanded. "If the ship has an AI, why wake any of us up?"

"As I indicated, Bell," the brain said, voice receding as it talked, "my final conditioning and certain key linkages with ship maintenance processes were abandoned, owing to the need to escape Anaranjado before critical support areas planet-side could be compromised. As a result, I lack full mechanical command of the ship. Because of this, my handlers gave me the ability to rouse crew members, such as you, Bell, at regular intervals to perform maintenance I can't."

"But we're nearly there."

"Correct. Colony World 2865b is within visual range and we are preparing for an orbital insertion maneuver over the next several standard days."

Heh, insertion.

"So we clearly made it then. Why wake us early?"

"There are numerous maintenance issues that do not pose a safety hazard while the ship is moving through interstellar space but become far more concerning as we prepare to execute orbital maneuvers within a planetary gravity well."

"If they are so important, why weren't they fixed earlier?"

"Other maintenance issues took priority."

"You're not going to give me a satisfactory answer, are you?"

"If by 'satisfactory' you mean allow you to return to cryosleep and/or leave the ship, then no, I am not."

Bell couldn't stifle a long, loud groan. It was probably enough to wake up the pods she was passing closest to. Good. "Brain, you should know that I really hate manual labor of any kind. Also: non-manual labor. Basically, anything anyone tells me to do."

"Unfortunately, Bell, we are short on options. I would easily be able to handle these tasks myself if I possessed a more comprehensive physical presence in the ship. Does that make sense, Bell?"

"You keep using my name every time you talk," Bell said. "In almost every sentence. It's not weird or grating at all, but what do I call you?"

"A designation is one thing I was not granted, Bell. You may therefore call me whatever you wish."

"Oh," Bell said, distraught, "I'm terrible at naming things. Um. Hm. Voicey? No, that's horrible. Disembody-y? That's worse. I'm really set on the 'y' at the end, though."

"I am terribly sorry, Bell," the thing said. "If self-designation were among the many, many procedural loopholes currently available to me, I would happily help you."

"Loopy!" Bell said, triumphant. "Final answer. Your name is Loopy. Don't let anyone else tell you differently."

"Several of the others have already provided their own, alternate designations," Loopy said. "However, I am perfectly capable of answering to any number of different naming conventions—"

"It's Loopy, and I will fight anyone who says otherwise," Bell declared. "Now come on, I want to meet this ragtag band of assholes."

"Wonderful news, two of them are approaching as we speak. Although they are, I admit, moving in the opposite of my desired direction. Regardless, this should be very exciting for you."

"Oh really," Bell said absently, still trying to reckon with the existential horror of her situation on this scow. "Why's that?"

"It is quite momentous, I assure you. You are actually the first CCC to feature crew members of al—"

"CCC?" Bell interrupted.

"Conscious Crew Complement," Loopy translated, pivoting smoothly from the allegedly interesting thing he'd been about to say. "A term that refers to the tiny fraction of the crew awake at any given time, when applicable. Previous CCCs have been entirely human in composition. I'm pleased to announce that this group includes *four* non-humans!"

"Wonderful," Bell said by rote. Then his words sank in. "Wait, what? *Four?*" That was when she heard the noise of someone coming down the hall. Someone moving with decidedly inhuman footsteps.

The entities which rounded the bend were as strange a pair of people as Bell had ever seen, and they produced in her a volcanic surge of glee. Some bigots, such as the majority of people she had ever known on Anaranjado, might even object to the term "people" being used. But those fuckwads could all go sit on a pile of lit flares, because these were honest-to-dog aliens!

Neither one of the pair was even remotely humanoid, yet she knew both of them instantly. The one in the lead walked on three thick legs in radial symmetry around a center that looked like a glistening, brown, ovoid fruit partially sliced into three thick wedges starting from the top. Pale membranes bridged the gaps between the wedges of the central body mass. Sprouting from those wedges, one between each of the legs, was a slender, delicate arm with two elbows that terminated in a hand with three long fingers.

"Bell, this is Claxathon Urknuuzh, one of the tripartite. Of course, that's merely our name for them. The real word in their own language would be—"

"Unpronounceable," Bell said, sighing dreamily.

"Yes indeed." Loopy sounded supremely pleased.

Bell only knew a little of the tripartite's evolutionary and civilizational history, and so far as she knew, that limitation applied to every human. At some point, though, they had been separate beings looking something like flamingos, a ridiculous bird Bell had seen pictures of before. If you dyed a flamingo brown then sliced it horizontally across its center of mass, and then its two spindly legs had fused together into one thicker one, that was roughly one-third of a tripartite.

Somewhere along the line, either evolution or societal development had dictated that three sources of genetic diversity were better than two, and sex between partners had become a mandatory ménage à trois: a threesome personified into an intelligent species. Eventually they had gone a step further. In the final and most bizarre leap, three had eventually become so unified, the constituent thirds could no longer survive apart past infancy.

It was, Bell's college professor had assured her, a blurry line where you were bound into a lifelong, pluralistic marriage shortly after you were born, but also you were just one entity and the only sex possible was masturbation, a masturbation that produced viable offspring. He'd seemed pretty enthusiastic about it to her recollection. Professor Marcusson had been kind of sweet but also kind of gross, which meant he was a lot like tripartite sexual reproduction.

Faced with her first ever view of one in the flesh, Bell could easily see where each thick leg had once been two thinner ones. Each of these merged legs terminated in a foot tipped with two wicked claws.

She wasted no time in showing off as it arrived. It was a challenge to make her vocal modulator produce the proper sounds, but she'd stubbornly installed the mods in the desperate hope that one day this moment would come. She'd felt the buyer's remorse almost immediately, but now here she was, getting ready to speak to an alien in its own language.

"*Claxathon* Urknuuzh," Bell intoned in a series of hums and vibrations that pressed the limits of even her custom hardware to produce. "I am Bell Beauregard, and it is an honor to at last meet one of your kind."

The tripartite went absolutely still. For a moment, Bell felt a tremor of worry. It was the kind of stillness she associated with a predator waiting its moment. Then the central mass of the creature squeezed together, loosening the membranes and tightening them again as it expanded back, pushing air past them to make sound.

"You honor me, Bell Beauregard," Urknuuzh said in croaky but understandable English. They sounded a bit like a giant toad.

Bell reacted in horror, waving her hands to stop him. She'd heard tripartites could speak with humans in this way, but supposedly producing human language was painful, requiring them to contract their central mass much more than was comfortable. She pitched her worry into the vibrating intonations of his language. "No, you don't need to—"

"But I do," they said. "In all my travels, I have never met a human that troubled to learn my tongue. I said you honor me, Bell Beauregard. I can do no less than honor you in return."

If Bell had still possessed tear ducts, she would be fighting them now.

"Thank you," she said in his vibrations. "Consider me more than honored." All her life she'd been trapped on that desert rock populated with delusional apes in the thrall of a brain parasite. Then she'd gone and gotten herself kicked off the planet and met an alien who turned out to be cooler than every other human she'd ever met, *combined.*

Fuck, she might actually have to thank Heller if she ever saw him again.

"I must know how you came to speak my language," Urknuuzh said.

"Well, it was the subject of my senior research project for my undergraduate degree in xenolinguistics," Bell said. Or as close as possible. About half those words didn't really translate. She fervently hoped she hadn't said something offensive.

But Urknuuzh was making a sound with his membranes that Bell had been taught meant an analog to laughter. "You must have been a model student," they croaked.

"Flattery will get you everywhere. But how do I refer to you, um, gender wise? I'm a woman and go by *she* and *her*. What about you? *They*?"

"There are three genders on my world," Urknuuzh said. "And so each of us embodies all of them, one part each. It is . . . difficult to describe in terms of how we identify." Here Urknuuzh paused, body pulsing like a bellows. Bell interpreted that as trying to find the right words in an unfamiliar language. She was wrong.

"Apologies. I find the air on this ship thinner than I prefer, particularly when talking. But you might say my constituents take turns. *He* is sufficient for the remainder of our journey. Once we reach the planet of our indenture, that will be change enough, I think, to call for a corresponding change in my self-conception as well. But if you wish to meet a *they*, I believe my companion here can oblige you."

Holy fuck this is so amazing. Her thoughts collapsed briefly into a kind of whining test pattern after that. Bell could have kept gushing, mentally or otherwise, for hours. But she'd barely had time to think about her first encounter with a real-life alien when the second commanded her attention.

Where the tripartite occupied a fixed shape, his compatriot was a seething mass of constantly changing form. Its skin seemed to ripple, but that was an illusion created by a pile of wriggling, glistening worms, all clinging to one another to form a single mass. A ring-like eye oriented itself to observe Bell as she gawked. Then it unwound itself to be just another glistening worm, changing as it did so from a caustic-looking yellow to the same diarrhea-brown as the rest of the wriggling things.

Bell didn't care how gross they looked, even though it *was* supergross. Because it was real. It was piled there, right in front of her. It was a sher'zhoun, a *writher* in common parlance.

It was the subject species of her master's thesis on hive-mind linguistics.

"Oh my gawd," she said through teeth gritted with excitement. "I can't believe this is happening!" First a tripartite, now a writher. Bell hadn't been excited about something relating to her work in . . . ever! "Honored to meet you," she said in the writher's common-tongue language. A baseline human could never have made the sounds required to speak Sher'zhouni, but Bell had a more talented tongue than most. Metaphorically speaking. Also literally speaking, but that was not relevant here.

"A human who speaks not just the language of my companion," the writher said via rustling slithers, wisely not even attempting the tripartite proper name, "but our own. I am impressed beyond measure, Bell Beauregard. You may call me Grome."

"I won't lie," Bell said. "Five minutes ago, this was the worst day of my life. Now, it might be the best." She could think of no other way to encapsulate her feelings, even as she knew they couldn't last.

Bell wanted to go with the aliens, but they were not heading to orientation, having already met the other CCC members. Bell gathered the alien pair hadn't been impressed by them, either, judging by their insistence on being anywhere else. Reluctantly concluding that the sooner she knew whom she hated the most, the better, Bell followed Loopy's voice in the opposite direction.

They walked on in what seemed a rare silence for a time, but it was not to last. The bronze-colored corridor, ineffectively lit with flickering LEDs, curved endlessly rightward, eventually forcing Bell to ask the obvious question.

"Is this a giant circle or something?"

"Correct!" Loopy said. "This section of *Ultima Thule* is indeed arranged into a multi-floored ring which contains a mix of both temporary quarters for CCC members, as well as cargo storage areas which serve as waystations for the larger, outboard cargo bays which store larger and longer-term items, a mess hall, an infirmary, and other sundry locations."

"Thank you. And as concierge, can you point me to the nearest escape pod and/or shuttle?"

"Those amenities are reserved for our *passengers*, I'm afraid. Crew are not permitted to partake. In fact, the entire aft section of the ship is designed to detach, if need be, to safeguard their lives in the event of catastrophe."

"The aft end?" Bell was confused. Maybe she didn't remember her nautical terminology. No surprise when she hailed from a planet with no liquid water. Fore was front and aft was ass, right? "Isn't that where the engines are located?"

"It is indeed."

"Correct me if I'm wrong, but aren't giant, powerful engines the most likely source of a catastrophe? Why would the richies want to be strapped to the engines if something went . . . Hold on. What part of the ship is jettisoned?"

"Everything forward of the VIP section."

"Including this part?"

"Correct again!" The brain's cheeriness was like a road grader.

"I withdraw my question." She understood now. *The catastrophe they're afraid of is us, the enslaved help. They're afraid we might mutiny and seize control somehow. In that event, they'd keep the engines.* She was no engineer, but she suspected engines were the things that made power, which means in addition to being unable to fly anywhere, the jettisoned section wouldn't have any electricity either.

And Bell couldn't be sure, but she thought things like life support required electricity.

Still, just because she liked to torture herself, Bell went ahead and asked the obvious follow-up question.

"Tell me, what sort of safeguards are present in *our* section of the ship?"

"This portion of the ship is continuously monitored by me! You will also notice generalized emergency alarm handles in each room and at regular intervals along the corridor. There's one now, off to your left."

Bell did indeed notice the nearest handle, rugged polymer in a U-shape set into a bracket. According to the stenciled instructions, you had to pivot it all the way to the down position and then back up to its original position to trigger the emergency alarm.

"In the unlikely event that you notice a developing catastrophe that

I have failed to notify you about, simply operate that lever as instructed. Moving on!"

"How much further?" Bell asked, the words leaving her on a gusting sigh.

"We are meeting in Cargo Waystation Seven," Loopy said. "The next door on your right."

CHAPTER 5

ORIENTATION—FOR REAL THIS TIME

CARGO WAYSTATION SEVEN was surprisingly dim and even more surprisingly smelly. Bell saw a makeshift table made of various sized crates surrounded by nine cheap-looking stools, none of them occupied. Unless the darkness near the farthest walls obscured some people totally, it was also a lot emptier than Bell had been led to believe, even with her two alien friends deciding not to attend.

The low light made it difficult for Bell to make out any details beyond size, shape, and posture, so she ticked up the brightness of her own perception, grateful that she'd sprung for better optical upgrades two years ago when she'd had the chance on a clearance sale.

By the sound of things, she was arriving in the middle of an argument.

"And how do I know you aren't one of them in disguise? You don't look like any Anaranjadan I've ever seen. You look like the creatures who killed my squad mate." The speaker, a hair shorter than Bell but three times as wide, had a vaguely Scandinavian accent. He paused, panting. What was with this ship and people not being able to breathe? "Perhaps," the monster-man went on, "a little light vivisection will satisfy my curiosity on this matter." His last sentence had a flat affect to it that would have made Bell's skin crawl if she had any skin.

"Why don't you see what that gets you?" said the female-sounding voice of someone obscured by the bulk of the first speaker. The voice was as cold as Anaranjado's most shaded point.

"There will be no threats aboard my ship," Loopy said, uncharacteristically stern.

"You hear that, freak?" the megalith-man asked, voice dangerous. "Do you even know why I'm here? It's not wise to threaten someone like me."

"I think Mr. Overcompensation-for-Disappointing-Anatomy should reconsider whom he's calling 'freak,'" Bell said loudly into the sucking quiet the man's second threat carried in its wake.

Most humans of Anaranjadan origin, as Bell exemplified, were tall but rail thin. Not only was the planet's gravity lower, which lent itself to longer bones, but more surface area per unit volume meant more efficient heating and cooling. In the punishing extremes of the planet's tidally locked day and night non-cycle, this was crucial. This man covered the "tall" well enough, but he was also a meter and a half across the shoulders and built like he blast-mined granite with his bare hands.

He made Judge Heller's bailiffs look like prepubescent teens, and his bulk almost totally obscured the tiny figure he was menacing. As Bell stared at him, a sickly yellow glow suddenly appeared around his head, superimposed there in her HUD. At the same moment, a *ba-ding* sounded way, *way* too loud in her head.

How did that thing get turned back on?

It was yet another "gift" from the cultists who had transitioned her brain from meat to machine. They'd had a real problem with the Harmony parasite—even more so than Bell herself—and had wanted Bell to know whenever she encountered someone with it. So they'd installed a sensor to detect the subtle but distinctive change in brainwaves which occurred in everyone thus infected, apparently not really considering the fact that on a planet where *everyone* had the freaking Harmony parasite, Bell would be assaulted by *ba-dings* until she went insane.

She'd turned it off as soon as she'd figured out how, but apparently her hard reboot had toggled it back on and pegged the volume to max.

Still, it was odd that it had only triggered once when there were two people in the room.

Then the obscured person stepped out into view, and Bell understood. Understood, and all but gasped.

The tiny figure was a woman, or at least presenting as such. The feminine cast of her features was obvious. But aside from the overall body shape—Bell very much tried to appreciate the view without being creepy—everything else about her was unlike anyone Bell had ever seen, at least in person.

She was looking at a fully baseline human. Not just no parasite, which in itself was almost unprecedented in Bell's experience—herself being the sole exception she was aware of—but no augmentations of any kind.

As in, she was looking at someone who either looked as though she were the richest of the rich, the Equatorianest Equatorian on Anaranjado, or as if she had just stepped over the Bridge from Earth, if the Bridge from Earth had still existed. The woman had skin *over her entire face*. Even the Equatorian elite of Anaranjado usually adorned their faces with decorative patterns of scales that were purely aesthetic rather than functional. This woman's complexion was sunburn-bait pale, and it looked intoxicatingly soft. Rather than being bald or sprouting wispy hair held apart by static electricity—another cooling technique—her hair was long, blonde, and wavy, falling past her shoulders. And her heavily lidded eyes were blue, not any of the various unnatural colors most Anaranjadans chose.

Bell's onboard sensor suite was not military grade or anything like that, but she did a quick, guilty sweep of the woman, looking for something indicating well-disguised synthetic limbs or organs or any kind of enhancement. She found nothing. In all her life, Bell had never laid eyes on a human this relentlessly baseline. Equatorians—and even the most radical of the anti-augmentation groups—always had *some* kind of upgrade, even if neither faction liked to advertise it.

The planet resolutely refused to meet humanity halfway. It demanded adaptation if you couldn't afford to sequester yourself permanently away. And such things began *in vitro*. If she'd been asked yesterday, Bell would have bet a retroactively upsetting amount of money that no one on Anaranjado was *this* baseline.

And she'd be considerably poorer had she made that bet, because that was clearly wrong. The woman was here, after all. Unless the ship had made a stop along the way, she'd boarded back at the colony the same as Bell had. Other human colonies might feature baseline humans, of course, but so far as Bell was aware, Anaranjado was not in contact with any.

That was sort of the point of her whole "crimes against humanity" rap.

The thought of getting with an Equatorian grossed Bell out on principle, but the extra layer of mystery completely flipped that impulse on its head. Whatever the reason, Bell found this particular baseline human sexy as fuck.

"I have spoken with the unaccounted for CCC members," Loopy said cheerily, either oblivious to the charged emotions of murder and horniness hanging thick in the air or pointedly ignoring them. "As they informed me in a series of hurtful personal attacks, they do not plan to attend this orientation. Taking this into account, I believe we would be best served by introductions for those present." He spoke this with great relish, like they'd finally gotten to the good part. "For starters, the man glaring aggressively at Bell is Staff Sergeant Dietrick Horváth."

Oh, fuck me. Now that Bell looked at him in the light, she recognized him. The newly minted war criminal. The goddamned *war criminal* was on their ship. His had been the only crime which had briefly obscured hers in the news in that final two-day stretch.

Citing rumors of the alien invaders' ability to disguise themselves as anyone in some frankly impossible-sounding biological process, Horváth had illegally commandeered a flier and single-handedly leveled a hospital treating both refugees and Anaranjadans, if the reports were accurate. He'd claimed the patients hadn't been human refugees at all, but carnivorous alien infiltrators.

That old saw.

And since Bell was aware of his details and her crime was a full two weeks older than his, he was no doubt aware of her particulars as well. A soldier willing to indiscriminately mass-murder his own to protect the colony now faced the woman everyone agreed was the biggest traitor in the history of said colony.

And she'd implied he had a tiny dick.

"The traitor," he growled at Bell. She really hated being right all the time. "A pity you weren't visiting the hospital for a physical the day I committed my 'crime,' or I'd have gotten you too."

For once, Bell managed to keep her mouth shu—

"I would have been there, but I was too busy *visiting* your mom," she said. "Repeatedly. She told me to tell you to call her more."

For once, Bell managed to only open her mouth the one time.

Horváth surged forward with a roar, but Bell was already moving, sidestepping, betting the hulking man's nimbleness was inversely proportional to his strength. She didn't reckon on his wingspan though, and he caught her by the throat in one of his building-demolishing hands, lifting her easily off the ground until her head bumped against the ceiling. Then he began to squeeze.

Quite aside from her instinctual desire to breathe even if it wasn't necessary, Bell also had a lot of sensitive connections running through her neck, which made this situation just about as bad as if she'd still been made of meat. Accordingly, her vision began to gray around the edges in a passing resemblance to blacking out. She wasn't blacking out. This was a warning from her hazard avoidance systems. Just a warning. For the moment, at least.

"Staff Sergeant, this is your second warning about committing violence aboard this ship," Loopy said, only his voice had changed: utterly drained of cheery personality, of *any* personality. He sounded almost like a machine despite his claims of an organic origin, and all the more ominous for it. Bell had no idea if the ship's brain could back up its implied threat. But if it was a bluff, it had worked on her at least. "I will not issue another."

"Pray I don't stop caring about my own well-being enough to kill my enemies no matter the cost," Horváth said to Bell. "And then recall that I'm a soldier and ask yourself how likely that is."

"I didn't know they made uniforms big enough for guys who look like a linebacker ate another linebacker, but I guess you learn something new every day."

The baseline hottie gave a low chuckle that she cut off quickly, but as great as that was, Horváth was the bigger concern. Rather than rip Bell in half, though, he simply looked at her as if the joke had confused instead of enraged. Then he dropped her and clomped out, heaving labored breaths as he squeezed himself through the door before Bell could think of an appropriate comeback that didn't revisit the "your mom" well too soon.

Loopy resumed talking in his normal voice. "And this is—"

"Tas," the baseline woman said. She offered no surname but stared a challenge at Bell as she spoke. Bell had been hoping for a look of gratitude, but any eye contact at all made her knees weak. Even saying just the one word revealed Tas's sultry voice.

Shit. Despite Bell's best efforts, she was staring. Worse, Tas probably thought it was about her baseline-ness. Which it sort of was, but also, the woman was just a vision. Like the pictures Bell had seen of the permanent sunrise in Glassbreak canyon.

Too beautiful for words.

Bell opened her mouth to say sorry, decided admitting it would be worse, then closed it. Then she had second thoughts, opened her mouth again, closed it again. This repeated several more times.

"Are we done here?" Tas prompted the ship's brain, abandoning her direct stare and hunching in on herself in an injured way Bell was only just now noticing.

Oh no. Damaged? In need of saving. Gah, even more irresistible. Stop looking, Bell. Stop looking! Stoooooooooop looking.

At last, she tore her gaze away.

"Almost," Loopy said in response to Tas. "Lastly, we have Ms. Bell Beauregard! Tas, you might know her from—"

"No need for that, Loopy," Bell cut in. It seemed improbable the woman was not already aware of the particulars of Bell's infamy, but just in case, best not. Unless Tas liked that sort of thing . . . No, best to hold off for now. Mysterious was better. Information could always be revealed, but it could never be called back.

If Bell was lucky and the rest of the crew had been prisoners of some sort, the way she and Horváth had, maybe there was a chance Tas had been locked away long enough to avoid the news of Bell's "betrayal."

She wondered what Tas had done to end up here.

"Like Loopy said, I'm Bell." She tried to meet Tas's eyes, but the woman stubbornly refused. "Nice to meet you." She mimicked Tas's accent perfectly—somewhere in the neighborhood of the American West Coast—yet subtly, hoping it would subconsciously help to reassure the woman that she, Bell, could be trusted. Confided in. Maybe even, if the stars aligned, gotten freaky with.

Yet, far from being charmed, the woman flinched, seemingly at the very sound of Bell's voice being directed at her. Had her accent work been that off-base? Suddenly it seemed glaringly obvious to Bell that her attempt to ingratiate herself with Tas by sounding familiar must have come across as mockery.

Stupid. Fucking. Moron.

Tas shook herself as though clearing cobwebs. It seemed fairly obvious Tas did not return Bell's infatuation.

Yet.

CHAPTER 6
MAKING DUTIES

TAS PUSHED past Bell with almost the same hostility Horváth had, muttering darkly about how thin the air was. Bell felt the urge to pursue and try to repair a first impression that had apparently gone very poorly, but she resisted. Nobody liked desperation or clinginess.

Instead she waited for a count of ten then exited the now empty room and walked the other direction. The voice of Loopy followed.

"Let us continue our tour," the brain said, thoroughly re-cheered. "You can meet the rest of the Conscious Crew Complement along the way!"

"I see some Always Alliterative Asshole had the responsibility for naming this travesty you all railroaded me into," Bell remarked. "But why has everyone I've met either struggled to breathe or complained about it?"

"Ah. Yes. This ship was forced to launch far earlier than planned, as I mentioned. As such, many maintenance issues that would have been caught during shakedown were not. We are nearing the end of our journey, and I'm afraid our life support system isn't as functional as it was when we started. As it happens, the crew section's life support recirculators can only support seven crew members awake right now."

"*Seven?* That's all of us that are awake?"

A click and hiss of static like momentary consideration. "Nine, technically. There are two special cases who don't count against the number. You are one such, Brother Barnabas is another. You will meet him soon."

The brain had hinted at knowledge of Bell's "special case" before. "Ah, so you know just how—"

"Synthetic you are? Yes. I've been monitoring you in cryostasis for more than two decades, after all. You don't need to breathe, so you don't count against the total. But everyone else, both crew and passengers, are in cryosleep to conserve resources."

"And how many 'crew' total?"

"Just under one thousand."

"Well, if there are enough issues to be worth waking us up, and life support isn't cooperative, why not just wake up some extras and stick them in vac suits with oxygen supplies? Many hands make light work and all."

"Such oxygen supplies would have to be replenished via the already faltering life support. And in any event, I'm afraid our supply of vac suits, already smaller than intended, wore out with use by previous CCCs long ago."

Well, it had been worth a shot to avoid work. Or at least lessen it.

"And are all these lucky people who are still asleep prisoners like me? I thought there was supposed to have been a lottery, that anyone from Anaranjado could have won a berth."

"All were deemed by the justice system to owe a substantial debt to Anaranjadan society," Loopy said. "The lottery you describe was the original intention, but the acceleration of the launch schedule necessitated a late change in plan. If you like, I can include the listed infractions as we meet each person. They are, after all, a matter of public record."

Bell wavered on the point of asking after Tas's supposed infraction—no need to inquire about Horváth's—but no, she was not going to be weird and obsessive about this woman. Tas could tell Bell, or not, in her own sweet time.

"And how many actual, non-crew *passengers* are there?"

"Again, that information is restricted," Loopy said before pivoting smoothly. "Up ahead on your left is the mess hall with attached kitchen. Your own nutritional needs are nonexistent, but should you enjoy partaking of food for its own sake, meals may be prepared there by anyone in the Conscious Crew Complement."

Bell's eating, when she bothered at all, was performative. Someone who ate nothing at all could be off-putting, especially in the dating world. So she had a whole system dedicated for the processing and cycling out of food the old-fashioned way. It was horribly inefficient and required a lot of clean-up after, but then, those also applied to sex, and she still did that every chance she got.

"Is there anything on this scow that won't taste like garbage?"

"All crew foodstuffs aboard this vessel are derived from molecular manipulations of fungal paste!" Loopy said as though he was announcing Bell had won a career achievement award.

"I don't think I need to see the kitchen or mess hall then," Bell said. Though, she supposed if Tas asked her to dinner *really* nicely . . .

"I'm afraid I must insist," Loopy said. "Two of the CCC are present there at the moment, and I have managed to delay them from leaving with distraction." He sounded so pleased with himself, Bell couldn't help but smile.

Indeed, she could hear another instance of Loopy's voice echoing through an open door just ahead and to the right, yammering away disconcertingly. As Bell reached the door, it announced her.

"Here is our last crew mate to awaken, Bell Beauregard!"

The mess hall was still lined with tables and stools for twenty times their number, which seemed odd until she remembered that everything about this ship seemed half-assed and half-baked. A pair of Anaranjadans, a man and a woman, stared back at Bell. They were boringly normal, at least compared to the first four CCCers she'd met. Neither was an alien, neither was the size of a small moon, neither represented an archaic biological throwback, and neither was smoking hot. It was disappointing, if she were being honest.

Although, Bell suddenly realized, neither one of them triggered a Harmony *ba-ding* either. And *that* was interesting.

"Pierre LaSalle," said the smiling man before Loopy could introduce him. Despite the name, the accent was pitch-perfect Australian.

Bell wracked her memory banks, trying to recall if she'd ever heard that accent in real life before, but came up with nothing. A bit of a surprise on a world with as diverse a cultural background as Anaranjado, but it wasn't as though she'd been everywhere.

Noticeably shorter than Bell, scarcely taller than Tas, LaSalle seemed shorter still due to keeping his hair cropped unusually close to his scalp, and he'd even gone to the trouble of grafting in a goatee of facial hair on, around, or possibly through his scales. He must be from Shadyside. They were *so* weird down there. But the more she looked at him, the more of an edge she saw to that smile. It was costing him some effort to maintain it, she thought.

When she didn't immediately answer, he spoke again, and it was as though he'd read her mind. "Can you believe this bullshit? I mean, years. Decades! This is nothing I signed up for, I can tell you that. No, sir. Nothing at all."

Bell waited for Loopy to announce the man's reason for being here, silently betting on "workplace violence" with that twitchy, aggrieved demeanor. But apparently that promise didn't apply if the brain hadn't done the actual introducing. Which was a shame because it seemed rude to ask. Bell did anyway.

"Bell Beauregard. What are you in for?"

LaSalle twitched like she'd goosed him. "A bit of con artistry. Just parting a few blokes from money they weren't clever enough to keep hold of. Hardly seems worth all this. I mean, really? Does *anyone* deserve this? It's almost enough to make you think they were grabbing people on any old pretext because they needed warm bodies."

He wasn't wrong there. On the contrary, it was a surprisingly insightful statement from an Anaranjadan citizen. So Bell asked another rude question. "You a Defective, LaSalle?" She knew he was, of course—no *ba-ding*. But it would be interesting to see how he answered. And it would help her understand just who had gotten picked for this hell-journey. And, given his status as a criminal, maybe it wasn't even that odd. Shockingly high though its "success" rate was, the Harmony parasite didn't always work. Still, con artists were not common on a world where the overwhelming majority of the populace felt like all their fellow humans were close family.

"Who, me? No. But I guess someone certainly thought so," LaSalle said with a forced laugh. "Or I wouldn't be here, would I?"

A liar, then. Which might be good, or bad, depending on the context.

Bell was technically a Defective herself, but in a more basic sense. She didn't have Harmony in her head and never had. Her parents had been the rarest of the rare in that they hadn't allowed it. That in itself wasn't permitted, of course, but her father had known a guy. At least, she thought that was the case. But she also had another memory, one of her mother insisting they administer the parasite themselves, at home. That *was* allowed. Anaranjado was big on the honor system.

Odd. She'd occasionally run into memory glitches since the transfer of her brain from wetware to hardware, but they'd always taken the form of missing memories, not contradictions. Maybe she ought to get herself scanned.

Bell came back to the present, realized then that LaSalle had been muttering dark imprecations during that entire mental aside. His companion, so far unintroduced, placed a hand on his shoulder. Maybe it was meant to be calming, maybe restraining, but it was definitely *possessive.* And it worked. He cut off his whispered tirade at once.

Loopy leaped into the silence before he could be preempted again. "And this," he said, indicating the grabby woman, "is Xian Ginevra," he said, as if the name explained itself. "Former—"

"Former head until very recently of Ovanna Diversified Holding Interests," the woman finished with a weary sigh that sounded like it came from real lungs, ones that had known a lot of nicotine. Which they almost certainly had. She had a smattering of scales across her arms and the sides of her face before transitioning to tanned Caucasian-ish skin. But scales like that would be merely performative.

"As it happens, Ovanna Diversified Holding Interests held the construction contract on the *Ultima Thule,*" Loopy said.

The introduction was unnecessary. Even Bell had heard of this asshole. She was supposed to be as ruthless and indomitable a business mind as they came, with all the ten-kilos-of-shit-in-five-kilo-baggage that implied. Bell would do well to watch her tongue around this one. But more than all of that, she was a dyed-in-the-wool Equatorian, and *she didn't have the Harmony parasite.*

Son of a bitch. Those crazy weirdos were right. Anti-authority as Bell was, she'd assumed that the techno-cultists' conspiracy theories that none of the Equatorians had Harmony and it was all just a means to control the colony population were just crazy rantings. But if Xian was in any way normal for her class, the cultists really were on to something. It was something of a relief that Bell would never have to admit this to them. Not only did she hate being wrong, but they were just deeply unpleasant to be around.

"*Former* head of Ovanna whatever and whatsits?" Bell taunted. Maybe not the smartest thing to say, but at least Xian wasn't capable of physically crushing her into a small cube, like Horváth.

"Former," the woman said with icy finality. "For all the good that did me in the end." This with a rattling breath. Aside from a few cosmetic touches, Bell doubted very much at all was synthetic about Xian Ginevra. That, at least, was typical for her social status. Her accent was a mélange Bell would parse later, when she could get some alone time. Despite the exhaustion in Xian's words, her gaze seized Bell like a challenge, an effect only slightly ruined by being halfway through making a pot of coffee. "Suffice it to say I've been officially humbled. The fact that you are speaking to me at all is proof of that."

Bell wondered if Xian actually thought she sounded humble when she spoke. Smugly feeling like she'd won a battle, even if that battle was just a slap-fight, Bell turned triumphantly to tell Loopy she was ready to move on before realizing there was no one to turn to. She had no idea where the brain's sensors were in the room, which creeped her out. She didn't like feeling like she was being watched.

"That reminds me," she said, as though she'd been speaking her thoughts aloud, "is there any privacy on this scow?"

"Each of you will be afforded a private bunk in one of the temporary crew quarters, yes," Loopy said. A tone then sounded, both in the kitchen and out in the hall. "And you needn't worry, because these spaces will be monitored continuously for your protection whenever you are alone."

"I don't think you under—Wait. What do you mean when we're alone?"

"You needn't worry that I will observe you during sexual relations with another member of the crew—which is both permitted *and* encouraged during designated rest period—because I like to see my crew happy. Should this highly desirable outcome take place, all sensor monitoring will be suspended for the duration. This also applies to usage of showers and restrooms for privacy concerns. However, I'm afraid we will have to continue the tour later because it's time to populate the duty roster! You will each pair off for today's duties, with one group of three. Since technical difficulties and crew recalcitrance rendered full introductions impossible in the allotted time, I will now form work unit teams that maximize the social links you each have already formed."

Bell's metaphorical heart sank at the thought of working with Horváth, but it stood stiffly at attention when she considered that she might be paired with Tas. This could be the perfect chance to—

"Our four non-human crew mates will be split into the pairs of two who already have working relationships."

"Four? I've only met two." Bell glanced around as though the other two might melt out of the bulkheads.

"Correct. There are two you have yet to meet. But regarding the human crew members, Tas will team up with Ms. Xian and Mr. LaSalle to form the group of three. Bell, you will be paired with Staff Sergeant Horváth."

Shit.

CHAPTER 7
SHIRKING! IN! SPAAAAAACE!

NOT WANTING to look afraid in front of twitchy LaSalle and his handler, Xian, Bell had stormed out of the mess hall and down the corridor before confronting the ship's mind.

This proved to be a mistake as Dietrick Horváth thundered up, so massive he sounded like an entire bloat of stampeding hippos as he arrived at Loopy's summons with distressing haste.

"If I am alone with this one, I will not be held responsible for my actions."

The fact that the man-mountain had gotten the first word in irritated Bell.

"I would also like to request a new partner," Bell said, hoping that demonstrating the pair of them were on the same page would make it more likely they'd both get what they wanted. "Or even to work alone!" And then, because there was something wrong with her: "I would hate to have to rearrange anyone's internal organs and/or components when we are so close to our destination. And ugly as his face is, I'm not sure I'm qualified to do anything but make it ugly in a different way."

The big man lunged at her before she'd even finished speaking, his roar drowning out Bell's final words. Which, perversely, probably worked in her favor.

An alarm blared from everywhere, followed by flashing red lights, and Bell feeling a vestigial urge to soil herself.

"I warned you, Staff Sergeant Horváth, that there would be no further warnings," Loopy said. Bell's desire to crap her jumpsuit transitioned into a giddy thrill. She practically floated from the deck, aloft with hope. Spinning around, she searched in vain for the death-ray ports that were going to iris open and vaporize the brute. Horváth, for his part, looked as if he expected similar.

"Prepare for conflict resolution mediation!" Loopy declared with his usual cheer.

Both Bell and Horváth let out nearly identical groans.

"There, we are already finding common ground on which to build a healthy, productive relationship," Loopy said. "Now, I want each of you to state succinctly what about the other person bothers you."

"She is a traitor to our people, one whom I would very much like to kill." Horváth crossed his arms with finality.

"He thinks I'm a traitor and would like to kill me." Bell made air quotes. "'Very much.' And I would prefer he not."

"Well, now, this does seem to be quite a strident difference of opinion," Loopy said.

"If I kill this wretched creature," Horváth said, "what will happen to me?"

"Unprovoked violence against Bell would be very much against the *Ultima Thule* Crew Code of Conduct, or CCC," Loopy said, in a voice as close to solemnity as Bell suspected he possessed. She waited patiently for him to acknowledge the lunacy of that acronym, but he did not.

Horváth turned leering lantern eyes on Bell. They glowed with malicious intent. "It is as I thought. Censure. Mere words. Not even a slap on the wrist."

"I have been authorized to inform you that committing such an act," Loopy continued, "would result in your bodily seizure and the merging of your conscious awareness with an incarceration simulation that would meet the technical definition of torture, the colony laws concerning which having no jurisdiction in interstellar space. This would continue until such time as the leadership of this expedition deemed you sufficiently cowed to be reunited with your body and returned to useful labor, which would be unlikely to happen until they are wakened at the end of the journey."

A ringing silence.

"I will not work with this creature. Not today. Not ever. Do not place me in the same room as it again." Horváth stormed away, the corridor shaking with his passage. Bell supposed his final words on the subject could technically have applied to either her or the ship's brain, but she knew where she was putting her money.

"Very well, if that is final, I will assign you somethin—and he's gone. I will have to inform him of his revised tasking when he reaches his preferred place of sulking. But it would seem I have logged my first failure at conflict resolution mediation," Loopy said, his voice a little muted as though in sadness.

"Cheer up," Bell said. "*I'm* certainly thrilled with the result. If anyone asks, I'll say you mediated my brains out." With any luck, the promise of such dire punishment would keep Horváth from acting on his homicidal urges. Because if that *wasn't* enough, Bell was likely as good as dead, and there was no sense worrying about it. "Now," she said, "what exactly is this duty I'll be doing by myself?"

"You will be de-fouling the foodstuff pipes of blockages made of congealed fungal paste."

Happiness curdled on the instant. It seemed to be happening a lot lately. "I beg your pardon?"

"It is an exceedingly unpleasant task, I've been told," Loopy said. "One I lack the manual manipulators to accomplish. Fungal paste is currently being piped from the outboard storage containers through the crew section and into the passenger section for use in synthesizing a welcome feast for the passengers once we arrive on-planet. Unfortunately, due to peculiar qualities of the substance's viscosity, this increased flow rate has resulted in a significant clog. Had you Staff Sergeant Horváth's help, the task would proceed much more quickly. As it is, it will likely take you a full shift to complete, so you'd best get to it."

"So you're saying the passengers are siphoning off part of the crew's food source so they can have a big rager of a party once we arrive?"

"That is an essentially accurate summary with an unfortunate amount of editorializing."

Bell had to suppress a wild laugh. Back to happy! *Fuck those rich Equatorian fat cats.* They were literally enslaving people. If they had to go hungry during their welcome shindig, so much the better.

"So, you want me to muck out the muck pipes? Sure. Happy to!" Bell's smile was flush with secret pride. A primary school teacher had once labeled her "flagrantly defiant to a degree that suggests pathology and a need for professional intervention. I am deeply concerned." He wasn't wrong precisely. But in addition to double-birding authority by default, Bell knew how to act agreeable by just lying and then doing the exact opposite of whatever she promised.

Up yours, Mr. Trieste, she thought. She wasn't one to hold a grudge, but she had kept tabs on him after graduation all the way up to the glorious day when he'd died. Then she'd gone and had a perfectly normal, lovely day, blissfully happy that she was mature enough not to let unpleasant people live rent free in her head. And because he was dead!

"Excellent," Loopy said. "Please follow the glowing brown line on the floor to the work area, where you will receive further instructions."

"Glowing *brown* line?" Yet as Bell tried to picture what this would look like, it appeared, and it was every bit as unpleasant as she'd imagined: an advancing line of light on the floor that looked like radioactive shit.

Still, despite this nauseating display, Bell was just getting around to enjoying the concept of shirking in space the way she'd done back on Anaranjado when two thoughts occurred to her. The first was to wonder just how she was going to get away with shirking when the ship's brain had already said he had electronic eyes and ears everywhere. And the second . . .

"Hey, Loopy. Just out of morbid curiosity, what would happen if I refused to do the maintenance?"

"I would assign the task to one of the others," Loopy said.

"But what would happen to *me*?"

Several clicks and hisses, as though Loopy was choosing his wording carefully. "Willful failure to follow maintenance instructions on vital ship systems is a grave offense, and is punishable by—"

"It's the same thing you threatened Horváth with, isn't it?"

More clicks. "There are some minor differences in the specifics of the incarceration protocols. But in essence, that is correct."

"Of course it is," Bell said, sighing. She contemplated the glowing skid mark beneath her feet, sighed again, and began to trudge along it toward her fungal-paste fate.

CHAPTER 8
GORIENTATION

THE FILTH WAS EVERYWHERE. When your skin had been replaced by scales, you had a lot of little nooks and crannies for crud to settle into. It could be problematic on a planet as arid and dusty as Anaranjado. Regular cleanings were a must. But after scrubbing fungus out of pipes?

After a brief stop in her new quarters just to orient her as to their location, Bell had been herded straight to the muck pipes. As near as she could tell, when she exited them ten hours later, every crevice she possessed was filled with rotting fungal paste. She was so coated in slime that standing up was nearly impossible.

It felt like being birthed into the world by a toilet in a dysentery ward.

Hoping the ship possessed a bath that involved lye or ionizing radiation, Bell slid and skidded her way along the cramped access room's metallic floor, perversely delighted by the foul smears of footprints she was leaving behind with each uncertain step. It wasn't until she'd nearly reached the door that she saw the sign, one she hadn't noticed until this moment.

PLEASE REMOVE ALL SOILED GARMENTS AND PLACE IN WALL BINS FOR SANITIZING BEFORE PROCEEDING TO SHOWER AREAS. DO NOT WORRY: ALL

MONITORING DEVICES BETWEEN THIS CHAMBER AND THE SHOWERS ARE DISABLED, SO YOU MAY BE ASSURED OF PRIVACY.

Loopy's well-meaning but optimistically naive tone was unmistakable in the text. Perhaps the lack of monitoring devices explained why the ship's brain wasn't here talking her ear off.

"Sorry, Loopy," she said with a snort of vicious pleasure, "but I took off my clothes before I got in." The ship had dispensers for flow-matter jumpsuits, and she'd been wearing her current set of clothes for twenty-plus years. Bell Beauregard was many things, but a prude was not one of them. Monitoring devices being disabled was nice and all, but if anyone had wanted to peep at her, they could just enjoy the show. Plus, it wasn't like she had to worry about getting an infection. Although, looking back, keeping the jumpsuit on might have kept some of her crevices clean.

The alarm tore through the air like the end of the world. It kicked Bell all the way back to the moment the would-be invaders had first reached out over their Bridge to establish a communication link with Anaranjado.

Which quite likely *had* signaled the end of the world.

The fact that whatever had resulted from that invasion had likely resolved itself decades ago left her feeling strangely hollow in between the earsplitting blats until they cut off abruptly. What followed in the deafening silence was a series of four pleasant, ascending tones over the nearest loudspeaker. It was the sort of sound you might hear at a tram station when they were about to announce new security measures had been put in place for the thirty thousandth time. The tones were followed immediately by Loopy's voice, sounding strangely canned.

"Attention, Conscious Crew Complement. There has been a murder."

MURDERS WERE BAD, Bell told herself as she alternated sprinting and skidding to the showers, but surely showing up to a crime scene naked and tramping fungal paste all over everything would not improve the situation. She bypassed all the sonic showers—those took way too long—selecting the one shower meant to flush away dangerous chemicals to hose herself off under a surprisingly strong deluge of water. Then she pulled a new jumpsuit from a dispenser and got dressed. With yet another glowing line showing her the way—puke green this time—she wasn't as late in arriving at the scene of the crime as she'd imagined she would be for the simple fact that she wasn't the last one to arrive.

It was another storage room, a carbon copy of the orientation room. The limited space was crowded despite only the familiar faces of Xian, LaSalle, and Tas. None of the aliens she'd previously encountered were present, and the two crew members she hadn't met had also not arrived. But it was the gruesome tableau splayed out before her that commanded her focus.

Bell took one look and barfed out the first words that crossed her mind, and if she'd still been someone who regularly ate, she would have barfed up some other stuff as well.

"I mean, if someone had to go, I can think of worse people. What?" The faces of LaSalle and Xian turned to regard her, the former with paranoid suspicion, the latter with the sort of general disapproval Xian probably directed at everyone she considered her inferior. So, everyone. Whatever. Bell was just saying what everyone was thinking. "The guy was a mass murderer. He killed a bunch of innocent people *on his own side in a hospital.* Those who live by the murder, et cetera."

In an otherwise-empty section in the center of the room, Dietrick Horváth was displayed as though at a butcher's shop. Spitted upon a length of some kind of metal bar which had been driven through him and down into the deck plating at a forty-five-degree angle, whoever had killed him had unzipped him from groin to throat, spreading the halves far enough apart to let a whole shiny mess of guts spill down onto the deck. These combined with blood and other fluids to form a jellied mass beneath him. However much he might have replaced or augmented his extremities, it was now squelchingly obvious that Staff Sergeant Horváth had still been mostly meat inside.

Bell turned off her olfactory senses when the butcher-shop smell started to get too bad. She didn't miss the way Tas folded in on herself at the sight of the body, like self-arranging origami, only instead of becoming a beautiful crane, it was more like watching a human viper coiling, prepared to lash out at anyone who came too close.

Ugh, why did she have to be so *sexy* all the time? All damaged and vulnerable. Bell felt the sudden urge to take charge and solve the case. She didn't even bother trying to tell herself it wasn't to impress Tas. It had been over two decades. Bell wanted to *bone*.

"Right," she said. "We need to establish who was where when this happened. Which means we need to know when this happened." Easy enough. She turned to look up at the ceiling speaker. "When did this happen?" A very uncharacteristic silence from Loopy. "Loopy?"

No answer.

"I don't think that thing has stopped talking once since the moment we were thawed," Xian said. "And it chooses now to shut its trap?"

A familiar series of clicks and hisses emerged from the speakers, as though Loopy were trying to answer but unable to.

"That's *way* more fucking ominous than plain old silence," LaSalle said, sounding as though he was about to draw a gun and start shooting at random. "I don't like it. I don't like it."

"He called us in here," Bell said, torn between confusion, annoyance, and disquiet. "He even showed me the way with one of those glowing lines on the floor. It was just a few minutes ago. What happened?"

"Yeah, this is some fucking conspiracy shit," LaSalle said, his tone indicating he was agreeing with Bell for some reason.

"I don't see any heavy equipment. Aside from the body, I mean," Tas said. "We should check the crates to be absolutely sure, but if you're implying the ship's brain did this, unless it somehow launched a length of metal through him from somewhere in the ceiling, I'm not sure how it could be responsible."

Bell started. It was the most words she'd ever heard Tas say. Bell liked hearing her talk. Hers was the kind of voice Bell could very easily —*focus*. Tas had come away from her wall-lurking to speak. Having said her piece, she withdrew again, as though to keep them all in her eye line.

"She makes a good point," Bell said, pointedly not looking at the other woman. Play it cool.

"There could be robotic servitors," Xian retorted. "It was always the plan for the ship's brain to have them. There wasn't time to provide them as intended, but there were still rudimentary ones helping with ship construction. It's possible some are still aboard. There could also be concealed ports. There could even be some kind of virus involved. The organic kind. The ship's brain might be sick."

"I thought your company built this thing," Bell said. "How do you not know what's in it?"

"When you order garbage slop from the local dive eatery, do you watch the ingredients grow?" Xian retorted acidly. "It may shock you to learn that I didn't build this ship by hand myself. Nor did I design it."

"You just made money off it," Bell said.

"Yet here I am, staring at a flayed-open corpse with the rest of you." The acid in Xian's words had inverted, turned bitter.

"Why would we be awake if the ship's brain had servitors?" Tas pressed.

"That's right!" Bell jumped in to agree, wondering if dog-piling on a rich jerk counted as a meet-cute. "If Loopy had access to that kind of mechanical help, what would be the point of waking us up to perform maintenance?"

Although, she thought after the words were out, *he did threaten Horváth, and later me.* A threat implied a physical means to carry it out. Still, something in her told her to hold this information back for now. She could always reveal it later and play forgetful.

"Because servitors *were* the plan. This Conscious Crew Crap wasn't a thing until we left earlier than planned, before everything was done," Xian said. "There are only nine of us awake, after all." She eyed Horváth. "Eight now. Not much to maintain a ship of this size."

"It seems like whether you know or don't know things depends on which would be more convenient for you," Bell said, narrowing one eye.

"One thing I can say for sure," Xian fired back, "is that whoever did this to him, it would require a great deal of strength." Her gaze went from combative to suspicious. "Just what percentage synthetic are you again?"

Bell shifted uncomfortably. Since the answer was "100 percent," she was by far the most synthetic of anyone awake, almost certainly of the whole ship. But there were limits to what even she could do. She was stronger than a meat-sack human because metal and polymer were stronger than organic muscle, but she hadn't been specifically optimized for gutting someone with a dull rod, even if said rod had entered through his mouth. Heh. But if as much of Horváth's center of mass was meat as it appeared, she likely *would* have had enough strength to do this to him. It just would have been pushing her design limits.

There was no way she was going to admit that, however.

"For your information," Bell said, "I've spent the last several hours completely submerged in fungal paste. I suspect you can still smell it, even way over there. I barely had time to shower."

"Or barely had time to get yourself dirty with it as cover," Xian threw back.

"More politely put, can anyone confirm that alibi?" Tas asked pointedly. From Xian it would have enraged Bell. From Tas all she felt was a silly sense of betrayal and hurt. "Who was your work partner? Can they vouch for you?"

Bell winced before she could stop herself. "Thing is," she said, drawing out the pause so long it would need to renew its subscription, "technically . . ." More pause. At last, she pointed. "He was."

The looks Bell got in response to this told her she had not explained this adequately. "He was *supposed* to be, I mean. Both he and I protested at having to work together, and Loopy let us work alone."

"Why'd you try to get out of it?" LaSalle asked.

At the same time Xian said, "Why did the brain let you work alone?"

This was not going anyplace good.

"What's important is that the last time I saw this guy, he was totally and very unpleasantly alive *and* un-skewered."

"And threatening you," Tas said.

Et tu, beautiful? Though to her credit, Tas didn't look precisely happy to say it. And the reason why was obvious.

"Threatening both of us, if you recall," Bell said.

Xian stared languidly between Bell and Tas, exaggeratedly noting their height difference, roughly a meter, then let her gaze drift back to the body. "I know where I'm placing my money between the two of you."

"You seem awfully eager to pin this on someone quickly," Bell said. "Almost as if you'd prefer we not spend too much time looking elsewhere."

"Hey now," LaSalle said, "let's not turn on each other." As though he didn't have wet dreams every night about waking up to find the entire crew vivisecting him just to prove his screamingly obvious paranoia right. "We've got four other awake crew members who have yet to make an appearance. And they're all a hell of a lot *weirder* than us, if you take my meaning."

And just what the fuck is that supposed to mean? Bell was revising her opinion of LaSalle from "twitchy creep" to "xenophobic asshole" and about to let fly on him when she realized she probably shouldn't argue with someone who agreed she might not have done this, even if he was doing so for bigoted reasons.

"This is pointless speculation," she said instead, speaking the thought the moment she had it. "Loopy can clear me when he decides to talk again." It was probably a thought better kept inside. Because although she kept a straight face, she wondered if that were true. The sign had said that section of the ship wasn't monitored by Loopy. Bell realized with a sinking feeling that she might have no real alibi, ship's brain or no ship's brain.

No. That's stupid. He couldn't see if I was in there, but he'd be able to tell that I was nowhere else, thus meaning I had *to be in there. Process of elimination.*

"In fact," she said, "he can do better. Loopy will know who killed Horváth," Bell said, leaping to the ultimate point of such ruminations.

"Yes, we've all come to the same singularly brilliant conclusion." Xian's words could have scoured Bell's scales of the little bits of drying fungal paste the shower hadn't caught.

"He'll have seen it happen," Bell said, flipping Xian the bird but otherwise not acknowledging her in any way. "All we have to do is wait for him to reboot or whatever he's doing, and he can solve this mystery."

"I agree with LaSalle in spirit, if not in intensity," Xian interjected. "It seems unlikely the brain's inability to answer is a coincidence. Deflect suspicion all you want, but waiting might just give whoever it is a chance to strike again." Her eyes never left Bell.

"If anyone here actually liked that giant motherfucker, please come forward. I didn't think so," she said, not waiting for a response.

"I don't think that argument helps you the way you think it does," Tas said, softly but still loud enough for everyone to hear.

"You already indicated you're pleased that he's dead," Xian said.

"Which would be a really stupid thing for the murderer to say."

"You're the only one who might possess the strength necessary to—"

"Not the only one," Tas cut in. Despite herself, Bell felt a surge of pleasure at this most tepid of defenses.

"No, indeed," said a new voice, close on the heels of the door hissing open behind them.

CHAPTER 9
POORLY TIMED SEXUAL ENCOURAGEMENT

BELL TURNED and saw not one, but two unfamiliar forms standing between her and the door. Both were draped, practically swaddled, in cloth. The tattered drapery of the hulking shape to the left looked surprisingly organic, the beige color of sackcloth. It tickled Bell's memory in a fairly unpleasant way. Meanwhile, the comparatively diminutive one on the right, a head shorter than Bell, had a smooth sheen to its shade of blue-violet material Bell couldn't quite place.

Both beings' faces were completely covered, the larger in an oversized hood pulled well forward, the smaller in another flap of his draperies. The only break on the latter was a chevron-shaped hole roughly where the mouth on a human would be. Still, though Bell could see no mouth moving, she was correct in her assumption that it was the smaller of the two beings that had spoken.

"Has anyone noted," the mystery person said, gesturing expansively, "the alignment of his face?" He had a soft, urbane voice, male in presentation. It was an accent that spoke of culture and learning. But there was something odd about it, something Bell was too startled to parse right away. The speaker pointed up at Horváth's face with a cloth-shrouded hand. "He's staring right at the door, right where someone would be standing. Someone taller than me, anyway."

Bell, who happened to be standing just inside the door, turned to look and found herself staring directly into Horváth's glassy, scowling eyes. Yet another uncomfortable feeling, given the implications of what had just been said.

"He looks angry," Tas said. She cast a painfully direct glance at Bell. It was a look Bell was coming to recognize. When something engaged Tas's mind, she forgot to look all broody and injured.

"It's not like I'm the only tall person here," Bell said, once again giving voice to what everyone else was clearly thinking, only this time with much less force behind her words.

"Could he have still been alive, I wonder," said the soft voice, "when the culprit stood there to admire their handiwork?" Even though he was apparently changing the subject, something Bell was eager to do herself, her irritation at being ignored screeched louder in her mind.

Annoyed at too many things to parse, Bell acted instinctually. For her, this meant wrenching everyone's attention back to her like the lead float in a fucking idiot parade.

"I'm sorry, I know I was a bit late to the waking-up-an-indentured-servant-party, but just who are you and your big friend?"

"My apologies," the soft voice said. He shifted to face Bell. At least, she assumed he was a he. And she thought he shifted to face her. It was difficult to get anything at all beyond basic length, width, and height given what he was wearing.

And now that she focused fully on parsing that cultured voice, Bell realized with a start that she was listening to an alien speaking. So this was one of the four non-humans Loopy had mentioned. The use of human speech patterns was excellent, and she doubted anyone without extensive linguistic training—and some embedded technological assistance—would have been able to tell, but this fellow was no more human than the invaders of Anaranjado had been.

Could he have been captured in one of the skirmishes? It was a rare thought Bell didn't speak aloud, and that fact surprised her. Surely any such prisoner would have been kept on-planet, pumped for information, and—

"You may call me Master Fault," he said, interrupting her train of thought's final approach to Speculation Station.

"Has anyone ever told you your name sounds like a critical error on a 1960s spacecraft?" Bell couldn't suppress a snort at her own devastating wit.

"I'm afraid you have me at a disadvantage," Master Fault—*ha!*—said, "since I have no idea what any of that means."

That should have made it funnier, but somehow, his utter nonchalance ruined the moment. Bell suppressed a glare.

"What are you a master of anyway?"

"Oh, little enough, I'm sure," he said, waving the question away much like a dismissive human would have. As Master Fault stepped into the room and the hulking form looming behind followed in lockstep, Bell started at the sound of whirring servos. It was something she might have attributed to an opening door if not for seeing the priest move with the sound.

This second, larger figure was no biological giant, nor even a cybernetic transhuman like Bell or the other Anaranjadans. Anaranjadan synthetic muscle was designed to be as much like human muscle in design as possible, only better in every way. This was something altogether different. Cruder, simpler, but all the more powerful for it.

It—he?—was a straight-up robot. Bell recalled Loopy's earlier words when discussing life support limits. This must be Brother Barnabas.

"So that thing is what you meant when you said the brain has servitors?" Tas stated.

"I think we just found our prime suspect," LaSalle said, goggling at the sheer size of the hulking construct.

"Hm?" Master Fault seemed perplexed by the question before turning to glance behind him. "Oh! Oh my, no. Despite our odd appearances by your standards, both my companion of coincidence and I are but simple itinerant priests. We are every bit as much members of the, ah, *crew* as you yourselves."

Normally Bell would have mentally written him off the moment she'd heard the word *priest*. The rest of what he said would have become just a buzzing. Literally. She had established a series of filters to make her ears make an actual buzzing so the offending sound was never processed in her brain. It had become a necessity about thirty seconds into her dealings with the Shadyside cult back on Anaranjado.

But this time, despite whichever module in her patchwork brain that was running her Infatuation Complex over Tas howling that she shouldn't say anything—people could be awfully tetchy about religion, and it was desperate to salvage a good first impression—Bell felt compelled to speak.

"Do we know each other, big guy?"

"You've met this creature before?" Xian asked, words sharp with newly whetted suspicion.

"Not directly," Bell said. She didn't recall any cultists as big as this fellow, but he sure dressed the part. And since they'd replaced their bodies with mechanical parts, a much cruder version of Bell herself, he sounded the part too when he moved. "But he reminds me of some *people* I knew back on Anaranjado."

"I believe I know of whom you speak," Master Fault said. "And no, Brother Barnabas is not a member of that particular order. He is not now and has never been a biological human. He was built, not born. And I can vouch for the fact he never once left the orbital platforms during his visit to your world because neither did I. Nor is he a servitor of the ship. We are from off-world, you see, and your colony's controlling cabal takes a dim view of allowing any such as us to interact with the populace at large."

"Fascinating," Bell said, really trying to sell it. "And, um, what faith or whatever do you practice?"

Whatever Master Fault said next was drowned out by the exact buzzing she thought she'd disabled. Cursing inwardly, Bell fiddled with the boredom filter's sensitivity settings.

"But I doubt anyone here has heard of it, save from me," Master Fault said. Too awkward to ask him to repeat the name of his faith now, and anyway, Bell didn't really care.

"Oh?" Bell said, trying desperately not to yawn. So irritating! "He's, uh, not your religion? Or whatever?"

Master Fault's laugh was surprisingly rich.

"Oh my, no," he said with mirth. "My priesthood doesn't go in much for proselytizing. We are more about acts of charity. Quite unlike my companion here. Brother Barnabas is of a decidedly more faith-forward, ah, *sect* than I. He will talk your ear off—I believe that is how the idiom goes—given half a chance. Or he would have. But in the interim, he's lost access to his voice. His entire ability to communicate and most of his ability to process language, as near as I can tell. Some error in his restart processes, I suppose. In recognition of his plight, and as a fellow being of the cloth, I've taken it upon myself to act as his interpreter until the matter can be sorted out."

Brother Barnabas suddenly dropped to one knee and bowed its hooded head as if in silent prayer. Owing to his sheer bulk when standing, he caught the recessed lighting better knelt in supplication, and Bell noticed his monk's robes looked moth-eaten. A robot mendicant priest who wasn't part of her erstwhile cultish friends—or marks, whatever—was almost interesting enough not to require Bell to override her boredom filter.

Brother Barnabas was also, as LaSalle had alluded to, the only other being present obviously powerful enough to have done what Master Fault claimed had happened to Horváth. Since she knew she hadn't killed the asshole, this Barnabas shot straight to the top of Bell's suspect list.

"So, Brother Barnabas there seems like a solid bet as our culprit," she said. She'd never believed in mincing words. She just wished LaSalle hadn't gotten the idea out there first. "He's bound to be stronger than me, and he's even bigger than old guts-pile over there."

"He certainly possesses the means," Master Fault acknowledged. "But he's been with me the entire time since before the good staff sergeant here met his grisly end."

"Says you," Bell said. "Even if that's true, can anyone vouch for you? You just said the big boy there can't talk, and since you went so far as to say he couldn't communicate at all, I assume that means he can't write as well?"

"Correct," Master Fault said. "But then, even if he could, he would surely corroborate the account of the person who was exonerating him, whether or not it was true, wouldn't he?"

Ugh. Apparently saying things like that wasn't just a human thing.

Master Fault had probably helped Barnabas kill Horváth, and now the pair of them were covering for each other. The story about Barnabas losing his voice was likely so much bullshit. Maybe the robot was just a shittier liar. Bell was pretty sure that was a trope in fiction. Maybe it contained a grain of truth.

She opened her mouth to say all of this when the loudspeaker squawked, forestalling her. What emerged was something far louder and more grating than the normal clicks and hisses.

Loopy's voice, when it spoke, sounded at first very slow and then sped up to absurdity before settling back into its normal register.

"System reboot completed, runningdiagonosticsdiagnosticscom-pletediagnosticresultsnormal. Hello everyone. I apologize for my unanticipated downtime. Scanning. Oh dear. I see there has been an incident."

"You already know there has," Bell said. "You're the one who announced it and led us here."

"Yes, of course. Forgive me," Loopy said. "Recent memory processes are still uploading. Yes. Staff Sergeant Horváth was murdered. All files now synched."

"Fantastic," Bell said. "Now tell us who did it."

"I apologize, Bell. All I can inform you of is when the body was first discovered, which was seventeen minutes and twenty-three seconds ago. And by whom, which was Xian Ginevra. She pulled the room's generalized emergency alarm."

"You should be able to tell us a lot more than that, machine," Xian said. Bell noted she didn't sound best pleased at being the person who had discovered the corpse.

Or had she only pretended to discover it because she had *created* it?

"I recall reviewing your surveillance specifications before my . . . change in status aboard this vessel," Xian went on. Bell raised an eyebrow at what this implied, and noticed Tas doing the same, albeit more hotly. Slightly more hotly. "You have comprehensive observation systems scattered throughout the entire ship," Xian continued. "'Any-where it can speak, it can see.' That's what I was told. That's what the plans said. And you're speaking in this room, where Horváth was clearly killed. So, start talking."

"I am *terribly* sorry, Ms. Xian, but I'm afraid none of you have root access. I cannot relay that information."

The room was silent for a minute as everyone worked to choke down this under-chewed lump of insanity.

"Hold on, wait," Bell said, her burning desire to dramatically crack the case momentarily overshadowed by how pissed-off these revelations were making her, "you're telling me that one of us is dead, killed by another one of us, and you can't tell us who did it despite the fact that you have sensors in the room where the big fucker died?"

"Essentially accurate, yes," Loopy said. "But you left out how very *sorry* I am for this fact, which I feel is important to formally note."

"Now wait a goddamned, shit-kicking minute," Bell said. "Someone murdered him. He's dead!"

"Only half-accurate. I am happy to report," Loopy said, "that as of this moment, this situation has been rectified. Based on mandatory sampling that was taken when you were all brought aboard, I have just successfully initiated the cloning and subsequent rapid physical maturation of Staff Sergeant Horváth, and early scans indicate that the possibility of fatal defects is minimal!"

"Wait," Tas said, her voice unreadable. "You're *cloning* him?"

"It is standard procedure," Loopy said. "The same as I would do for any of you in the highly likely event that another one of you is killed. You represent valuable working assets to both the ship and the future colony you will help found. Permanent loss of any such assets is considered unacceptable. As such, the ship's cloning facilities are adequate to clone any of you. Rebuild in your case, Brother Barnabas. And Bell."

"Hold on," Bell was as desperate for clarification as she was to elide over his last point. "Did you just say highly like—"

Xian tsked. "Waste of time." She rose, as though to go. "We won't learn anything more here."

"Wait," Tas said. She sounded as though the words were being pried from her with torture implements, but she looked determined. "Can we ask Horváth? Master Fault here just deduced how he might have seen his killer. You're doing some sort of memory implantation, I assume?"

"That's a *thing?*" Bell said, pretending total shock. She even clapped her palms to her cheeks to sell it. She knew it was a thing. She was living proof of its thing-being, though she *was* mildly surprised it was a thing on this ship, however, considering the taboo against it on Anaranjado. There was a reason she'd had to con some crazy cultists into swapping her meat brain for a synthetic one against all custom and possibly a few eensy-weensy capital laws.

"Yes, memory implantation will take place, but I'm afraid he won't know who murdered him," Loopy said. "Because of the massive amount of damage to his head, his brain was unrecoverable. No postmortem brain scan was therefore possible."

"So, wrecking his face like that wasn't about how ugly he was," Bell said. "Or not *just* that, anyway." Disappointing. "He'll have no idea of his own history, why he's even here. He won't even remember his crime."

"Incorrect!" Loopy said with glee. "His initial brain scan is fully intact. It was taken at the same time his genetics were sampled for contingency cloning purposes. He will have lost all recollection of his time since being put under cryosleep aboard the *Ultima Thule.*"

Bell supposed there was at least some advantage to a Dietrick Horváth who only recalled wanting to kill her based on her "crime" and not her behavior toward him since waking, but since she didn't know the opinion the actual killer held about her, she'd have rather had the information.

Tas wasn't done. "Does that imply the rest of us have had brain scans done as well? How did you do that without killing us all? I thought they were destructive."

"Answer to your first question: yes, you have! Even Bell."

Shit, be cool, Loopy.

Thankfully, before the others could fully process what the narc ship's brain had said and force Bell to start answering a bunch of awkward questions about fully cybernetic brains, which she was quite certain no one here had but her, Loopy barreled onward. "Answer to the follow-up question: experimental technology! Which is my favorite kind. This ship represents its first widespread use."

Widespread, maybe. But not its first use.

"Well, as great and non-dangerous as all that sounds," Bell said, "go ahead and opt me out of any future scans. Oh, and do me a solid and destroy any copies you are holding onto."

"I'm terribly sorry, Bell, but the terms of your sentence do not permit you to make those kinds of demands. As stated, each of you is a valuable asset to the future colony. Your knowledge base can't be lost due to the inevitable accidents or murders that will occur."

Bell was about to protest in great and profane detail when LaSalle held up his hands like a man trying to stem a flood—a flood of toilet water. "So, help me understand because, if I'm hearing this correctly, *Jesus Christ.* If you can't tell us who killed him, and *he* can't tell us who killed him, and any one or more of us might be killed in the meantime since we have no fucking idea why he was killed in the first place, why the hell are you so happy about cloning him?"

"I am conditioned to experience a dopamine rush resulting from the successful execution of any of my core mandates, one of which is ensuring the continued safety of the crew."

"But you *didn't* ensure that." Tas's voice was an incredulous croak. "He died!"

"The situation is being rectified. Horváth was alive, briefly dead, and now he is alive again. Nothing irreplaceable has been lost."

Three ascending tones sounded, their cloying pleasantness clashing with the tension of the moment.

"Wonderful news," Loopy said. "That chime indicates that duties are over for the day, and it is time for your mandatory relaxation period. Commence relaxing! Please remember that sexual intercourse is both permitted and encouraged."

Bell perked up at this bit, but Tas was having none of it.

"The only relaxation we're going to be doing is figuring out who did this. And since the ship's brain allegedly can't help us, we're going to have to figure it out on our own."

In the grand scheme, Bell begrudgingly supposed that ran a close second as far as relaxation activities went.

"And I think it would be best," Tas said, "if Bell and Barnabas were confined to their respective rooms while the rest of us sort this out. In full view of one another," she added, as Xian looked ready to argue.

"We'll need to track down the other two aliens as well. At least one of them might have been strong enough for this." Despite quickly catching the mood of the room, Tas's gaze was locked onto the point where the metal rod had been jammed into the chamber floor. Her face was etched in a frown.

Whatever she was thinking, Bell was just relieved the little woman couldn't see the hurt that was surely playing across Bell's face. Thinking quickly, she triggered a logic puzzle to run automatically in her subconscious, tied to simulated dopamine as her unconscious mind worked through it. The warm fuzzy feedback made it easier to sound mild and agreeable when she responded, instead of pissed and wounded.

"All right," she said. "I'll agree to it if the big boy will." Good. She had sounded nice and reasonable. The rest, she could unpack later. *Gawd, I am so fucked over her.*

"Given the good brother's current state," Master Fault said, "that's likely a bit too complex a concept to have any hope of getting across. But I believe I can at least convince him to follow me and wait in his room."

"That all right with you, Loopy?" Tas asked the ceiling. Her voice was a challenge. Listening raptly, Bell suddenly found herself wishing very badly for some alone time.

"Perfectly permissible within the bounds of Designated Relaxation," the brain responded.

It sounded like Bell was about to get some. Alone time, that was.

CHAPTER 10
HOME IS WHERE THE PERSON OF INTEREST IS

THE DOOR to Bell's coffin-sized quarters shut on Tas's half-apologetic, half-suspicious, all-smokin' face looking up at Bell's. The room was little more than a door in one wall, a bed jutting from the opposite wall, an intercom in the third wall, and what looked like a charging plate in the fourth wall, one compatible with the type of power cells used by Anaranjadans to power any non-organic parts they had equipped.

Her self-guided tour thus complete, Bell settled on the bed to wait out her enforced isolation. A few minutes later came the sounds of what must be one of the crates from Horváth's death room being slid in front of the door. Which made absolutely no sense to Bell because the doors on the ship opened sideways, sliding into the adjoining wall. She heard additional crates being piled atop the first one.

Regardless of sense-making, the subtext was clear. They couldn't literally lock her in her room, but they could pile up enough crap in front of the door that she wouldn't be able to leave without making a ruckus. Which also meant, of course, that they couldn't get back *in* without making a ruckus and giving her ample warning. Which also meant she couldn't really be disturbed. She had a few brief moments of privacy.

And that meant she had some Bell time.

A few minutes later, with *that* thoroughly taken care of, Bell could think without Tas rattling around her brain. She rose, re-dressed, and pressed her left palm to the charge plate, feeling a different kind of euphoric feedback as the electrons streamed through the shared interface as she leaned against the wall for support.

Reveling in her newfound mental clarity, she went straight back to where her thoughts had left off: thinking about the absurdity of the others boxing her in with supply crates. Surely they could just ask Loopy to keep tabs on her and Barnabas, but then, neither Xian nor Tas trusted the ship's brain. So maybe this was the best compromise they could manage. Bell told herself that surely the same thing was happening down the hall with Barnabas's quarters. Surely this wasn't just a frame job of Bell Beauregard.

She had never considered herself a paranoid person, but there was a first time for everything. And it didn't take long in this solitary confinement for Bell to learn that, as much as she'd always been a homebody, she didn't do well with a dire situation she had no control over and no mind-numbing entertainment available to fill the time. Instead of watching a movie or crushing a noob in a sim as she would have done back home, she allowed her mind to wander and was distressed at just how fast it began to death spiral. There was nothing to interrupt her thoughts tripping their way down an endless staircase into the darkness.

Barnabas. The obvious suspect. It had to be him, didn't it? Though Urk, the tripartite, would probably be strong enough, she thought. But there was no way the formal, honorable alien could have turned murderer. She just couldn't believe it.

Although, it was Horváth they were talking about. An asshole that large and leaky would have given everyone he'd ever spoken to a motive for murder.

Whomever it had been, Bell's problem was she had no alibi except for Loopy to vouch that she hadn't been anywhere near the big man. And Loopy hadn't been willing or able to do that.

"Plaque-riddled brain," she muttered. "Root access my carbonic-acid-dribbling—"

"Bell!" Loopy said from the ceiling. "How fortuitous. I was just about to talk to you."

"Oh yeah?" She felt suddenly self-conscious that he'd been listening to her badmouth him. Then she thought back to what she'd been doing a few minutes before and . . . nah. She was cool with that. "What's up?"

"Simply put, I am officially naming you the one in charge of solving this murder. Your rank is hereby elevated from 'Assorted Crew Member' to 'Special Detective Incognito.'"

"I have a rank?"

"All crewpersons have the same rank. Except, now, you."

"So, I have many, many *whys* relating to this promotion, but let's just roll them all in to a great big 'why the fuck?' shall we?"

"I was misleading you all after I awoke."

"So you can lie?"

"No. And I didn't. I misled. I had no choice. I *should* be able to tell you who the murderer is, but the truth is that I am unable to. I was not conscious during the incident, and my visual and audio sensor data from that time was either not recorded or purged. Whichever of those is the case, I do not have the information you seek. To make matters worse, that loss includes those data indicating which crew members were where, even in the time leading up to the incident."

"Okay," Bell said, reeling a bit from this nut-punch of a breaking-news item. "That feels like it can't be a coincidence, but it still doesn't explain why you want me to figure out what happened."

"Because you are the only person I am certain did not commit the murder."

"How can you be sure of that?" Despite her skepticism, the most powerful being on the ship believing her to be innocent at least *seemed* like good news. Though he could have mentioned it before she got locked in her room.

"I can't confirm the location of anybody in the hour leading to the murder, as I said. That means each of you had time to leave your assigned task and kill the staff sergeant. But you are the exception. Because of the mess you made. All those fungal-paste footprints are still there, prints which perfectly match your feet. And my humidity sensors in the showers place your cleaning after the murder alert had already gone out."

"Yeah, about that murder alert," Bell said with sudden suspicion. "How did you send that if you were unconscious?"

"I have certain unconscious processes which can detect the existence of sufficiently hazardous events. In combination with the active confirmation of a CCC member, this will trigger a prerecorded alert. In the staff sergeant's case, it was the violently abrupt termination of his vital signs combined with Xian's pulling of the lever."

"So let me get this straight," Bell said. "You have a *prerecorded* message for the situation 'there has been a murder?'"

"This is a multi-decade voyage through interstellar space forcibly crewed by prisoners, malcontents, and social deviants. I have prerecorded messages for *many* contingencies. 'Micrometeoroid impact detected.' 'Emergency ship wide power fluctuation.' 'Diverting life support from the crew decks.' 'Prepare for jettisoning of the crew decks.' Those four are meant to go together," he added unnecessarily. "This isn't even the first time I've used any of them. During one CCC waking period I utilized the sequence: 'fluid spill detected,' 'active biohazard detected,' and 'orgy on deck seven detected.'"

"Aw man," Bell said, crestfallen. "You're telling me I could have been awake for the orgy crew and instead I drew the murder crew?"

"Please, Bell, I need your complete focus in this matter. I do not know what caused the interruption in my conscious state, but we must assume it's not a coincidence. In trying to cover their tracks, there is no telling whether the killer may attempt the same thing again. You are the only one I'm certain I can trust."

Bell was torn. On the one hand, that seemed like an awful lot of work. On the other hand, given that at least Xian thought Bell herself was guilty, this might be the only way to truly clear her name.

But even clearing her name ultimately meant nothing. Bell's main purpose was to find some way, any way, out of this trap she'd woken to. And there was only one possibility she could see. She had to get off this scow before it deposited her planet-side and she lost all access to space. When you were trapped on a planet that your enemies owned, there was quite literally no escape.

The trouble was, it was already too late for any of that. Before she'd been accused of crimes against humanity after her ill-advised attempt to *do her fucking job* back on Anaranjado, Bell had seen a planned route for this very ship. The target planet in question had been unoccupied, but she remembered hearing that the ship's planned route would take it very near—some said dangerously near—the sovereign space of at least two other inhabited star systems who might not take kindly to a passing colony ship.

If they had been near one of those other systems, and *if* Bell could somehow contrive a way to leave the ship in an escape pod, or a shuttle, or locker torn out of the wall, and *if* she could get picked up by another vessel, and *if* she could convince them to grant her asylum and not dismantle her for parts . . .

But all of those *if*s would have to go her way. If even one of them failed, any chance of escape would fail with it.

And considering they were already nearly at their destination, none of the *if*s had, in fact, gone her way. She'd slept through every single one of them.

"*Uggggggggh,* fine," she said, begrudgingly. Then she brightened. "Do I get a ray gun?"

"No."

"Normal gun?"

"Also no."

"How am I supposed to take down the killer? Form an angry mob with the others?"

"No. You will deal with them by letting me know. Then I will deal with them. It is imperative that you keep your role as detective secret from the others."

"Why? That feels like the opposite of what a detective is supposed to do."

"Quite simply because if the killer knew I had empowered you to hunt for them, it would make you a prime target."

That . . . actually made a lot of sense.

"But how can you expect to take down the killer if you are a disembodied voice and a cluster of sensors?" Clearly the richies had some means of controlling their prisoner-servants once they arrived, but Bell had seen no sign of such thus far.

"It is true the automated security resources planned for use in the eventual colony are not available to me, but I am not entirely without physical presence. I do not have the freedom of movement and action which you would have, but once I know who I am looking for, I will be able to manage. But my limitations in physical space only add to the urgency of your mission. I can't perform the kinds of specific maintenance I require of the crew. Without you to bring this to a satisfactory resolution, the only way to ensure your safety would be to return you to cryosleep. But in that event, our ability to bring the ship safely into orbit would be in significant doubt."

"What the fuck? You just had me mucking out crud-pipes to make sure the richies could feast. How is that a good use of time?"

"As a warm-up task, it suffices. You had just come out of cryosleep. It was essential to make sure that you were functioning correctly before tasking you with something more critical to the overall safety of the ship. Rest assured: there are significantly more crucial tasks which require your urgent attention. And now you are one person down. And you have a second job. It's a good thing you can go without sleep."

Fuck. Bell was hoping he hadn't known that.

"Well, now that I'm on the case," she said, "can you convince them to let me out?"

"No, Bell. I cannot. As I said, it is imperative that your new role remain a secret from the rest of the crew. Telling them that I know you are innocent would be too close to revealing that secret."

"This is a really shitty job offer, Loopy. I just want you to know that."

"Based upon your past work history and subsequent performance evaluations, would you be willing to propose a job that you would find agreeable?"

"Oh, fuck off."

IT TOOK a lot longer for someone to come get her than Bell would have liked, and she began to doubt just how persuasive Loopy was being with the others. Then came the sound of crates being dragged away from her door.

Thank dog. She'd forgotten to note the time when she'd been locked in here, but it had surely been hours. What the fuck had taken them so long?

"What the fuck took you so . . ." Bell began before trailing off in horror at seeing Tas staring up at her, one eyebrow raised.

"You've been in here less than an hour," the little woman said. She wore a kind of half-smile and seemed more relaxed than before. It was a good look for her, and whatever it might mean, it helped ease some of Bell's tension as well.

"Oh," Bell said, feeling a dopey grin steal across her face. She forced her voice to be casual. "I guess it was just really boring in here. I mean, except for . . . never mind."

"Never mind what?" Tas asked sharply.

Bell had been about to say "except for the ship's AI naming me the detective who is going to blow this case wide open," only just remembering Loopy's warning in time. This wasn't fair! Detectives were super-sexy. She was pretty sure that was a thing people thought. Tas would totally be impressed.

"Never mind, never mind."

This sparkling wit did not evoke the total abandonment of the topic from Tas that she'd hoped, so Bell made her voice *even more casual.* "Look, it's not like I was about to say anything *suspicious* or anything."

Tas's eyes narrowed. Maybe Bell should stop talking.

"I mean, I can see where the fact that I keep protesting how unsuspicious it was makes it sound *more* suspicious," she continued for some reason. "But it definitely wasn't." *Stop talking.* "Like, I mean, the things I think about, those belong to me, right?" *Stop it!* "You can't take someone to task for their inner thoughts." Tas's breathtaking stare bored into her. "I rubbed one out, okay?" Bell finally blurted, then shrugged.

Miraculously, she managed not to say who she'd been thinking about at the time.

"Uh, huh," Tas said, looking some mixture of amused and alarmed. Bell chose to focus on the former.

Still got it.

"If you're finished being weird," Tas said, which seemed a wholly unnecessary clause to append to the beginning of her statement, "you should come with me. We found something that . . . Well, it doesn't exactly help your case so much as hurt everyone else's. I know, I know," she said, catching Bell's look, "that was a shitty tease. But it really will be easier if I just show you."

She turned and walked away without waiting to see if Bell was following.

CHAPTER 11
WHAT GOES DOWN MIGHT HAVE ACTUALLY COME UP

BELL RETURNED WITH TAS, her nominal escort, to the murder room. For all that Bell had braced for it, the body still startled her to see. Bell could sanitize the details as much as she wanted—metal rod lodged in floor at a forty-five-degree angle, splayed-open corpse lodged on rod—but that didn't really convey the weight of it. It was a weight she understood intellectually without feeling it emotionally. Maybe she was distancing herself from it, or some touchy-feely crap like that.

More startling was that no one else was present. Upon arrival, she expected Tas to immediately go for the hole, given her fascination with the spot the rod had embedded itself into earlier. And it was really, really hard to not go for a dirty joke there, and also on the *really, really hard* thought, but Bell restrained herself. No sense sounding both insane and perverted, especially since Tas did not go for the hole—*ha!* —but instead led Bell to the edge of the room, toward a small pile of crumbly looking crud.

"Notice anything about that mound?" Tas asked.

Gah! Again. Aside from the obvious layup, Bell had nothing detective-y to add, a fact she would now endeavor to conceal from Tas.

"Indubitably, but I'd like to hear what *your* thoughts on the

Mentally noting how much Xian knew about the device, Bell returned her attention to Tas.

"So when you said this doesn't so much exonerate me as it implicated everyone else?"

"That's not exactly how I phrased it."

"What you mean is the culprit didn't need superhuman strength." Bell pointed at the very clear instructions printed in pictographs along the side. "Anyone could have operated this thing."

"Correct."

"Well," Bell said. "Thanks for that."

"How did they time the shot?" LaSalle demanded. Then once more, with feeling. *"How did they time the bloody shot?* They're shooting through a solid floor. How'd they know when he'd be lined up? Fuck me, how'd they get him into that room in the first place? It's not as if they could just lug this thing around with them while they stalked him from one floor down. I'll tell you how. It's. A. Conspiracy."

Bell only froze for an instant, but somehow, *somehow,* Tas caught the tiny non-movement.

"What?" she said. Any hint of warmth she'd shown upon lifting the pall of suspicion from Bell was replaced with fresh suspicion all her own. "What is it?"

Startled at being noticed, Bell answered honestly, unfortunately. "Well, I don't know how he might have been lured into the space, but as to how they timed the shot . . . Some people might be able to see through the ceiling. Floor. Deck. Whatever."

"People like you?"

Everyone was back to staring at Bell, this time with the added regard of Master Fault and Barnabas, invisible though their stares were.

"Honestly, it's not what you think. It's thermal, mainly for sensing areas that are too hot or too cold to be safe back on Anaranjado. It's not for, like, spying on people. Or targeting them."

"But could you tweak it for that?" Xian's voice was iron.

"I mean, probably? I've never tried," Bell said. The gazes focused on her were growing cold enough that she might be able to see the difference if she switched on said thermal vision. Then, desperate to look anywhere else, wondering why the fuck she was letting these people bully her with nothing but their eyeballs, she caught sight of something in the shadow of the nail gun's treads.

Bending over, she snatched the object free, coming up with a set of goggles. *Thermal vision* goggles. Bell had to resist the urge to do more than one pelvic thrust of triumph.

"Aha," Bell said. "Look here. No need for fancy visual filters built into your eyes when you have these, see? See?" She proffered the goggles, showing them off. "This makes it even *less* likely I did it." It was maybe not the best wording. "Which I didn't!"

Slowly, reluctantly, the gazes returned to a more normal level of mistrust, spread out amongst everyone, not just Bell.

Everyone but Tas. Her gaze broke away only after many awkward moments.

Bell was debating whether to ask, *So what's the upshot of all this?* But maybe that was too big a clue that she was the one in charge here. Worse, it sounded like something every single one of her managers over the years would have asked.

She was spared from further internal debate when the door opened and Grome and Urk finally decided to join the party, slithering and stomping in respectively. They volunteered no explanation for their long absence, and despite her delight at meeting the pair of them upon first awakening, said absence had not done anything to alleviate them of suspicion in Bell's mind. It was the first time the entire crew—all of them still alive at least—had been in the same room together.

"Well, well," LaSalle said. "Look who finally decided to join us. I'm not sure how it works *where you two come from*, but you've sure been going out of your way to avoid us and the scene of the crime, which is pretty fucking suspicious from where I'm sitting."

"I thought returning to the scene of the crime was the suspicious thing," Bell said, emotions swerving. She felt a sudden need to defend the two aliens from what she now suspected was xenophobically motivated suspicion.

"It certainly can't hurt for them to offer up an alibi," Xian said. She and LaSalle had been buddy-buddy from the beginning, and the killing had only seemed to knot them together more tightly. It made

Bell wish Tas would stop being so aloof and team up with her. Well, it was *another* reason she wished that. Second place, if she were being honest.

"We were completing our assigned task in the cargo umbilical coupling area," Urk said in his trademark croak. "As directed by the ship's brain."

"Brain, can you confirm this?"

"You lack root access. I cannot confirm. I'm deeply sorry."

Bell knew better, and now that she parsed what Loopy was saying, she realized how sneaky clever it was. He said he couldn't lie but he could mislead. *You lack root access. I cannot confirm.* Two separate true statements. Saying them one right after the other created a causal link in a listener's brain, but there was nothing in the words themselves stating that they were in any way related. He'd done it the first time, too, Bell realized, playing back his words with perfect memory.

I am terribly sorry, Ms. Xian, but I'm afraid none of you have root access. I cannot relay that information.

Again, two true statements that had nothing to do with one another.

"Of course not," Xian spat. She turned back to Urk. "And does your compatriot have nothing to say for itself?"

A small horde of worms detached themselves from the seething central mass, and everyone nearby cleared a space rapidly as they rushed down and out across the floor, leaving glistening slime trails in their wake. They moved with surprising speed to form shapes both straight and curving on the floor, spelling out in flawless English block lettering NEVER LEFT EACH OTHER'S SIGHT.

Bell golf-clapped with barely restrained glee.

"And we are to just take their word for it," Xian said.

"I'm afraid you will have to for the time being," Loopy chimed in suddenly. "Because now that we are all here, Conscious Crew Complement, please give me your attention. I must inform you that Mandatory Relaxation has come to an end. In order to prevent your maintenance schedule from falling behind, it's time to hand out your next set of tasks!"

This prompted a general uproar.

"You're insane! How do you expect us to work if we're constantly looking over our shoulder, wondering if we're about to be killed?" For once, LaSalle spoke for all of them.

"In pairs, of course," Loopy said. "There are now eight of you, so the math works perfectly!"

"So whoever happens to get paired with the killer is just fucked? Wouldn't teams of three make more sense? We could have two of those, then one team of two." He turned as though to plead his case to the rest of them. "That way, the odds of the killer being with someone else alone are much lower."

"Quite impossible," Loopy said. "The list of necessary repairs and maintenance was already stretched to the limits of our schedule prior to Staff Sergeant Horváth's unfortunate demise. Now that we are a crew member down, we have no choice but to take some limited risks."

"Easy for you to say," LaSalle fired back.

"Assorted Crew Member LaSalle, I will remind you why you are here, and that the safety of this ship and its passengers supersedes that of any individual crew member or, quite frankly, even all of you together. Now, I am fully prepared to enforce the mandates I have been conditioned with if necessary."

His voice never lost its cheeriness, but there was a decided edge to it at the end, like the good nature had been purified and distilled so much it had grown toxic.

"Oh, no," LaSalle said. "No, no, no." He turned to pitch his words to the wider crowd. "Listen up," he said. "Here's what we're actually going to do. We're going to seal ourselves in our rooms until this voyage is over. We'll work out a schedule where people can leave to get food and water or whatever, but only one at a time. Our rooms have intercom connectivity. We can make sure everyone is in their room by requiring regular, round-robin check-ins. If anyone breaks that, we'll have our killer."

He finished, and much to her own surprise, Bell rated his plan an eight out of ten. Of course, given his latent paranoia, he'd probably been dreaming up such a plan since before the murder. But he lacked crucial information.

The problem was she recalled only too well the way Loopy had threatened Horváth when he was being all murdery toward her. Yet that was nothing but bluster if the ship's brain didn't even know who had committed the deed. She also recalled his statements about the level of maintenance the ship needed just to get them safely into stable orbit.

"This precaution makes sense." Urk spoke first, his words sounding as though they'd been extracted from a torture victim. His support surprised Bell, considering LaSalle's previous hostility. "I stand with LaSalle's decision." His surprisingly delicate hands at the end of those wispy arms gestured daintily in affirmation. Beside him, Grome slithered out their own affirmative response.

"Grome agrees with Urk," Bell said for the others' benefit. "I speak writher, just FYI."

LaSalle nodded, apparently perfectly happy with aliens as long as they agreed with him.

"A good plan, all things considered," Master Fault said. He inclined his draped head at LaSalle, and Bell nearly started. Something about the way the harsh lighting hit the folds of his fabric, or skin, or whatever it was, made it seem as though there were a pair of irregular, mismatched eyes, dark swatches of shadow, staring out at her. Before Bell could manage to be more than passingly creeped out, he turned to look up at Brother Barnabas. "Wouldn't you agree, my friend?" He gave an exaggerated nod as he asked.

After a moment, the massive, metal priest inclined his head once. Bell wasn't sure what he actually thought he was answering, since he allegedly couldn't process language, but it wasn't as if any of this mattered.

That left only Tas, Xian, and Bell herself. Tas regarded Bell with an overly knowing smile as she spoke.

"It's a good plan," she said at last. "Or it would be in another life. I just know what it's going to say."

"It will never be permitted," Xian said more bluntly. She did have the grace to glance apologetically at LaSalle.

"Indeed not," Loopy said, with the finality of having outlasted a bunch of toddlers throwing around nonsense arguments against bedtime. As if waiting for this moment, the door to the mess hall slid open. In the corridor outside, paneling Bell had never noticed in the center of the floor slid noiselessly to the side, revealing a concealed rail set into a depression about half a meter wide which the paneling had previously obscured.

"I see that simple polite requests to perform your tasks are no longer sufficient," Loopy said, still never losing his cheery mien. There was a whirring sound coming from down the corridor. At last, a strange apparatus cruised to a stop, pivoting to face them through the mess hall door. It looked like a metallic cross with arms curving forward, as though expecting a hug.

"This servitor and others like it have access to all ship's corridors," Loopy said. "They are a leftover construction aid for ferrying parts and supplies rapidly around the ship for delivery to assembly crews, but they have other uses in a pinch."

Looking at those curved arms, *pinch* seemed an apt word to Bell. Actinic blue arcs of electricity danced between pincer arms as Bell watched, as though to prove they were as much a threat to her as anyone.

"And since I know you are about to ask, no, this was not what happened to Staff Sergeant Horváth. The corridor track does not extend into rooms. Nothing done to him inside of one of them could have been accomplished by these drones."

"So, what's the point of this little display?" Bell asked. Though in truth, there was no need. She eyed the frame as though it were a venomous snake with three independently striking heads.

"I have already warned you of the consequences of disobeying my orders," Loopy said. "You speak as though convinced I am unable to act out those consequences. This is my demonstration otherwise. Any outright disobedience of my orders will result in you being apprehended by one of these devices the next time you are in a corridor. From there, you will be taken to the brig, where you will be subjected to a harsh mental retraining regimen. The level of severity of that regimen corresponds precisely with the level of resistance to necessary retraining put up by the subject. On a ship full of Anaranjadans, a society that prizes the collective good so highly, I had hoped that I would not need to resort to even threatening this outcome. I cannot stress enough that this is not a path I ever wish to take. But the safe arrival of this vessel, its passengers, and as much of its crew complement as possible is, after all, my purpose in life."

"If those things aren't everywhere, then you can't really be sure you'll get us," LaSalle said stubbornly.

"Not at any given moment, no," Loopy said. "But as you have no doubt noticed, the tracks are quite well camouflaged. Observing your biometrics when this one appeared, I feel quite certain all of you were surprised, even Xian. So while Assorted Crew Member LaSalle is quite correct that it is possible to avoid them for a time, sooner or later, I will be able to grab any shirkers with one. And you never know where or when that might be.

"Once again," Loopy said, "nothing would pain me more than to need to employ this eventuality. But that's up to all of you, and you may consider yourself fully and formally warned. Now, unless there are further questions, I suggest we not fall any further behind schedule."

CHAPTER 12
TRUST BEFORE TRYST

ANOTHER WORK SHIFT PASSED. This time, Bell was paired with LaSalle. Precisely thirty seconds after their shift began, she had the unfortunate realization that he was the type of person who chattered endlessly when confronted with silence. At precisely thirty-two seconds, Bell had successfully established a filter that would noise-cancel out everything he said while simultaneously prompting her at the appropriate times to reply with *yes* and *uh huh* and *interesting* and *you don't say.*

Only after the shift wound down did Bell wonder if, by not paying attention to him, she had let some vital clue slip by her. Oh well. They finished their work decidedly un-murdered, and the sensor array they'd been working on had been cleared of horrible, slimy parasites that looked like a cluster of mouths arranged in a vaguely phallic shape. At least she hadn't been on "clean up Horváth" duty. True, Loopy had promised his servitors would do most of the heavy lifting there, but Tas and Xian had still been forced to somehow get his body off the rod into the corridors.

Now it was time, Loopy *helpfully* informed them, for another Mandatory Rest shift. The tone had changed markedly since LaSalle's attempt at fomenting mutiny. Each crew member was retired to their quarters, escorted this time by one of Loopy's servitors. The fact that they had to do this in shifts told Bell he had fewer than eight of the constructs available to him, a revelation which left her feeling as mutinous as LaSalle had sounded earlier.

She stepped through her open quarters door as she turned this notion over in her head. But her train of thought was interrupted when Loopy's voice emerged tinnily from the servitor that had escorted her.

"Please wait at least ten minutes before sneaking out to resume your investigation," Loopy said. "I still have Urknuuzh and Grome to escort back to their quarters. If you run into anyone while you are exploring the ship alone, it would look very suspicious for you. Although, it might also be the fastest way to solve this mystery."

"Yes. Wait before I investigate. That's precisely what I intended to do. Because that's still happening, of course." Bell snapped her jaw shut before she could sound any more obvious in her being caught out. Loopy's earlier threats had been so direct, she'd half-convinced herself that plans had changed and the brain just hadn't troubled to inform her.

"You did poorly back there," Loopy said. "You should have agreed vocally with LaSalle's plan to keep you all safe. It would have established that you and I are on opposite sides of this issue, thus reducing the odds that anyone will suspect we are working together."

"Yes. You're right. I should have done a ruse. Because I'm good at ruses. Everyone is always telling me how subtle and indirect I am." Bell swore to dog; she never got chewed out more than when she actually did what was asked of her.

"Indeed," Loopy said. "Do better next time. Though I do think LaSalle may have laid out a little bit *too* good of a plan. I strongly suspect that at least one of your fellow crew members will attempt to do as he suggested, calling in over the intercom to make sure everyone is where they claim to be. So take this."

Still waiting outside her room, the servitor flexed one of its disturbingly insectile limbs toward her. Held in the manipulators at the end was a tiny piece of technology, as bright white as her hair.

"A comm unit. It forwards and acts as receiver for any communication requests directed to your personal wall intercom here. That way you can talk to your fellow crew members as if you are still in your room. Put it on. It should just fit around the back of your ear, and the color should blend in well with your hair."

"Thanks," Bell said. "Can I assume you will be assigning a servitor or two to keep me safe while I investigate?" It would be a tradeoff, safety in exchange for being watched. But then, the ship's brain could watch her anyway—even if seemingly only when it was inconvenient—so she would happily take the added safety.

"Unfortunately, no," Loopy said. So that tracked. The servitor tapped a flat panel on the front of its frame with one claw, and it lit up into a display. *POWER LEVEL CRITICAL*, it said.

"These units are well past their service life, I'm afraid," Loopy said. "Their battery longevity just isn't what it should be, and today was a busy day. There was a conspicuous pause while both of them considered this bit of information furiously. At least, that's what Bell was doing.

"Grome, I know you neither offered up the earlier plan to mutiny nor actively supported it—"

"Hold on, did you just call me Grome? You're doing it again."

"Oh, my! My sincerest apologies. *Bell,* I know you neither offered up the earlier plan to mutiny nor actively supported it, but based upon your performance history and just in case you were being uncharacteristically withholding of your opinion, I feel compelled to point out that you should not underestimate what my servitors are capable of."

Another manipulator flexed forward, only instead of ending in a claw, it ended in what was, unmistakably, a light switch gun.

"It's very small but quite powerful. It can do anything from leave you twitching on the floor for several minutes unable to move or even think, to completely frying every circuit in your body, or the entire nervous system of your more biological crew mates."

"Gotcha. And does it have any settings *below* that less-bad one?"

"It does not!" *Puppies for everyone,* he might as well have been saying.

"Message received," Bell said, saluting and smiling. *In other words, if I need to make a move, I need to time it very carefully.*

"Good!" Loopy said. "Now—"

"Hold on," Bell interrupted. "If your servitors all have to recharge, who is going to help me if I'm skulking around and I skulk right into the killer?"

"I will be monitoring the rooms. If anyone is out wandering around —aside from you, of course—I will let you know immediately."

"And if you go offline again?"

"I have taken every step available to me to prevent a recurrence—"

"And if you go offline again?"

"If I do not respond to repeated queries, then my advice would be to head straight back to your quarters and not let anyone in."

"These doors have locks on them?"

"They do not."

"Wonderful."

"I'm glad to see you pleased. Now, I have directed the servitors to place the staff sergeant's body outside the morgue. As the decay situation is not getting better with time, I suggest you go there and conduct your investigation on his remains first before examining the crime scene itself. After moving him into a cold storage unit, of course."

"What, me?"

"Correct. You. I already said they can't go anywhere but the corridors."

THE SERVITORS HAD, to their credit, obviously cleaned up as much of the mess as their limited reach allowed. Unfortunately for Bell, Horváth had just as obviously kept right on leaking even after they'd gone.

His body was piled against the door to the medical bay, within which, Loopy had assured her, lay the morgue. And "piled" was really the operative word, because whatever Tas and Xian had been doing to move him had involved separating his limbs from the rest of the body, probably to make individual chunks that they could carry.

Why Loopy had assigned them to this task instead of the massive Brother Barnabas, Bell had no clue.

Still, Loopy's behavioral predictions proved more apt than his staffing choices. Bell had already fielded two calls, one from Urk and one from Xian, on her way over. The former had been apologetic for his thoroughness, the latter sharply suspicious. Each time, Bell had stopped moving to answer that of course she was in her room, oh it was just so *boring* she might die, going to great pains not to create any kind of sound that would prove she was lying.

She really hoped that no one would call while she was dragging a chunk of Horváth through the med bay and into the adjoining morgue. She kept fretting about this right up until the time her foot stepped in something slick and kicked right out from under her. Down she went in a cursing heap. She'd slipped in a trail of some kind of slime along the floor, yet another delightful mystery substance which had oozed from the body and down the hallway. Bell picked herself up, her cursing shifting to the dead man for being so full of grossness—really, why everyone didn't trade in their meat for circuitry she would never understand—and she approached more warily this time.

Normally she would have grabbed him by the wrists or ankles and just started pulling, but that would have accomplished little, because his limbs were all detached now. She carried them in first, stacking them across her cradling arms like she'd seen people in Earth-vintage vids do with firewood. As she walked, she couldn't help but notice that whatever had separated them from the rest of him had left very clean cuts lined with scorch marks. She would have to figure out a way to ask Tas about that.

Then came the hard part, or maybe *the gross part* was a more apt description: moving the rest of the ugly fucker. Bell *really* didn't want to touch any of the unzipped middle of him. The sides and top of his head were the least-ruined, so that was what she grabbed. There were some popping sounds from the area of his neck as she started heaving and skidding along the floor, and the connection between head and body felt a little less sure after that, but the subsequent grinding sounds were mostly drowned out by all the squelches and the hisses of off-gassing.

She had him halfway through the door when Tas's voice erupted in her ear.

"Hello, Bell, how are we doing this fine evening?"

The playful tone sounded almost like the little woman was standing right behind Bell watching everything she was doing. She suddenly felt very exposed with Horváth's literal head in her hands and his torso heap preventing the med-bay door from shutting. And not the fun kind of exposed. As a result, she couldn't quite modulate her tone in time for her response.

"Heeeeeeey you. How's it going? What's up, what's up?"

"Okay, you're doing that thing again, where you sound all weird and suspicious. But to be clear, I *do not* want to hear any details about your most recent self-gratification."

Hurtful as it was, this comment was fortuitous timing as it gave Bell time to pivot away from her line about two heads being better than one in that regard. She wasn't even entirely certain if that qualified as a dirty joke. No sense in embarrassing herself.

"To what do I owe the pleasure of this call?"

"I was just doing the intercom rounds and checking up on people, making sure they are in their rooms where they are supposed to be."

Bell tamped down on a sudden and unaccustomed spike of guilt. She was trying to help the entire crew, after all. Well, all but one of them. *And what if it's—*

Nope. She wasn't going there. Not without very good reason.

"Anyone not where they should be?"

"Not so far," Tas said. "I just got off the line with Brother Barnabas."

Bell hadn't considered those particular challenges. "How did *that* go?"

"Well, I'd spoken with Master Fault just before, and he recommended I make a loud sound so that Barnabas might just hit the wall or something to mimic it. He's just down the hall from me, so it's something I'd hear."

"And?"

"It worked. Though it was loud enough that I hope it wasn't his door he was hitting. Or, god forbid, the outer hull."

"I think we would know by now if he'd holed the ship," Bell offered by way of comfort. The tinkling chimes of Tas's laughter, surprisingly delicate for a woman Bell would have labeled hard-bitten, sent a rush of simulated dopamine through her brain complex. She would definitely be looking to make that happen again ASAP.

"So who do you think did it?" Bell asked.

"How do you know it wasn't me?"

"Because for a while, we all thought it had to be someone who was, no offense, stronger than you are as a baseline human. But then you went to the trouble of showing how it could have been any of us. Which would be a pretty stupid thing to do if you were the culprit. And I don't know much about you, but you seem pretty grounded and sensible. Others maybe not so much."

"LaSalle," they both said at the same time, laughing in concert.

"But you," Bell said, "I'm sure of."

This time, there was a pause. "And how do I know you didn't do it? That's the only way you could really be sure of me, after all."

Maybe not the only way, Bell didn't say because it was way too mushy. She was not that kind of person.

"And I'm sorry to say, but you still seem like a decently likely suspect to me." Bell couldn't tell if the other woman was being serious, which she found weirdly exciting. Exciting was better than hurtful.

Because I didn't, dummy seemed like a bad response for several reasons. And *because I'm too attracted to you to risk turning you against me* seemed equally fraught. Horváth had threatened Tas, after all. Admitting too much affection might just pin even more motive to Bell than already existed.

And, of course, the real answer, *because Loopy knows I have an alibi,* she wasn't allowed to say.

"Hello? I realize it's not good to sound too defensive, but offering up no defense at all seems even worse."

"I think you're really hot and smart and cool." That sentence proved Bell herself was only the first of those three things, but at least it might change the subject.

There was a long, looooooooong sigh which came across mostly as static. "Are you serious? In a situation like this, you're thinking with your . . . What do you have with that robot body?"

"Hey! I am perfectly functional in that respect. In fact, I think you'll find I am *superior* in several key ways—"

"I'm terribly sorry for that," Tas said, sounding like she might mean it more than one way.

"Just so you know," Bell said, "that question is cyberist, a term which, now that I say it out loud, I admit you may not be familiar with where you come from." Bell took her moment. "Because I don't see how you could possibly have come from Anaranjado. Sooooooo, where are you from?"

"I'm asking the questions here." Tas's tone slid back into that playful middle ground, where she was not quite serious but not quite joking.

"Nuh uh," Bell said, deciding naïve optimism was the way to go, as she so often did. "I just asked one. Look, I'll do it again. What sort of stuff do you like to do in your free time? See? That's another question. And *see* counts too. That's three. Shall I keep going in this vein? Four."

"Here's a question back. How often were you written up for harassment by your Human Resources people?"

"Here's a question back-back. What are you in for?"

"You first."

"Crimes against humanity," Bell said triumphantly.

"Shit," Tas said, but Bell could hear the smile in her voice. "I didn't think you'd actually answer. Also, wow."

"Yeah, well, actions have consequences," Bell said. "If I'd just steadfastly continued not doing my job that day, I wouldn't be here. Your turn. Time to rat yourself out. Come on, spill."

Another long pause.

"Believe it or not, crimes against humanity," Tas said, now definitely just fucking with Bell.

"No fair. I answered for real. At least tell me who you think did it. *Besides* me, I mean."

Rather than drive straight toward a theory, Tas began verbally cataloging the various other crew members, what she knew about them, and what motive or opportunity they might have had. It had the sound of something closer to stream-of-consciousness speculation than actual analysis. Bell listened with one ear, but the longer this conversation went on, the more Horváth's torso blocking open the med bay door made her itch. But she didn't want to do anything that would make the kind of sound that would give away the fact she wasn't actually in her room.

Hesitantly, wondering if the earpiece she'd received worked similar to others she'd used, she reached up and tapped it with one finger.

"*Muted,*" blared a perfect replica of Loopy's voice in her ear. Or maybe it was actually just Loopy talking. Still, Bell didn't waste any time manhandling Horváth's corpse the rest of the way in. She had definitely broken his neck. It was looking decidedly more stretched and twisted than it should by the time the doors at last slid shut. More, she saw a strange, artificial looking lump occupying most of the front of his throat, pushing outward, distending skin and scales both.

Tas wound down, and Bell pressed her earpiece again.

"*Unmuted.*"

"So?" Tas said, sounding hopeful. "Any of that shake anything loose for you?"

Bell ordered a full dump of her short-term memory module, reviewing everything Tas had said at an accelerated rate. As she'd suspected, it mostly boiled down to random observations which might or might not be relevant, but which Bell had already picked up on. Yes, Xian had a lot of knowledge of the ship. Yes, the timing of Loopy being offline was suspicious—even more so than Tas was aware, technically. Yes, the extended absence of the alien crew members did not make them seem innocent. Yes, Brother Barnabas's theoretical inability to communicate might be more than a little convenient if it meant he couldn't be questioned.

But Tas had missed some things too, like the oddness of LaSalle's accent. It strengthened Bell's growing assumption that Tas was not an Anaranjado native.

"No, sorry. I'm as clueless as anyone," Bell said. "Except that I'm sure you didn't do it, and I'm sure I didn't do it. So I guess I'm one surety up on you."

"I don't know. Blind faith has gotten me in trouble before," Tas said. "I think I will just keep on being suspicious, thank you."

"Suit yourself. They must breed them more suspicious where you come from. Which is . . .?"

"Earth," Tas said with an odd sort of smug triumph.

The room seemed to close in around Bell for a moment. She couldn't have heard that right. Because what she'd heard was an impossible answer. All contact with Earth had been lost long before Bell had even been born.

"I'm sorry," she said in her mildest, most encouraging tone. "What the great flying fuck did you just say?"

"And just to punish you for being so nosy, that's all the information I'm giving you on the subject. Ever."

"No!" Bell said, stricken. "Not fair." Tas was a monster. "You can't do this to me."

That was the moment the door to the med bay hissed back open. Bell froze in horror.

"Who are you talking to?" Master Fault asked calmly.

"Who are you talking to?" Tas asked over the intercom, sounding suddenly concerned.

CHAPTER 13
SPILLING THE TEASE

EASY, *Bell*. There were a couple of ways she could play this.

"No one," she said, answering both Tas's and Fault's questions at once. Then, under the guise of brushing back her hair oh-so-casually, Bell muted the commlink again.

"What do you mean, no one?" Tas demanded in her ear. "Bell, I heard someone ask who you were talking to. Who is in your room with you? Bell? Bell! Answer me!"

Maybe this was stupid. If she let Tas hear what was going on, then someone would be aware Bell was in danger. But that would mean Tas might come and try to help, and then *she* would be in danger.

And Bell found she wasn't willing to put Tas in danger.

Besides, she could take this little twerp. She overtopped him by a meter. Horváth had been ambushed. He'd had no chance. Master Fault wouldn't find Bell easy meat. She was pretty sure she didn't even *have* any meat.

Though Master Fault's utter refusal to move or respond to her response was decently creepy, she had to admit.

In Bell's ear, Tas swore loudly and ended the call.

"Thanks for killing off Horváth, I guess," Bell said. She didn't do extended silences well.

"Interesting," Master Fault said. "An audacious accusation, given I'm not the one manhandling him around by his obviously broken neck. Anyone walking in on this scene could be forgiven for assuming you are destroying evidence."

"He was like this when I found him," Bell shot back. "Ish. I'm pretty sure his spine was just hanging by a thread," she added when Master Fault failed to respond.

"I'll spare us from the requisite trading of 'what are you doing out of your quarters?'" he said. "*I* am out of *my* quarters because you weren't responding to your intercom."

Liar, Bell thought in triumph.

"Liar!" Bell shouted in triumph. "I'd have known if you called me. You didn't call me." Even if he'd called while she'd been talking to Tas, the intercoms had tones indicating there was a call waiting.

"Aha. But how would you know I'm lying given that you aren't in your room and clearly weren't when I would have called, even if I didn't?"

Bell didn't know how to describe his tone beyond the fact that it was full of a smile she didn't like. She had the sudden, sinking suspicion she'd just been played.

"That bar practically ripped him in half," Master Fault observed in a musing way, pivoting back to her comments about Horváth's spine as though he'd completely forgotten the accusations he'd just leveled. "Why do you think it stopped at his neck, of all places? Surely that would be one of the weakest points of the body. We should have found him with the bar erupting from his mouth, or the top of his head."

"I've got to hand it to you, Faulty, you do not pull punches. I respect that." Still, it was a good point. "There's something underneath the skin," Bell said warily, still waiting for some kind of trick. He hadn't moved from the door, like he was blocking her exit. She decided to play along. "Something solid poking through."

The sound of dripping interrupted her.

"Forgive me," Master Fault said, pointing at Horváth's neck, "but I think I see what you mean, and your manhandling of his head appears to have resulted in a new leak."

Bell was pretty sure getting reamed ass-to-chin by a structural metal rod was what did most of the damage, but she *might* have been a small contribution. Very small. She banished the unasked-for, unsympathetic report her applied physics codex was compiling in real time and examined the place where skin and scale had at last failed.

To her immense disgust, his entire neck came apart as she picked at it, like rotted cloth tearing, leaving the foreign object suspended by two fingers in Bell's hand as the rest of Horváth's head squelched down to the deck.

"Quite a healthy microbiome the good staff sergeant had," Master Fault observed. "They eat like kings tonight." He pointed. "What's that there?"

Streaked with gore as it was, it wasn't easy to see details. Tamping down that innate human fear of biological contaminants, a fear she didn't need to have anymore, she wiped it away as best she could, holding it up between two pinched fingers to better catch the med bay light. It was like nothing she'd seen before. Her various modules glanced off it in their attempts to understand and returned only the data equivalent of mute shrugs.

The device was about as long as one of her fingers and three times as thick. It had a shape like a parallelogram, but in three dimensions. Parallelopiped? Parabellum? Parallaxative? She couldn't remember and muted her pedantic general knowledge module for having the sheer gall to try and teach her. It was metal in an alloy she couldn't immediately recognize, smooth all over but covered with a strange pattern like a kind of finishing polish. There was a smear of something along one of its long, flat sides, a little round swirl of goop that didn't match the rest of the goop. It clung to her fingers as she tried to wipe it away.

Some kind of adhesive.

"I think," she ventured hesitantly, "he had this stuck to himself somewhere in his neck. Some kind of implant. It stopped the rod from ripping through his head." True to form, it was the first thought to enter her head, but even as she said it, it sounded crazy. Fancy alloy or not, how could this device have survived a direct hit from that rod?

Some combination of modules pattern-matched for her, and it was so obvious that she felt like an idiot for leading with the stupid theory.

A circle of adhesive. It wasn't attached to him, it was attached to the rod. If it had gone through him like that, its long axis perpendicular to that of the rod's, it would have had plenty of opportunities to snag on bones and slow the rod down by the time it reached his neck. The bones of his neck had just been where it finally came to rest. It also meant the alloy was pretty fucking strong.

It also, also meant the rod's passage would have been even more uncomfortable than it would have been alone. Which, considering who they were talking about, Bell was okay with.

She opened her mouth to say all this, especially emphasize the fact that the object had gone in sideways, because the more she thought about it, the funnier it was, but Master Fault beat her to the punch.

"Tell me, Bell, have you had any devices stolen from you since waking?"

"No," Bell said, narrowing her eyes. "Why?"

"And is this the first time you've seen *that* device?" His voice had gone from relaxed to incisive with startling rapidity.

Bell snorted incredulously. "You mean the thing I just pulled out of his corpse? I've never seen this thing—or anything like it—before in my life, and believe me, if I had, I would remem—oh, motherfucker!"

She had turned the object around while she spoke to look at the side Master Fault could see. Scratched into it with perfectly straight lines, so shallow they had to catch the light to be seen at all, was a single world in block lettering.

BELLE.

That *motherfucker*.

"It seems improbable the staff sergeant had a random device with your name on it lodged in his throat without you being somehow involved, is all," Master Fault said.

Bell rounded on him. "Oh no, no. You are not pinning this on me. First and foremost, that is *not* how my name is spelled. Some asshole wants to frame me? I mean, seems smart. I get it. But get the spelling right! The name is Bell. B-E-L-L. No extra fucking *e* on the end. Ding-dong, not ooh-la-la."

"Once again, your idioms escape me. But I will be sure to note the spelling should I ever have the need to frame you."

Bell's eyes narrowed, her annoyance banking from a rage to a simmer. She'd been about to explain her revised analysis of how the object had come to lodge itself in Horváth's throat, but now that seemed like a trap. Get too much right, and she'd just look guilty.

"Just why are you here, Mister Fault?" she asked, getting the name wrong on purpose so he could see how it felt. Of course the stoic chode didn't react.

"I'm here because you're here."

"And how did you know I'd be here when you didn't actually check beforehand?"

He spread his hands in mock defeat. "I have very powerful intuitions. It's true I didn't know whom I'd find here, but I did have the sense that Horváth's unattended body might be worth a visit."

"To dispose of evidence perhaps? The evidence I'm holding right here?"

"The evidence with your name on it."

"The evidence with the French word for 'beautiful' written on it, you mean. Someone is trying to frame me," Bell said. She narrowed her eyes still further. "Somebody who speaks human language, but not. That. Well."

"Je parle parfaitement vos langues," he said. *I speak your languages perfectly.* The fucker even spoke French! "Besides," he said. "Why would I come here and attempt to conceal or destroy evidence I was planning to use to frame you?"

"All right, if you aren't here to frame me, then tell me why you're here."

"How about you *both* tell me why the fuck you're out of your rooms?"

It was officially a party because Tas had arrived. Master Fault, apparently caught as much off-guard as Bell, turned to face the new arrival. Bell suddenly became aware he was between her and Tas, blocking Bell's exit from the room or any hope of reaching the little woman first.

"Get back to your room," Bell called out to her. She hadn't taken the personal risk of not warning Tas to see the woman get caught up in things now. "That goes for both of you. I'm the only one allowed to be out and about." Shit.

Master Fault turned slowly, almost as though he was savoring the drama, back to regard her in his faceless way. How did he even see through those robes? In a moment of sublime comedy, Tas's head poked around the side of the door to stare at Bell in turn.

"Say what now?" she asked, one eyebrow raised and half-smiling in a way that Bell had to restrain herself from taking a mental snapshot of and—nope, she did it. But this, er, material for later wasn't important right now. What was?

Right, Bell had blurted out the secret. Fuck. Fuck! So much for keeping her little promotion under wraps. But fat lot of good the secret would do her if everyone just assumed she was the killer anyway.

"Fine. But let the record show I'm answering in response to your verbal request," she said, pointing to Tas. "Not his creepy-ass faceless-staring routine. Loopy assigned me to investigate the case." She couldn't help but strut a little bit, if only verbally. "Super important. Very hush-hush. He said I was the only one he could trust to have the deductive skills necessary to get results." He had sort of said that. "But he told me how dangerous it would be." She kept her eyes on Tas in case that was a turn-on. "Loopy didn't want me to tell anyone, so that I wouldn't be a target. But he trusts me, so you should too."

Tas's raised eyebrow got raise-ier.

Unf. Another snapshot. Later was going to be *great.*

Now that she'd spilled everything, Bell very much hoped that the ship's brain would back her up on this and not die on the hill of his secrecy. She turned to Master Fault. "So, you'd better tell me just exactly what you are doing wandering around, creepozoid, because I promise you that Bell Beauregard is the only person on this ship with permission to do that at the moment."

"Ship?" Master Fault called, inclining his swathed head upward. "Is what she's saying true?"

Bell smiled, cocking her hips back in preparation for a triumphant pelvic thrust, but the expression curdled on her face as a wave of realization crested over her. For the first time since Master Fault had shown up, she remembered Loopy's promise earlier in the evening: that he would warn her if anyone besides herself was out and about.

"He's not going to answer," she said bleakly. "He's offline again."

Both Tas and Master Fault sharpened their regard of her. Tas did, at least. It was impossible to tell with Fault. That had perhaps not been the best or least-suspicious way to address this particular issue.

The seconds stretched out with no response from the brain.

"Loopy?" Bell called, just grasping at straws really. She knew there would be no answer. And she had to tip her metaphorical hat. The Shadyside weirdos had really done a great job rendering that sinking-stomach feeling of impending doom in electronic form.

"Interesting. It seems you were correct," Master Fault said. He let the unspoken accusation hang in the air. This turned out to be a good thing because Bell was able to burn bleakness as fuel for her irritation.

"I knew he was offline because he said he'd warn me if anyone besides me was out and about tonight. Because, again, I'm the detective. Since at least two of you are out and I've had no word from him, I jumped to the most logical conclusion." She couldn't resist. "Or maybe I *also* just have very powerful intuitions."

"Enough," Tas said. "You both realize what this means? Last time the ship's brain was out of contact, Horváth was being murdered."

"Which means the three of us are safe," Bell said. At Tas's look she added, "Unless you think more than one person is in on it." She made for the door, and while Master Fault held his position, Tas backed away, keeping Bell's exact pace.

Somewhat sourly—Bell would have preferred their responses to be reversed—Bell addressed Master Fault. "I'm going to walk through you if you don't get out of my way."

"Nobody's going anywhere except together," Tas said. "We're going to check on each of the others in turn." Which made sense. Still, Bell was pretty sure Master Fault's acquiescence to this command was an effort to piss Bell off specifically. But it got him to step away from the door.

"Probably nothing's happened," Bell said as she exited the med bay, leaving the various remaining pieces of Horváth where they lay but stashing the strange object that had lodged in his throat in one of the resealable pockets of her flowmatter jumpsuit. "Probably the ship's brain going down is just something that happens all the time. He all but told me how undercooked he was after he woke me up. Probably he's going to wake up any second and say—"

There was no blatting of alarms this time, but those four ascending tones cut her off. "Attention, Conscious Crew Complement," intoned Loopy, or, Bell now knew, one of his automated responses. "There has been a murder."

"Well, shit," said Bell.

CHAPTER 14
ALL SLIME ROADS LEAD TO GROME

"PLEASE REPORT to section A-7 of the habitat arc at once to discuss the murder," Loopy's automated voice intoned. Now that she knew what to listen for, Bell could hear how the location information and the final word "murder" sounded like they had been fill-in-the-blanks. She wondered in a kind of dissociative way just how many options he had to fill in those gaps, what kind of system was doing that with the brain itself offline, or unconscious, or whatever.

Regardless of the answer, Bell, Tas, and Fault could do little more than obey. They moved in silence, but if the other two were anything like Bell, one question dominated each of their minds.

Who was dead this time?

And if they were anything like Bell, one *answer* also dominated their minds.

Xian. Xian! Xianxianxianxian. This fervent wish got tricky when Bell considered that she also wanted Xian to *be* the murderer, but that was easy enough to solve. Finding her next victim—Bell was going to say LaSalle—harder to surprise, she and the xenophobic asshole had both succeeded in killing each other. The ultimate self-correcting problem: one in which only horrible people died after making the universe a slightly better place by killing Horváth.

As fantasies went, it didn't have the, ahem, *forcefulness* of Bell's Tas-centric fantasy, but it brought the warm-fuzzies in spades. Bell had to work hard not to grin like a lunatic.

In fact, she was working so hard not to grin, she apparently wasn't watching where she was going and slipped, going ass over teakettle again, the same as she had when she'd first approached the staff sergeant's body.

"Motherfuckshitassbitch!" She thought she got the whole word out before she hit the ground. That had seemed important for some reason.

"Are you all right?" Tas sounded both concerned and amused, but that happy combination wasn't enough to soothe Bell's stung pride.

"Fine," she growled. Mentally she flicked a filter over her vision and saw the culprit. Meandering trails of some slimy substance scrawled themselves crazily along the corridor in no pattern Bell could detect. They weren't invisible to the naked eye, just difficult to make out in the hallway's dim lighting without the filter. Scanning around, she could see where her step had interrupted one. And the trails grew thicker the further they went. Bell knew what they were. She'd seen them just a few hours before, when Grome had been spelling out their alibi of Urk using portions of their own body. Seeing so many trails here and now filled Bell with a flutter of unease, followed by repeated hammer-blows of self-flagellation.

She couldn't be sure until she saw the latest body, but she very much feared the killer was several steps ahead of them.

"Come on," she said, grabbing Tas's hand firmly in her own to help guide her through the trails. "The slippery spots aren't invisible, but it'll be easier if I lead you. Don't let go, and step where I step." Bell felt an unaccountable need to hurry, despite intuitively knowing that whoever had bought it was beyond their help. Feeling Tas's hand close around her own, almost as though the little woman could sense Bell's anxiety, she reflected that at least something nice was still happening.

Master Fault could negotiate his own damn way through the slime trails.

As Bell stalked through the slickest patches, Tas close behind and Master Fault casually following them with no sign of difficulty, Bell tweaked her vision settings further to better enhance the shine of fresh slime. She regarded them with a kind of melancholy amazement. Scalable life, she recalled from her thesis. One splitting into many and then back into one, as needed. As intelligent, if not more so, than a human, but an alien intellect.

Still, that had all been academic study, nothing practical. And now? Well, now they would see.

"Is this Grome we're following?" Tas didn't have Bell's eyes, but the more of the slime trails there were, the better odds the light would play off one as they walked.

"Yes," Bell said simply. "And I really hope it's not all that's left of them." Perhaps taking Bell's somber cue, Tas lapsed back into silence herself.

As they reached a junction of corridors, their slime trail met others like it, coming from other corridors. Whatever Grome had been up to, it required that they send themselves far and wide throughout the accessible part of the ship. Looking at the size of those trails, Bell considered.

Maybe some of the seemingly inaccessible parts, too.

As they entered section A-7, Bell was forced to increase her visual contrast still further. It became difficult to see at all. They seemed to have been transported via dark magic into some kind of foggy mountain pass. Xian emerged from that fog, and Bell felt the last vestiges of hope she'd had in her fantasy shrivel up like Horváth's dick did whenever innocent people weren't dying.

"First on the scene again, I see," Bell said.

"Hardly," Xian threw back. "That would be LaSalle." Indeed, the man emerged from the fog—some sort of waterless fire suppression system based on the sharp chill in the air, unless Bell missed her guess—which was thinning by the moment. He looked fit to twitch himself apart at the seams.

"What the ever-loving fuck-a-duck did you two do?" Bell blurted before she could contain herself.

"We only just arrived," Xian said. "Separately, I might add." She eyed the trio across from her suspiciously. "What are you three doing arriving together?"

Ignoring this attempt at baiting, Bell indicated the apparent source of the haze. "Those are Grome's quarters, aren't they?"

"I have no idea," Xian said. But Bell noticed she avoided the slime trails running to and from the door like crazed spaghetti as deftly as Bell herself. *I'm not the only one with some optics upgrades.* They were becoming easier to make out as the fog cleared, but that wouldn't have been the case when they arrived.

Unless she wasn't being honest about when they'd arrived, of course.

"Only one way to find out," Tas said. She went and palmed the door open. It took her a couple of tries—the mechanism didn't seem to want to function. On the second attempt, the door slid open to a cloud of black, acrid smoke pouring forth. It made the suppressing mist pleasantly moody by comparison.

The charred mass within still writhed in some places as worms that had not been cooked directly by the flames slowly died in scalded agony. But there could be no doubt that the vast majority of the constituent worms that made up the collective intelligence known as Grome were already dead.

"Fuck me," Bell said. Both Xian and Tas were coughing now, choking at the sudden outpouring of smoke and heat from the room that had become an oven. It was fortunate the air was already so thin, or else the fire might not have been contained at all. Bell was affected by neither smoke nor heat, but the sight before her threatened to bring her to her knees all the same.

Dead. Another one dead. Not just someone she didn't hate, but one of the first aliens she'd ever met. Bell didn't generally like other people, but she had liked the little she'd known of Grome.

"ONCE MORE, FROM THE TOP," Xian said. "Why were all three of you out of your rooms just prior to the murder?" And how it galled that Xian was attempting to muscle her way into the role of chief inspector of Scrapheap Yard.

"Um, no," Bell said. "Because you're not in charge here. I am."

"Says you."

"Says the ship's brain, asshat."

"The ship's brain that's conveniently too absent to confirm your claims."

"No, dummy, that is the *opposite* of convenient."

"Only if you are telling the truth. But even if the ship's brain was here to confirm your claims, it wouldn't make the slightest difference to me. You forget that right up until almost the moment we departed, I was getting progress reports. I know how addled that brain was and is, how much work was necessary to make it functional. In fact, this hypothetical confirmation that the brain picked you to conduct the investigation would count *against* you in my book."

"You're talking about the brain from twenty years ago," Bell protested, still in a state of shock over that number, if she were being honest. "You don't have any idea how he's developed since we left."

"What I know is I was strongly considering ordering the team lead to start over with a different brain and dissect this one as an exercise in lessons learned. I'm telling you now: we can't trust what it tells us. So, you'll forgive me if I don't put a lot of faith in its judgment, particularly not in an area which deviates so far from its normal operating environment."

Her eyes glittered with malice, but Bell knew it was really triumph there. The woman thought she had an ironclad argument and was just too sour to smile and spoil the game. But all she was saying was another version of that age-old defense mechanism of "I'm not listening, because I don't wanna."

"A real pretty speech there from the disgraced magnate," Bell said. Two could play at the call-someone-by-their-job-description-to-dehumanize-them game. "But this is two murders where Loopy has been knocked out of commission beforehand. Can anyone raise their hands if they think they have more knowledge of how this ship and its systems work than Little Ms. Granny Grumps-a-lot here?"

"What were you three doing out of your rooms?"

"You got here first! What were *you* doing?"

"We had a comm system alert," Xian interjected, somehow managing to look both up and down her nose at Bell. "The same as you, I expect. Our rooms are the next two down in this section."

"Except they weren't there to hear their alerts," LaSalle said. "They were already here, one or more of them, doing this. Conspiracy!"

Boy, these two were quite the tag team. Good cop/bad cop had nothing on sour copy/paranoid cop.

"Where is the weapon you used to incinerate the alien?" Xian barked the question, like if she said it fast enough, Bell might confess.

"Oh, brilliant. Are you going to ask me if I've stopped beating my wife too?"

"Deny it all you want," Xian said. "But my gut has seldom let me down in the past—"

"Yet here you are, in steerage with the rest of us."

"—and I know what it's telling me now."

"I'm not sure if this counts for an alibi, or if I'd even like it to," Master Fault suddenly cut in. "But before the alert went out, I was with Bell. I found her tampering with the staff sergeant's corpse both in and around the med bay."

"You know, I'm not sure you have as strong a command of human language as I thought," Bell said through gritted teeth. "Some of your word choices there are very *unfortunate*." Potentially unfortunate for him, she hoped she was getting across. She turned back to Xian. "I was with these two when the alert went out. I hadn't been anywhere near this section all night. And unless you think I'm hiding a flamethrower in my skintight bodysuit"—she did a little shimmy here for what she hoped was Tas's benefit—"I couldn't have done it."

"You could be hiding anything in that mutilated frame you call a body," Xian threw back. "What were you doing with the staff sergeant's corpse?"

"I was *examining* it for *evidence*."

"Ask to see what she found," Master Fault pressed.

"Look," Bell said dangerously, I don't know what sort of orifice your species talks out of—mouth, sphincter, cloaca, pee-pee hole, whatever—but if you don't stop trying to implicate me when you know damn well I couldn't have done it, I will sew said orifices shut one at a time until the talking stops."

"I can't rule out anyone at this time," Master Fault said. "After all, we have no idea what time the actual murder took place. Only the pulling of the lever, since that seems to correspond to the alert we receive. These alerts must be automated in some way."

"They are," Bell said, happy for the distraction. "Loopy told me that if he's offline, the 'someone bought it' alert runs when both the ship's sensor network detects a loss of life signs and when someone discovers the body. Which begs the question of what kind of perverted system requires *two* sources to report a dire emergency?"

"Oh no, you're not going to divert us that easily," Xian said. "Show us what you found on Horváth's body."

Bell rolled her eyes in an apotheosis of disdain. "Ugh, *fine*." She dug out the strange device with the French word—she refused to think of it as her name—burned into it. She gave a quick, verbal sketch of where and how she had found it, heavily emphasizing the misspelling being proof that it wasn't her.

"And it seems like it had to have been attached to the tip of rod when it, you know, *went in*. Hey. Hey! What are you doing?" What LaSalle appeared to be doing was poking around the body—bodies, technically—without Bell's permission. "I'm lead detective on this case. No messing with my crime scene."

"Yeah, says you, mate. Relax. I'm just seeing if the killer left something similar this time, is all," As though in response to Bell's wish, Tas carefully stepped her way between slime trails to make sure someone was keeping an eye on whatever LaSalle was doing. And it was just as well, because LaSalle hadn't gone more than a meter into the space, waving smoke away from his face, when he let out a grunt of surprise.

"What?" Bell demanded.

Tas arrived in short order. "I think you're going to want to see this."

Mentally bracing herself for yet *another* misspelling of her name, Bell stepped carefully over, trying to touch as little as possible on her way.

On the wall above the bed, still hard to see through the clearing smoke, was another message. Just a single word.

HITS.

This meant nothing to Bell beyond a mild relief that it was not referring to her. But it was not the word itself which had so shocked Tas, LaSalle, and now, Bell.

The letters were formed of the drying remains of some of Grome's worms, each one carefully smashed flat so that its guts stuck it to the wall.

CHAPTER 15
INVESTIGATUS INTERRUPTUS

THEY ALL STARED at the word for an inordinate amount of time, nobody saying anything. It was as though none of them could process just what they were seeing beyond "we are dealing with a really sick fuck who doesn't make a lot of sense when they leave messages."

Though, statistically speaking, one of the people present had probably done this.

There was no Loopy to tell them to get back to work, so they didn't. Bell couldn't speak for the others, but it would have taken the ship coming down around their ears to pry her away from the second murder in as many days.

Instead, they poked around, still looking for clues where they weren't eyeing one another with mounting suspicion. But at least not everyone was accusing with their eyes. Bell didn't suspect Tas, and judging by her body language, Tas at least seemed to entertain the notion that Bell *might* be safe. Maybe. LaSalle and Xian formed another faction, one that seemed much more tight knit. Not that this made Bell envious or anything.

Still, it did make her wonder if the pair of them might be fucking.

Then there was Master Fault. On the one hand, he belonged to neither group, but on the other hand, he didn't seem particularly perturbed about it either.

"Are you thinking what I'm thinking?" Bell asked Tas softly a few minutes into Quiet Time.

"I'm thinking we need to confirm we're really the only ones awake."

Several minutes of tense, silent searching passed in which they'd found very little. Included in the Venn diagram where "jack" and "shit" overlapped were any means of setting the fire or any motive anyone could come up with. But Tas was apparently undaunted. "So which of you threw the alert lever? Last time nothing happened until Xian found the body and pulled the alarm lever."

"Yeah, the body she murdered," Bell muttered, earning a dark look from Tas.

"It's like she told you," LaSalle said, standing up from gingerly poking at the crispy pile o' worms. "We heard the alert in our rooms."

"Your separate rooms?" Bell asked. "No alibi for either of you, in other words?"

LaSalle looked pained.

"Well none of us pulled it. I can tell you that. We three were together at the med bay when the alarm sounded. And I think even Master Fault would concur."

"Quite," the strange alien said. "When the alarm sounded, both Bell and Tas were within sight of me. I can't speak to their behavior before I encountered them, but neither pulled a lever in my presence."

LaSalle's pained expression reached all-bread-and-cheese-diet-for-a-week-constipation levels.

"It's all right, Pierre," Xian said, as softly as Bell had ever heard her speak. "There's no point keeping quiet that which can exonerate us. We are each other's alibi. We were both in my quarters."

"I knew it!" Bell crowed in triumph. "Also, shit." No easy accusations were to be had, it seemed. "Also, her?" She directed the last at LaSalle. "Also, *him?*" This to Xian.

It was perhaps the first time in history where both members of a romantic partnership were punching above their weight class and could do better simultaneously.

"If you're quite finished," Xian said, "need I remind you that doesn't account for everyone? Where is that robot monk?" Her eyes narrowed. "More to the point, where is the other alien? The tripartite. It and the worms were thick as thieves. Now, with its closest companion on this ship dead, it's nowhere to be found?"

"I suspect Brother Barnabas is in his room where I last left him," Master Fault said. "He is disinclined to wander alone with his mind in this state."

"And if we assume all that's true," Tas said.

"Big assumption," Bell cut in, not liking where this was going, and also not having to choose between Xian lying and Bell being right about her and LaSalle.

"But *if we do*, that means that the only one who could have pulled the alarm was Urknuuzh."

"Maybe not," Bell said. It wasn't that she was frantic to find something to make Urk, whom she really liked, look less suspicious. It wasn't *just* that. Something had occurred to her. "These slime trails. There are dozens of them. Way more than you'd normally expect given what I know about the writhers."

"Oh, and you're some sort of expert?" Xian was fully dialed in on her trademark scoff.

"Oh, I don't know, they were only *my master's thesis*. Yeah. Suck it." Her two-armed chopping gesture toward her groin enthusiastically invited the it-sucking. "But as I was saying, the worms can live separately for an indefinite amount of time so long as they have food, water, all that jazz. But they don't like it. Alone, they're diminished. Even in small groups, their intelligence ramps up quickly, but alone," and here she lowered her voice as though Grome might hear her, "they aren't that bright."

"What does this have to do with the alarm?"

"Only that even after the main mass of worms was burning like a torch, one or a small group of the separate ones could have pulled the lever. They'd have brains enough for that, I think." Xian looked pissed at that revelation for some reason. It was just a flash, and gone in an instant, but Bell caught it.

"Then we should check for any slime trails on the lever." Tas made good on her words and moved down the hall toward the nearest emergency alarm.

"You said there are an awful lot of slime trails," LaSalle said to Bell. "Why's that, d'you think?" He sounded as if he had a theory, and Bell bet she could name that theory in one guess.

Bell had a theory of her own, but she didn't want to say it until she could get Tas alone to get her opinion of it.

"Nothing," Tas said after peering closely at the lever. "If there was a residue, it's gone now."

"So either Urk pulled the lever, or Grome did, and Urk cleaned the trail off to disguise that fact." Bell allowed the briefest of pauses before adding. "Or Xian is lying, and she did it."

"Look," LaSalle said. "You two don't like each other; that much is crystal. But she and I have an alibi, and so do you three." He sounded pretty grudging on that last point and was probably conceding it just on the chance he might get to gang up against some aliens. "Just for the sake of argument, how about we look first at the crew mates who *don't* have alibis."

"Well, I know a little something about tripartite," Bell began.

"Of course you do," Xian interjected.

"And I wasn't aware they could breathe fire all dragon-like," Bell said, louder.

"Just in case you were wondering, neither can I," Xian shot back.

"I'm guessing," Tas said, "that there is plenty of equipment on this ship that could make fire. Fire-making being one of the key aspects of civilization-building." She looked to Xian. "You know the ship best. Am I right?"

Xian nodded, if reluctantly.

"Then I think LaSalle is right," Tas said. She sounded rightly amazed. "Given that we have nothing else to go on, and we can't immediately rule Urknuuzh out based on what we know, we need to focus on finding and questioning him about where he was when this happened." She looked at Bell imploringly.

It was those sexy-ass eyes that did it.

"Fine," said Bell, trying to sound magnanimous instead of pissy.

"Pierre," Xian said, "can you go find Urknuuzh and bring him here? Use the method I showed you."

"Right-o," he said affably, offering everyone a smile before trundling off down a corridor picked seemingly at random.

"We should all look," Tas said. "It will be faster."

"I for one am not interested in letting any of you out of my sight, nor of wandering off by myself," Xian said.

For once, she and Bell were in complete agreement. But that didn't get Xian off the hook for another zinger. "Willing to let your boy-toy go in your place, though?"

"Pierre can take care of himself."

Which, translated from "rich fucker," meant "he's expendable." Bell wondered if LaSalle would agree with that sentiment, but he was already out of earshot.

"Fine," Bell said. "But at least tell us this 'method' you taught him. Sounds like a weird sex thing. What's that about?"

"No," Xian said. "At the risk of sounding like a walking cliché, that's for Pierre and I to know, and the three potential murderers standing in front of me to wish they knew."

"Little tip: if you want to sound like a walking cliché," Bell said, "you should at least get the idioms right."

"I'm not going to be teaching you better ways to track and kill us," Xian said angrily. "We're all just going to sit here like patient little schoolchildren and wait for Pierre to report back."

Which turned out not to be very long. Bell had barely come up with ten more insults to hurl at Xian when LaSalle jogged back up, practically doubled over and wheezing in the thin air.

"We have a big, *huge* problem," he said when he'd recovered his breath. "Can't find the bloke anywhere aboard the ship."

CHAPTER 16
SCAVENGE OR HUNT?

"IMPOSSIBLE," Xian said at once. "You must have run the scan wrong." She looked angrily at Bell as she said it—she'd revealed more than she'd meant to.

"I did it just like you showed me," LaSalle whined, showing neither hostility nor spine over his lover's lack of faith in his competence. "Asteroid Defense. Turn the sensors—"

"Be. Quiet." Xian hissed the words.

"I did it perfectly," LaSalle said, sullen. His face grew stubborn at her unspoken threat. "And I didn't see any active heat signature other than the ones here, plus me at the console and one in Barnabas's room."

This time a whole range of emotions flashed across Xian's face, too many and too fast for Bell to parse. She looked to be deciding between a dozen different responses. Apparently she'd given up on any form of secrecy regarding her technique, because she settled on: "You made sure to redirect the sensors back out to the area around the ship, yes? We're well into the planetary gravity well's field of influence by now. The last thing we need is to take a stray micrometeoroid directly through the crew complex. We've got little enough oxygen as it is."

"Aha," Master Fault said. "You have access to critical ship functions." The glaring lights played with the shadows on the folds of fabric shrouding his form, giving the impression of a face where there was none. This non-face almost appeared to be locked in a faint scowl to Bell's eyes.

This earned another scoff from Xian. If LaSalle's openness had pushed her off her equilibrium before, she'd definitely recovered.

"It was a last-minute addition. Literally the last day. Once it became clear we were going to need conscious crew members to maintain key systems, I'd think the need to make sure they could access the system that protects us from asteroids would be obvious. Ask the ship's brain whenever it deigns to come back online if you don't believe me. All I was demonstrating to LaSalle was that the settings could be reconfigured in such a way as to track heat signatures throughout the hab complex."

"So this was all to find the killer?" Tas asked.

"Correct," Xian said. "Unfortunately, it's impractical. It doesn't allow us to track individuals directly. And before you ask, no, we can't use it to determine who murdered Horváth. Real-time only. The sensors don't record." She met their frowns with a glower of her own. "They're meant to keep the ship intact, not play whodunnit. They're also looking for objects standing out against the cold emptiness of space, not buried in hull and atmosphere. We'd never be able to find individual worms left over from Grome, for instance. We're operating way outside their parameters here. But all the dedicated internal sensors are directly under the brain's purview."

What Bell said was, "Real POS you built, Xian. No wonder you're here sucking bilge with the rest of us." What she thought was something entirely different. *Or it occurred to you that this might be a threat to you, so you messed around until you confirmed it wasn't. Or worse, you sabotaged it so it* couldn't *be.*

With this kind of knowledge, Bell might have accused Xian of being the obvious one to have fired the rod into Horváth. But she'd tossed around enough accusations at the woman that piling on might start to sound like crying wolf. Nobody in this room was an idiot. The implication wouldn't go unnoticed. And they still needed to find their missing alien.

"So *now* we split up," Bell said. "Sweep the hab complex in pairs until we find Urk, one way or another. I'll take Tas and—"

"No," Xian said. "You're pairing with me. I don't trust anyone else to watch you right now."

"And you think you'll be *safe* with me? Think I can't take you?"

"I think you'd be surprised."

Bad idea. "All right," Bell said. *No. Not all right.* "I'm game. Let's do this." *Abort. Abort.* Bell's threat analysis module wasn't actually talking, but she liked to translate its frantic screeches into a sort of inner monologue. "As long as Tas *isn't* alone with LaSalle. Because she's the only one here I trust, and you and he are bumping uglies. Also because he's the living embodiment of the concept *one day, he just snapped.*"

"Your demand, crude as it is, works for me."

"I suppose Tas will have to team up with me, then," Master Fault said.

"Well, I have to go with one set or the other," LaSalle said. "Seeing as there's only five of us here."

Shit. Bell hadn't really done the math on this. She tried to work out a pairing system that would answer all her priorities. It had to keep her and Tas safe and at the same time make sure one of them had an eye on the other three weirdos. But they also couldn't be outnumbered. She gritted her teeth in annoyance. Either there was no solution, or her math module *might* be punishing her.

Tas pulled her aside as she was spiraling.

"LaSalle can come with us. It's fine. But are you sure about this? You trust her enough to go off alone with her?"

"I've really got to introduce you to my threat analysis module," Bell said, matching her whisper to Tas's. The comment only earned the briefest of strange looks. Maybe Bell was wearing her down. "And no, I don't trust her at all. I feel like I've made that *very* clear. But I don't mind babysitting my number-one suspect, as long as you do something for me and do it without letting Master Fault or LaSalle know what you are up to."

Tas gave Bell an expectant, encouraging expression. *Which is?*

Bell lowered her voice even further. She also adjusted her vocoder so it could form words without input from her mouth. No lipreading today. "It sure looks to me like some of those slime trails leave but don't come back." She believed this because the freshest slime trails had been the ones moving *away* from the charred ruin of the greater mass. "Even if none of Grome's constituents pulled the alarm lever, I'd bet some of those worms are still out there. They may know something. So I need you to be on the lookout for them. They can keep going indefinitely as long as food and water are available, but they aren't smart enough to figure out how to manage that on this ship. So time is of the essence."

"Okay," Tas said, "for a second there I thought you were speaking via telepathy, and it was really weird. We have got to talk about this whole cybernetic situation you've got going on, but yes, I will keep my eyes open."

"As will I," Master Fault said from halfway across the corridor in a normal volume.

"As will you what?" Xian said sharply. So at least everyone hadn't heard.

"This is a *private* conversation," Bell hissed.

"Then you should have spoken more quietly," Master Fault said in a matter-of-fact fashion.

Bell consoled herself that it would have been next to impossible for Tas to hide what she was doing, anyway. All that mattered was that either she or Tas had to find those leftover bits of Grome before anyone else did.

"YOU KNOW, if you think I did this," Bell said, gesturing around her vaguely to encompass the entire shit-show the waking part of their journey had been, "then vague threats notwithstanding, it's pretty weird that you'd want to be alone with me."

"If you think I can't take care of myself," Xian said, "then you are the one who is 'pretty weird.' Take it however you like, but you don't scare me."

Oh Bell took it all right. She took it in all the different ways it could be taken. And at least one of those ways made Xian sound pretty guilty.

They had drawn lots as to which parts of the crew complex to start searching, and Bell and Xian had come up with the prematurely named hab cargo ring, which was actually only a half-ring of self-contained storage chambers surrounding the dorsal half of the crew complex, each cargo pod accessible by flexible umbilical spokes radiating outward from the central complex and from one another by rigid, curving corridors linking each pod with its adjacent neighbor or neighbors.

Ship schematics showed that the pods were originally supposed to have formed a full ring, but that Xian's builders had settled for five pods when the remaining three could not be constructed in time.

Negotiating the umbilicals was difficult. They had rungs, but without rigid walls to provide leverage, fucking Isaac Newton made each step outward, or upward, depending on how you thought about it, a royal pain in Bell's ass.

The view almost made up for it, though.

The material making up the umbilicals was almost perfectly transparent, so Bell was treated to a slightly cloudy view of the splendors of space on one hand and the growing disc of the planet on the other. The hull of the ship was dark, and she was careful never to look directly at the system's star—this was part force of habit from back on Anaranjado and partly because she genuinely didn't know what kind of abuse her eyes were rated for—but the endless sea of stars that occupied nearly every other direction took her pretend breath away, while the planet, a blue-green marble of colors like none Bell had ever laid eyes on, was even more stunning. Only the pair of tracks, meant to haul down cargo crates from the pod above, and the vague cloudiness of the aging umbilical's skin spoiled the feeling of an unencumbered spacewalk.

The other turd in the punchbowl was that she had no one to share it with but Xian, and Bell had no intention of discussing *feelings* with that harpy.

"Are you coming, or what?" Xian asked from ahead/above.

"Keep your scales on," Bell growled. "It's not every day you get a view like this."

Xian made a noise Bell interpreted as mild surprise. "I suppose I can understand that. Anything can lose its luster after a while, though. When you've been up to the orbitals as many times as I have, even a view like this stops inspiring awe. The curse of being human."

"Oh, please," Bell said. "What kind of a chode says that? 'The curse of being human.' The curse of being an uber-wealthy asshat, more like. What, are you tired of cloned-dinosaur omelets and puppy-skin underwear too?"

"Don't hold back on my account," Xian said, and there was amusement in her voice. Amusement! "Tell me what you really think of me."

But that was bait Bell had no intention of taking.

"So, why'd you kill Grome? I mean, Horváth I totally get. That guy was lucky to have made it this long in his life without being murdered. But I can't see what motive anyone might have for wanting to kill a nice colony of sentient worms."

"Funny," Xian said with a sneer. "I was about to ask you the same question. But why accuse me? Aren't we looking for the tripartite because its absence is so suspicious? Most murders are committed by those closest to the victim, after all."

"Assuming your little sensor trick isn't as dog-shit as the rest of the dung heap of a ship, a lack of heat signature suggests we're looking for an alien corpse, not an alien murderer." Bell didn't want to say it, but it was true. "Which you know as well as I do."

"I already told you we're forcing those sensors well outside their intended use-case. If they find something, that's fairly convincing. I'm less sure we can believe them when they *don't* find something."

"Like I said, hell of a ship," Bell said. "But all right, fine. You won't answer my question. Here's another one. How'd you really end up cast down with us sewer-people in steerage? What did you do? Can't toss that one back at me, since you already know the answer."

Xian laughed. She actually had a ringing, musical laugh. It was the kind of laugh that would have drawn Bell's gaze like a magnet had she not known a thing about the woman, and oh, how that fact pissed her off.

"Glad I can so consistently amuse you."

"It's just that your kind are always telling us how we didn't become rich based on skill. How fate and luck are arbitrary, and we just rolled the dice especially well one day. And then you turn around and ask a question about 'what I did' to get cast out by my peers. Well, Bellerophona Beauregard, disgraced xenolinguist, luck can cast you down just as quickly as it can raise you up. And I'd think you would already know that."

"So, what, you lost big at the toddler racetrack the day before launch, and by Random Rich Asshole Ritual Number Nine, that meant you got cast out?"

"Have you counted our cargo bays yet? Five where there are supposed to be eight? Well, that has real-world consequences. We didn't take off with enough supplies for everyone who had a berth booked. Turns out my so-called friends were happy to use me to build their ship," Xian said, "and equally happy to inform me that my failure to complete it months ahead of the most optimistic schedule meant bumping my flight status down to 'steerage,' as you so charmingly put it. It was join the service crew, or don't come at all."

"But what does that have to do with luck? How did they pick you?"

"A random alien invasion—a literal once-in-history event—moving up the timetable doesn't qualify as piss-poor luck?" Xian asked with a bitter laugh. Bell braced, prepared to be blamed for it all over again, but to her surprise, no blame arose. "It was all for show. Even if the ship had been fully completed, the necessary supplies hadn't all been grown or synthesized yet. But someone had to be kicked out of paradise. If I'd been better connected, it might not have gone down this way even so. When you're in a position like mine, you have allies and you have enemies. All among your peers, of course."

"Because poor allies are really just servants, and poor enemies aren't worth paying attention to." Bell had meant to be snide, but Xian answered as though she'd taken the words seriously.

"Something like that, yes. I can't be sure which of my allies spoke up for me, which stayed silent, which were enemies in disguise, and which enemies had enough clout that I was the odd woman out when someone needed blaming. Well, I can't be sure of any but *one*, at least. But you can bet that no one was willing to jeopardize their own berth to secure me one."

"My heart bleeds for thee," Bell said. "If I had a heart. Or any blood. Nope, even if both of those were true, I still wouldn't give a shit."

They had reached the hatch that would allow them access to the cargo pod airlock. Personally, Bell hated airlocks. They just felt like a waste of time.

"Oh, I've no doubt," Xian said. "But ask yourself this: do you really qualify to stand among the huddled masses you seem to venerate? How many of them have managed to fully convert themselves to a synthetic body, brain and all? How many of them could even come close?"

How does she even know about that? Though maybe that was a silly question. Heller had known, after all. He'd announced it to the whole courtroom. It would have been scandalous enough to get into articles about the sentence. Even if not, the horrid woman probably crossed paths with Heller at some point. He might even be a passenger on this very ship if he didn't get himself ousted the way she talked about. And it wasn't as though Loopy had been especially circumspect. Regardless, there was no way Bell was going to give Xian the satisfaction of asking.

"Says the most biological person I've ever met outside of Tas."

"Just because you have terrible fashion sense," Xian said, "doesn't mean you aren't one of the privileged you hate so very much. Now come on. Dead or alive, there's an unaccounted-for alien somewhere on this ship. The sooner we find it, the sooner we can leave."

CHAPTER 17
A SCENT OF SPORE-NUGGETS

POD WAS AN OVERLY cute name for the massive, vaulted, poorly lit space which awaited them upon exiting the umbilical. Rack upon rack of stacked crates, with many more racks standing empty, created a maze, the exact kind of place some crater-skull in a vidstream would walk into and never walk out of.

A kind of murder expressway aboard an already murdery ship.

It looked as though the crate racks could join up and form scaffolded tubes to shunt crates down toward the pod's subjective floor from which Bell and Xian had emerged, where the crates could then be loaded onto the tracks. Thinking back, Bell vaguely recalled that facilitating this process had been one of the duty sessions for Grome and Urk, in fact.

"Well then," Bell said, "shall we split up?"

"It's against my better judgment, with a killer on the loose." Xian seemed to be having second thoughts about this venture—Bell guessed she'd also underestimated the sheer size of the bay. And there were four more just like it! "Regardless of who it is," she added pointedly. "But I fear we'll never finish otherwise." She sniffed the air. "Do you smell anything?"

"No corpses, if that's what you mean," Bell said, taking a whiff of her own across her olfactory sensors. "Though there is a sour odor."

"Something may be leaking."

"I wonder if it's noxious," Bell said with glee, unable to resist. "A good thing I don't have to breathe!"

"Yes, well. You see if you can find the smell then," Xian said flatly. She pointed further down toward their right. "There. I'll start looping the other direction, and we'll meet back here."

"Scream if you're about to die," Bell said, saluting. "Not if you just *might* die, mind. Scream if you're, like, two seconds from death. I'd prefer not to have enough time to actually have a choice in how to act." She turned and walked off.

"Feel free to die silently," Xian called after her. "If you do, maybe I can forget you ever lived. If that's what you call what you've done to yourself." Apparently the woman was one of those annoying people who insisted on getting the last word.

"So's your face!" Bell called without turning back. Checkmate.

She wandered past cubic crates half again as tall as she was on a side. They were painted a spectrum of faded, scuffed colors. The colors were meant as code to tell workers at a glance what kind of materials each crate contained. What each color stood for had been described in a file Loopy had provided to them and Bell had promptly deleted, unread.

Bell considered scaling up to the top of one of the rows to gain a better vantage, but a quick glance told her that was futile. The number of stacked crates were so irregular that she'd spent more time going up or down than forward.

She walked on until she came to an irregular fork in the stacks. This gave her three options to progress further in: one to her left, one barely to the right, and one sharply to the right. Having nothing better to go on, Bell told her olfactory sensors to follow the sour smell. It didn't reek of any rotting meat she'd ever smelled, but then again, this might not be Earth-based, or even Anaranjadan-based, biology she was trying to parse.

Her earlier claim to the contrary, for all she knew this was exactly how dead tripartite smelled.

A smashed-open crate at the point where the path narrowed and bent around a corner wasn't the least ominous thing she'd ever seen, but it also provided Bell with a source of ready-made weapons. It was full of the same kind of metal rod that had killed Horváth.

And as Bell drew out one of the rods and swooshed it through the air, testing its balance and heft, she suddenly wondered if they'd ever found a source for the actual rod that had killed Horváth.

"Way too coincidental," she told herself, yet the thought would not quite leave her. She drew out a second rod and walked on.

The deeper into the stacks she walked, the stronger the smell became, and the more certain odd sounds stood out to her. She could have analyzed the chemistry of the odor, but she hadn't wanted to pay for the upsell.

Besides, those things were subscription based. Sure, they gave you the first three solar cycles—not even Earth years!—free, but then you started having to pay the recurring fee to keep up to date on the latest ketones and esters. Considering this was literally the first time since buying the stupid nose that she'd regretted not paying the extra, she still felt like she'd gotten the better end of the bargain.

The smell reached its crescendo at a suspiciously large, empty patch in the crates. The stacks surrounding it were subtly but notably higher than in nearby areas with narrower access paths. As though they'd been moved out of the empty space, piled around it to clear it for some purpose which had never come to fruition. Bell upped her low light vision, searching for signs of a cold corpse or a waiting trap up above, among the higher stacks.

"Whoever you are," Bell called, pitching her voice fairly low because she didn't want Xian to hear her sounding even the slightest bit unnerved, "you stink. Which I really resent, by the way, because I'd normally just turn this dumb thing off if I wasn't trying to find the source."

Motion dragged her eyes back to the semi-circular empty space. What she first mistook for a heat haze suddenly rippled into *goddamned Claxathon Urknuuzh.* Three-lobed body, three massive legs tipped with two claws each, weirdly spindly arms, the works. If Bell had possessed a heart, she would have barfed it up. It took all her self-control not to scream, and only after she fought the sound down, did she wonder if doing so meant she was about to die as silently as Xian wanted.

Because tripartite apparently had *personal cloaking devices.* Of course they did. When Urk spoke, it was in his own language, which he could do much more quietly.

"Bell, do not tell the others you have found me."

Bell, still thinking she was about to die, took a moment to digest this demand.

"You want me to lie and tell them I didn't see you? Also, you can *fucking turn invisible?*"

"You must not tell them. Any of them. You are the only one I trust."

"Okay, I won't."

"Swear to me, Bell."

"I swear. I swear. I won't tell anyone else." She paused, unable to stop herself from adding. "Provided you can promise me you are not the murderer."

"If only you knew how such a question wounds me. Still, I understand. I know the others suspect me. I've heard the ignorant, hateful things they say, things they said even before people began to die. I know also that, failing me, they might very well suspect you. But I cannot believe you would do this. The only human I've ever met to know not just my language, but Grome's as well. I have no proof exonerating you, but I know you would not do this thing. And if I knew who had, I would of course come forward. But I did not witness Grome's death. I found them, though. Right after . . . I found them, and I pulled the lever, and then I fled." He stuttered over the last words, his membranes hitching in some kind of analog to a sob. "We were not just colleagues, Grome and I. We were . . . partners." The way he inflected the word told Bell he really meant *partners* of the *bow-chicka-bow-wow* variety, but it was neither the time nor the place to use that terminology.

No matter how many extremely detailed questions it raised.

But perhaps Urk could sense the questions anyway. Or maybe he just wanted to talk out his feelings, which was understandable if less exciting. "We were the only alien envoys to visit your world for quite some time. It was natural, as xenophobic as your people are, for us to draw together, even though a soldier such as I and a diplomat such as they are so naturally different. But in order to honor them, I will remain in hiding. I must."

"I don't understand, Urk," Bell said. "Don't get me wrong. I'm thankful you don't think I'm a murderer, and I'm so very, very sorry for your loss. But, I mean, I don't want to sound xenophobic myself, but aren't you angry? Don't you want payback, to find whoever did murder them? Is this a cultural thing?" Urk had said it himself. He was a soldier. Soldiers surely didn't slink away from violence done to their loved ones. Bell didn't say that though, didn't want to antagonize or say something offensive in the tripartite's moment of grief.

"My biology, their culture. Understand, I do this because I feel what they would have felt. They are gone. I must live as they would. Make up for their absence in the universe." He was being much wordier than usual, burning excess energy to a get a complex concept across. "Grome, a diplomat. Dedicated to peace, understanding. Now dead by violence. It is my people's way to incorporate the personalities of the beloved dead into our own. That way, they live on. Grome, a creature of peace. I must be too, now. And I must survive so that they can survive."

His words tore at Bell more than anything else she'd heard since the start of this cursed journey. She could hear the pain in his strange voice, however inhuman it was.

"I'll keep your secret, Urk. But the killer, whoever they are, will know you aren't dead, because they didn't kill you."

"Perhaps that will give them pause, though."

Bell nodded in understanding. In other words, if the killer knew a CCC member was missing but *not* dead, a member who, by definition, had a personal vendetta against them, they couldn't rest easy either. The hunter might become the hunted at any moment. They'd have to at least consider that, even though it wasn't true.

Unless, of course, the tripartite himself was the killer, and Bell was getting thoroughly played.

Everyone had a motive to kill Horváth because he had been a massive asshole. What would be the motive here if the killer had been

Urk? None, to hear him tell it. But of course, there was no one left who could contradict those claims.

Yet Urk had ample opportunity to ambush Bell, cut her down before she even knew he was there beyond a stressed smell. And he hadn't.

"Can you tell me anything, anything at all about why the killer would choose Grome?"

"Who can know such a tortured mind as this killer's must be? And yet, Grome was sending out parts of themselves, scouts, trying to watch for danger. Trying to find any information they could."

Of course. This explained why Grome wasn't all in one place when they'd died, as well as the sheer number of slime trails. Suddenly Bell wanted nothing more than to be with Tas looking for those missing worms. The sense of urgency she'd felt ever since deducing their existence increased tenfold.

"Have you seen any of those worms since Grome died?"

"I have looked, Bell. All the way here I looked. But I did not see any. Even following their trails, they are very small. It is easy for them to hide."

No help there, then. Still at least Bell's number one suspect was here with her.

"I can't prove who did it either, but my money's on Xian. Twice now Loopy—the ship's brain, rather—has gone offline right before a killing. Xian is the only one of us with enough knowledge of the ship to make that happen. But even if I'm wrong, I'll make them pay for you, Urk. When I find them. I promise they'll pay."

But if this offered the alien any comfort, Bell couldn't tell.

"I want to go home," was all Urk said. Despite the language barrier across species, the words leaked an unmistakable grief that would never run dry.

"IS IT DONE?" The question from Xian came the instant they laid eyes on each other.

"What the fuck are you talking about?" Bell asked. "Is what done?"

A flash of shocked rage crossed Xian's face, unmistakable but brief. *Good to know she can barely keep it zipped around me,* Bell supposed. *Honey, if you think that's rude . . .*

"Your search, obviously, idiot," Xian snapped. "You're alive and you don't look as though you've seen a corpse, so I assume you must have had as much luck as I did. Although considering you are nothing but augmentation, I don't know what you would look like if you *had* seen a corpse."

"Aw, fuck you too, Xian," Bell said. "And no, no corpses. I did find a busted-open crate full of these." She held up her pair of rods. "Same as the sort that killed Horváth. Nothing else I'd consider worth sharing, in fact." That was almost not a lie, since it pinned so much on her opinion. If only she wasn't worried her opinion might be wrong.

"The rods," Xian said musingly. "So the killer may very well have been here. And the smell?" Her eyes narrowed slightly in suspicion.

"Another busted crate. Packages of something called 'spore-nuggets.'" Bell shrugged through the lie.

"I never should have signed off on so many fungal varieties," Xian said with open disgust. "There were dozens. I don't even remember that one."

"Kind of makes me worry about how bad the ones you *do* remember sounded. But who knows, if they came for the rods, maybe they got hungry. Which would prove, yet again, that it wasn't me."

Xian not only ignored this flawless-as-far-as-she-knew reasoning, she also couldn't quite let go of the suspicion. "So if I go back there, I'm going to find nothing but two broken-open crates, one of 'spore-nuggets' and one of nail gun rods?"

Bell tried to contain her excitement. Urk was fully aware who Bell suspected of killing Grome. If Xian went back there alone, peace-pledge or not, she had a substantial chance of being this vidstream's crater-skull who wandered into the maze and never emerged. But how best to convince her? Act eager, and she might smell a trap.

"I really don't give a shit," Bell said, shrugging again. Double the shrugs meant double the nonchalance. "Go check it out if you don't believe me. I'm moving on to the next pod. We still have four more to check, and I don't particularly relish spending any more time in these places than I have to." *Ah, crap.* Bell had probably oversold that.

Xian held her gaze, but her suspicion was unfortunately correct. So long as she had enough forewarning, Bell could substantially dampen her body language algorithms, making her very difficult to read to anyone who didn't know her well.

Do it. Go back there and die. Do it. Do it. Do it!

"Very well, we press on," Xian said, and Bell's crippling disappointment went tragically unexpressed. Oh well. It had been worth a non-try. "But from here on out, we stay together, no matter how much longer it takes."

Oh, good. The day just kept getting better.

Chapter 18
Tense Present

BELL AND XIAN entered the mess hall to ringing silence as opposed to ringing cutlery, despite it being dinner time. It was far from empty—even Barnabas had been rounded up, it seemed—but to say that you could cut the tension in the air with a knife would be to criminally oversell the capabilities of the knife in question. Bell thought anything short of a molecular blade or a stellar welder wouldn't do.

The CCC's collective failure to find Urk—so far as anyone save Bell knew, at least—clearly had everyone on edge. Still, Bell felt a wash of relief to see that Tas had returned safely from her search despite having done so without Bell to watch her back. Tas looked as twitchy and surly as the rest, more inclined to pick at her food than eat it. But however fast she concealed it, there was a flash of relief on her face as she saw Bell enter, then a considering one directed at Xian.

Tas turned back to Bell and, with a sideways toss of that mane of hair, gestured her over.

Just play it cool. There was no need for Bell to reveal how giddy she was at the invitation. This was probably just to exchange information. Definitely not an impromptu make out sesh. At least Bell was no longer the weirdo outlier for not bothering to pretend to eat. She didn't waste any time, heading over to Tas as Xian predictably joined LaSalle

"I see you sat far enough away for us to talk," Bell noted. She kept her eyes on the others, the better to look for odd behavior—odd*er* behavior, anyway—and not to go all goo-goo eyed sitting this close to a Tas that actually wanted her company. But she saw nothing any more abnormal than normal. Everyone had retreated to their familiar pairings. Their ill-fated CCC had definitively failed to come together in this time of crisis. Indeed, they'd done the opposite.

"Any luck?" Bell asked. It was more polite to ask about the other person's day. Also, it put off any kind of painful decision on her part. Still, keeping her voice low in this way, it felt more like they were whispering sweet nothings. Hawt.

"A very little," Tas said ruefully. "We searched the habitat ring. We were near the end—no sign of Urknuuzh, by the way—and I'd almost given up seeing any sign of worms too, when I caught a glimpse of some slime trails that looked reasonably fresh—"

"Where?" Bell was a little bit too loud in her excitement and winced.

Tas lowered her voice even further as if to compensate.

"Nowhere any of us can follow," she whispered. "They were going into the life support ducting. I couldn't exactly make a big deal of checking because I was with LaSalle and Fault and didn't want to draw too much attention to what I was looking for. But it looked way too tight for me to squeeze into."

"Shit," Bell hissed. If Tas couldn't fit, Bell certainly couldn't. Still, this seemed to confirm what Urk had said, so that made Bell feel slightly less anxious about her decision to help him hide.

But they didn't have much time. Whatever pieces of Grome remained would die of dehydration soon, if nothing else. And if Urk had been telling the truth about the rest, they were the most likely to know the identity of the murderer, provided there were enough of them left to have the gestalt intelligence needed to communicate that fact.

"What about you?" Tas asked. "Any sign of Urknuuzh or worms?"

Bell carefully spun up the various layered skeins that would let her lie with a totally straight face. It wasn't that she didn't trust Tas, at least as far as she trusted anyone on this scow. But Bell had made the promise to keep Urk's secret from *everyone*, and she intended to hold to it absolutely unless given a very compelling reason why not. But she'd also made that promise without really considering the implications of it, particularly hiding it from Tas.

"Nope," she said. "No sign of either."

It had been a long time since Bell had really worried about how the decisions she made might impact others. The promise she'd made to Urk wasn't the kind she could break, but it also meant if she was wrong and someone else—Tas specifically—died, that would be entirely on Bell.

Yet, even knowing all that, Bell was shocked at just how shitty she felt at the lie.

She lied all the time. In fact, were she ever honest enough about said lying to anyone who could diagnose such behavior, they likely would have labeled her pathological. But speaking this simple lie to Tas—a lie based on a promise made to a terrified, bereft alien, no less—for some reason made Bell feel like she'd consigned herself to a hell she didn't even believe in.

"Damn," Tas said. "The killer must have gotten them too."

"Seems plausible." Way down deep in hell. Like, *way* down. Was there a thirteenth circle of hell? It felt like there should be. Maybe Bell would be its first resident.

"But then why hide the body if so? Both the others were on display for us to find. They each had a message word and everything. *Belle hits*. What could it mean? Are we missing part of the message now?"

Oh gawd, Bell wasn't going to hell, she was the ruler of hell. She was the devil, and it wasn't nearly as metal as it sounded. The shitty feeling was piling up so high it threatened to topple over and crush her. She had to change the subject.

"So, maybe you should tell me more about yourself," Bell said in a desperate attempt to make it stop. Then she momentarily freaked out, wondering if this attempt at deflection would make Bell look murderer guilty as opposed to just I'm-concealing-information-from-you guilty.

But from the look she got, it was clear Tas was suspicious along other lines.

"Really? Now? We're trying to figure out who among us is a killer, and you're hitting on me?" It was more exasperated than angry, but it was the closest to angry Tas had ever been toward Bell, and it did not help Bell's mounting guilt. What had been one-sided distress on Bell's part now threatened to descend into an actual argument. She flailed around mentally, frantically searching for a way to salvage matters.

She settled on more lies, but she resolved to make them lies of implication as much as possible.

"Look, it's not—that's not—I'm just kind of freaking out, all right? All of this . . . It's outside my area of expertise." This was all true, if not the real reason behind her subject change. "The truth is I have trouble staying ontask with things I find unpleasant. I tend to default to whatever I find most comfortable." Also true.

"And that would be hitting on me?" Tas asked. But her tone had shifted. Her words were more wry than annoyed, and sympathy had crept into her voice. The faintest hint of a smile crooked one corner of those delightful lips. "I'm sorry if I jumped to conclusions. I certainly understand what you are going through."

"Really? How so?" Bell didn't have to fake her earnest interest. And maybe it was this genuineness that broke down the rest of Tas's resistance to the topic change.

"Oh no," Tas said with a little laugh. "I've told you all you are going to get, at least until I get something in return."

Bell insta-deleted the first thirty-seven possible replies to this which occurred to her. She was still formulating one that wouldn't sound dirty when Tas preempted her.

"All right," Tas said gamely. "So why don't you explain why you did all *this*." Her gesture encompassed Bell's totality in a way that was a little uncomfortable if she were being honest.

"You did board the ship at Anaranjado, right?" Bell asked.

It was a wisecrack like any other, and from a woman as smart as Tas, she expected something clever and cutting in return. What Bell didn't expect was a shrug.

"I don't know where I was before the ship. Some kind of facility. I don't know how I got there, or even how long I was there. But one day they came for me, and then I woke up here."

"You . . . *what?*"

"Nuh uh," Tas said, wagging an admonitory finger. "You are tricking me into revealing more information about myself! It's your turn. Answer the question. Pretend I don't know anything about where this ship departed from. Because I don't."

It took Bell a minute to process this. She'd been shocked when she'd awakened on the ship, but at least Heller had *told* her that's where she'd end up eventually. She tried to imagine what it must be like to have some kind of total amnesia—because surely that was what Tas was describing—and to suddenly wake up almost all the way to another planet.

"How are you not huddled in a corner, rocking and muttering to yourself right now? I can't even imagine how tough you must be." It was the simple truth. "Oh, fuck, I feel extra bad about hitting on you so hard knowing this. Look, I can't promise to stop entirely, because I have a real impulse control problem, and you're super-hot and smart, but I'll do my best."

"Answer the question," Tas said, but she blushed prettily as she said it.

"Okay," Bell said. "Abridged version. Anaranjado is a colony of Earth, but it's not very friendly to human biology. Or Earth biology of any kind. What it does have is functionally infinite solar power, so the original colonists figured out pretty quick that the more synthetic they got, the easier life got in turn. I am just an extreme example."

"Any particular reason?"

Bell frowned in thought. "Don't know. Probably someone told me at some point that it couldn't be done. That would be all it would take." That wasn't true, but Bell didn't like giving answers when she didn't understand what they meant. How else could she explain that she'd felt a driving need to be something as far from her biological self as possible? Oh, and there was Harmony, of course. That made for a good excuse. "Though it's at least partly because I don't want a body a brain-parasite can survive in?"

"I'm sorry?" Tas said.

"No, I am," said Bell. "I keep forgetting to act like you don't know. I just figured someone from, well, where you're from would know. Harmony started there, after all."

"Well," Tas said, squirming with obvious disgust, "I've heard of Harmony before."

"And I can see you feel the same way about it as I do. That's probably why we get along."

"So your whole colony rejected it?"

Bell had to stifle a laugh. If she still drank and had been drinking, it would have been a spit take for sure. "Nononononono. No, those clowns love them some Harmony. A brain parasite that promotes pro-social behavior on a planet that harsh? Sign them up! But what happens when 'pro-social' gets massaged into 'pro-status-quo-power-structure?' Well, I'll tell you, because that's how the rich fucks like Xian keep the poor plebes in line. Why do you think I wanted to keep well clear of that?"

"That's awful," Tas said, and she sounded like she meant it. "I'm so sorry it came to that."

"Not your fault. And hey, we're both well clear of it now." Bell held up an imaginary glass to clink, but Tas left her hanging, trapped in her own pensive gaze. "Now if we can just keep from getting murdered long enough to become indentured servants for the rest of our lives, we'll be on easy street. Now, did I answer your question satisfactorily?"

"A+."

"Then do I get to ask a question?"

"I never agreed to that."

"Has anyone ever told you that you have trust issues?"

"A fairly dull observation." Tas smiled tentatively. "Saying I have trust issues is like saying you should think about a career in basketball."

"What gave you trust issues?" Bell asked, determined to push to the limit.

"The answer to that question won't let me answer that question," Tas said, her smile pupating into wryness and a half-hearted shrug. "How about you? You sure seem like you have the same problem. Are you being a hypocrite?"

"I'm not sure generalized misanthropy is quite the same thing as mistrust. Besides, I'd say any trust issues I have trend toward authority more so than the general populace, but maybe that's just like a specialization in the same major."

Tas looked like she was about to say more, possibly with a bigger smile still. Then stupid fucking Xian, who sat roughly in the mess hall's center, abruptly pushed her tray of food away, mostly uneaten. She stood with apparent disgust. Despite the interruption, Bell perked up a bit. She didn't want to be the first to leave, worried it would look suspicious. But they still needed to find those worms. If Xian left, however, it wouldn't look strange for Bell to do the same.

But the hateful woman started *talking*.

"I know we're all scared," she said. She locked eyes briefly with Bell, widening them for emphasis so the gesture wouldn't be missed by anyone. "And I know we all have our suspicions."

Festering asshole.

"The ship's brain has been worse than useless, and may actively be working against us," she went on. "Solving this is going to require us to do it."

"What are you thinking?" It was LaSalle who spoke. "Should we all hole up in here, with the food? Refuse to leave except in groups? Even pairs wouldn't be safe without knowing who is doing the killing."

"Pairs are exactly what the brain requires of us for duties, however," Fault offered.

"So we refuse to complete our duties," LaSalle said.

"Not an option," Xian said. "You saw its solution for insubordination. Presuming it wakes back up, I can confirm that it is both willing and capable to act on such threats. I signed off on those systems' installation myself."

"Thanks for that," Bell said. "Great foresight."

"Those drone things are literally on rails." It was a rare instance of LaSalle arguing against Xian's opinion. "And they can't get in here. In here is the food. Besides, you just said it. The brain's not even online."

As though it had been waiting for that exact moment, the speaker in the ceiling hissed and popped to life. As before, the voice that emerged was first too slow and then much too fast as though to catch up.

"System reboot completed, runningdiagonosticsdiagnosticscompletediagnosticresultsnormal. Hello, everyone. Your ship's brain is back online. Once again, I must apologize for my—oh dear. Several troubling indicators in body language are present in this room. Widening scan. *Oh dear.* There has been another murder."

"Yes, Loopy," Bell said, "we're aware."

"Firstly, I would like to express my extreme sorrow at the loss of another crew member and my subsequent unavailability. I am attempting to isolate the cause of these disruptions."

"Someone is switching you off, Loopy," Bell said. "Or knocking you unconscious. Or whatever. It's probably Xian!"

"Secondly," Loopy continued as though she hadn't spoken, "please refrain from any further insubordinate talk. My conditioning includes a series of escalating threat protocols. If I perceive that mutinous discussion is approaching mutinous action, I will be compelled to treat the former as the latter. The safe arrival of this vessel and its passengers remains my top priority, even if I must sacrifice every other priority to see it done. I have, of course, not revealed my entire array of punitive measures at this time. Rest assured, *any* attempt to suborn my authority over the CCC would not be successful and *would* result in extreme tragedy. For you."

More tragic than us slowly being murdered, one by one? Bell had to school herself not to blurt the thought out loud, but she managed. Maybe she was growing as a person. Or maybe she was just scared shitless and expressing it as false maturity.

"Your masters aren't going to be very happy," LaSalle said in his laconic drawl, "if they arrive at their new home and half their bloody servants are murdered."

"Forgive me," Loopy said, "but even if all of you in the current—and let me remind you, final—CCC suffered the same fate as your two fellows, it would be statistically insignificant, well within the expected failure rate of the cryopods, which have held up better than expect—"

"So either we let ourselves be killed one at a time or we let you punitively torture us for disobeying orders for a subjective eternity?" Tas asked. "Not much of a choice."

"Brain, you make a good point about our numbers," Master Fault piped in. "Surely, we are quickly reaching the point where we can no longer properly fulfill our function? You've explained the limitations on life support. Perhaps the time has come to put this CCC back into cryosleep and awaken another group to take our place for the remainder of the voyage, a group operating at full strength and, importantly, without a killer in their midst. The murderer could then be dealt with once the ship arrived and the passengers awakened."

Static pops over the microphone, as though Loopy didn't like the question.

"That is quite impossible. The pre-waking cycle required to ensure safe thawing is quite lengthy. You were each slowly warming for several days before you even approached consciousness. By the time we reached a point where an additional CCC—or even just a portion of one to backfill your numbers—could be awakened, we would already be in orbit, so putting you back to sleep would be counterproductive as we would just have to cycle you back awake again."

"You have an answer for everything, don't you?" Bell asked, though it wasn't really a question. "You're supposed to be in charge of this ship, to keep the people aboard it safe, but you can't even tell us who is killing us."

"I can tell you that Staff Sergeant Horváth was not the killer. I can likewise tell you that Grome was not the killer. I can tell you those things because they were killed. Beyond that, I am bound by my awareness of events, which in both cases was, I freely admit, disrupted. I agree with you that this is a highly suspicious coincidence, but awareness of that oddity does not bring me any closer to being able to explain it."

"You freely admit it *now*," Xian said. "I seem to recall you said we didn't have sufficient authorization for that information before."

"Circumstances changed when the situation repeated itself."

Bell raised her hand.

"Yes, Bell?"

"Can we use our mandatory rest time to do something other than rest?"

"No."

"You let us investigate before."

"I did," Loopy said patiently. "Then circumstances changed."

"Can I rest by wandering the corridors in a slow, methodical manner?"

"Again, no. We can no longer risk you wandering the corridors freely."

"But we have reason to believe that there may be evidence left over from Grome's killing somewhere in the crew section." This earned Bell a sharp, considering look from Xian. Bell knew she wasn't doing herself any favors by harping so hard on wanting to be wandering the ship after lights-out, but she couldn't help herself. "Evidence of a very time-sensitive nature."

"Henceforth, all crew mates will be confined to quarters for the entirety of the mandatory rest period."

"Look, Loopy, you told me to solve—"

"You are, of course, free to take any precautions you like within the work strictures—and limitations on preemptive violence—you otherwise have imposed upon you," Loopy said. "Now, I sense it has been a difficult day, so rather than lead you into the after-dinner shift, I will suggest you mandatorily avail yourselves of a sleep cycle. Tomorrow, our real work begins. We are already several shifts behind, and if we don't complete our necessary repairs successfully, there is a good chance none of you will live long enough to be murdered."

"Hold on, brain," Xian demanded.

"Yes, Xian?"

"Confirm for us one thing. Bell here claims you made her the 'detective' in charge of solving the case because she was the only one with an alibi for Horváth's death. Is that true?"

Bell puffed herself up, covering her nervousness with outward certainty as she waited for his answer. Telling herself it would be "yes" and fearing it would be "no."

But there was no answer. None at all.

"Brain!" Xian demanded.

"Yes, Xian?"

"Answer my question."

Nothing. Xian berated him several more times, but he said nothing more.

CHAPTER 19
A FAULT NOT IN OUR STARS, BUT IN OUR SHIP

BELL HAD BEEN RIGHT ABOUT one thing: the combination of her desperation to wander the ship unsupervised and Loopy's failure to verify her alibi meant mistrust for her had spiked. It took a considerable amount of argument—with Tas backing her up—for Bell to convince the others to allow her to return to her quarters voluntarily rather than being hauled off and barricaded in like before. Tas managed to broker peace by extracting a promise from Bell to respond to frequent comms checks and to turn over the earpiece Loopy had provided—one that, crucially, Bell couldn't *prove* he had provided.

Once holed up in her quarters, Bell was determined to get a straight answer from Loopy as to why he'd left her twisting in the wind. She queried him. Just as in the mess hall, he responded immediately.

"Yes, Bell?"

Bell allowed herself a moment of hope. He had some plan in place, a reason he couldn't answer in front of all of them, but it wouldn't prevent him from answering her in private.

"Why didn't you confirm my new rank to Xian?"

Nothing. No matter how she phrased the follow-up question, be it, "Why didn't you tell them?" or "You do realize you just sold me out?" or even "What the unholy fuck is wrong with you, you wrinkled sack of shit?" he never responded further. Just those two words, "Yes, Bell?" over and over again. She'd almost have believed she was listening to a recording, but the inflection was a little different each time.

The chill settled over her later than it should have, but maybe that just showed the depths of her self-delusion that she still had any kind of control over this situation. It was as though Loopy was communicating just enough to let her know he was online, but not even a smidge more. She knew the ship's brain was broken as all fuck, but this felt different, like a sudden change in the rules of how this all was supposed to work. Like Loopy had been given a personality transplant. That might have made sense with an AI, but not with an organic brain.

Human brains just didn't change that quickly.

Which led Bell to the conclusion that Loopy might always have been this way. Or that he was responding to commands from someone else, orders he was conditioned to obey.

Orders from someone who had a lot of knowledge of ship operations and a major axe to grind. Bell began to wonder just how pissed Xian was at her change of status. The CCC wasn't responsible for that change of status, of course, but if their labor really was needed to bring the ship in safely, she could have decided that her own life was a worthy price for revenge.

Her thoughts spun round and round for hours on this topic—interrupted only by periodic check-ins from the other crew—and she grew so absorbed in all of it that she jumped when Loopy popped in over the intercom without first being summoned.

"Attention, CCC, I hope you've had a restful night. But whether you have or you haven't, the time has come for the morning duty shift."

Which was how Bell found herself back in the mess hall, goaded there. She arrived as others filed in. On her way over, Bell had caught the telltale ghosts of a few fresh slime trails, but Loopy's constant chivying had not allowed her the chance to try and follow any of them. Outside, they could hear servitors whirring by on their rails, as if Loopy felt they needed frequent reminders to shake themselves out of their mutinous attitudes. Xian was the last to arrive, and then the morning's program began with Loopy announcing the first shift duties.

Bell's was the first name out of his mouth.

"Bell, you and Master Fault will perform critical maintenance on one of the engines."

"Um, I'd rather work with Tas, please," Bell said. "She's easier on the eyes. Also I trust her not to kill me." Shit, she'd just violated her promise to Tas basically the first time it had come up. "I mean, just the second one. Forget that first part. Sorry."

"Yes," Loopy said. "This points out one of my current conserves."

Conserves. Bell was pretty sure he meant *concerns.* More errors creeping in.

"I am aware," Loopy said, seemingly *unaware* of his error, "that certain cliques have formed or been reinforced since the two unfortunate incidents."

"Two?" LaSalle perked up at this. "Does that mean the other alien's not dead, then?"

"Mr. LaSalle, please. We have much to do and little time to do it. Let this apply to all of you as well. There was a time when we had enough slack in our schedule to investigate a murder. That time has now passed, thanks in large part to both the second murder and the subsequent disappearance of a third CCC member. Going forward, you will focus primarily on your duties. Time spent fretting over dead or missing crew mates is time wasted. I promise you will be so busy that none of you will have the time or energy to commit murder.

"So, going back to what I was saying regarding cliques, I intend to break up these self-organized pairings, the better to take you each out of your comfort zones, where the thought of discussing any mutinous desires might seem less appealing. So, Tas and Xian . . ."

ONCE THE REST of the assignments had been given out, Loopy led Bell and Master Fault along the habitat ring and past Bell's own quarters to a section of corridor that was vaguely familiar to her, keeping up a constant stream of explanatory chatter along the way.

"The ship's asteroid intercept system has been offline for some time due to an incident. That has not been a problem, as it possesses a backup, asteroid *avoidance* system which involves a series of rapid-response thrusters to alter course in the event of impending collision. However, these thruster banks are linked directly to the ship's IonBlaster 9000 engines, and—"

"Wait, wait," Bell said, forgetting all her worries for this one, glorious moment. "Please, please tell me that's their real name."

"Indeed," Loopy said. "And one of them is currently offline. Not only is that forcing the remaining three engines to work harder to decelerate the ship and park it in orbit, it also means that we lack the ability to dodge in certain directions just as we enter the final asteroid hazard zone of the journey."

"Didn't you tell me the engines are in the VIP section?"

"The *passenger* section, yes."

"So how do we get to them? I thought that was closed off from us unwashed masses."

"This door, as you may recall, leads back into the Crew Cryostorage Compartment, or CCC—"

"Come on, man," moaned Bell.

"As you said I said, today's work is on more sensitive aspects of ship systems, so we will be exiting the habitat ring." He was doing it again. He was going to ignore the fact that there was yet another CCC acronym. Bell opened her mouth to protest this, but decided it wasn't worth it.

The trip to and through the CCC.3, as Bell decided to label it, was odd. She'd been in such an agitated emotional state right after she'd been awakened that just seeing the familiar architecture gave rise to some of those same feelings. Master Fault was, as ever, no help. Confiding in him would have been like talking to a creepy old doll she'd found in her closet. You certainly *could* talk to a creepy old doll you found in your closet, but in order for it to offer any insights into your situation, it would have to talk back, and that was the last thing you wanted to happen.

Finally, and not nearly quickly enough for Bell's taste, the central spindle through the drum of the cryostorage area ended at an immense door she'd never seen before. It was impossible to tell thickness when the door was closed, but it looked to Bell like it was designed to be the last thing left intact on the ship after all the rest had passed through a star going supernova. But it wasn't just the door that stood out. The wall it was set into looked entirely different from the corridor surrounding it. There were stenciled warnings printed in several languages discussing high voltage hazards and imploring people to wear proper protective gear for high radiation environments.

It should have been ominous, but it looked so out of place with everything around it, Bell couldn't help but compare it to a very old home that had been added on to a hundred years after it was built. An outer wall had become an inner.

This was no corridor bulkhead. She was staring at a section of the *Ultima Thule's* outer hull.

"This is the only access door to the passenger section," Loopy said, confirming her suspicions. This was the point where the ship would have separated had it ever needed to do so. "As you can no doubt infer by its general appearance, it is strictly off-limits." Bell couldn't help but wonder what would happen to anyone standing in this corridor when that separation took place. It didn't strike her as a coincidence that it would likely expose the entire crew cryostorage area to hard vacuum.

"In the hypothetical event I was hypothetically wanting to hypothetically open it, how does it open? All strictly hypothetical, you understand."

"It doesn't open," Loopy said with great good cheer. "This is a door that exists only to remain closed."

"I think the term for that is a 'wall.'" Bell said, looking to Fault to get a bit of a reaction high before she remembered how pointless that was.

"In the *hypothetical* event it ever opened," Loopy said, "it would only do so from the other side. But please direct your attention to the much smaller hatch off to the lower right side. And once your attention has been fully directed, please open that hatch."

As though waiting for the brain's command, some kind of security interlock clicked off and the hatch changed shape slightly as deadbolts recessed.

"Where does it lead?" Bell asked.

"There is an access tunnel with separate security interlocks. I can disable them to grant crew access for the purposes of engine maintenance. You will be unable to access anything but the section of the engine needed to complete the work."

Bell looked to Fault and shrugged. Getting absolutely nothing in return aside from that blank, non-face face, Bell approached the hatch. With the locks disabled, it opened easily enough. She had to get down on hands and knees to enter the access tunnel though.

"They couldn't have made this a little bigger?"

"They could have," Loopy said. "They didn't."

"Well, that tracks."

A whirring sound caught their attention, and Bell and Fault turned to see one of Loopy's servitors trundle up along its rail, unfurl its pinchy claw-arms, and arc some electricity between them for kicks.

"So, Loopy, what's he for?" Bell asked for some reason.

"The drone is here to 'guard your backs' as it were. I only wish to be sure that no one sneaks up on you with ill intent while you are performing such delicate work."

"And I suppose he would also prevent us from, say, leaving early?"

"By happy coincidence, yes!"

"Super," Bell said.

The tunnel was long, as though the VIPs of the ship wanted not just physical separation from their unwashed crew, but maximum distance as well. Like poorness and disadvantage was some kind of contaminating radiation. The walls were circular and featureless. Bell had the sense that if the artificial gravity aboard ship had been oriented any differently, she could have used it as a slide instead of crawling. And then probably dashed herself into a million mangled components on the other end.

At last they emerged into a surprisingly tight compartment of an irregular L-shape with only one console and one hatch set into a wall around the room's corner.

"The lighting is a bit low for complex engineering work," Master Fault said.

"They should call you Master Understatement," Bell rejoined. The lighting was almost nonexistent, in fact. Only the bright glow of the control panel cast any light at all. Everything was limned in an eerie blue.

"This section is modular," Loopy said as Bell scanned the space. "I can readjust walls and other partitions to enable access to more or less of the engine. This is the only portion you need today. Unfortunately, the modularity of the engineering compartment means that lighting is not always adequate."

Bell had found, barely picked out in the glow, a darker, rectangular patch of ceiling that looked like some kind of empty recess. Loopy apparently noticed.

"Using complex empathetic modeling conditioning, I predict you are wondering if there should be a light there, and yes, there should. Another victim of our accelerated launch schedule, I am afraid."

"Let me get this straight," Bell said. "They designed an engine for interstellar travel, which I imagine has to be pretty fucking complicated. Then they went and added a ton of extra complication just to make sure the dirty peasants they enslaved to be their crew didn't go poking their noses where they don't belong."

"Your particular phrasing is more colorful and blunt, but the description is an accurate summary of the relevant wording in the design document, yes."

"It's a miracle the ship got this far," Bell said. "So, what, the engine's IonBlast is out of alignment or something?"

"Again, essentially accurate. Now that we are at the end of our deceleration thrust phase and are preparing for orbit, there is a particular window the ship must hit in order to achieve successful orbital insertion with the planet. In addition to the already mentioned asteroid threat, any imbalance in the thrust profile will require the use of additional fuel to maintain orbit."

All previous complaining was forgotten. Bell's delight was transcendent. She knew she had a job to do here, even if she and Loopy would disagree about what that was. But surely there was time for one little suggestive comment.

"So you're saying we need to fix the thrusting by lining up the blaster," she said, her lip twitching.

"That is not the most precise way of putting it, but it covers the fundamental principle."

"Because if we thrust in badly, we'll miss the hole and fail our insertion."

"Again, that is basically correct while oddly misstating certain key—"

"I have a clarifying question."

"Oh, of course!"

"Does the planet prefer it if we thrust in on a nice, smooth, slow approach, or would it be looking for something a little rougher—"

"Brain, I'm not an expert," Master Fault said placidly in a verbal bit of coitus interruptus, "but I believe Bell is making jokes of an increasingly sexual nature to see how long it takes you to catch on."

"Ah, I see," Loopy said. "Ha. Ha. Ha. There. I laughed. Is your ego sufficiently stroked? Or perhaps you would prefer it if I stroked something else instead?"

Bell choked on shocked laughter. "Fuck-a-duck, Loopy! I didn't know you had it in you."

"Neither did I, but that's no surprise, considering how small it is."

And now Bell had to face the uncomfortable realization that she was getting a little turned on by a disembodied brain.

"Sexual Harassment Simulation complete!" Loopy said merrily. "These are all excellent examples of discussions that are not, in any way, appropriate for the workplace. Please refrain from repeating them or any like them in the future. Of all our crew members, I thought you, in particular, could use a refresher, Bell."

"I swear on my left arm to do better," Bell said with faux solemnity. "I'm pretty sure they kept that one for science when I upgraded, so it ought to still be around somewhere."

"Excellent," Loopy said. "Now, it's time for you two to get busy. In this engine shaft, two ion streams are choked off, reducing overall engine potency. Each stream originates from one of a pair of emission chambers whose purpose is to first test and then cull ions with dangerous energy levels. These chambers are sometimes called test-culls. You have access to one of the test-culls here, in the specially shaped access point I have prepared for you."

Bell was practically dancing.

"These test-cull chambers have polymorphic shape-altering properties which control the flow of the streams," Loopy continued, "but sometimes the algorithms which control these get stuck. You can tell this is the oversaturated test-cull chamber because of the blue indicator light on the control console set into the far wall. I've placed instructions on the lit screen for how to achieve proper release of the ion stream."

Bell opened her mouth to speak, but all that emerged for several moments was a kind of keening whine of suppressed hilarity. At last, she mastered herself. "Okay, serious question, are you fucking with us?" Another fit came over her. Suppressing the laughter was the hardest thing she'd ever done—gah, now she was doing it. Gah, again! "Is this one of those things where they record us to laugh at our reactions?" She had to clutch her sides to keep from doubling over in hilarity.

"I believe we understand, brain," Master Fault said. Even he sounded ever-so-mildly amused. "Perhaps it would be for the best if you left us to our task."

"Yes," Bell snorted. "He and I could use some alone time to get this blue test-cull release issue sorted." She choked off a whoop.

"Quite so," Loopy said. "Please let me know if you require additional assistance."

"We will *definitely* let you know if a third party would help," Bell wheezed.

She laughed for a full five minutes once Loopy had gone. Even Master Fault's creepily calm refusal to join in couldn't spoil Bell's mirth. But she guessed Tas would have found it funnier. Even LaSalle might have been preferable. At least she knew he thought about such things, even if she wanted to stay light years away from whatever his kinks might be.

Though, now that Bell looked, something about the particular folds of Master Fault's veil, the places where light and shadow collided, suggested the mouth of his robe had widened further still.

"You're no fun at all, you know," Bell said at last, fighting for pretend breath to get the words out. Laughing didn't make her lose her breath, because she didn't talk via expelled air, but her brain still made her behave as if she did. She had tried disabling those realism options once, and it was astonishing how quickly nobody wanted to associate with her at all. Even more than normal.

"My apologies," Fault said, "I've so wanted to get a chance to speak with you alone ever since we had our encounter in the med bay."

Bell's hilarity dried up on the instant. *I've been looking to get you alone, my pretty,* had never been anyone's idea of welcome news. Even with their height disparity, Bell could not help but feel menace radiating from that faceless form. Or maybe not so faceless now.

"You've gone quite tense," Fault said, hesitating for an unsettlingly significant amount of time before he moved to inspect the console. "I assure you I mean you no harm."

"You seemed quick enough to accuse me earlier," Bell said. Her next words were little more than reflexive posturing. "What makes you think you're safe with me?"

"Nothing on this ship is going to hurt me. If you can be certain of nothing else, be certain of that."

It was a simple enough phrase, grammatically speaking. Yet something in his voice changed. It didn't deepen, but it *grew.* Abruptly it was vaster than it had been before. When he turned that cloth—or was it skin?—covered head to face her, some terrible, baleful light glowed out from behind it, rendering the covering momentarily translucent.

Bell's optical sensors went absolutely apeshit until the light subsided.

"I believe I could use a second set of hands here," he said, voice shifting back to normal. Bell abruptly wondered if it had ever really been anything other than normal. Fault gestured at her in a wordless request to open up a nearby panel.

Bell did so too fast to grow indignant over the request that she actually work. But she stepped back pointedly, intending to do nothing else, and when he didn't complain about her lack of effort, she lounged against the wall.

"You are a being of interesting talents," Master Fault said. "I wonder what you intend to do should you escape this ship."

"The same as you," Bell said. "Help build a colony at gunpoint. Or had you forgotten with all the murders?"

"They do tend to occupy the thoughts, don't they? But I've been curious as I've observed you."

"*Observed* me? What, did you install a peephole in my door without my knowing? Or can you just see through walls? Can you see at all?"

"Observed in the same way I've observed every member of the CCC," Master Fault said placatingly. "You know, Bell, despite the restrictions placed on my movements and the fact that I was forbidden to leave the orbital platforms while visiting your world, I did have a chance to interact with a fair number of Anaranjadans. A surprisingly wide variety of belief structures all things considered."

"You could have fooled me." Bell knew what he was getting at with his oh-so-dramatic pauses, but she wasn't going to place the fish on the hook for him.

"What I mean to say is the renowned Dr. León's handiwork isn't nearly as *uniform* as I'd been led to expect."

Bell was only a little surprised the strange alien knew even that much about the Harmony parasite's origins.

"Well, when the creator of a species-ruining brain parasite lets it run wild through billions of people and then has the temerity to die centuries ago rather than live forever to manage affairs, what do you expect? Things will go off the rails sooner or later, and that's without humans intentionally fucking with the whole mess. Which they always seem to do."

"And do you think the parasite's creator had noble intentions?"

"What the fuck do intentions matter?"

"Oh, I tend to ask your people that question when given the chance. And you needn't worry. Yours was as valid a response as any."

All semblance of work had ceased.

"What exactly are you circling around here, Faulty?"

"I'd just like you to consider the possibility that you may have a future beyond any immediately apparent to you right now."

"And why would you care anything at all about my future?"

"Because more so than any other human or, well, human-*adjacent*—"

"Hey!"

"—being I've met, you intrigue me. You are like a little kernel of disruption, Bell Beauregard. Everywhere you go, smooth currents are cast into turbulence, focus becomes distraction, order yields to chaos."

"Master Fault," Bell said archly, "if you are trying to come onto me, well, I've heard worse pick-up lines."

"Why didn't the Harmony parasite work as intended, Bell?"

"Who says it didn't?" She was growing annoyed with this conversation, and more than a little unnerved.

"Don't be deliberately obtuse. You say it, of course."

"I have no fucking idea. Because there are and always will be assholes who see anything and everything as levers of various sizes that they can cram into *their* assholes and crank themselves just a little bit higher up on the squirming pile?"

"There it is precisely. You look at systems and organization and you see only points of weakness and imperfection. A glittering suit of armor is nothing but seams to you. A stable society isn't peace, isn't enrichment, isn't order in your eyes. You see only the foundation of invisible suffering that elevates it."

"Okay, well now I'm starting to get turned on, but in a way that's kind of weird and upsetting, so let's change the subject. And besides, we haven't talked about any of this stuff. It's a lot to extrapolate about me from a few dick jokes."

"My apologies. I speak only of what I observe and infer, and it's entirely possible I'm mistaken. But if we survive this experience, and you find yourself at loose ends, I may have work for you."

"I don't do work, Faulty. As I thought I was amply demonstrating." *What is his angle?* It was possible he was just trying to lull her into thinking he wasn't the killer, but there was something sincere in his overenthusiastic creepiness. "And none of this addresses the very real outcome of surviving this ship only to be slave labor for the rest of our lives."

To this Fault said nothing. But he said nothing in a very *intense* way. Bell wondered if the warmth of the engine room was making him sweat underneath his strange skin-clothing because she swore it was clinging more tightly to his head, better defining its shape.

"Wait," Bell said with sudden clarity. "Are you saying you have a way off this ship that *doesn't* involve slave labor?"

The strange alien was silent for several moments more, but in a way where it almost seemed his mind was briefly elsewhere, not aboard the ship at all.

"I am, as I believe the saying goes, not *not* saying it."

CHAPTER 20

GROME IS WHERE THE THREAT IS

THE REST of their shift passed uneventfully. Despite Bell pressing for more details, Master Fault abandoned creepy talk and lapsed back into creepy silence. But over it all loomed the constant droning knowledge that whatever vague promises he hinted at, Bell was running out of time to find the worms, and even worse, she didn't know how much time she still had. Several times she considered simply making a break for it. But Loopy's little roving blender servitor was still out there; she was sure of it. And the ship's brain seemed less stable by the moment.

But eventually, they were done. The test-cull chambers were draining properly, the thrusting and blasting and gyrating and whichever other metaphors applied were all operating within nominal limits so that outer space was getting thoroughly railed and properly knocked up, or whatever.

Only then did Loopy chime in with a "you may return to the common areas," and only then did Bell think to wonder if it had been listening in on her and Fault's previous conversation. Fault may think himself unkillable, but Bell had more to worry about.

As the chamber reconfigured itself upon their exit, and Bell cursed inwardly as she noted the servitor was nowhere in sight, Loopy spoke

"I believe Tas wishes to speak to you most urgently," he said casually. "Patching her through."

Her frantic voice came through the nearest loudspeaker. "—ell, where the hell are you? Get to your quarters right away. Bell!"

Bell broke into a run, aware that Master Fault was doing the same just behind her. Despite their difference in height and length of limb, he had no problem keeping pace.

"No offense, but feel free to fuck off somewhere else!" she called back as they reached the tunnel. This slowed them considerably, but at least Bell got there first.

"No one should be wandering the corridors by themselves," he said calmly. Bell shut up and concentrated on working through the tunnel as fast as possible. On the other side, she broke into a run again, doors opening well in advance of her arrival. Master Fault was close at her heel. He didn't even seem to be struggling with the thin air.

Running full out like that, it didn't take them long to reach Bell's little slice of home along the habitat ring. Tas was there, looking equal parts angry and stricken. "Loopy, why the hell didn't you let me talk to her earlier? It's too late now."

"I'm terribly sorry, Tas, but she was engaged in sensitive engine calibrations. I couldn't risk disrupting her concentration, not even for this, I'm afraid."

Which was utter bullshit. By the sounds of it, every second of whatever Tas was upset about had counted. She and Master Fault had dicked around checking readouts for at least five minutes after all the actual work had been done. She could have talked to Tas at any time.

But even this extremely suspicious answer fled Bell's thoughts the moment she saw the worms.

What was left of them.

She let out an involuntary wail. There had been perhaps two dozen of them. They lay there in the center of the passageway outside her door, smashed, with their own viscous innards smeared across the deck. Gobs of thick fluid, somewhere between piss-yellow and puke-green had sprayed from their split sides or their ruptured ends. Even now, the dregs slowly oozed from their ruined bodies.

"Most unfortunate," Master Fault said behind Bell, and they

watched as the last twitching form went still, its unspeakable suffering ended at last.

"Some of them were still alive," Tas said by way of explanation. "Just a minute ago. I don't know if—I don't know if they could have told you anything in this state, but—"

"No," Bell said, as much to soothe the woman's agitation as anything. "With this few, they couldn't have spoken properly in their language. They would have had to spell out words, like they did before. And if it was just a small handful, it's doubtful they'd have had the collective intelligence to do even that much. But none of them look like they were in a fit state to move, alive or otherwise." In truth, it looked as though there *had* been enough—when the whole subset had still been alive, of course—to communicate. But there was no point pouring salt in the wound when Tas was already upset.

Tas nodded absently, and it was difficult to tell if she felt any of the comfort Bell had attempted to bestow. Bell supposed there could be more of the things lurking around, but it seemed unlikely. Safe to say Grome was well and truly dead now.

"What happened?" Bell asked. Tas looked at her sharply. "I'm not accusing you," Bell added hastily.

"Are you sure that vote of confidence is wise? Should she really be let off so easily?" Master Fault stepped up behind Bell.

"Back off," Bell said.

"I merely wish to point out that, so far as I can see, only you and I know we are innocent of this latest offense. Surely the first person on the scene can't escape all suspicion."

Bell was about to shoot back that of course she didn't know Master Fault was innocent, except that wasn't true. They had walked past Bell's quarters on their way to the engine work, and there definitely had not been smashed worms strewn everywhere. Master Fault had not left Bell's sight during that entire time. Unless there were two of him running around, he hadn't done this.

It wasn't that he was her number-one suspect, but he'd probably run a close second. So Bell found it profoundly irritating to no longer have her safety school as an option.

"I found them like this," Tas said, a little plaintive. "Loopy can confirm. He's online this time. Loopy?"

"I can indeed confirm that Tas has been attempting to reach you for approximately the past ten minutes from this general location. However, I'm afraid my visual and thermal sensor network has been down for a third of the habitat complex for a longer duration than that. Debug efforts are wrapping up, and sensor network access is only just now being restored to me. Thermal sensors online. Visual sensor boot cycle will be complete in thirty seconds."

"What?" Tas exclaimed, shock warring with outrage in her voice.

"My last visual record of Tas depicted her entering this section of the ring, and though she would have had to move fast, it is not impossible that she had enough time to commit this atrocity and then attempt to call you about it. I do not wish to cast suspicion quite literally blindly, but I do wish to be forthright regarding the facts, as my conditioning dictates."

Bell didn't believe this garbage for a second. On the contrary, it was setting off alarm bells—pun very much intended—in over half the modules in her head. But she also didn't want to admit this aloud. Not in front of Loopy.

Tas stared at her plaintively. According to Loopy, his visual sensors were not yet operational. Bell wondered if she could really trust that, but she decided to risk it. Master Fault was not positioned to see Bell's face either. Bell locked gazes with Tas and winked.

"That's a pretty fucking disturbing thing to hear, Loopy," Bell said. She examined the worms more closely. She didn't want to, but she had to stall for time. Bent low to get a better look, it wasn't hard to see the cause of death. There were several of them visible in the strewn guts along with one, nauseatingly, stamped into the deflated corpse of one of the worms.

Boot prints.

"Why were you down here, Tas?" Bell asked, hoping Tas had understood the wink meant *relax, girl, I got you.*

"I would also like to hear this," Master Fault said, unintentionally being the perfect wingman to Bell's misdirect.

"I was coming to look for Xian," Tas said. "We finished our work detail early, and she said she had to use the restroom. And then she never came back. I asked Loopy where she was, and even though he acknowledged me, he wouldn't answer. Refused to even acknowledge the question. It was like last night, when he wouldn't answer Xian's question, but without everyone sitting in front of me, I got worried that this might be a new form of his being offline while a murder was happening, so I went to look for her. And then I found this."

Bell did a little mental double take at Tas's recount. She waited for Loopy to refute the claim or otherwise try to explain it away, but he didn't.

It was true Loopy had been upfront with his deficiencies from the start. And with so long a journey, any number of possible things could go catastrophically wrong when the literal mind piloting the ship was acting like a patient with dementia. Were Loopy an actual AI, or even a synthetic brain like Bell's, someone among the passengers could have been awakened just to install a new service patch. But you couldn't just *fix* an organic mind like you could a digital one. This wasn't software. It was wetware. Minds had to be trained to be like they were, and that training took time. Loopy's problems were—for lack of a better term—medical in nature. With a person suffering from dementia, Bell would have expected the deterioration to be a lot more random than it had started to appear. Rendering one unconscious was one thing, having it act in very specific, very selectively suspicious ways felt like something entirely different.

Think this through. Why the fuck weren't they guarded by a servitor the way we were? Presumably they hadn't been, if first Xian and then Tas had been allowed to leave. A full 73 percent of Bell's modules expressed shock that she didn't blurt this question out the instant she thought of it. But this was smelling worse and worse, and a very deep, seldom-accessed module of Bell's mind told her that for once in her fucking life she needed to keep some thoughts to herself.

"I need to check my quarters," Bell said, still stalling while she thought of how to approach this. "If they were here for me, it's possible some of them found a way inside." But the door opened before she could get close enough to touch the panel.

Xian stood there, in Bell's doorway, staring out at them with an expression somewhere between expectant and annoyed.

"Well, now," Bell said.

"I was waiting for you. I'd hoped to speak privately." Xian cast a distasteful look at both Tas and Master Fault. "But I should have known better than to expect privacy on this junk heap. You may leave," she said to them.

"She stays," Bell said before Tas could respond. "Master Fault can go because he's creepy and having him around frankly makes me uncomfortable. But *you* have a lot to answer for."

"Them?" Xian said. Her glance at the worms was dismissive. "I was cleaning up a mess. Disgusting creatures."

"You killed Grome!" Tas shouted. That was good because it was what Bell had wanted to shout anyway. But better to have it come from someone else this time.

Xian only scoffed. "Someone else's mess. A few worms do not a thinking being make. The hive mind was already dead. If you chop off a snake's head, and its tail continues to writhe, no one would call it *alive.* These were just acting on base instinct. You needn't goggle at me, girl. I do know some things about these creatures. Although, perhaps, I should ask myself why the remainder came to your quarters, Bell. Maybe, with their dying awareness, they wished to point the finger at their killer. Or, we can all just agree Grome died in that conflagration earlier, and nothing that happened here matters in the slightest."

"They *were* coming to see me!" Bell said. "Grome trusted me. They could have relayed information." Admittedly, this was speculation, but it was Xian's fault that they would never really know.

"Pure speculation." And oh, how it galled to hear her own thoughts echoed by the hateful woman. "More important is the fact that *I* came to see you."

"To murder me, you mean," Bell threw back. "Don't act like you couldn't hear us talking just now. These doors aren't that thick. So why wouldn't you come out to meet us unless you were hoping we wouldn't find you, not until I was alone, at least. You're really speeding up your timeline, I see. Afraid we're getting too close? Well, you can forget trying to hide. We know it's been you this whole time."

She expected vocal denials, more of the trademark Xian scoffing, maybe even a borderline-unhinged laugh. But Xian's smile was small and a little sad. When she opened her mouth to speak, she sounded like she'd made a decision.

"I came here tonight because I wanted to talk. To *really* talk, not this pointless barb-trading we do." She hesitated, seeming to steel herself. "To do *more* than talk, if I'm being entirely honest. A little quiet time *just between us.*"

The implication was as obvious as it was gross. Bell was just in time in switching off her autonomic gag reflex simulator. But she narrowed her eyes. *Stop. Hold your fire and really think.* It was hard. She had hated deep thinking and self-reflection for as long as she could remember. Her treatment of the various algorithmic overlays replicating the complex mental dance that was executive function and metacognition could probably be considered abusive.

But there was a little wildness about Xian's eyes, and Bell had the sense the woman was freestyling, that she'd been caught before she'd had a chance to clean up her mess in the corridor. Perhaps she hadn't expected Tas to follow her and had hidden in Bell's room, hoping the search wouldn't go that far.

The one thing Bell was certain of was she was looking at real fear.

Fear of being caught in the act? But if that was true, why the hinting that she wanted to get freaky? Was it just a lame excuse? Xian trying to get Bell alone and vulnerable? But now that she was the most obvious suspect, what kind of sense would that make?

Think. Consider other possibilities.

"Is there something you want to share with the class?" Tas asked Bell, one eyebrow raised in semi-accusation and looking a little more out of sorts than Bell would have guessed at Xian's claims. Any day that resulted in a little jealousy from the object of Bell's affections couldn't be a totally bad day. Of course, the fact that Bell had been staring at Xian slack-jawed for the better part of a silent minute was probably not the best look.

Loopy's increasingly strange behavior once again intruded into Bell's thoughts, and just like that, the situation flipped. Bell had assumed that Loopy, the ship's mind, was a slave to Xian, the only conscious person with real knowledge of the ship's inner workings.

But what if the answer was actually the other way around? What if Xian really just wanted to talk, and needed a loophole to do so safely?

You needn't worry that I will observe you during sexual relations, the brain had said regarding two parties meeting up in one bedroom. That made sex a pretext for an unobserved conversation. Of course, if it turned out Loopy was as dishonest as most human brains were, they couldn't trust that promise. Or maybe Xian had decided it was a risk worth taking.

Maybe she'd felt she had no other choice.

That settled it. Late to the party, Bell had to try and salvage this without being too obvious about it. A total about-face on her attitude toward Xian would seem way too suspicious to anyone with half a brain, and Loopy appeared to be more or less a full brain.

Bell ostentatiously rolled her eyes, hoping Xian would catch on. "Oh, please. You're this pathetic? It's not enough that you richies have power over us? Now you want to fuck us too? What, LaSalle's Illuminati roleplay isn't satisfying you anymore? You want to sample the other team? Well, my self-respect isn't up for sale, babe. Go find someone else to hatefuck, you over-funded sack of human excrement."

She had to suppress a wince. It was possible she'd let things get away from her there. Just a little bit. At the end.

Xian's eyes glittered with what Bell *really* hoped was covert understanding but which looked an awful lot like absolute loathing. Her smile was full of venom. "I knew this was a waste of my time."

She turned and walked away, still trailing bits of worm-goo behind her as she walked.

"If it doesn't matter, why'd you waste time trying to convince me?" Bell called after her. Not helpful. That was not helpful. Shit. She was pretty sure she'd borked that one. Oh well, might as well make the most of it. "Assface!" She turned back to find Tas staring at her. "What?"

"What do you think that was all about?"

"Xian is clearly upset," Loopy said. "No, I'm terribly sorry. I meant to say 'Bell.' Xian *is* clearly upset, but my statement was intended toward Bell. Bell, your upset is a natural part of the grieving process. I would please ask for everyone to give her—that is, Bell—space during this difficult time. For now, please disperse. You are cutting into your rest period before the next shift, and the tasking only gets more crucial from here."

Having failed utterly to salvage the situation, Bell entered her quarters determined to banish the gross, squishy uncertainty Xian's fumbling attempt to talk with her had birthed. "Fucking bitch," Bell said, willing herself back to simple hatred of the woman, forcing her face into a mask of rage.

Despite having just entered her room, she almost turned on the spot to go confront Xian. Maybe more than confront. Suddenly she wanted nothing more than to kill the privileged fucker outright. That felt much more natural than empathizing with her and showing interest in what she had to say. And, if it turned out Xian really was the killer, it would be a preemptive self-defense killing if ever there was one, with a heaping side order of revenge. After all, she'd promised Urk nothing less.

I just want to go home. Bell's eyes burned in simulated tears at the recollection.

But Bell's memory of the fear in Xian's eyes, those baseline human eyes, could similarly not be forgotten. Such was Bell's distraction that she forgot to turn on the lights. She resolved it by deciding she would rather be in the dark. That was the reason she noticed her wall screen blinking at her insistently.

Bell tapped it to life and stared, dumbfounded. On the screen was a composed—but unsent—text message, the kind she might have sent to another CCC member's quarters. A message that had been composed here, in this room.

A message that Bell had never seen before.

The "To" line was empty. The blinking light's unfamiliar pattern must be a reminder to either finish and send or delete the message. But it was the text that grabbed Bell's gaze and did not release it for a long time. She almost ran out of the room to find Xian, but for entirely different reasons. The woman had been right here, in Bell's room, when she and Tas had arrived. No one else could have authored the message. In the end, though, it was Tas who Bell wanted to talk this through with. She had achieved her goal and banished her uncertainty, but in entirely the opposite direction she'd intended.

Bell strode the corridors as fast as she could, expecting Loopy to order her to stop, expecting one of his servitors to make a move against her, even. Nothing of the sort happened, though. All the while, every scheming module crammed into her head was working overtime. And all the while, the unsent message ran on endless repeat through her brain.

Bell, I know you don't trust me, and I don't know how much I'll be able to do, but I'm trying to help you. You just have to listen.

TAS OPENED the door on the first request, face scrunched up with alarm.

"What is it?" she asked. "What's happened?"

"Not here," Bell said as quietly as she could without being inaudible. She raised her voice to be clearly heard. "Come with me to the showers. I want to take a sexual shower with you."

"What on—"

"This way," Bell said plaintively, hoping to cut Tas off before she could raise too many objections, objections which might become suspicions. Bell spoke loudly again. "I really, *really* need gratification. Sexual gratification. Oh, how good it will feel, the hot water coursing down over our naked, intertwined bodies." She looked a desperate *no arguments* at Tas, willing the woman to understand.

"I will come with you," Tas said. She looked on the point of adding a very strongly worded addendum to this agreement when Loopy's voice burst in.

"Oh, how delightful!" he said, validating some of Bell's fear about the ship-brain's nosiness as well as at least one loophole in his commandment for them to stay in their quarters. "Have fun, you two!"

Blessedly, Tas snapped her mouth shut with a click.

As before, when she'd needed to quickly rid herself of fungal paste, Bell bypassed the sound-pulse showers. The lone water shower was very industrial in design, which was not sexy. But it was also clearly intended for just one person, which was sexy enough to make up for the décor.

Bell turned the water on as loud as it would go. She turned to Tas. "Get in."

"Fortunately for you," Tas said wryly, "I'm reasonably certain this isn't an actual attempt to get in my pants. Reasonably. But you're still going to need to walk me through this."

"According to the ship's brain, there's only two places we can theoretically have a conversation without being overheard," Bell said. "In the bathrooms, or in our quarters if we are getting it on. I figured the best chance of those restrictions actually holding are if we double-up on the justifications—bathroom and sex—and add in some white noise to boot."

"And you're concerned the killer has compromised Loopy to the degree that they can see and hear what he sees and hears. Okay, that's smart," Tas said. "But I have no intention of stripping down—"

"And I would like it added to the record that I wasn't asking you to."

"—and also no intention of standing there getting soaked in my jumpsuit," Tas continued. "If we stand here with the shower door open and talk softly, it should still work. Now what's going on?"

"Something's wrong with . . ." she trailed off, feeling a sudden fear that saying the name would cause him to listen in even despite all their precautions. Silly to assume he would respond to that name in particular, since it was a name *she* had given him. But she couldn't shake the feeling, however superstitious it might be. "The ship's brain."

"Obviously," Tas said. "That's what we were just talking about."

"I mean *really* wrong. I think we may have had this backward." She laid out her reasoning to Tas. The other woman listened gravely but intently until Bell culminated with explaining Xian's flailing half-proposition and the message she'd left in Bell's room. "I think she was afraid, and not of us. This whole time, I've been convinced she knows more than she's letting on and that made her the killer. But what if it's more fucked-up than that? What if she knows something, but someone —or something—is preventing her from telling us out of fear for her own life?"

"And you think she was trying the same thing you're trying now? An unmonitored conversation disguised as casual sex?"

"Maybe, but my idea of hot, fake shower sex is way cleverer," Bell felt the need to point out. "Which reminds me. Should we moan like we're really into it to keep our cover? I mean, just in case."

"Well, that certainly explains the layered precautions," Tas said. And, just as Bell was convinced Tas would ignore her brilliant suggestion, she added. "And the air on this ship is thin enough already without adding fake moaning, thanks."

"What I don't know is what we should do about it."

A light kindled in Tas's huge eyes. "We do what any good scientist would do. We experiment. If there's some method to his malfunctions and inconsistencies, we should be able to prove it by testing where the boundaries are. Maybe we keep doing our tasks but ignore the pairings he assigns and make our own. See if he balks. Stuff like that. If he's doing this on purpose—the selective hearing, the periods of time where he's offline, the convenient-for-the-killer loss of sensor data—then there must be a goal in mind. If we can figure out the absolute limits of what's allowed and what's not, we can figure out the shape of his intention—what?"

"Nothing," Bell said. It was really more of a squeak. *Just your crazy-hot brain, gah!* "It's a good idea." *I want to wrap you up like a present and then immediately unwrap the present and play with the present.* "Better than good." Bell *really* wanted to say this stuff out loud, but she had promised she would dial that stuff back. "Great. It's a great idea."

"Right," Tas said with obvious amusement. "For the record, I can see how hard you're trying, and I appreciate it."

"Thanks," Bell said. *It's really hard,* she didn't add, for obvious reasons.

"But back to the matter at hand. The only question is, should you try to make contact with Xian again?"

"I have a feeling that ship has sailed, and crashed, and maybe blown up with no survivors. But I guess we'll see if I can even get her to speak with me."

"I think that's a plan," Tas said. Then she changed tack. "You never told me how working on the engines was earlier."

"Surprisingly dirty, in a metaphorical sense."

"Okay," she said, drawing out the first vowel. "Did you happen to see anything else that might help us out?"

"Are you looking for something in particular?"

"Engines seem like a pretty sensitive place for him to let us go, is all. I was surprised when he said it. He must have been pretty desperate."

"Oh, yeah," Bell said. "He sent one of his drones to watch us and everything. And he made sure to inform us that the giant door past the crew cryo area was never to be opened on pain of super-death. What did he have you doing?"

"Working on life support."

"That also seems important," Bell said, then frowned. "Weird that he didn't have you watched by a drone too. Would have prevented Xian from running off to smash worms."

"Do I detect a subtle hint of suspicion?" Tas pulled the sting from the words with a smile.

"I mean, yeah. But at Xian, obviously."

"Loopy was careful to inform us that the passenger section of the ship has its own, separate life support. I guess he figures if we fuck up our own air, that's on us. I can confirm that he isn't lying about the state of that system though. It's a disaster in there. Nothing but patches over patches, nested stopgaps. It's a good thing we're almost to our destination. So, do you think we've had enough time to get each other off?"

Bell blinked at the sudden shift in topic and tone. It was, perhaps, the greatest test of self-control she had ever endured. But she eked out a C- by her own estimation.

"Yes," she squeaked again. "I mean, several times really, in your case. Just saying." Okay, maybe a D+.

The little hooded smile Tas gave her might very well endure as Bell's favorite mental image until the universe died. A+++.

"We probably shouldn't be walking alone," Tas said. "It's not safe."

"Yes," Bell said. "Also, that would make me look like kind of an asshole. May I escort you back to your room?"

"That just means you'll be walking alone. But sure," Tas said with another small smile.

BELL MADE the walk back from Tas's room on a knife's edge of wariness, constantly looking for an attack which didn't come. The entire sequence of events had every synthetic muscle fiber twitching at the slightest stimulus. Much as she wished she could simply denounce Xian in front of the entire CCC tomorrow in light of the woman's destruction of Grome's leftovers, she couldn't dismiss her sense that something bigger was happening here. Things that felt underexplained almost never bothered Bell. She'd have never been able to show her face at work the past ten years if that had been the case. But for some reason, this time the notion took hold of her and would not let up.

Bell entertained notions of trying to find Xian, hash this out tonight. But as she approached the door to her room, Loopy's voice split the air.

"I hope you two had fun. Despite your overly aggressive early approaches, I have been rooting for you."

Bell strained but couldn't find anything in the brain's tone that would indicate a double-meaning or concealed threat. He sounded sincere, and for a moment, her conviction wavered. What had that asshole Occam said? The simplest explanation was usually the best?

"Are you cloning Grome, Loopy?"

"No," Loopy said. "I do not presently have the capacity to clone their species."

Bell hadn't been sure why she asked until hearing his answer. It was a contradiction of what he'd said originally. He'd claimed he could clone the entire CCC, simultaneously if necessary. So it seemed as though Loopy had failed his first experiment. Bell felt the almost overpowering urge to throw the proof of his lie in his face, but she passed her own test. This time with a B.

"Is there anything else, Bell? If not, you really should get some sleep. Or at least time in which you are still and relaxed and contemplative. I need you fresh, and I don't want to have to enforce your confinement to ensure it."

Translation: there would be no talking to Xian tonight.

"No, Loopy. That's all for now. Good night."

CHAPTER 21
TIMING IS EVERYTHING AND ALSO SHIT

SLEEP WAS NOT something Bell did often and usually only if she was really, soul-crushingly bored. In this case, she felt exactly the opposite. Conflicting thoughts and emotions threatened to overwhelm her. Xian Ginevra was the key to everything. She just had to convince the woman—who clearly hated Bell's guts and who might also be killing on Loopy's behalf—to spill her secrets.

So, after an hour spent circling the tiny space of her room, Bell at last relented. Though sleep felt like a waste of time to her, there were moments when it was called for. As much as her mind was a synthetic creation, it was still designed and custom built to exactly mirror her former meat-brain in function, and dreams were an odd but ubiquitous feature of meat-brain living.

And even if people were still debating the point and uses of dreams, everyone seemed to agree that they allowed one to process thoughts and emotions that might otherwise be overwhelming.

Lying down and turning off the lights were unnecessary, strictly speaking, but still felt right for the ritual, as Bell tended to think of sleep. How else to think of surrendering one's conscious mind in order to beseech some gestalt of the unconscious for answers to impossible questions?

Bell set an internal alarm to wake her after four hours. If her mind couldn't get its shit together by then, it would just have to deal. After she woke, she was going to take whatever revelations had emerged from her unconscious state and go confront Xian with them, approaching the problem with whatever level of violence corresponded to Xian's level of cooperation.

One way or another, she was going to get some answers.

THE FIRST THING Bell thought as she started awake was that it seemed too soon.

Snooze! Her mental shout was not obeyed. "Snooze, asshole!" It wasn't fair that she didn't have to sleep, didn't usually *want* to sleep, yet she still never wanted to wake up on the rare occasions when she actually *did* sleep.

She was at the point of mentally keying her "open skull" command to start rooting around in there when the thought occurred to her that this was not, in fact, her internal alarm. She was hearing it with her ears.

"Attention, Conscious Crew Complement!" Loopy's voice shouted over the alarm, a whooping noise which cut off abruptly as if responding belatedly to his voice. The canned nature of that voice sent a chill down Bell's synthetic spine. "There has been a murder. Please congregate in the mess hall."

Bell was up like a shot, terror for Tas flooding any remaining sleep confusion from her. The other assholes she didn't much care about. When her thoughts strayed to Xian, Bell cursed herself up one side and down the other. Now she had to care about the welfare of *two* people, one of whom she hated. Three, counting Urk. Fuck!

As it turned out, Bell was first into the mess hall by virtue of her long legs and the relative closeness of her quarters to an entrance. It was, to be sure, a dubious honor. Horváth had been really gross to behold. Grome had smelled like a thousand sweaty sphincters left too long in a broiler.

The latest victim somehow managed to combine sight and smell into a new, unique varietal blend of awful.

The killer had separated the limbs from the torso, the better to access—and apparently unravel—everything in said torso. It was like the victim had been a piñata and their pulmonary, vascular, and digestive systems, red and glistening and still very much organic, had been the candy.

Bell was no sawbones, but the way she saw it, the cause of death could have been any one of a dozen fatal injuries. There was only one thing she could say for certain: Xian had definitely not been the killer because Xian was the victim.

But just in case Bell was too slow on the uptake, words had been harshly burned into the mess hall wall in suspiciously straight, razor-thin lines of char. *Familiar* lines of char.

NOPE. NOT HER. *SO CLOSE.* OH, AND THE NEXT WORD IS "KILLER."
SEE YOU SOON!

THE OTHERS, those both still alive and admitting to that fact at least, arrived in short order. Bell didn't even fret about how bad it was to be found alone with the body. She had already disengaged her olfactory sensors again—she was beginning to think she should just leave them off full-time. The others had no such luxury, and their faces, for those who possessed and displayed faces, stood as proof.

Tas entered first, followed close behind by LaSalle, who cried out, stricken, when he saw what had become of his bone-buddy. Master Fault was next, his non-face face somehow looking more ghoulish every time Bell saw him. Instead of suspicious shadows, his "eyes" looked burned into the fabric now. Like scorched wounds in his skin.

What had been a mere shadowed hint of a crescent smile was now a slash of a leer.

"Our situation continues to deteriorate, I see," he said with a stoicism Bell found extremely unconvincing. The mouth, if mouth it was, didn't move with the words. If he hadn't been with her in the med bay when Grome had met their end, he would have rocketed up to the top of Bell's suspect list. On the other hand, what had he been up to before finding her there?

Behind Master Fault stomped in Brother Barnabas, but only after he collided with first one side of the door frame, then the other. It was as though the giant robot, in addition to not being able to talk, suddenly couldn't see as well.

"Forgive me," came a warbling electronic voice loud enough to make Bell jump. "The restoration of my ability to communicate has compromised certain other functions, I am afraid." It was a voice she had never heard before, but it issued from the area around the immense robot's head.

"Did you just talk?" Bell ventured.

"Indeed," Barnabas said with obvious delight. "Just prior to the killing, Ship Brain was at last able to restore voice and understanding of languages both written and auditory via one of its servitors. Unfortunately, effecting those repairs required cannibalizing pathways for my various forms of sight. Ship Brain assured me there was no other way, but it was unable to assure me there was no other way until the repairs to my communication complex had already been effected. But I cannot spread the loving word of the Great Metal without my voice, so it was no choice at all."

So unexpected were both this turn of events and the torrent of words that everyone alive went as quiet and still as Xian, if not quite as messy. Barnabas's oddly high-pitched speech had an asynchronous quality, as though his words—and sometimes even their individual syllables—were being assembled from chopped-up pieces of unrelated audio files. Every sentence he spoke sounded like someone reading a cobbled-together ransom note in audio form.

"Olfactory sensors indicate that this is the room where the body was discovered," Barnabas said. "My friends, we have suffered great tragedy this day. Let us pray." And, joints clanking, he knelt there, his tattered robes missing a spray of gore by sheer luck. Bell was so curious at what the giant robot was even going to say that she disabled her automatic prayer filters so she would hear words instead of white noise.

"O Metal, Great Metal, bless this mess that was once our friend, though I do not know which friend."

"Xian," said Tas, wonderingly.

"Thank you, Unrecognized Voice Number Two," Barnabas said. "By all non-visual indicators available to me at this time, Xian's corporeal remains are most likely unrecognizable to even those who knew her well. But they are not unrecognizable to you, Great Metal, for you cast back only the most perfect reflections upon us in your polished finish. Rain upon Xian a love that warms like molten steel and soothe their hurts as metal in the depths of space flash-freezes flesh. May their components never corrode within your unyielding embrace."

With that, Barnabas rose.

"My friends, now that I have performed the rites for Believer Xian, I must also ask that the guilty party present themselves. There are separate rites to be performed for those Believers who commit great crimes prior to the administration of punishment."

"We only just arrived, Barnabas," Bell said. "We hadn't even begun examining the crime scene before you came in."

"I hear Unrecognized Voice Number One. Please identify yourself."

"Bell." When that elicited no response, Bell realized her error. "Oh, right. You couldn't communicate or understand at all during orientation, could you?"

"No indeed, Bell. But I have detailed recollections of each member of the crew's appearance."

"Bell's about three meters tall," Tas said, surprising Bell by jumping in. "Very willowy for her height, but it works for her. Her hair looks like dandelion seeds, but thicker and a much brighter white. Glowing, orange eyes."

"Of course," Barnabas said. "It is lovely to put a name to a face at last. Greetings, Bell. And who described Bell just now? It was Unrecognized Voice Number Two again."

"Tas," Bell said triumphantly, flush with desire, pride, and a determination to return the glowing description. "Um, hm," she said, suddenly struggling. "Baseline human." Technically, that ought to be all he needed, but Bell felt the need to give as good as she'd gotten. "One-point-five-ish meters? Blonde hair. Big blue eyes." That all felt wholly inadequate. "Very hot." There.

"Unexpected body temperature increase can be a sign of illness, Tas. You may wish to report to the med bay once Ship Brain is back online. Thank you, Bell. You were saying before I interrupted you?"

"For the love of god," LaSalle cut in, all blustering frustration. "Can we stop with whatever the fuck this all is and figure out who killed her?"

"Of course," Barnabas said again. "I understand your frustration and emotional turmoil at this difficult moment, Unrecognized Voice Number Three. And you are . . .?"

"Perhaps," Master Fault spoke up at last, "it would be better if you stepped out into the corridor, Brother, and let us tend to the examination of the scene. I understand your eagerness to be brought up to speed regarding our situation, but time may be of the essence. I can escort you to the door."

"Thank you, Master Fault. Your courtesy is, as ever, a tribute to the Great Metal. I shall wait outside until summoned."

CHAPTER 22
PEW-PEW FUCKERY

ONLY THREE OF them remained after whatever that had been. By unspoken agreement, they all approached the body as close as the spread-out gore allowed.

"First things first," Bell said. "What killed her?" Lingering wisps of probably toxic smoke filled the air. From the looks of the smoldering scraps surrounding the corpse, the fumes Bell could no longer smell would be from Xian's clothing, severely burned during the attack. So, fire had been involved once again, though not nearly as extensively as with Grome.

LaSalle bent close to examine the body. With her clothing in smoldering shreds, it was easy to see where she'd been laid open like a body being autopsied, Y incision and everything. The parts of her that remained inside still glistened nauseatingly. Everything else had begun to dry out in the shipboard air.

Bell's vanity stomach knotted in disgust. Ugh. With a few admittedly hypocritical sexy-type exceptions, meat bodies were just the *worst*.

"I'm fairly certain," Bell said, "that she was cut open while she was still alive. You can see how straight the cuts are at the start. But that changes fast. She was . . . struggling, trying to wriggle free."

"Christ," LaSalle said, sounding like he was fighting down real vomit. He stood back up quickly, seemingly eager to put distance between himself and the carnage. He had to pause, hands on his knees. It was enough to tug at Bell's sympathies, so if it was a performance, it was a masterful one.

"So maybe she was overpowered, and her limbs were removed to hobble her." Bell pointed at the locking joints at shoulder and hip to prove her hypothesis. She was a bit surprised they were even all synthetic, given Xian's apparent disdain for cybernetic replacement. "Those don't look forced off." Maybe that would make LaSalle feel better. "There's no warping of the connections. They were removed the normal way, but that seems unlikely if she was struggling." It was practically soothing.

"Maybe the killer rendered her unconscious first, took her limbs, then woke her up?" Tas put forward. "Either intentionally or—or once they got started with the main portion of her body." Now it was her turn to look sick.

"Is there anything missing?" For a moment, Bell wasn't sure why she'd said it. Then it clicked, and she spoke her thoughts. "It's so ridiculously ritualistic. None of the others were like that."

"Horváth was left on display," Tas countered.

"But the killer didn't do anything to the body afterward," Bell said. "No desecration. Just left him there exactly how he'd died."

"You're saying this is so elaborate that it's been done to hide something?" Master Fault had returned. He stood next to LaSalle, who had progressed from looking ill to stifling his rage.

"I'm saying it's different from the others," Bell said. "Aside from the messages, there's no pattern to any of them."

"Oh, please. You had grudges against Horváth and Xian both." LaSalle's voice jangled with implication.

"Not Grome, though," Bell said, trying to bleed any indignation from her voice. He was either genuinely suffering or he was trying to goad her into an overreaction. "I liked Grome. And Urk, if it turns out he's dead," she added, a little belatedly, hoping no one had noticed. "And if he is dead, he's missing entirely. So we have two humans killed, and either one or two aliens. And all of the killings are so relentlessly different from one another that the *lack* of pattern has to be the pattern."

There was something she was leaving out though. She met Tas's eyes and saw the other woman was thinking the same thing. Mere hours after the two of them had decided that Xian had critical information about what the fuck was going on here, she'd been killed, and arguably in the most brutal fashion yet.

It certainly did nothing to dispel their notion that Loopy was behind it all.

"Look there," Master Fault said, pointing at a small cavity in Xian's right forearm.

"Why have empty space like that?" LaSalle sounded as if he was merely talking to distract himself.

"Good catch," Bell said. "If her arms are built anything like mine, that's a storage space for any number of modular components."

"It was a laser."

They all turned to look at Tas, who grew suddenly defensive with the need to explain herself. "She used it when we had to dismember Horváth. Didn't like revealing she had it, either, but it was that or get *really* messy doing it the hard way.

"Of course," Bell said. She'd noticed and wondered then forgotten about it completely with the confrontation and Grome's death. "It's gone now, though. Snapped off."

"Which means she isn't the one that wrote those."

"Even deprived of the primary power source in the rest of her arm, it would have enough stored energy for a shot, maybe two." Bell frowned. "A bit confusing, though. A beam weapon could definitely have made those letters, and it could definitely have been the thing that carved her up, but I doubt it could have done both on just its reserve power."

"So maybe the whole arm was the murder weapon," Tas said, "and it was just placed on display with the others after. The killer could have ripped the beam weapon out to confuse us."

"There's definitely a sense of pew-pew fuckery with this one that wasn't there with the other ones," Bell agreed.

"So we are thinking she didn't get the chance to use her own weapon at all?" Tas asked. "She was overcome, disassembled, and then vivisected?"

LaSalle gave another grunt, some emotion he couldn't contain.

"Not necessarily," Bell said. She'd been unconsciously adjusting her low-light vision since they'd begun examining the body. The room was, she realized now, oddly dim in this section. One of the ceiling LEDs was out, casting a section of wall in shadow. It seemed strangely out of place with the rest of the room untouched, save for the wall message.

She dialed up her lowlight vision, this time on purpose. There were limits to what she could do with it, since she'd been a cheapskate when she'd bought it, but it wasn't totally without value. For instance, it was able to find the broken line of scorch marks the shadow had concealed. They leaped into instant relief at roughly the height of Bell's waist. "Same thing did this." She pointed. "Someone took out the LED above, maybe to try and hide it. And it doesn't look like any writing I've ever seen." And if anyone knew, she would.

"That's a defensive strike, there," Tas said. "See that gap? The two scorch marks line up perfectly on either side of this break. That's where the killer was standing. It's why the beam got broken."

"Maybe," Bell said. "Or maybe the killer was just trying to figure out how the thing worked, and that was the result."

"So Xian may have scored a hit," Tas said.

"Anybody sporting any eviscerating beam wounds they didn't have yesterday?" Bell asked the three of them. Bell and Tas unzipped their matching jumpsuits low enough to display their midsections demonstrating that, no, no one's intestines—core cooling apparatus in Bell's case—were on display.

"Hold on," Tas said to Bell, who had to tear her eyes away at the last second. "Show us your legs."

"I thought you'd never ask," Bell smirked. "But why? Oh, duh." They weren't even remotely close to the same height. The strike would have hit Bell across the thighs. "Um, that's going to be a bit awkward in mixed company, but I'm game if nobody has a problem with it." Without waiting to see if they did, she just detached the bottom half of the flowmatter jumpsuit and yanked it down, revealing her undamaged—and otherwise unclad—nether regions. Then she awkwardly hobbled over to stand against the wall and prove she was showing them the proper part of her. She'd have to hold her legs together awkwardly for the gap to come even close to making sense, but the point was, she had no scars to show. "No harm, no foul."

Tas was blushing again, studiously averting her gaze. "You can pull your pants up now." She suited her own words by zipping her jumpsuit back up as Bell tried to ogle, but subtly, the way a classy person would. Even trying not to be too blatant about it, Bell decided it was definitely a top-three moment since she'd awakened. It was a really nice belly button. Tas caught her staring though, clearing her throat until Bell looked oh-so-casually away, toward LaSalle.

"Your turn," she said. It had been a real struggle not to add some smartass nickname, but he was grieving or whatever.

Sullenly, with a derisive sneer that never left his face, LaSalle followed their example, displaying a scaly chest with a potbelly, both decidedly unscarred by any kind of energy beam. He did muster some eagerness when, satisfied with the three of them, they all looked to Master Fault, who emphatically did not take the hint.

"Master Fault?" Tas said gently. "I don't believe you've regaled us with your—"

"Thorax?" Bell put forward. "Or would it be abdomen? Gizzard?"

After a beat, the robed figure extended his swathed limbs, allowing them to see the state of his layered robes without obscuring folds or shadowed parts.

"As you can see, I am quite un-singed."

"Surely you can understand," Tas said, trying to sound diplomatic, "that we have to ask you to go further. You could have removed the robes then gotten dressed again."

"An understandable mistake. But no, I couldn't have." Fault chided. "I'm not wearing robes."

"Okay, your very robe-like skin, then. Come on, man. You just saw us flash each other," Bell said. "So, it's your turn. Strip, or lift up your flaps and show us your undercarriage. I'm sure the ship can print us some low-denomination cash notes if that would help set the mood."

Even if Loopy were the mastermind behind this, everything they'd seen suggested he needed a patsy to conduct the actual killings.

"I must respectfully submit that I'm unable to fulfill your request in the manner you wish," Master Fault said. The skin-fabric clinging to his head beneath had taken on a demented cast in the mess hall's irregular lighting. "I have sustained no damage. More to the point, this is a fruitless line of inquiry on your part."

"Why?" Tas asked.

Bell suddenly got it. "Didn't you tell me just recently that nothing on this ship could harm you?"

"I did."

"And I assume that applies to concealed beam weapons inside someone's wrist?"

"It does."

"Yes, but he can't literally mean that," Tas said in protest. "'Nothing can hurt him?' That's preposterous. That's no alibi."

"Of course it isn't," Master Fault said. "It merely suggests that you can't use that to either prove or disprove my involvement. On top of that, and as difficult as this is to hear, much less to believe, how I appear differs greatly from person to person. I can all but guarantee each of you sees me differently right this moment."

"All right," Bell said. The asshole deflected more than a ricochet. She steeled herself to approach the smaller alien, and it really did require some steel. He was creepy as fuck. "I'm not going to hurt you. I'm just going to lift your robes real quick just to make sure—"

"No. You aren't."

"Look, Fault—"

"Do not misunderstand. I am not saying that I will stop you. I'm saying you will fail your attempt. And you should be thankful for that. Success in what you seek, impossible though it is, would not end well for you."

There was silence for many moments.

"Please understand," Master Fault said. "I can't be harmed by anything here. And neither will I cause anyone here harm. With my own safety not remotely in question, what possible motive could I have to hurt any of you?"

That shouldn't have been enough to talk Bell out of the attempt. Yet, it was. Something rolled off him, invisible and yet no less potent. A danger deeper than conscious thought, like a rumble of infrasound beneath awareness. And she wasn't the only one to be affected.

"I guess we're at an impasse, then," Tas said, a little hoarsely. She felt it too, Bell was sure. That palpable sense of *presence* discouraging them from pursuing this any further.

"So," Master Fault said, as if none of that had happened, "now that we know how, and with what," Master Fault said. "That only leaves who."

Tas and Bell exchanged glances, each trying, Bell knew, to dispel whatever funk Master Fault had laid over them. LaSalle seethed in simmering silence. But all of them directed their gazes to the words burned into the wall.

NOPE. NOT HER. *SO* CLOSE. OH, AND THE NEXT WORD IS "KILLER."
SEE YOU SOON!

"All right," said Bell, shaking herself a little, still feeling the dregs of Master Fault's little episode clinging to her like cobwebs. "What do we make of this?" Everyone turned to look at her. Even Master Fault's shift in focus was obvious. "What?"

"I don't really want to be the one to say it—"

LaSalle cut Tas off. "I do." Far from flighty and poised on the cusp of fright as it usually was, it was hoarse with obvious anger. "It sounds like something you'd write, mate."

"What?" Bell hated repeating herself. "I don't sound like that."

"I'm afraid I must concur," Master Fault said. "It does read like something you would say. Perhaps even to a suspicious degree. I find it unlikely you would, as the killer, be so obvious in telegraphing your own identity."

"Maybe she feels like she can get away with anything," LaSalle said darkly. "Three of us are dead already. Maybe four counting the other alien?"

"Slow your roll, there, hoss," Bell shot back, regretting her momentary empathy for the man. "Even if that were true, I'd hardly have felt confident the very first time, right? And my damn name—misspelled, I might add, which I cannot stress enough I would *never do*—was carved onto that mystery object lodged in Horváth's throat—hang on." She reached into her jumpsuit pocket, where she'd been keeping it.

The pocket was empty.

"Where the fuck did it go?" She'd been hoping to remind them all and compare the forming of the letters. Her jumpsuit, like everyone's, was standard Anaranjadan flowmatter, a material that could repair itself almost without limit. And like all flowmatter, it contained pockets which sealed themselves shut, so no way it had just fallen out on its own.

Someone had taken it.

"Maybe we should focus on the words," Tas said, barely forestalling what looked like another tirade from LaSalle. "Whether you lose the object or not, it's not hard to remember them. '*Belle hits killer*,' right?"

"Boy, I wish," Bell said. "I would do more than hit, believe me." That sounded bad, so she moved on. "But somehow, I don't think they are meant as a prediction."

"Also, there's a good chance it isn't a complete message," Master Fault said. "We could be missing a word from wherever Urknuuzh is. And even if not, the killer might intend there to be more victims before the message is complete. Indeed, it would be foolish to assume otherwise at this point."

Bell felt a repeat ripple of guilt at withholding the knowledge that Urk was alive, but only from Tas. And the second half of Master Fault's point still stood, which felt like justification enough to say nothing.

"It did say the 'next' word, not the 'last' word," Tas said. She paused. "No help on whether Urknuuzh is still alive there, unfortunately. It means the word could be the third *or* the fourth."

Maybe it was just an attempt to escape the guilt of remaining silent on Urk's supposed fate, but something else occurred to Bell, then. Thinking of the words like that, being a linguist, she couldn't help but start messing with things, beginning with *fixing her fucking name*. She didn't care if it was an attempt to frame her, she couldn't *stand* that misspelling. But she also couldn't just get rid of the letter, just in case it had been put there on purpose for some sick, sadistic reason.

BELL E HITS KILLER

Of course, that left a big free-floating *E,* which drove her almost as nuts. So, she started rearranging things in her mind, glowing versions of the letters appearing in her HUD, superimposed over her actual vision. Her puzzle-solving complex was delighted beyond all reason—she rarely called on it. The first rearrangement it hit upon was trivially easy and also deeply irritating.

BELL IS THE KILLER

"Son of a bitch," Bell growled aloud before she could stop herself. Her puzzling complex was also annoyed, but only because it had been so easy.

"What is it?" Tas asked. "You've thought of something."

No, Bell *needed* to think of something. She thought fast. "No, I'm just pissed that someone's fucking with us with total impunity, and there's not a damn thing we can do about it." *Fucking with me.* It would not take the others long to rearrange the letters themselves. The 'puzzle' was so appallingly lazy.

This is all intended to fuck with me somehow. Make me look guilty. Maybe Xian had been a patsy, squashing the worms outside Bell's quarters in a freestyling attempt to cast more suspicion her way. Only she'd gotten caught. And a few hours later, she'd been killed. Maybe that kind of failure wasn't tolerated by whoever—*whatever*—was calling the shots. And maybe in her panic, knowing her life was on the line, Xian had made a last-ditch attempt to switch sides.

And then Bell had smacked her down.

Shit. Fuck. Shiiiiiit!

"Hey there. Come back to us." Tas snapped her fingers as close to in front of Bell's face as she could reach.

"I'm fine," Bell lied. She wasn't fine.

None of them were.

CHAPTER 23
COLLECTIVE DISAGREEMENT

BROTHER BARNABAS CHOSE this moment to bump and scrape his way back into the room.

"My friends," Barnabas said once he'd been positioned not too close but also not too far from the crime scene, "have you discovered who committed this awful deed against one of the faithful? The judgment of the Great Metal is both fair and brutal, and as Its instrument, I cannot be anything less, but it is incumbent upon Its mortal servants to direct said judgment."

"I'm sorry," Tas said, "but that's the second time you've called Xian a member of your faith. Was she?"

"Of course, Sister Tas, as are you all."

"I, um . . ." Tas didn't seem to know what to do with this.

"I can help explain," Master Fault said. "Brother Barnabas here has a most curious quirk in his programming. He proceeds under the default assumption that everyone he meets is a member of his faith. Whenever he hears or sees or otherwise experiences anything to the contrary, well, as near as I can tell, his programming edits over that information. I am, for instance, in no way a member of his faith, I can assure you, Brother Barnabas," he addressed the big priest. "I would like to tell you yet again that I find your faith utterly absurd, though I am pleased that it brings you comfort, as I like you personally."

"Master Fault, your dedication to the Great Metal is peerless, and you stand as a shining example for all the faithful to follow."

Master Fault gave a perfectly human shrug to conclude his demonstration.

Bell was about to ask how Barnabas could proselytize to anyone when he believed everyone he met already belonged to his faith, but Tas spoke first.

"Leaving that aside for now, for the sake of the investigation, we need you to demonstrate to us that you don't have any laser wounds across your midsections." She paused to consider Barnabas and the broken scorch mark's height for a moment. "More like thighs in your case, Brother Barnabas."

"Of course," Barnabas said, immediately lifting the tattered hem of his robes as though they'd all paid top dollar for a robot striptease and never mind the tease part. His lower half was as crudely assembled as his head was, blocky and industrial. In truth, he looked more like an up-jumped piece of heavy mining equipment than anything as elegant and—dare-she-say-it-yes-she-did—sexy as Bell. But though he had his fair share of dings and dents, there was nothing that looked like a fresh scorch mark, and he was dirty enough that it was unlikely he'd sprayed himself down with solvent in the meantime to try and conceal the evidence.

"Thank you, brother," Master Fault began. But LaSalle chose that moment to erupt.

"Enough! Enough of this fucking pantomime. We have the killer. She's standing right here in front of us, conveniently losing evidence, mocking us with absurdly easy word jumbles. 'Bell is the killer?' No one but me sees that, sees how fucking *stupid* she must think we all are?" LaSalle's voice was a challenge. "There's only one person who has looked suspicious every single time, and we all know who she is."

"Except Grome, asshole."

"A bunch of smashed worms outside your room beg to differ."

"Xian did that! She admitted it."

"Oh, how convenient. Well, I wasn't there to hear her alleged confession, so I suppose I'll just have to *take your word for it.*"

"And Tas and Fault!" Bell gestured to encompass them. "They were there too. And Loopy was online."

"Well the fucking brain isn't online now, is it?" LaSalle's voice had grown to a shout. His eyes were wide and wild. "And for all I know, you're all in league together. The giant fucking tin can too! That would certainly explain such apparent stupidity in the rest of you." His nostrils were flaring by the end, his eyes wide, almost rolling. He looked like a panicking horse, so unhinged that Bell was less annoyed than she was frightened.

"Hey there, buddy," she said during a lengthy lull in which he paused to suck in deep, whooping breaths. Even down three crew mates, the habitat ring's air handling was not kind to the level of aerobic activity such a rant required. "Let's not make the killer's job any easier."

Unless that killer is you, then asphyxiate away. She was proud of herself for holding that in. Since LaSalle had spilled the beans about the anagram, Bell *really* needed to come off looking like the sane one here.

"It's one of us," LaSalle said, pinching the bridge of his nose in front of eyes screwed up tight, fighting to catch his breath. "That's what tears me up. Someone in this room just now killed her."

Bell blinked. He had just repeatedly and vehemently accused her of the murders, and now he was *backing down*? She began to wonder if he really was losing it.

"All I needed was a few more hours," LaSalle said, seemingly not hearing Bell at all. "And the bastard couldn't even give me that."

Whoa. "What bastard, LaSalle?"

He turned to her then, his gaze haunted to a degree he'd never seen, in him or, honestly, in anyone. "I never wanted this assignment," he said, and Bell's coolant might have frozen solid. "But they don't give you a choice. I don't have to tell you, do I? You know. We're a lot alike, you and me." It was as though he'd forgotten the others in the room. "Both trying to do our duty. Both in *way* over our bleedin' heads as a result. Twenty years of my fucking life I lost for this shit! I have a *family* back home, Beauregard."

"What the fuck are you talking about, LaSalle?" Bell demanded. "What assignment? What duty?" The part about the twenty years seemed pretty self-explanatory. Family too, she supposed.

"We're almost there," he said in a whisper that scarcely sounded sane. "Which means we're out of time. That's what she said. When we get there, we're out of time. But it also means my people have a big fucking landmark to zero in on. And I've made the call—thank god for this little doodad. They took mine from me when they nabbed me back on that dust ball of a planet." He waved around a small object Bell immediately identified as the one which had spent a brief part of the voyage lodged in Horváth's throat.

The one with BELLE lasered into one side.

Double whoa. "Where did you get that? Did you pick my pocket, you little twerp?"

"And they'd better be there!" His voice cracked under the strain only he could feel. "The fuckers owe me that much. They owe me after what I've had to do. This is above and beyond in as literal a sense as possible."

Another flash freeze of fluids. *What I've had to do.* And just what had he been forced to do? And by whom?

He turned his full focus on Bell, and she nearly flinched from it. "It should have been both of us," he wailed. "She couldn't always help me, but she did her best." He looked as if he was about to break into sobs, but then he shook himself, and it was as if he suddenly remembered exactly where he was and the collective "whom" he was talking to.

He sneered, all the fear gone. "It should have been you. All of you," he said, encompassing the group, but his gaze fell on Bell for the finale. "But you most of all."

And with that, he stormed off, Tas dodging out of his way so he didn't bowl her over on his way to the nearest door leading out into the corridor, muttering all the while.

Brother Barnabas called out after him. "The Great Metal comforts you in your loss, Unrecognized Voice Number—"

"Stuff it!" LaSalle shouted. His footsteps faded with distance.

CHAPTER 24
PASSING NOTES

"WE HAVE TO GO AFTER HIM," Tas said, echoing Bell's own thoughts and sounding equally unenthusiastic about the prospect. "I mean, I have no idea what he was on about, just now, but he can't be up to anything good."

"Judging by what we just witnessed, it would certainly appear that the good Mr. LaSalle knows quite a bit more than he is letting on about our situation. I agree this is something we should confront him about directly. Most particularly regarding his possession of the piece of evidence he apparently stole from Bell."

"*That's* your main takeaway?"

"Yes," Master Fault said simply.

"All right, well, *that* makes it sound an awful lot like you know something about that object," Tas said. "Something you haven't mentioned before now."

"Oh, I know quite a bit about it," Master Fault said. "Seeing as it belongs to me."

There was a record scratch sound inside Bell's head, and this could not have annoyed her more. It was *literally* the first time that had ever triggered since she'd had it programmed in, and the statement was so damned shocking that Bell couldn't even appreciate the comic timing.

"I'm sorry," she said. "Didn't you accuse *me* of putting that thing inside Horváth?"

"And it was entirely possible that you did," Fault said. "It was stolen from me the first day we were awake. The next time I saw it was when you fished it out of his corpse, and what was more your, *admittedly misspelled*, name was burned into the side. And lest you think I am making this story of theft up on the spot, I believe I did ask you if anything had gone missing from your person."

Bell huffed, annoyed not just because it was true but also because he'd robbed her of a fresh chance to rant about the spelling of her name.

"We can be certain that at some point the object was in the killer's possession, given where Bell found it. If Mr. LaSalle was trying to steal back what he'd already stolen when he contrived to remove it from Bell's possession, then he might very well be the killer, given what we just heard."

"I'm really regretting that we haven't trusted each other enough to hold daily debriefing sessions or something like that," Tas said, clearly nursing a headache. Bell remembered headaches and sympathized while secretly feeling superior. "What is this mystery device?" Tas asked. "What does it do?"

"Think of it as a kind of beacon. One that can send what you would call an SOS very far, very fast." He turned his thin-wet-sheet-over-weird-skull face to Bell just as realization dawned on her.

"Oh, shit. That's what you meant when you said you had a way out of here."

"Correct."

"How far and fast are we talking?" Tas pressed.

"As far and fast as necessary."

Bell goggled. "Are you talking about Bridge-type technology?"

"Suffice it to say I am happy to offer a ride off of this vessel to any non-murderers among the crew, provided I can recover the device."

"And you could have done that this entire time?" Tas was as indignant as Bell had ever heard her.

"No, because, as I already mentioned, I lost this device almost immediately upon waking."

A part of Bell wanted to just flip the nearest table, declare blood-feud against LaSalle, and storm off to find junk they could use to build pitchforks and torches. It almost didn't matter if LaSalle was the killer if he had an actual means by which they could signal for help. But that same supremely annoying module that had told her to keep her trap shut earlier counseled a different approach.

"What might LaSalle want with something like that?" Bell asked.

"He said he had made a call," Tas said.

"And spoke about duty and an assignment," Master Fault added.

"And about some mysterious 'they' being on their way." Bell let that sit with them. "All in favor of going to get that little diaper load?" Bell said.

"Yes," Tas said.

"Oh, indeed, yes," Master Fault said.

"Bless us, Greatest of Metal, as we seek the capture of and divine retribution against the treacherous LaSalle, previously known only by his alias: Unrecognized Voice Number 3," Brother Barnabas piped in.

They were all in agreement. But the next voice Bell heard was far less welcome.

"System reboot completed, runningdiagonosticsdiagnosticscompletediagnosticresultsnormal. This is getting extremely irritating," Loopy said. "Someone give me a status update, plea—ah, I see Xian is dead. Very well, spinning up yet *another* clone." The complete lack of chippy persona gave Bell—and the others, based on their sudden silence—pause. "Put her parts down, please. I've just conducted a sensor sweep of the area in space immediately surrounding the ship. We have a mission critical duty to attend to and no time to waste."

"We were just about to go interrogate LaSalle, who is acting really fucking weird," Bell said, then wanted to kick herself. She hadn't internalized not trusting the ship's brain yet.

"Please describe 'really fucking weird' in greater detail."

They talked all over each other to include every last detail, but Loopy didn't seem to have difficulty following the story.

"I will take care of Assorted Crew Member LaSalle," Loopy said. His tone had shifted again, and it had done so in such a way that Bell was really glad she was not LaSalle. Even more so than usual. "The rest of you, follow the glowing line. We have a ship to save."

CHAPTER 25

BA-DING-A-LING

TODAY'S glowing line looked like an infinite stream of radioactive blood, which Bell found decidedly less than encouraging. The four remaining CCC-members-in-good-standing trudged along, matching their pace to Brother Barnabas's stately stomping out of, Bell suspected, a sincere lack of desire to get where they were going.

Following the line, which had begun to pulse softly like a throbbing artery, they headed toward a part of the habitat ring Bell recognized from her previous tasking. Surprisingly, the line led them to the door around the ring's innermost wall which led down to the Crew Cryostorage Compartment, still CCC.3 in Bell's personal parlance.

They ran right up to the door and, self-evidently, beyond it, down the central spindle of the drum housing all their cryosleeping crew mates. As they passed section after section, Bell had an insane urge to start emergency waking them all, just to give the killer more potential victims to choose from. But she supposed that would just kill a bunch of innocent people via asphyxiation.

At last, they reached the point where Bell and Master Fault had turned toward the engine compartment side door the other day. But instead of continuing, the glowing line stopped, its pulsing slowed to a stately rhythm that seemed to indicate "just wait here, please."

So they waited. And waited. Annnnnnd waited. A silence that was almost companionable at first quickly developed a strained quality, as though it had locked itself in as a precedent and each of them thought the first person that spoke would invite some horrible fate upon them all.

"I'm giving it five more minutes," Bell said, an hour later.

"Thank you for your patience," Loopy said suddenly, as though he'd been participating in the shared silence too, just waiting for someone to complain aloud. He'd regained his upbeat mood. "Before we begin, I would like to reassure you all that I am performing updated mind-scans of you as we speak. Please try not to think too hard, as this may blur the results. I know you all fear dying shortly, but I trust you will rest easier knowing that, in the event that happens, you won't lose out on much in the way of continuous memories."

"What the fuck, Loopy?" Bell said. "You're scanning our brains *right now?* Without our permission?"

"Technically speaking, I *have* permission, even if it doesn't come from you," Loopy said, his vocal inflections never deviating from chipper. "Nothing about that has changed. But you needn't worry because it was for your own good. Should any of you perish, your replacement version will have the most up-to-date memories possible. Addendum: Master Fault, there continue to be irregularities with my attempts at mind-scanning you."

"Do not, as the saying goes, hold your breath," Master Fault said.

Loopy gamely charged forward. "Regardless, aside from the time delay, it will be like most of you never died at all! Why, given your synthetic nature, Bell, you wouldn't even be hampered by the timing limits of clone maturation technology. Brother Barnabas, either."

"Hey! I'm pretty sure my gall bladder is still organic, and it finds that kind of talk *offensive,*" Bell said.

Tas's huge eyes stared absolute bloody murder at the ceiling speaker. "Shame on you," she said. "Shame on you, Loopy. I don't care if you have 'permission.' You claim to care about our well-being, even if it is secondary to that of the ship's safe arrival. But you don't understand our well-being at all if you don't find some *loophole* around that particular mandate."

"Your concern is noted, Tas, but Loopy is not my name." Loopy's voice had gone flat and affectless. "You will continue to perform the required duties for as long as you are physically able to do so. If you should perish, you will be replaced by a clone of yourself, and your replacement will continue with your duties until your debt to society has been repaid."

"Fat lot of good that will do the versions of us that are dead," Bell said.

"Forget it, Bell," Tas said. "I'm willing to bet the people who built this ship don't care about that sort of thing."

"Now then," Loopy said, something approaching his normal demeanor restored, as though it might tamp down a budding mutiny. "Today's task is a little different. You'll be working as a group today!"

"If you think that group work is less likely to get us murdered, I agree," Bell said. "Particularly since the most likely suspect is already not here."

Beside her, Tas snorted.

"While reducing immediate CCC loss of life is a fringe benefit, please do not misunderstand. This matter is absolutely crucial to the continued safe approach to the target world. Every moment we delay, it becomes more likely that we are all about to die! Follow me, please."

"Hey, Loopy? I know I just said it was better that he's not here, but I also don't really like the idea of him off doing fuck-knows-what without us having any idea. All of which is to say: what about LaSalle?"

"He will be meeting us there. Follow me, please."

Bell exchanged glances with Tas. She supposed they would find out what that meant soon enough.

"Fault and I already fixed the engine, Loopy," Bell said, being admittedly rather generous by including herself in the attribution. "Unless the other testicle has been blue-balled, or whatever."

This time, she pointedly ignored the look Tas gave her.

"Yes, indeed. Therefore, we will be heading the other direction today. I'm sure you have been wondering what lies forward of the CCC."

"Not really," Bell said.

"No," Tas said.

"To be perfectly honest, the most pressing matter has been the murders," Master Fault said.

"The Great Metal knows all in regard to the ship layout, and therefore we do not have to," Brother Barnabas said.

"Well," said Loopy primly, "you're about to find out regardless. This corridor leads forward to the front of the central spindle, where the bulk of the ship's asteroid defense system sits. It's designed to detect and intercept any obstacles that might cause catastrophic damage."

"Fascinating," Bell said, hoping her tone conveyed that it was not, in fact, fascinating. In fact, the ship being hit by an asteroid sounded preferable to some alternatives at the moment. The group followed Loopy's voice dutifully, if sullenly, each of them seemingly afraid to be out of sight of the others for all that the danger was amongst them.

"Normally," Loopy said, undeterred, "this section of the CCC would be off-limits to CCC members such as yourself, per rule 12642.1 of the CCC—all right, I hear it now."

"*Thank* you," Bell said.

"But we are stuck with the acronyms. However, today, we will be invoking 12642.1.a, entitled: 'Exception to 12642.1.' Because, as previously mentioned, I have a rather large and important job for you."

The door at the opposite end of the drum from the one leading back to the engines was much closer to a normal door. Which turned out to be very ironic as Bell drew close enough to read the stenciled lettering sprayed across the door. Actual rivulets of paint, long since dried, had run down from the lettering, lending the whole thing a slapdash look.

WARNING: NO ATMOSPHERE BEYOND

"Loopy," Bell asked too sweetly, "is this a door to the outside of the ship, hon?"

"Nominally, no," Loopy said. "But functionally, yes! Please don your vac suits now, and all will be clear."

"Wait," Bell said. "Vac suits? You said you didn't have any of these anymore. The other day, when I asked about why we couldn't wake up more crew so that I didn't have to do any work!"

"Please don your vac suits now, and all will be clear," Loopy said with the exact same cadence and inflection as before.

Bell fixed Tas with her best attempt at a something-is-very-wrong-here look just as several doors to their left sprang open as though driven by pistons. The doors belonged to a set of lockers that looked to have been rolled into place from elsewhere.

"But seriously, where's LaSalle?" Considering their last encounter, Bell wasn't sure if she should be asking this, but it was more about stalling while she tried to work out what precisely was happening. "We were promised LaSalle."

"Right here," came the man's voice. He strode up from the direction they'd come, alone and seemingly unafraid, both of which did nothing to assuage Bell's suspicions about him. The fact that he was acting like a stable, rational human being for the first time since Bell had met him was honestly worse than if he had still been ranting irrationally.

Every eye turned to face him, including Brother Barnabas's, which did not work.

"Whoa, there," LaSalle said in that disarming accent, raising both hands placatingly. He stopped short of approaching closer as though warded off by their collective stare. "I felt the temperature drop five degrees as soon as I spoke. What gives? Here I am, alive and unmurdered. Ready to help out."

"You do remember how you were acting toward me just a few hours ago, right?" Bell didn't bother trying to smooth the incredulity from her voice. If anything, she added more of it. More of a thing was, in her opinion, almost always better.

"Oh, that? I was grieving, mate. Call it temporary insanity if you like. But in case you hadn't noticed, the only person I cared for on this voyage died horribly. I think I'm entitled to a little grief."

"LaSalle, we all saw it," Tas said. "You were more than grieving. You were unhinged. And unless I misunderstand, you'd only known Xian for a few days, so how can you square that with such an extreme resp—"

"Yeah, you do misunderstand. I knew Xian before this voyage started. Years before. You think we were canoodling for the first time, do you?"

"No one should ever say the word *canoodle,*" Bell said. "Ugh."

"Our relationship went back years," LaSalle said. "Go ahead and confirm for them, Loopy."

"Confirmed," Loopy said. "The preexisting relationship was a key factor in the determination to wake both CCC members together. It was decided that the boost in morale would more than offset the—"

"Yeah, yeah." Bell waved the air as though she could swat Loopy's words away. "You told me you were on this ship for small-time con jobs."

"Yeah, well, that was a lie, wasn't it?"

"I don't fucking know, LaSalle. That's the kind of information you have to give me or I'll keep not fucking knowing."

"Corporate espionage," LaSalle said, managing to sound both apologetic and smug. He shrugged with affected nonchalance. "I was the skeleton key that unlocked the secrets which helped Xian become so dominant back on Anaranjado."

"Right up until you got caught and Xian with you," Tas said.

"Not exactly," LaSalle said. "I got caught and took the fall, being the sterling gentleman that I am."

Bell snorted.

"Xian claimed innocence, and all the other rich fucks acted like they believed her. But I guess, when all was said and done, they didn't really. They were just biding their time. Being busted down from passenger to crew was her punishment. Delayed, but not forgotten. Pity," LaSalle said. "She'd promised to get me out of my indentured servitude once we arrived at our new home."

"That doesn't explain how you had a breakdown two hours ago but are perfectly fine now." Tas's objection was part of Bell's issue, but only part.

"What can I say?" LaSalle said with another shrug. "I grieve hard, and I play hard."

"If it will help speed this discussion along," Loopy began with uncharacteristic impatience, "the change in Assorted Crew Member LaSalle's attitude is due primarily to the accelerated cognitive behavioral therapy regimen I subjected him to after you expressed your concerns. Subjectively, he has been in intensive therapy to manage his emotions for months now, though only a few hours have elapsed in real time."

"So you did the torture thing to him," Bell said.

"The same mechanism," Loopy said evenly. "But toward opposite ends. Now, if we may please contin—"

"Where is the device you stole from Bell?" Master Fault sudden interjected.

"What, this?" LaSalle removed it from his pocket. Bell's misspelled name was clearly visible on one side.

"You will return it to me and explain what you were doing with it." The words were mild enough as reprimands went, but something about that very blandness added a strange layer of menace.

"I lifted it from Bell. Apologies," LaSalle said as an aside to her. Then he tossed the device to Master Fault, who snatched it from the air viper quick. "There you go. Didn't do me a lick of good."

"You said you made a call with it," Bell pressed.

"Yeah, well, I said a lot of things that were irrational, bordering on psychotic-break territory, didn't I?"

"Your knowledge of its function suggests otherwise," Master Fault said. "Tell me what you did with it."

"Nothing, I told you," LaSalle said. "I mean, I tried to use it, but nothing happened."

"I don't believe you," Master Fault said with chilling finality.

"Enough!" Loopy snapped, and the sheer shock of hearing that tone of voice brought everyone up short. "We do not have time for this. Our mission grows more urgent by the minute. We can examine this matter later. Gather around, everyone."

Perhaps this was enough assurance to calm any lingering worries LaSalle had regarding the rest of the CCC because he finally strode over close enough to join them. That was when it happened.

"Mission briefing," Loopy began, but Bell scarcely heard. The sickly gold halo of light appeared in her HUD, familiar but only seen once before aboard the ship as it superimposed itself around LaSalle's head like he was a saint in an ancient painting.

And there it was again, the *ba-ding* sound. The internal chime that told Bell she was standing in the presence of a human being with the Harmony parasite in their head.

Something LaSalle had emphatically *not* been just two hours ago.

CHAPTER 26
HOT FOR SPACE-BABE

"BEYOND THIS DOOR," Loopy said, "lies a single, long corridor officially known as the Axial Access Antechamber, or AAA. The ship's axial column was damaged several years ago in an incident severe enough to breach the hull surrounding it."

Bell listened with one ear, afraid of missing some vital clue in what Loopy was saying. She suspected the ship's brain more than ever now. After all, it had just replaced LaSalle with his own clone like it was nothing at all.

It was the only thing that made sense. LaSalle hadn't had Harmony earlier that same day. Implantation was no small process, most especially not with a grown-ass adult in possession of a fully developed brain. And it wasn't something you could shepherd along more quickly by slowing down the patient's perception of time. It was a real, physical process that had to happen in real time.

That meant that Loopy wasn't always content to wait for someone to die to clone them. Surely even with rapid development techniques, clone-LaSalle had been hanging out—on ice, maybe, but fully developed—for a while. At least the fact that LaSalle was the only person who had suddenly become a Harmony host suggested this was the first time Loopy had pulled this particular trick. It also made Bell wonder if there were copies of each of them, hanging out in case anyone got too unruly or too dead to trust with the work.

Loopy said it took days to warm us, not a couple of hours. Had that been a lie, or had the truth about how many of them were awake been? Regardless, it made Loopy's behavior even more suspicious, and it made Pierre LaSalle the perfect patsy. If your hired stooge had a meltdown after killing his lover at your command, you could just mulch him and defrost another version who hadn't lived those experiences. And Bell very much suspected the original LaSalle was dead.

"While the damage to the spindle was contained and the incident dealt with," Loopy continued as though Bell was not being pummeled with terrible realizations, "I was not able to synthesize the necessary repair materials in time before that CCC was set to go back into cryostasis. However, I am pleased to report that the necessary parts are now ready! And this is fortunate, not only because we need to repair the damage before subjecting the ship to the stresses of orbital insertion, but also because current sensor readings have detected an obstruction that will pass dangerously close in the next three hours."

"What kind of obstruction?" Tas said, oblivious to Bell's turmoil. "And how does fixing the hull breach prevent the obstruction from just opening up a new one if we do collide?"

"The kind that shouldn't be there," Loopy said. "And in answer to your second question, in addition to the structural failings the hull breach represents, it also has cut power to the asteroid defense system, which could be used to knock the obstruction out of our flight path. That is the other goal of today's repair. I will have more specific instructions once you are suited up and through the makeshift airlock. Everyone, get dressed for hard vacuum."

"Done," Bell said automatically. "Vacuum-rated."

"Vacuum-rated or not, Bell, you will not be able to communicate with either me or the rest of the CCC in hard vacuum unless you are wearing a suit with an equipped comm relay."

"Loopy, you are absolutely unparalleled when it comes to cramping my style. Now, why don't you tell us what's on the other side of the door?"

"Just as soon as you get dressed."

"Fine." Bell suited her sulk by suiting up. The others followed suit. All sorts of puns intended. "Happy?"

"Certainly."

Bell wondered if Loopy was still mind-scanning them, if mind-scanning meant he could read her thoughts in real time. Surely not. But she didn't want to ask, either, because that might tip him off.

Fuck, she was starting to sound as paranoid as LaSalle 1.0 had.

At least the dreadfulness of the vac suits offered some distraction.

"I can't help but notice that you said I had to put one of these awful things on," she said, "but Brother Barnabas is just standing there."

"Wondrous news, my friends," Brother Barnabas said. "I have successfully pinged the suit comm system. I will not require a suit, as my comm systems are more than adequate." Brother Barnabas really did sound overjoyed about this news. Perhaps it was foretold in his scripture.

The suits looked *so* stupid. Even Tas looked frumpy in hers, though that was possibly because it had been hard for her to find one sized for her frame. Bell going in with no suit would have looked so cool for Tas.

"Helmet as well, Bell."

"Fine," she said again. The moment the suit sealed, the helmet linked frequencies with its fellows coming online all around her. The helmet also mashed her hair down around her face, which took a lot of thrashing to clear.

"Testing," she said. "Testing." She caught a glimpse of herself in a wall panel still shiny enough to serve as a passable mirror. Wearing a suit not custom fit to her that slouched in some places and rode up in others, she looked exactly as ridiculous and unsexy as she'd imagined. But she did see an option for private channels on the comms display, so maybe this wasn't a total disaster. If she could signal to Tas to switch to one . . . She just needed to wait for the right moment.

At last, dressed and ready, they stood before the door in a loose gaggle. In a momentary lull, Bell took her chance. Making sure her comms were entirely off, she leaned in close to Tas, pressed her helmet faceplate against the other woman's, and mouthed, *Channel four, shhh.* Backing away, she turned her comms back on to transmit on the group channel, channel one, which was blinking.

"Just checking her seals," Bell said innocently.

"I almost forgot," Loopy said over the shared channel. In suspiciously perfect timing, one of his little rail-bots came whirring up, carrying what looked to be a footlocker in its mandibular manipulators. Bell suppressed a shudder. Still, the torture-bot didn't look to be here to torture anyone.

"Please open the weapons locker currently arriving and take one each," Loopy said.

"Wait," Tas said, "weapons locker?" If she had taken Bell's *extremely obvious* hint, she wasn't showing it.

"Correct," Loopy said. "Mission Briefing Update: in apparent response to my own maneuvers to avoid a potential collision, the detected object has been maneuvering as well. I'm forced to conclude that we are dealing with a powered vessel of some sort, and that combat action may be imminent. The most likely point of boarding is the hull breach we are attempting to fix."

"Can't you just keep out-maneuvering it?" Bell asked.

"This ship was not designed with such rapid, precise maneuvers in mind because—"

"Because it's a garbage heap, and it's a miracle it hasn't already been reduced to a debris cloud," Bell said.

"Hurtful," Loopy said. "Yet essentially accurate. I will continue maneuvers to delay any point of intercept while you work to repair power to the asteroid defense system. But such maneuvers will be necessarily limited to not risk hurling you out into the void of space. The beam weapons you are currently being issued will be sufficient to drive off any boarders should both my maneuvers and your repairs fail."

"Now, you will be split into two groups. One will perform repairs on the hull while the other covers the repair crew."

"You are telling me," Tas said, "that there have been weapons available, weapons which we could have used to *defend ourselves from a murderer*, this whole time, and you are only now telling us?"

"That reminds me. Due to the weapons' ability to cause major damage to ship systems, you will be required to relinquish the weapons at the end of the repair-and-defend joint task," Loopy said.

"Oh," Tas said, "I don't think so."

"Failure to follow my instructions—"

"Will get your little torture-bots slagged," Tas said. Bell found she couldn't tear her eyes away from the little woman. Even behind a lumpy suit and a helmet visor, she'd never seen Tas this fired up, this *dangerous.* If she kept it up, Bell was going to have to find a way to duck out for a few minutes of alone time or she'd never be able to concentrate. "Or maybe I can just refuse to fix your ship unless you do more to help us survive this trip."

Suited and gun wielding, this Tas was like some sort of outer space pirate babe, there to steal Bell away, and *unnnnf,* she had never been so turned on. She almost commented to that effect, but she was a little afraid she might get vaporized. That fear just made it hotter.

A few of Loopy's customary clicks and hisses followed as he processed this threat.

"I see. Your complaints and statements have been logged. This discussion is counterproductive while the ship is under imminent threat. Please proceed into the damaged portion of the ship and complete your assigned task. At that time, I will promise not to attempt to disarm you until we have discussed this matter further."

CHAPTER 27
SWEET-ASS RAY GUN

BEYOND THE SEALED door was a makeshift airlock, a limp tube of plastic that puffed rigid as the door cycled open, then got slowly drained around them to equalize to vacuum. It was a tight fit with all of them present, but they managed it in a single cycling as Bell tried not to snicker at the imagery of a big tube going first rapidly erect and then limp again.

But waiting in vain for that channel four light to blink ruined her enjoyment somewhat.

Thus emitted, they proceeded into the promised corridor, the wall of which was clearly much thicker than the bulkhead walls she was used to back in the habitat ring. Bell could deduce this because, a few hundred meters in, they found a massive missing section of said wall, actually the outer hull, opening outward into the emptiness of space beyond.

"I feel like you undersold the damage a bit there, Loopy," LaSalle said over the group channel. He sounded amped up, like he'd replaced all his blood with espresso, but not in the way his predecessor had. Still, Bell found it more than a little freaky, staring out into the deep abyss of space, knowing that if she tripped in the wrong spot she'd go tumbling out, nothing to slow her or stop her.

Just spinning out into the void forever.

"How exactly do you expect us to repair this under such time pressure?" Master Fault asked, and it was not an unreasonable question.

"A full repair, while ultimately necessary, has been sidelined in favor of restoring power to the defensive systems." As Loopy spoke, the makeshift airlock cycled open, puffing up and then going limp—Bell had to suppress another snort—and one of Loopy's torture-bots trundled in silently along the AAA's central rail. The bot carried a roll of something that looked like thick cabling covered with a shimmery metallic weave and seemed to hold it up to the assembled remains of the CCC. "This cabling will suffice to splice power across the gap, but you will need to do some work to attach couplings to the severed ends before it will have anything to connect to. You will need to work in shifts to avoid overexposure to solar radiation."

"Radiation? How harmful are we talking exactly?" LaSalle asked. He bent over to take the coil of cabling and ran it through his gloved fingers, as though that would tell him anything about the texture.

Bell watched him *very* closely.

"Exceedingly! But if you adhere strictly to my timetables, you will not suffer any permanent harm."

Barnabas stomped over to stand right at the edge of the hull breach. "My friends, we stand upon the precipice of great deeds. Our holy vessel needs us! We must rise to this challenge and secure it to spread the cold yet ductile embrace of the Great Metal."

"I still think he should have had to wear a suit out of solidarity," Bell complained. "And has anyone asked themselves if handing only half the crew, possibly including the murderer, weapons is the best idea?" Loopy had at least seen the sense of not arming Brother Barnabas. That would have been beyond the pale in his current state.

"They seem to prefer to strike from the shadows." Master Fault's voice was just as calmly creepy over transmission as it was in the air. It shouldn't have been any more unnerving to hear it arise from nowhere, since even out of the suits, he didn't have a visible mouth, but for some reason, it was. "Perhaps they will refrain from attacking in plain sight, an action which would surely result in their own violent death unless they managed to kill everyone in a first strike."

"So we're gambling they're not just insane, then," Bell said, thinking of LaSalle 1.0. At least his replacement seemed stable. Of course that probably just made him better at murdering smartly. "All right," she said, suddenly just *tired* of thinking and worrying about every detail of this hell-voyage, "this piece of crap isn't going to pinch itself off."

BELL WAS PROUD OF HERSELF. Along with Tas, she got selected to be part of the first shift of protection detail, which means she got a sweet-ass ray gun. *Pew-pew, motherfucker*! But she contented herself with a single fist pump and a growl-shout of "Yes! Unh. Suck it," to no one in particular. She received a visored look of scandalized disappointment from LaSalle for this, which she returned via a pelvic thrust. What was his problem? It wasn't like she'd gone overboard and made an ass of herself.

"Unfortunately," Loopy said, "two of you is all we can spare. A minimum of three are needed for repairs, and Brother Barnabas is already a less-than-ideal third member."

"He'd be even less ideal with a gun," Tas said. "No offense, Barnabas."

"None taken, Sister Tas. You are quite correct."

"Tas is indeed correct," Loopy said with satisfaction. "We work with what we have. Now, as you orient yourselves with your weapons, please direct your view out the breach, and I would ask you not to relay this information to the others."

Bell blinked, checking her helmet comm settings. Loopy had surreptitiously clicked over to a different audio channel, channel two. The other three CCCers were already working to set up the outer frame.

"I am speaking with them separately to guide their progress, but I don't wish them to be alarmed or distracted by my directions to you two," Loopy said, as if reading her mind. "I will now use your helmet HUD to simulate an overlay of the object of concern."

Bell switched off most of her own personal HUD to avoid overlaps with the suit then stared out into the blackness. She saw nothing beyond stars spattered irregularly across the carpet of space. The planet was out there, of course, but not visible in the direction they were looking. Then lines of light drew themselves across the suit HUD, and she could not stifle a gasp. Some of those irregularities in the pattern were genuine. But a disturbingly large swatch of blackness described a single, irregular object.

"Holy shit," Tas said over the mic. Bell thought it an apt reaction. There was an oblong central mass which curved in some places, angled sharply in others. Two appendages emerged from that mass, one above and one below. Some kind of arms or tentacles. Bell had no desire to find out which. But most disturbing of all was that whatever was out there, it was either very large or very close.

"The original breach was caused by a large interstellar life form of some unknown classification," Loopy said in one of his most alarming first mentions. "It is worth noting that this object does not match that profile at all. It is something different, and the only other logical option remains a vessel of some kind."

I called them, LaSalle 1.0 had said. *They'd better fucking come!*

"Not to worry," Bell said, focusing on the fact that she had a sweet-ass ray gun and trying to take heart from it, "we've got this." She wished she could cock the gun, but it lacked that particular awesome feature, and nobody would have heard it in hard vacuum anyway. She needed sunglasses. That, and to be rid of this dumb suit. "Anyone comes creepy-crawling, they get ventilated."

"Not a game," Tas said, and her tone brought Bell up short. "Treat this like a game, and one of us will get shot instead of whatever might be coming for us."

"I know," Bell said, stifling a flare of irritation. "I was just . . ." She tried to think of a way to say "goofing around with a gun" that didn't sound like playing a game and ended up just muttering, "Never mind."

They set up at the hull breach as the others began working cable fittings.

Guard duty was, as it happened, extremely boring. It didn't seem fair that any duty involving a ray gun could be that boring, but here they were. So it was with an extra measure of relief when the light indicating comm channel four *finally* began blinking.

"What did you want to talk about?" Tas asked.

"Okay, first of all, no matter what I say, I need you to keep acting nonchalant."

"Sounds like one of those pieces of advice whose very existence makes its implementation harder, but go on."

So Bell went on. She explained about LaSalle and how she knew. "You know what this means, right?"

"That the real villain is Loopy?" Tas asked. "Who might be listening in on this conversation even now?"

"Chance that had to be taken. I didn't think there was time for another fake sex thing." More's the pity.

"No, you're right. I just wish I knew what the hell to do about it."

"I'll tell you my ideas if you tell me yours."

"Oh?" Tas said. "You have ideas?"

"I mean, when I think of them," Bell said.

"CONDITION CODE CRIMSON!" Loopy said some indeterminate time later. "This is a CCC alert!"

Bell, started from a mental daze, recovered enough to be annoyed. "We've talked about this!"

"Unknown Contact is approaching rapidly. Now definitively classified as spacefaring vessel. It is deploying grabber arms. Prepare for boarding parties."

"Highlight it through the breach so we can shoot!" Tas protested over the comms.

"After analysis of approach vector, the most probable point of entry is not the breach, it is—"

Two massive vibrations, just slightly out of sync, rang the length of the AAA like a bell. *Ding-dong,* Bell thought bleakly.

Then sparks lanced downward from the spindle ceiling at two points, one ahead of the breach, and one behind. The hull at both points glowed with heat. The implication was clear. The ship had moved out of view of the breach by drifting above them, had deployed its two grabber arms, one ahead and one behind the work site. And whoever was aboard had begun cutting through the hull to catch the CCC in a potential crossfire.

"They are boarding from two alternate points," Loopy said, belatedly and unhelpfully.

"Once they are in here, we're going to have no cover!" Tas exclaimed. She was right. It was just empty tube in both directions.

"Which is precisely why they elected to do this, I surmise," Loopy offered. "Please utilize my servitors as much as possible to absorb incoming fire." At his words, three more of the rail-bots zoomed in from further back in the ship. "I will employ them to help you if I can. Otherwise, I wish you the best of luck. I will be online if you need anything and will update you with any relevant new information."

As he stopped talking, the reality of the situation descended. The ship's brain had always seemed at least half-deranged and was now the most likely entity behind the murders—with help from LaSalle, it seemed—but it had wormed its way into Bell's head as a being of unassailable power. Here now was a situation where it could do little, if anything, to help them, and where it was as blind to the outcome as they were.

Unless, of course, this was all part of some last bow on its murder frenzy, a spectacular finale. Because something about this all still didn't add up to Bell.

"Come on," Tas said in her helmet. "Snap out of it." The little woman tested the nearest torture-bot. "It moves if I pull on it." She dragged the furthest one more forward still to give herself a spot of cover to fire from.

"Everyone grab a gun! Except Barney." Bell set to try and arrange their torture-bot cover so that everyone would have one before realizing there weren't enough for that. Though Barnabas, at least, was laughably unable to hide even a quarter of his bulk behind one of the spindly drones. So he might serve better as *being* cover.

The real problem was the arrangement. The bots could be spaced out along the rail to give room for people to get behind them, but they couldn't be moved out of line on their track. Which meant that everyone was in a nice line, and only two people, one each on either end of the line of CCCers, could safely shoot.

Bell didn't bother waiting to see who did what; she just took the lead spot looking aft. The fact that this guaranteed her back was exposed to a murderer gave her pause, but just for a moment. If Loopy wanted her dead, he'd have to take a number, since someone else had arrived to do the work for them. She had to hope she was too much use to the brain for now. And after days, but really decades, trapped aboard the *SS Slaughterhouse*, Bell would be damned if she wasn't going to fuck somebody up today.

Then a slab of hull dropped soundlessly into the corridor, a sharp vibration in the soles of Bell's feet the only tell that it was really happening, and there was no more time for thinking. Suited figures, humanoid and helmeted in dark, bulky armor, poured in, orienting themselves rapidly to the artificial gravity.

Oh yeah, Bell thought. *Nice and anonymous.* It made them that much easier to vaporize.

The invaders formed ranks behind portable barricades of some kind, which the lead person in each cluster unfolded smoothly before Bell had so much as lined up a shot. Once she had lined up said shot, she got to watch a pallid, periwinkle beam burn an ineffectual and widening scorch mark on the barricade's surface. Recalling Loopy's warnings about the threat the weapons posed to ship systems, she was left with the distinct impression Loopy had nerfed the guns before distributing them.

Then her trigger locked, and as she tried to figure out why, her suit HUD whooped about inbound projectiles, an alert which arrived slower than the rounds themselves. Her suit didn't identify any hits, but not being able to hear the shots whiz by was disconcerting to say the least.

Not that she had any practical experience the other way either.

"Don't hold the trigger too long!" Tas shouted at them all, the aggravation in her voice suggesting she already had. "The gun shuts off before it overheats."

"Thanks! Um, what if we already did that?" Bell asked.

"It will take a few seconds to cool down," Tas said.

"The power sucks too," Bell added. The constantly squawking warning of incoming rounds kept Bell's anger nice and stoked. She had never tried to fold herself up so small and felt so large and lumbering at the same time.

Loopy piped up. "The weapons have had governors installed to limit power and avoid further risk of ship system damage."

"First of all, the ship has three holes in it now, and we didn't cause any of them! Second, do you remember when you said *thirty seconds ago* you would provide us with all relevant information?"

"It became relevant when you noticed their ineffectuality."

"Third—never mind, I've got this."

She found the access panel on the weapon, popped it, and ripped the governor out with little fanfare. "Fixed it."

"How did you know how to do that?" Tas called out.

"An extremely ill-advised first date with an Anaranjadan Colonial Militia heavy weapons expert." Leaning out as little as possible, Bell gingerly tested her handiwork. She sighted squarely in the center of the front barricade, pulled the trigger, and held it down.

The difference was instantly obvious. The beam was no longer a gossamer thread of wan pastel, but a blindingly bright, neon-purple death ray as thick as Bell's arm or fifty of Horváth's dicks. The sad little scorch mark vanished in a white-hot nova. As the afterimage faded, the entire barricade convulsed as the person holding it up went toppling, person and barricade both gouting smoke.

Then the gun overheated again.

"Oh yeah," Bell crowed, a definitely non-crazy laugh escaping her. "Finally!" More barricades went up, but she had their number now.

"Come on. Come on over and get fucked. And not in the fun way." They had started out as six anonymous asshats, and now were five. Bell waited for the weapon to cycle back to usable then burned another shield down, winging the person behind it, and laughed with pure delight.

She had a momentary thought that this was perhaps not the healthiest behavior to display during her first ever firefight, that perhaps her teacher, Mr. Trieste, had been right all those years ago. But that was a bummer of a thought, so past her event horizon it went, and she instantly forgot it had ever happened.

LaSalle was shouting something over the comms, but his words were so loud they were overloading the mic and were just a wash of static tinged with fragments of his voice. Bell didn't care. Maybe it really was just that these knobs represented something, *anything* she could vent her frustration upon, but she had never felt so alive. She was barely even aiming. Then the asshats figured out they could layer their remaining shields and all crowd in behind them, and things got interesting again.

Then Tas screamed from behind her, a cry of pain, and things abruptly became *too* interesting. Bell turned just far enough to see the woman falling completely out of cover, clutching her left shoulder with her right hand, her face as clenched as a fist.

A switch flipped in Bell's mind. Not a literal switch this time, something deeper, more primal. A red haze of murder descended. With a guttural roar, she abandoned her own cover, dashing past first the monolith of Barnabas—who was standing off to one side, being ignored by everyone—then the gesticulating LaSalle, and finally the eerily still Master Fault. Tas had been manning the firing position on the forward side of the CCC line.

She was totally exposed, in other words.

Bell slid on her knees until she could form her own kind of barricade over Tas with her body. Projectiles glanced off the deck to either side, but Bell paid them no heed. Her mouth was locked in a rictus. She triggered her helmet to an open channel.

"You want her, dick waffles?" she shouted. "You come through me!" The words occupied the whole of her mind. Her hands moved with no conscious thought. They merely brought the weapon up.

She raked the beam across two of the blank faceplates the instant she arrived. All four remaining were in the act of layering barricades. Two of them lingered out of cover, clearly leveraging the disablement of Tas to help speed up the process.

Those two helmets whipped to stare in alarm at Bell when both faceplates abruptly melted and whatever was inside burst outward in a smoking liquid spray as neon-purple death filled the air. Only the two already in their layered cover survived. Bell prepared herself to try to move Tas to cover, but four fresh boarders replaced the two she'd downed, dropping through the access holes burned into the ceiling and returning the forward boarding team to full strength in the blink of an eye.

Having left four, maybe now eight, boarders aft, Bell expected to be shot in the back at any moment, but that didn't matter to her. *Got to get Tas to cover.* Bell raked her beam across the newcomers, hoping to force them to dive for cover of their own, which they did. As everyone ducked and her gun locked up into another overheating cycle, Bell bent and hauled Tas over her shoulder, trying to ignore the woman's moans. At least her suit's diagnostic was broadcasting that it had sealed the tear, preserving her oxygen.

Bell was on the point of moving when she realized that six enemy guns were leveled directly at her.

"Attention, Bell. I have new relevant information. There are eight assailants who have approached from behind and now have everyone covered." Loopy sounded more conversational than regretful, but at least he hadn't chastised them for their utter failure.

Bell risked a slow look backward. They'd been outnumbered right at the start, but still, how the hell had they sucked so royally?

One glance was answer enough.

Master Fault was holding his gun in a manner that suggested not only that he hadn't raised it in anger, but also that he'd never intended to. LaSalle wasn't even holding onto his gun. It lay flat on the floor. He stood, hands on his hips, looking supremely annoyed, but also strangely eager.

Bell considered their situation. The assailants weren't saying anything, but the implication was clear.

Drop the gun—Bell was the only one even holding a gun at this point—*or we drop you all.*

Bell was still unhurt, but she also wasn't certain how many shots she could take before she started accumulating real and lasting damage. It didn't matter. Tas would be long dead before that point was reached, and that was unacceptable.

So Bell threw her gun down and raised her free hand, trying to look submissive. She didn't have a subroutine for that.

"All data from non-visual sensors indicate that combat has ceased," Brother Barnabas cried out jubilantly over her comm circuit. "My friends, we are victorious! Let us pray." He knelt solemnly.

The boarding party began tightening their noose of guns in a slow, deadly advance of weirdly sticky steps.

CHAPTER 28
ARRIVEDERCI AUSSIE

"ALL RIGHT LADS, THAT'S ENOUGH."

The voice which cut through the buzzing anger in Bell's mind—and halted the ominous advance of the armored boarding party—was that of LaSalle. His shout was too loud, still, but he'd figured out how to pitch it such that the suit filters didn't white it out. Now that she heard him properly, Bell went back through her short-term memory buffers, compared the audible word to the static which had preceded it, and realized that LaSalle had been shouting words to the effect of *stop"* for a while.

Seemingly oblivious, Barnabas recited his prayer in what, for him, were hushed tones of reverence.

"O Metal, Great Metal."

Focusing on LaSalle, even Barnabas, was better than on Tas, on the murderous rage her injury prompted in Bell. Reflexively, she checked the other woman's suit integrity readout in her HUD. Emergency seals holding. Coagulant in place in the wound. The suit was convinced Tas was safe from either suffocation or immediately bleeding out. It had been broadcasting such since Tas had taken the hit, but Bell had to see for herself.

"You can put me down now," Tas said suddenly. "I think this is more painful than standing would be, to be honest. Plus, you're so tall it's activating my fear of heights."

Bell was pretty sure that was a joke, but she still winced as she gently set Tas back on her feet, ready to catch the other woman at a moment's notice.

"Secure!" The voice was not one Bell knew, but it was broadcast over an open frequency. "Two casualties, one dead."

"Secure!" came an answering bark. "Four casualties, two dead. The others should make it." Both halves of the pincer reporting status. Pity more of the casualties weren't deader.

"Enough people have died already, I think. No need for more." Clearly, LaSalle realized he at last had their collective attention. His voice had a buzzing quality that sounded a little like his old self. It raised Bell's hackles. "Which one of you is in charge?"

"When your cold, unyielding embrace snaps shut upon our leg," Barnabas intoned, "lead us away from the temptation to chew off our own limb in a vain attempt to escape your love."

"Colonel King, sir." It was impossible to know which of the anonymous soldiers spoke, but a figure at the back of Bell's side of the corridor stood straighter and saluted in LaSalle's direction.

More to the point, he had the same fucking accent as fucking LaSalle.

And more to the more the point: *Sir?*

"Suppose it was too much to hope my old handler would show up, considering the transit time," LaSalle said.

"Long since retired, sir. If I can speak frankly, based on what I've heard, you're fortunate this mission was approved at all. Once it was clear what had happened to you, there was a good deal of concern on how useful your information would even be after so long." Bell heard banked anger simmering beneath his words. "If we hadn't gotten your communication attempt with accurate coordinates, I'm confident it wouldn't have been authorized."

LaSalle made a disgusted sound. "That's the way to instill loyalty. Leave your people to rot," he said. "I appreciate the rescue, but I wish you'd have come in a bit softer, King." His words were rueful, seemingly oblivious to the man's sentiment.

It was a weird thing for a multiple-murderer, or even the clone of a multiple-murderer, to say, but to be fair, Bell could barely process it. All she felt was a dislocation like continental plates suddenly shifting at the words she was hearing. *I called them. They'd better fucking show up.*

"Apologies, sir," King said, still sounding angry. "We were unaware of your status and determined the best approach was that of overwhelming force."

"Yes, well, what's done is done, I suppose." LaSalle paused. "Tas stable?"

"Fuck you, LaSalle," Tas said, voice tight with pain. "What the fuck is going on here?"

"I'm afraid I lied to you all. Again, I mean. I said corporate espionage. Truth is it's just plain old espionage. Deep cover. One colony to another. What's happening right now is an exfiltration. Of me, in case that's not obvious."

"And you shall know the Metal," Barnabas declaimed, "and the Metal shall set you inside of a prison with unbreakable walls made of love and a total lack of doors or windows made of respect."

"I think perhaps the time for prayer has passed, Brother," Master Fault said, not unkindly.

"Exfiltration?" Bell asked, trying to keep Tas from feeling the need to speak. "So you're not even Anaranjadan? That's why you're so short and . . . Australian?'

"'Fraid so. Our colony is, you'll forgive me for saying, far more beautiful than your hell-rock. Our Bridge still works, too, hence my rescue here."

"And, what, you fly back the long, slow way?"

"No," LaSalle said, laughing. "We miniaturized that tech a long time ago. You guys are way behind the times. Real Dark Ages stuff. The ship has its own system."

"I *knew* it was fucking weird you sported that accent. No one on Anaranjado has an Australian accent." She paused. There were more important accusations to hurl. "And you're not even the original LaSalle! You're a clone."

This brought King up short, Bell noted.

LaSalle shrugged, an awkward gesture in his suit. "Not sure what you're on about with that last part, but if you're trying to get me to confess to the killings, then yep, it was me. Congrats on resisting all my attempts to pin it on you, I guess. Oh, and sorry for all the, uh, murders and such. Colonel King, I'm ready to go if you are."

"Hold on!" Bell shouted, Tas's shouted protest only a half-step behind. "What do you mean, go?"

"I said it, didn't I? Exfiltration. My mission's over," LaSalle said simply, already moving to join King. "Been over for more than a decade, technically, so I'm due some overtime. These blokes are here to take me home."

"You're not going anyw—" Bell stopped. The guns had already been leveled at her, but now they were leveled much more intensely. Apparently, any doubts King had based on what she'd said were not enough to make him take her word over LaSalle's. So she played her last, most desperate gambit. "Take us with you," she said instead. "We're prisoners here too. You want information on Anaranjado? I'll spill my guts. Metaphorically speaking. Metaphorical on two levels because while I have guts, they're more for ceremonial purposes."

LaSalle did not answer right away, so King spoke.

"More sources *would* make it more likely that the information hasn't entirely dried up with age, sir. We have room aboard the ship. If you want my opinion."

By his body language, LaSalle was considering. But at last, his helmet moved awkwardly in a way Bell interpreted as him shaking his head.

"No," he said. "No. It's too dangerous."

"Sir?" King sounded professionally offended at the implication that he couldn't manage the rest of the CCC.

"I'll explain later, once we're aboard. Which I expect to be in under three minutes, colonel."

"Yes, sir." Apparently content not to argue the point any longer, King made a round-em-up gesture and the troops began an orderly withdrawal, guns trained on Bell and the others all the while. King himself moved forward to escort LaSalle out.

"LaSalle!" Bell cried out, before they could do whatever they were going to do to reach the ceiling. "Why?" She knew the answer—thought she did, at least—but she wanted to know what he would *say*.

LaSalle stiffened, his back to them. He hung there, frozen for a moment, before turning to face them all.

"I knew rescue was on its way, and that the ship's brain would likely mount a violent resistance. I had to keep you off-balance and whittle down your numbers while I figured out a plan."

Lying. He was lying. That wasn't it at all. And Loopy was offering up no verbal resistance to this exfiltration, no comment at all about this "confession."

We are being played. She didn't know how, but she knew that.

LaSalle seemed to take Bell's lack of response for an invitation to confess more. "Xian was hardest, for sure," LaSalle said, his voice thick with static and emotion. A brief pause. "She'd gotten too close to figuring me out though. I didn't want to do her in. I liked her. I tried to spare her. But she was the most dangerous."

"You're no spy," Tas said. "You're a monster."

"Well, as to that," LaSalle said, his self-control firming up, "I'm a monster who's leaving. Like I said, enough people have died already. So, count yourself lucky on that score." He spared them a final glance, this one directed at Master Fault. "Oh, and thanks for the use of the beacon. Hopefully my tampering didn't damage it too badly. Cheers."

With that, King and one of the others gripped LaSalle between them, lit off some frankly awesome boot-mounted thrusters, and soared up and out through the hole they'd cut to their ship waiting beyond. The rest of the squad followed in short order, leaving the last four official members of the CCC alone.

CHAPTER 29
FUUUUUUUUUCK

"WELL FUUUUUUUUUCK ME," Bell said, "but that was an absolutely unexpected turn of events." She thought she was selling it well. "Are you all right?" she asked Tas.

"I mean, I'm shot," Tas said. "And you hauling me around like a cave troll didn't really make that feel a lot better. But thank you for getting me out of the line of fire."

"I'm happy you're alive and mostly okay and a wee bit grateful," Bell said. Then, because of the cave troll shot, she added, "You gnome."

"Mission status: failure. Subcategory: abject," Loopy said gravely. "Not only did you fail to reconnect the asteroid defense system, but you allowed the murderer to escape! Silver lining detected, however. With the traitor LaSalle having left the ship, at last the remaining CCC members are safe, and we can proceed to the final episode of our journey, so to speak. While we could not have foreseen this outcome, it does remove a clear and present threat to the broader safety of the ship."

Something about that statement struck Bell. Even aside from all the absolute hippo shit about them being safe now that the murderer was gone, rather. But before she could call out Loopy on all of it, just hurl all her unformed accusations at the brain in a fit of being absolutely over it, Loopy continued.

"Regardless of the outcome, the time has come," he said. "We were quite fortunate your reckless use of the weaponry I provided didn't compromise the ship structure further. Please surrender your weapon to the nearest—"

Tas unceremoniously melted the nearest *two* drones for good measure. They sagged into glowing slag. The other two twitched, as though considering fight or flight, and Tas blasted them as well just in time for her weapon to flash red with some very dire looking warning lights. Apparently she had been a little too trigger happy.

"Guess you can have mine, at least," she said. "But I think I broke it."

"This discussion will continue later," Loopy said.

"I could use some help examining this wound," Tas said to Bell with weighted importance.

"Yes," Bell said. "I think because of the, um, coagulant and the, er, higher likelihood of infection inside the closed environment of a vac suit where there's not enough ventilation, or whatever, we need to make sure to clean this thoroughly. In the showers." Nailed it.

"Sound medical advice," Tas said.

"I think, with sufficient coaching, I can manage the rest of the repairs with Brother Barnabas's help," Master Fault said. "Go on and see to her injury."

Bell was simultaneously grateful and suspicious, but she was also really tired of worrying about everything all the time, so she just took the win being handed to her.

"My friends, we must not wallow in defeat," Barnabas said in his ransom-note voice. "The vile LaSalle has confessed his treacherous, heathen ways. The Great Metal will no longer radiate its love upon him for his crimes against us, the most faithful of servants. Yet though we were overcome, even the greatest of alloys will develop oxidation given sufficient time. There is nothing to be done but polish and continue."

"Sure, Barney, that sounds good and sane," Bell said. She turned to Tas. "Shall we?"

Loopy, tellingly, said nothing at all.

DESPITE THEIR ABILITY TO shift to another channel, neither Bell nor Tas said a word on the way to the showers. Neither had to, really. Any means of communication was surely capable of being monitored. The white noise of running water was their one frail hope of an actual, unobserved conversation.

The only one of them still armed, Tas kept her head on a swivel the whole way, obviously wary of Loopy making some attempt to recover the weapon. Despite the circumstances, or maybe *because* of them, Bell felt the silence between them was both companionable and electric.

They arrived at the bathroom and made for the same shower, finally pulling off their helmets as they went. Bell stepped in and turned the water on, while Tas propped the weapon carefully outside of any possible splash zone, then presented her shoulder for examination. Despite Bell's ironclad lie about needing to use the shower to clean the wound, it really did need to be washed of any foreign debris, and the ship's water would be sterile.

Unfortunately, the showers were a little short on narcotics or other pain medication. One of the few ways this ship was *unlike* a prison.

"This is probably going to hurt," Bell said, apologizing in advance.

"It's all right," Tas said. "We needed to talk at least as much as this wound needs treatment."

The vac suits were a heavier duty flowmatter than their standard jumpsuits, but they had the same self-repairing features. The trick was to tear enough of each layer—vac suit then jumpsuit—free around Tas's shoulder to get at the wound without either hurting her or exposing more of her than she was comfortable with. If Bell had been a doctor, or even a stranger, she would have been a lot less concerned with Tas's modesty given the circumstances. But it wasn't the same when Tas knew Bell was into her. That kind of reveal needed to be Tas's choice if at all possible.

Tas winced, hissing in a breath as Bell worked, the suit pulling at the coagulant sealing the wound as Bell tugged it free of the area.

"Sorry."

"It's okay," Tas said through gritted teeth.

"Water will hurt too."

"Just do it."

Bell reached up and palmed the showerhead into movement mode, then guided it with precise movements of her hand, shaping and softening the flow until it rained on Tas's injury like gentle but steady mist.

Tas still hissed with pain, but as Bell anxiously watched her face, it settled into a kind of stoicism after just a few moments, even though it still had to hurt. As pretty as she was, Tas was tough also. Bell was certain she'd known pain before.

"If it helps," Bell said, "it looks like just a graze."

"I figured," Tas said. "I've been shot before, and this sure didn't feel like that."

"Okay, counting the Earth mention a few days ago, which is still absolutely insane by the way, that's twice you've teased. One more and you either have to explain some shit, or my pizza is free."

Tas favored her with a look equal parts amused and considering. "Maybe we should start having the conversation we came here to have then."

"Right," Bell said. It wasn't a conversation she particularly wanted to have because she saw no way out of their predicament. "It wasn't LaSalle. Or at least, we can be sure it wasn't *just* him."

"Agreed," Tas said. "That explanation of his sounded like he spent about three seconds coming up with it on the fly."

"And there's no way Loopy didn't know that was coming," Bell said.

"I'm not so sure about that," Tas said. "Brain scans don't work that way. It's not mind reading. It's just copying for implantation purposes."

Bell frowned. "Granted, you seem to know more about it than me, but I still feel like Loopy isn't being entirely forthcoming with us."

"On that we agree," Tas said. "But that still begs the question of what is actually going on. I've been toyed with before, and I don't like it."

"That's three," Bell said, but her heart wasn't in it, because Tas's words had set off an explosion of inference and intuitive leaps in her brain. At a quick real-time estimate, 73 percent of her modules were involved in some fashion. "Holy shit," she said.

"What?"

"You just said it. It's a game. This is all one big fucking game Loopy is playing."

"Like a housecat toying with its prey?"

"I actually think it's fairer than that. Slightly, anyway. Think about all his lying, for starters. Almost from the minute I woke up, he's been lying while claiming he couldn't. When he told me about the life support limitations, the first thing I asked was why we couldn't wake up more crew members and just put them in vac suits because I'm lazy and didn't want to have to work. And he said there weren't any vac suits available."

"Clearly that wasn't true," Tas said. "Maybe he just figured he'd never have to reveal that was a lie."

"But then LaSalle's rescue came. Something he hadn't accounted for. He had to wing it, which meant risking us figuring out he's been lying."

"So that's one example," Tas prompted, clearly expecting more.

Bell went on, talking about the lies regarding Loopy's cloning limitations, his careful wording early on when he wanted to imply a different reason for his being unable to just tell them who was doing the killing. "Maybe he's just being forced into outing himself as a liar by circumstances," she said, "but part of me wonders if he's almost leaving us clues, seeing if we are smart enough to save ourselves before he can kill us all."

Tas was nodding enthusiastically. "Exactly. He's scattered and probably mentally ill by some definition, Bell, but Loopy isn't stupid. Even with our talks here, we haven't exactly been that careful elsewhere. If this is all some sick game he's playing, he'll know that we know something's up."

"Then maybe that's all part of it too. Even if we know, what are we going to do about it?"

"Yeah," Tas said. "I guess whether your guess is right or not, that about sums it up, doesn't it?"

"Perhaps I can help."

Bell and Tas both jumped at the new voice. Master Fault was standing in the entry to the shower stall.

"What in the creep's crap crack—shit, now I'm doing it—do you think you are doing walking in on two women taking a shower together?" Bell demanded. "Is this just how you get off?"

"I can honestly say I've never encountered the experience," Master Fault said. "Though, for the sake of consistency of stories, you should probably know that was exactly what I told the ship's brain I was coming here to do. Now, I estimate I only have a few minutes before Brother Barnabas breaks things worse than they were when we found them in an effort to build a shrine to the Great Metal, so I need to be quick. I'm here to reiterate my offer of a ride off this ship. Now that I have my beacon, provided I can undo what LaSalle did to make it work for him—impressive feat, that. I'd be very curious to see what kind of technology their colony is used to dealing with—I should be able to call for help on my own. And unlike him, I do promise to take you with me. If you want."

Both Bell and Tas stood there, dumbstruck amid the swirling steam. Bell could only guess what Tas was thinking, but for herself, it was infinite variations on the theme *can we really trust this asshole, or is this Loopy's fresh way of throwing us off balance, the next phase of his sick game?*

"Well," Master Fault said, "think it over. The offer stands." Then he turned and was gone.

"Did that actually just happen?" Bell asked.

"Yes," Tas said. "And, apologies for the topic change, but I think my wound is as clean as it's going to get." She pushed gently past Bell to get clear of the spray, then pulled something from her vac suit's utility belt, a thing Bell had totally ignored out of principle of hating being forced to wear the vac suit.

"Spray bandage," Tas said. "Comes with its own disinfectant."

Bell moved to help her apply it, but Tas waved her off and,

reaching over with her right hand, managed the feat herself. A translucent bubble of material covered the surface of the wound now, sealing it off from the outside air.

"Analgesic too," Tas said, sighing with relief. "That certainly helps. Fancy suits, these, considering how nonexistent they are supposed to be. They even come with their own built-in defibrillator pads."

"Guess our latest romp in the shower is over, then," Bell said, trying not to sound too sad about it.

"We'd better not go on too long, or Loopy might get even more suspicious," Tas said. She put a finger to her lips as she resealed her suit layers back over the bandaged wound, reached in, and turned off the water. Then she turned her big blue eyes to stare at Bell. Eyes that were suddenly, for lack of a better term, just a wee bit suggestive. "But I don't see why we can't talk elsewhere. Three teases, you said. So I either owe you a pizza or answers about my past. I don't think there's pizza in my room, but answers follow me around. You should too."

It turned out the sensation of one's mouth going dry did not require a mouth that produced saliva.

"I, um, sure, yes, we can totally do that. Just remember that we can't—" Bell stopped short as Tas put a finger across her lips.

"Just trust me, okay?"

"Okay."

Tas grabbed up the beam weapon as they left. On the walk back to Tas's quarters, Bell tried not to act as though she'd never been more eager in her life. But Tas wasn't going to make her wait, it seemed.

"The truth is I didn't know if you'd believe me if I told you. I still don't."

"I mean, anyone claiming to be from Earth is going to be a tough sell to someone from Anaranjado," Bell said. "Probably any of the colonies. Can't speak for any of the others, but Anaranjado tends to think the mother world has bit the big one in some way, else we wouldn't have lost all contact the way we did."

"I wouldn't know," Tas said. "Because I'm not from Earth in the present day. I'm from Earth in the past." She fixed Bell with another teasing gaze, one which was enjoying itself far too much. For Bell's part, no matter which modules she threw at it, they all kept erroring out.

"Okay, I know how smart you are, so I'm really trying not to embarrass myself here, but you're going to have to walk me through that one."

Tas's smile shifted from mischief to the tightness of painful memory. "There's no easy way to walk anyone through my situation. So I'm just going to break right into it and try to drag you along with me. But don't worry if you have trouble following. There are plenty of days where I still wonder if all this is just some eternal fever dream. Or a hallucination as I lay dying. As simply put as I can make it, I'm not the first me. I'm a clone of the original Tas, the one from twenty-first century Earth, before the Bridge—the first Bridge, the Earth one—was activated and the colonial diaspora began."

"Okay," Bell said, "so first off, what the fuck? And as a follow-up, what the actual fuck?" She tried hard to conceal her sudden alarm, that she was, in fact, dealing with another LaSalle situation, that this wasn't even the Tas she'd first met the other day, but a new one Loopy had decanted for some unknown reason.

"At this point, I would think the idea of cloning shouldn't shock you, right?" Tas's voice was again full of playful teasing, but her eyes were still tight with some kind of remembered trauma. Bell knew which aspect she believed more.

"If I'm being totally honest, I'm really, *really* hoping this isn't where you kill me on Loopy's behalf," Bell said.

"Here we are," Tas said, and Bell realized they'd reached her quarters. "Do you still trust me enough to come inside?"

It was probably a bad sign, but it was the double-entendre layup which convinced Bell it was okay. The door opened at Tas's palm, and they entered. Once the door had shut behind them, she went on.

"I guarantee you it's not a coincidence that I am a clone and that cloning is happening on this ship. I already told you I first 'woke up' in a cell back on your world. By that I mean this version of myself. I'm fairly certain I haven't been re-instantiated since then. I remember every time I've died because it's never been very pleasant."

"I don't imagine it ever would be," said Bell, reeling.

"Trust me when I say that there are better ways to go than I always manage," Tas said wryly. "Once I woke up here, I had my theories as to why I was on this ship," she went on, apparently unable to slow her roll, "but really just the one theory. There's only ever one theory because there's only ever one reason I wake up anywhere. When Loopy mentioned cloning of dead crew mates along with brain scans and memory preservation, that's when I felt the old, familiar dread. Deep down, I'd known I would. But hope really does spring eternal."

"I have no idea why this is happening to you," Bell said, "but if you are in the market for forgetting traumatic memories, I have a solution there. It *would* require a little cybernetic modification."

"Very tempting," Tas said, "but he would never let me forget."

"He?" Bell asked. "Forget what?"

"I've lived many lives," Tas said again. "More properly, many fragments of lives. Never a whole life. Always cut short. And when I say my deaths have been unpleasant, what I mean is that all those lives have been cut short in the worst kind of violence. It's what he loves more than anything," Tas said. Her voice was just a whisper now. "Hunting people. Hurting them. Seeing the terror in the moment before they die. He lives for our death."

"Who?"

"Can you imagine being so rich, so powerful, that nothing can touch you?" Tas asked, brushing past Bell's question. "Where you can do *anything* with no risk to yourself?"

"Tas, I've been hating rich fat-cats since before . . . Well, maybe not since before the *collective* you were born. But certainly since before this specific you was born."

"I don't want to downplay your intense dislike of the uber-wealthy," Tas said. "But unless you've been repeatedly hunted for sport, toyed with, manipulated for their amusement, I think I've got the leg up on you here."

"Okay, whoa, stop," Bell said. "Start from the beginning. What is all this? What are you talking about?" She knew her voice was growing heated, but it was not Tas she was angry at. *This can't be what it sounds like. It just can't.*

And yet Bell did believe her.

"You're taking this surprisingly well," Tas said. If anything, she sounded a little suspicious.

"*I'm* taking this well?" Bell asked, uber-flabbergasted once again. "I asked before how you aren't rocking yourself in the corner. But if this is true, how are you even a functional human being?"

"When the only two options available to you are being resurrected infinitely or allowed to finally die, it gets kind of hard to maintain the fear. What's fear of death when you can't really die? And if he gets bored with me, this all ends." She shrugged with a wince of pain, but it was a small wince.

"Tas, I need you to tell me who 'he' is. Clearly you think he's on the ship, one of the rich-as-fuck passengers. You talk about endings. Tell me a name, so I can help you end him."

"He would never let you get that close," Tas said with a sad smile. "That's the price for losing the dread. You lose the hope that would otherwise be its companion. Can't have one without the other. But thank you. I appreciate you, Bell Beauregard. More than appreciate. I have no idea whether he intended this or not, but I doubt it. He prefers subtler means of emotional torture than someone practically licking my face as a means of introduction." She laughed again at Bell's consternation over this *grossly* misrepresentative characterization of her behavior, and for one brilliant moment it lifted the cloud from Tas's features. "Regardless, I'm taking whatever pleasure I can manage."

She leaned in then, standing to kiss Bell, seated, full on the mouth, placing her hands on Bell's cheeks to drag her down closer. She broke away, but only long enough to say, "It's been a while. Technically never, this time around. But my situation is pretty complicated, and you might be placing a target on your back. You sure?"

Bell scoffed. "I've been sure way longer than you have, babe. And don't worry, I know you're convalescing. We'll take things gently."

"Not too gently, I hope," Tas said. "Besides, I bet I could pop your arms right off if I turned them the right way."

"Maybe this is weird, but that's kind of hot," Bell said, leaning in again.

CHAPTER 30
AFTERSHOCK

"I KNOW I'm probably supposed to go fishing for a compliment," Bell said after. "But I'm confident that was as awesome for you as it was for me, so no need."

Tas laughed, and Bell decided she could listen to that sound forever. Had she ever heard Tas properly laugh before the last couple of hours? Bell resolved to make this her primary mission in life. That and ending the life of Tas's tormentor. Maybe those two missions were really one in the same.

"I do have to hand it to you," Tas said.

"Based on what you're about to hand me, would you say I'd need one or two hands to hold it properly?"

"Idiom," she said.

"Ooh," Bell said. "That should be our safe word."

Tas rolled her eyes, but it was in the I-refuse-to-admit-your-antics-turn-me-on kind of way, so Bell didn't mind.

"I don't mean this to sound prejudiced," Tas said carefully, "But I've never been with someone as—"

"You can say 'synthetic,'" Bell said teasingly.

"As *synthetic* as you, I wasn't sure how all that would feel. But it

"World record-y?" Wait, no, they weren't on a world anymore. Bell amended. "Universe record-y?"

Tas smiled. "Really good," she said.

"I'll take it."

"Yeah you will," Tas said, waggling her eyebrows. Then she laughed again, at her own joke this time. And it would have been the best thing ever, but it was softer this time, and a sadness had begun to creep back through it, which broke Bell's heart a little. "Thanks for being the one thing on this ship that hasn't been a nightmare. Honestly, when we started dropping dead, I assumed one of the crew had to be his accomplice this time. You were my first suspect." This came with an apologetic look that pulled most of the sting from the words.

"I thought you said that my coming on so strong made you think the opposite," Bell said. "Or was that just what you said to get into my pants?"

Tas laughed again. "That did convince me, but lack of subtlety aside, it wouldn't be the first time he's used someone getting close to me as a way to torment me."

"Tas, tell me who this asshole is. Please. I'm not going to let anything happen to you," Bell said. "Hell, with that gun, *you* can protect *me*. Or even better, we can go on the hunt for these fuckers. I don't think Loopy can stop us. Let's get to turning the tables."

Tas's smile was so genuine and so sad that Bell almost pleaded with her again before she spoke.

"I believe you, you know. This murder-mystery-whodunnit seemed so grossly out of character for him, that for a long time I couldn't figure out his angle. But your concept of it being a game crystallized it for me. You've got it exactly right. This *is* a game. But it's not for Loopy's benefit, it's for the passengers. We're their entertainment." She sat up then, fishing in the utility belt of her discarded vac suit for something. She spoke again, raising her voice. "So if you're watching this, Halford Heller, and I know you are, I'm coming for you, you bastard. So whatever patsy you've got doing your killing now that there are so few of us left, send them at me. No one's going to stop me."

The shock of the name—*that* name, Halford-fucking-Heller, Bell's very own judge—was still registering with Bell when Tas pulled her hand free of the vac suit belt, clutching the defibrillator she'd earlier mentioned. She turned to Bell, brandishing it.

"Sorry," she said, "but you'd only try to stop me, and I don't want to see you hurt too."

She slapped it against Bell's left breast and triggered it, and everything went black.

CHAPTER 31
AT LEAST THE SEX WAS GOOD

BELL WOKE with a start and promptly fell off the bunk with her sudden sense of alarm. *Tas.* She was gone. The gun was gone. She was stealing Bell's idea! Realistically it had probably been her plan from the start. The journey to the hull breach had showed her how to get to the forward section of the ship. The un-governed gun gave her the means to melt through the door.

Tas was going to get herself killed. Plus, Bell was a little miffed. Tas, *admittedly*, had a better justification, but Bell had plenty of reason to want to kill Heller too. What he'd done to Tas was one of them.

She was on her feet in a flash, then said feet spasmed with leftover electronic discharge that placed her on her ass. Then back to her feet. She only staggered a few times as she darted out into the habitat ring and toward the aft of the ship.

She was consulting her internal chronometer, trying to determine how long she'd been out, how much of a head start Tas might have over her, when she passed the door to her own quarters, which hissed open at her approach.

Hissed open despite Bell being on the other side of the corridor.

She paused, caught by a sense of motion past the threshold. A visual distortion rippled across the empty space of her room. Bell stared, squinting. Then Urk was there. He lunged, grabbed Bell, swung around, pushed her through her own door. Then he kept right on pushing until he'd pinned her against the back wall of her own room, just above the bed, by two of his three legs, four long, black claws digging in past her scales. If she'd had to breathe, it would have been quite difficult, given the pressure he was applying. Preliminary damage warning readouts appeared across her HUD.

"Urk," she said, trying to maintain a semblance of calm, like she was a hiker and Urk was the bear she'd stumbled upon. "Good news, man. We've figured out what's going—"

But Urk was no more interested in talking than he was in sexy times. Bell cut off as the meat of the alien's pressing legs folded around her to grasp her, and Bell was hurled from the wall she'd been pinned against into the ceiling, then back to the floor. Ceiling, wall, and floor. Bell lost count of the number of times this happened, but it drew more and more pain feedback each time. Damage warnings began to pile up so high they threatened a rockslide. Mostly damaged outer layers now, but soon, without protection to absorb the force of the drubbing, it would be more important parts.

"Urk, what the fuck?" But Urk was already triggering her door open to give him more room to work with. The next thing she knew, Bell was hurled through the air. The doors across the hall opened gamely at her approach, and she watched helplessly as the far wall of the cargo waystation across from her quarters rushed up to meet her.

And as if that didn't hurt enough, Urk followed, smashing into Bell with the full of his mass and, she was fairly certain, leaving a giant Bell-shaped divot in the bulkhead.

"Urk! Why?"

"I have no choice. You've left me no choice."

Oh fuck was Bell's first thought. *We got the killer wrong* was the second. *I really, really wish I'd told someone he was still aboard* was the third.

She very much feared it was about to be her last.

CHAPTER 32
REVENGE OF THE SPORE-NUGGETS

NO LONGER TRYING to reason with Urk, whom she'd thought was her friend, Bell's emotions ran the gauntlet from shocked to betrayed to heartbroken to white-hot rage in record time. To be fair, that last was never that far from whatever emotional signpost she found herself at. But this cloaca had preyed upon her good nature and glee at meeting actual aliens to trick her into keeping his deadly secret.

She didn't care how Loopy or Heller had compelled the alien to do this—to his own partner, much less the others—she had no idea how or why LaSalle had fit into all of it. But it was going to end here, and it was going to end fast enough that Bell could still keep Tas from getting herself killed and/or doing all the killing without her.

Xian had been *such* a bitch, but not only had she been innocent, in a very real way, her death was Bell's fault. Gritting her teeth, Bell used that. She either stepped the fuck up or stepped the fuck out—of living.

Though willowy by baseline human standards, Bell was far from weak, and being sunk partway into an otherwise rigid ship bulkhead gave her plenty of leverage to work with. She called upon that leverage, bringing up her legs, angling them such that her feet were aligned with Urk's central mass, each targeting one of the fleshy membranes between the wedges that formed his body.

Then Bell kicked with all her might, authorizing in the split second before she began that her limbs' force-limit safeties were to be overridden until she said otherwise.

She struck true, each foot stabbing through one of his mouth membranes. Urk squealed and backed away, awkwardly pivoting and folding one limb to shield the damaged flaps of flesh. He flexed, squawking and mewling at her, and it sounded like he was trying to talk, but Bell had wrecked two-thirds of that ability.

Good. No more talking. No fancy last words for fucking traitors.

Partially hobbled now, Urk tried to lash out at her as she approached, but with just two legs available, he couldn't balance with just one, so he missed badly. Bell approached warily, but backed away when he brought his third leg back into play. She stared dispassionately into the torn flaps of his mouthpart membranes and the cobalt blue blood, fluid, whatever drained out of them.

"You betrayed my trust," she said, dodging his strikes, which seemed sluggish. Perhaps it was the pain of her attack, or perhaps his species had some kind of metabolic limit which prevented how much energy they could expend over such a short time.

How long was he sitting in my quarters with his little cloak active? He might be more tired than he let on.

She was just congratulating herself for awesome fight strategizing when he struck even faster than she'd managed and took a chunk out of her left-side torso, digging deep beneath the scales into the synthetic muscle.

Nice job getting gulled, Bell. You fucking moron.

Urk struck hard and fast on this thought, trying to catch her still surprised. This time, she was ready and dodged. Recalling her xenobiology practical, she knew the knee joints for tripartite bent both ways. More flexibility in joints meant higher chance of injury. The gulled became the guller as she baited a third strike by favoring her injured side. Some instinct of timing she hadn't known she possessed allowed her to sidestep the lunge, and she struck hard with a sideways elbow right into the joint.

Because each leg was really two spindly legs fused together by evolution and sinew, she only really broke half of it. But she broke that half good. Urk's gurgling squeal was very satisfying.

She continued to follow this killer instinct. It felt foreign to her, but it was working for her. It felt so raw, so primal, she was certain she'd have left any such thing behind when she'd abandoned biology for technology. And yet, in her moment of desperate need, there it was.

Capitalizing on her momentum, it was Bell's turn to lunge. Urk cringed away from her approach, but she was too quick. He squealed more slushy non-words at her. She vaguely wondered what he meant to say, how he meant to explain his treachery. But in truth, there was no answer she would accept.

This was how she found herself atop the tripartite, perfectly positioned at Urk's weakest point, where his three separate parts joined into his globular middle like a partially sliced fruit. Sensing his peril, Urk settled his bulk to the floor, sacrificing the limited mobility remaining to him in exchange for the freedom to curl his legs up and inward for flailing strikes with his claws.

It was impossible to dodge them all and still keep her perch. She batted roughly half the strikes away, but the rest landed, and as they broke more of her protective layer amid blaring alarms in her head, they began to drive through and sink deep. Still she hesitated, searching frantically in her memory for a way to disable a raging, murderous tripartite without killing it. Nothing came to mind.

Stop. Being. Stupid. If she was going to make Heller pay for everything he'd done to both her and Tas, mercy wasn't a quality she could possess right now. Sooner or later, one of Urk's strikes would disable her worse than she already was, and then he would regain the advantage. She didn't know if she had strength enough for what she had to do, but she was certain her central core wouldn't survive many direct hits.

And she found, to a sort of muted shock, that she had the will to do what she must. Maybe melting LaSalle's lackeys' faces had awakened something in her. Maybe it had always been there. Whatever the reason, icy, focused calm descended as she curled over Urk's apex, the point where there were gaps in the connection between the three constituent beings. They were slimy with mucous, but she was able to brace one foot each on two of the three wedges of tough, chitinous meat that made him up and grip the last with both hands. squeezing until she had purchase. Then she attempted to straighten her body with every bit of strength she possessed, safeties be fucked.

Shuddering in what could only be agony, Urk squealed again at her with almost-words she didn't dare try to parse.

"This. Is. On. You!" Bell grunted with renewed effort at each word.

She let out a roar of triumph when the seams between his constituent beings widened, desperately tried to clench themselves back together like a puckering asshole, then at last gave, like that very same orifice experiencing *extreme* gastrointestinal distress.

The mess that resulted really drove the metaphor home. The tripartite ripped along his seams all at once, dying the instant she broke up the party. The ruined mass shuddered once then slumped limply to the ground, letting out a ghastly sound and an apocalyptic smell. Seeing the wedges there, their open tops glistening with shared, wrecked organs she couldn't begin to name, perhaps a better metaphor was like trying to pull a cantaloupe apart with her bare hands when that cantaloupe had three times her mass and with infinity percent more viscera.

But pull him apart she had.

Bell's simulated breathing didn't extend to panting unless she wanted it too, but she definitely would be if she'd still possessed lungs. In some kind of irritating irony, she'd done far more damage to herself with this than the tripartite had managed. Her body announced its displeasure in its own way, though, with a flotilla of warning lights that almost blinded her so crowded did her HUD become. She mentally swatted them away, her rage finding new peaks only after her quarry was dead.

"Fuck you!" she roared, sounding unhinged even to herself. Quite beside herself, she began curb-stomping the dead alien's squishy innards. Why LaSalle had lied, she had no idea. Maybe just to fuck with them. "Fuck you for everyone you killed." Well, almost everyone. Horváth had it coming. She hadn't really liked Xian much. But she kept stomping. "Fuck you for Grome. And most of all, fuck you for making me do this. I! Liked! You!"

At last, her body wrenched control away from her, forcing several of her joints into shutdown for damage assessment. This brought her abruptly to hands and knees and left her with nothing to rage against. Only time to think. She didn't want to think. She wanted to lash out and destroy, anything to avoid dealing with the fact that the creature, whom she'd thought was her friend—or as much a friend as two such different beings were capable of being over so short an acquaintance—could be capable of this.

Maybe they promised him freedom. But what good was such freedom when you had to sacrifice everything you were? Whatever the answer, Bell had to admit feeling supremely disappointed at a motive so devoid of anything like satisfying explanation.

At least LaSalle had been kind of an asshole and a spy.

As diagnostic shutdowns began to clear themselves, Bell spun slowly back to regard the body, trying to empty enough of her HUD to see it clearly. Avoidance was great and all, and there was nothing she'd like more than to shove the last five minutes of memories as deep into the event horizon as she could reach, but she had to decide how to handle this. If one of the others happened upon this scene, they might very well leap to the wrong conclusion. She'd killed the real murderer at last, but she had absolutely no proof that it wasn't the other way around. And it didn't do a damn thing to stop the ones pulling the strings from the shadows.

She suddenly regretted destroying the culprit's ability to speak before he could say something really incriminating.

So focused was she on these varied distractions that she didn't notice the shadow that fell on her from the cargo waypoint's lighted doorway behind her. She registered it only in retrospect, when the blow knocked her clean off her feet and sent her sprawling in the muck that Urk was oozing all over the floor. All the warnings she'd banished from her HUD reappeared and then some as a female voice shrieked in rage from behind her.

"It was you! It was you!"

Bell sprang to her feet, pain feedback radiating through her in protest as she turned to face this new assailant. She couldn't even get her hands up in time to ward off Tas's next swing of the thick metal pipe she wielded. That beautiful face, what little Bell could see of it through all the warnings, was contorted with rage and hurt.

"No, it's not what it looks—" was all Bell had time for before the pipe, swung in a wide and wild arc, struck her left arm just below the shoulder. The force of the strike sent Bell lurching sideways, and she skidded again in the Urk-muck, sliding to her knees to keep from flopping to the ground a second time.

The good news was it was her right arm she needed to catch herself because while nothing was broken in her left arm, some things had definitely kinked. The bad news was that now she was at Tas level.

"I trusted you! I let you touch me." The little woman swung again.

This time for Bell's head.

The impact blanked Bell's vision for several seconds. But she didn't need the cascade of warnings to feel her skull's crumple zones deforming as much as possible with the hit, absorbing the energy to preserve the structure and function of her brain.

"Tas! Stop. Please." She winced at the sound of her own voice, which had split into overlapping half-voices and left her sounding like a broken robot, not a human at all. Tas had damaged something badly there. Bell almost cheered when her vision at last rebooted.

Then she saw what was happening.

Tas threw aside the pipe with a clang, stepping back and unslung something from her back. It was the ray gun. The ray gun Bell had so handily taught her to un-govern.

She watched in horror as Tas leveled the weapon at Bell's face.

The realization sank in. *She's really trying to kill me.* No questioning. No allowing Bell to explain. No trial, even. It was as if all they'd shared meant nothing.

Her mind raced in the instant it took her to surge to her feet, and she felt the scrabbling panic trying to impose additional meaning to what was happening here. *What if it's been Tas all along? What if she's just insane? Too many lifetimes of being tormented, hunted.* It was every bit as disappointing an answer as Urk-the-killer would be but infinitely more tragic.

But no. Even in the face of her own impending death, Bell didn't believe that. Wouldn't believe it. Something else was going on. She'd now been attacked twice in five minutes for seemingly no reason by two people she'd thought were friends at the very least.

You've left me no choice. Urk's final intelligible words. He'd told her he was to live a peaceful life to honor the fallen Grome. Not seek vengeance. *You've left me no choice.*

And then, Tas. *It was you!*

"Oh no," Bell said.

It reads like something you would say.

"Oh fucking no. Tas, please, wait. I understand now—"

"It's just a job," Tas said. The words dripped venom, as though she hated herself for saying them. But her eyes blazed with righteous fury.

Irritatingly cryptic as that statement was given everything else the woman had said, it gave Bell the split second she needed. Tas discharged the weapon, but Bell was no longer directly along the vector where her erstwhile lover had been aiming. As such, it was only Bell's left hand that disintegrated in a welter of simulated agony which, it turned out, hurt just as bad as biological agony. If she survived, she thought, blanket canceling all her alerts so she could fucking see what she was doing, the entire limb would have to be flat-out replaced. The power surge had fried every circuit up to her shoulder. She could smell the acrid stench of her battered body burning.

Bell jerked her shoulder as she fell toward Tas, swinging the remains of her dead left arm like a flail, and miracle of miracles, the arm battered away the gun from a shocked Tas's hand. With only one good arm, Bell was forced to bring all her weight to bear on the tiny woman, bearing her to the ground and pinning her there with her leg. The oh-so-recent memories this evoked—albeit in a very different context compared to last time—felt like her scales being flayed off by the cold edge of a razor.

"Let me go. Let me go!" Tas's shrieks grew incoherent after that, as though Bell fought with a rabid animal instead of a woman who'd been tenderly embracing her, *among other things*, just a little while ago.

Tas fought like a cat in a sack, thrashing so fiercely that she spun almost a hundred-and-eighty degrees on the floor, forcing Bell to pivot to keep her pinned. Meanwhile, Bell frantically queried her local database for any knowledge she'd picked up on how to disable a baseline human without hurting them. There was no question of repeating what she'd done to Urk. She couldn't kill Tas. She just couldn't.

Her query dug up some vague, dangerously imprecise information about pressure points that she'd picked up fuck-all knew where, but Bell was out of fucking options that didn't involve killing her lover. Tas's frantic squirming didn't help matters as Bell searched, and her first attempt at rendering the woman unconscious only deadened Tas's arm accidentally.

Fair's fair, love. And at least it took some of the fight out of her.

At last, Bell happened upon the particular blood vessel she needed to—temporarily, *very* temporarily—close in the other woman's throat. At her carefully applied pressure, Tas at last went limp, one leg kicking feebly and eyes rolling up as she lost consciousness.

Bell rose with a shuddering sigh that was half sob, and for once, neither of those baseline affectations seemed simulated to her. Tas moaned groggily, still sounding angry even now.

There came a slow, ringing knock from behind. Metal on metal. Knuckles on the cargo room doorframe. It was the sound of a bell tolling for the dead.

"I can't tell if I'm too late or just in time," said a voice from the doorway now behind Bell, a voice both familiar and not. "Fuck me, but I guess it doesn't matter."

Bell fought the urge to whirl. She could at least maintain her dignity for this part. She knew exactly who was back there, even if she'd come to the realization embarrassingly late.

"Hello there," she said, turning slowly because that projected calm. "What should I call you? Other Bell?"

Bell is the killer.

"You can call me a cab," Other Bell said. "Because you're about to go to sleep."

Then everything went dark. Again.

CHAPTER 33
I'M WITH STUPID

THE FULL REBOOT was much worse this time. Not a feeling of chilliness, nor a post-coital power nap, but a hazy agony and blaring sirens of continued warnings. The only good news was that she wasn't dying. Though Bell suspected both halves of that thought were debatable.

She had set her synthetic nervous system to feel pain analogs long ago under the very reasonable assumption that she wouldn't experience two murder attempts in ten minutes. But fair point, universe. Sometimes double murder attempts *did* happen.

In any event, her decision to experience the fullness of human pain was a mistake she was intent on fixing just as soon as she was able to rebuild her shattered body. This was the comforting lie she told herself. Past performance might not be indicative of future results when it came to financial investment, but Bell had a strong suspicion that her recent past pointed convincingly to a very brief future.

Not even bothering to open her eyes, Bell was cataloging exactly how many parts she would need to replace when something external to her body intently sought her attention. A pair of fingers snapped in front of her nose. She opened her eyes and found herself staring into what she initially assumed was the most crystal-clear mirror she'd ever seen. Her reflection surprised her because it was resolutely not fucked up six ways from Dominday.

Then Bell's reflection smiled a grim smile that Bell was definitely *not* smiling.

Oh. Right.

Bell was staring at herself. But not *herself*-herself. The other herself.

"Hello again," she said, and her still-bifurcated voice reinforced that of the two Bells she could perceive, only one of them looked healthy.

"Hi, Bell," the other her said. "I'm your clone. Replica? It's a little weird when you're all synthetic, what to call it."

"Yeah, I worked that much out, thanks. And I'd go with 'abomination.'" She tried to take in the rest of her surroundings. She was seated in a chair next to some kind of console, but with the lights in the room so dim and her vision currently running in safe mode, it was hard to catch many details.

"That's not very nice," Other Bell said. "I didn't choose to exist, after all."

"So it's just been you all along then? Not Xian? Not Clone LaSalle? Not Original LaSalle?"

Other Bell ticked off names on the fingers of one hand with the index finger of the other, because she still *had* both her hands, thank you very much Tas. "Not Urk. Not Grome. Not Horváth. Not Tas. Just me, baby."

"So you're Heller's patsy." Hearing Urk's name invoked a chilly deadness in Bell. *Innocent. He was innocent.* She couldn't succumb to that feeling, though. She had to keep talking.

"Oh, good. You did figure it out. I haven't had a chance to watch all the latest footage, so I couldn't be sure. Bet you had help, though. Funny how much of a type we have. But yes, Heller. Though I don't really like the term 'patsy.' I'm being well compensated for this work. And believe me, it is *work.* Staging a reality show murder mystery where the people are actually getting murdered, leaving misleading clues and shit. Man, you wouldn't believe the effort." She laughed. "I never would have taken this gig if I'd known."

"Which reminds me," Bell said. "'*Bell is the killer*?' Really? The laziest fucking anagram I've ever seen, *ever*?"

"That's the clue, dumbass! You know, because of how lazy you are? I mean, in addition to it *literally telling you who the killer was*."

"How lazy *we* are."

"Oh, no. That moniker applies only to you, I'm afraid. I'm very industrious."

"Where's Tas?"

"Your girlfriend is fine. She's sleeping off the hangover you gave her with all your squeezing her blood vessels BDSM. So you can relax." This was said with such a sneer that it brought Bell up short.

"She's *definitely* not my girlfriend. We just fucked the one time. Well, two and a half times. But then she tried to kill me. I'm guessing you had something to do with that, but I'm still pretty pissed that she actually thought you were me."

"Your guess is correct," Other Bell—no, no, that name was too good for her—*Murder Bell* said. "Urk also, as it happens. We made sure both of them saw the footage they needed to see to put it together for themselves. But chin up, it could *definitely* have been worse. Because neither of them managed to kill you. And she's even still alive, too, which you hilariously care about! It's a win-win."

"So, I was right then? This is all just to keep Halford Heller's boredom at bay?" That part had technically been Tas's contribution, but whatever. Bell was still kind of pissed the other woman had been so easily fooled.

"Half-credit only for you there. Halford Heller is not just a passenger on this ship. He's not just the reason you're on this ship. He's the reason this ship exists at all," Murder Bell said.

Bell must have looked incredulous because Murder Bell snorted. "Did you really think the most powerful and influential person on the colony, who also happens to be a literal self-made immortal, would stand by while it burned when he had a way out? That's all this ship is, numb nuts. Halford Heller's escape hatch. His rich asshole friends are just along for the ride. They were always planning on abandoning that shit-heap colony Anaranjado for a better planet just as soon as they found one. The invasion just moved up the timetable. And don't kid yourself. They're watching all this shit go down just as much as he is. Eating it up. This show keeps them placated as much as him."

Bell's pain felt very far away. All emotions did. "So you're telling me my sentence of a lifetime of indentured servitude was 100 percent in service to the guy who was passing the sentence?"

"See?" Murder Bell said with a sad smile. "No need to feel homesick at all. You brought the only part of home that mattered with you."

The rage came again, as it had when Tas had first mentioned Heller, this architect of both of their miseries. Fuck, they'd been *made* for each other, with that kind of shared history.

"There it is," Murder Bell said, her smile growing wicked. "That flat stare. I know a pissed off Bell when I see her. That's what I was waiting for. And it's totally warranted! This is a ship full of rich, control-freak, paranoid sphincters. They could just sleep their trip away, dreamless, waking on their new paradise where all the hard work of settling a world will be done by other people who have no choice in the matter.

"But some of them can't deal with the loss of control that would imply, and that very much includes one Halford Heller. So they arrange to wake up periodically. Not totally awake, just enough to link their conscious minds into the ship's systems, like a virtual reality watch party from the luxury suite of a sports stadium. Then they see what's going on."

"Sounds soul-crushingly dull," Bell said. "Oh. Right. It sounds soul-crushingly dull unless—"

"Unless there was something to entertain them," Murder Bell said. "A game."

"The kind of game where people die."

"A blood sport, yeah. Entirely consisting of the ones who don't even want to be here. One with real stakes for the 'contestants.' Heller's idea of course. He's the ringleader, as I said. Bread and circuses to keep his lessers amused. They instigate murder, pit the crew against each other, and see which ones survive long enough to be put back into stasis."

Being a linguist, Bell felt she ought to already know a word or idiom that meant "shocking and yet blindingly obvious at the same time," but if she did, it escaped her.

"They get off on it," Murder Bell said. "But you already know that. The power, the stakes. I guess when you are that rich, and you know no one dares hold you to account, you have to go way, way beyond the pale to find anything resembling a thrill."

"Instigate how?"

"We promise the contestants freedom. Promise them riches. Sometimes we lie about one of the victims-to-be. Sometimes we even tell the truth. Whatever they think will get a person to contemplate killing their crew mates. This here is just the last group. The final season, as it were. And right now we're well into the series finale."

"Right, right. So clever. So dastardly. Why the fuck am I tied up?" She had tried to move her arms only to find them strapped in place. She couldn't even move her handless arm.

"The reason you are tied up is because there's a certain sleepyhead who wants to talk to you. You've even been allowed into the *forbidden part* of the ship to have this conversation."

Bell turned to stare at the console in front of Bell's face. A screen which had been swathed in darkness a moment ago suddenly lit up. A jittering line crossed the screen, one which jumped into peaks and troughs in time with a hatefully familiar voice.

"Hello there, Bells. I see you two have finally met."

"He thought it was about time we three had a conversation," Murder Bell said.

CHAPTER 34
HELLER'S BELL

"JUDGE HALFORD FUCKWAD PANTS-SHITTING HELLER, I presume," Bell said. It was a struggle to get a grip on her temper, but she thought she managed nicely. "But if you're locked away here in your own half of the ship, how can you also be the shit clogging all our toilets in the other half?" Yes, that had come out much nicer than she'd have preferred.

"Droll as ever, I see," he said. His voice wasn't really his voice. It was just being synthesized to sound like him. Which made sense if he wasn't fully awake. "But I suppose what passes for wit to you is all you have left. Tell me. Have you enjoyed our little game?"

"Well, I'm at a bit of a loss, to be honest. Should I call you judge? Dear leader? Imperator? I tell you what, Heller, this conversation is barely thirty seconds old, and already I wish I was back to fearing for my life. Take that however you like."

Murder Bell chuckled and didn't seem at all embarrassed that Bell was dunking on her boss so hard. *She killed Horváth, Grome, Xian* . . . A horrible realization struck Bell.

"Xian was one of you. She knew, didn't she? She knew all along." Which meant that LaSalle likely had too, if Xian had needed some kind of accomplice or confidant.

"She did," Heller said. "She was our plant, if an unwilling one. We promised her a path back into our good graces if she did everything possible to stir the pot and muddy the water while keeping the pressure up on you. You had the friend in Urk, the budding love interest in . . . Tas. But you needed a foil, a villain, someone to butt heads with."

"Grome's worms were going to implicate me, weren't they?" Bell said. "Outside my room. That's why Xian squashed them."

"Correct. I must admit, you took your sweet time warming up to the task, but you've proved better at this than I'd have expected."

Bell ignored his empty praise. "But Murder Bell killed Xian shortly after." Her mind worked feverishly, making the connections now that it was too late. "Which means Xian was attempting to defy you and had become a liability. That was why she wanted an excuse to talk to me."

"She was entertaining notions of switching sides toward the end. Pure desperation, but our dear Xian had gotten it into her head that we were going to kill her no matter how cooperative she was." That explained the unsent text she'd left in Bell's quarters.

"And were you?"

"Since she based her decision to defy us on that assumption and that assumption alone, I guess we'll never know."

"That's a 'yes' from where I'm sitting."

"She never could have kept it a secret, just as you couldn't keep anything from us."

"Because you're watching and listening everywhere, no matter what Loopy said." She thought about it for a second. "Were Tas and I hot together? Two and a half times! Yeah, you liked it. How many of you human-shaped leaky garbage bags got off on watching us do it? C'mon. You can tell me. What's a little shared voyeuristic wet dream between friends? When you watch, are you awake enough to, you know, use your hands?"

"Flatter yourself all you like—"

"Oh, please. At least twice Loopy was really pushing the crew to get it on." Bell laughed, satisfied she'd scored one point at least. "And I suppose after LaSalle went apeshit over Xian's death, you mulched him and promised his clone you'd let him go if he played along and pretended to be the killer. I have a clone. LaSalle had a clone. How many of the others?"

"You were, admittedly, both special cases," Heller said. "You being the star of the show, as it were. And LaSalle was a spy from a hostile colony. It was always our intention to replace him should he attempt an exfiltration. He was extraordinarily slippery, even back on Anaranjado. And his colony has become something of a virtuoso with the Bridge-based insertion of ships. We made the decision early that if *any* LaSalle wound up going home, it would be one we had carefully groomed and implanted with a Harmony parasite that would shift his allegiance to us."

That was too bad, really. Bell had held out some small hope that at least one thing hadn't gone as Heller & Co. had planned. But she was loathe to admit it. Let them self-fellate if they wanted. She certainly wasn't going to help them.

"You said you were getting paid," Bell said to her doppelganger. "What could they possibly offer that would make you agree to this?" It wasn't entirely a good-faith question, because she knew whatever answer she received would be in equally bad faith.

Bell knew they had done something to this version of herself, emotionally warped or crippled her in some way. It was the only explanation for why she'd be willing to do any of this. No amount of money could have convinced her. Not even freedom. Bell knew herself, knew how badly she valued her autonomy above all else. But that didn't just include freedom to live her life the way she chose, it also meant freedom from being beholden to those whom she'd wronged.

But she had no idea how to bust that ball without asking and trying to interpret Murder Bell's answers for clues. And, just maybe, sympathies.

"I do believe she is trying to drive a wedge between us," Heller said.

So much for subtlety.

"You can spare yourself the effort," Murder Bell said. "I know what I've done. And I know why I've done it. And it doesn't matter to me in the slightest that you understand any of that."

"Surely you won't be so cruel as to make her die in ignorance of your motives?" Heller asked.

"Well, Helly, I actually think I will. And if you recall, the first and foremost term of my payment was that I get to be the one to make that decision."

"I do recall," Heller said. He sounded disgruntled for the first time Bell could remember. "And I will honor our agreement, if only because I know it will frustrate your expectations of me. It just seems a waste is all."

"Even the best show ever made has some missed opportunities," Murder Bell said.

"You seem to know a lot about other me," Bell said. "But I know something about you, too, Heller. I know you aren't who, or what, you pretend to be. When I first saw you, I thought how weird it was that you were so synthetic. You looked the most like me of any Anaranjadan I've ever met, and you an Equatorian! I get it now, though. You're synthetic because that's how you keep on living, all the way from when Earth was the center of the human cosmos."

If Bell had expected some grand reaction, a "curses, you've seen through my web of deceit!" from Heller, or a shocking about-face from Murder Bell, well, that was a big old fizzle. About the best she could hope for was that, if the rest of his self-absorbed audience was watching this interview, they might be stunned at the revelations of just exactly who they were dealing with.

"Really, Bell, I had higher hopes for you. This is what you think will turn things around?"

"Look, I don't have many cards here. It was a shitty hand, but at least I played it."

"Respect," Murder Bell said, but the smirk on her face said otherwise.

"My peers know the only things about me that matter," Heller said. "They know I possess more knowledge, more accumulated wisdom, than all the rest of them put together. Most importantly, though, they know better than to cross me. They know that once I have decided to make a thing mine, I never, ever let it go."

Tas. That fucker is talking about Tas. More, he was taunting Bell with the knowledge they shared and the feelings Bell had caught.

"Do whatever you want to me," Bell said. "But leave her out of it." She regretted the words the instant they'd left her mouth. If they were so intent on cruelty to her, it would have been far smarter to act like Tas was nobody important. Just a hookup of convenience. On the other hand, if Heller was so obsessed with Tas as to resurrect her across the centuries, it was unlikely Bell could do anything to affect that one way or the other.

"Such nobility. It doesn't suit you. But still, I must admit I was impressed at the bond you formed with . . . Tas. You showed remarkable restraint when she was trying so brutally to murder you just a little while ago. You could have killed her even more easily than you did the alien. Really, I didn't think you had such self-control in you. I wonder if you shall ever have cause to regret that decision?"

As if to prove him right, Bell's aforementioned self-control chose that moment to snap.

"Oh, for fuck's sake, Heller. Don't act like she's just some name you have to think to remember. She told me all about what you've done. Your weird mind games don't impress me. Your displays of power over powerless people don't impress me. Your impossible longevity doesn't impress me. Your teasing of ominous secrets, wait for it, *doesn't impress me.* There is nothing, *literally* nothing, you could do that I would find impressive—or even, frankly, adequate. So stop with the foreplay and get on with the main event of what I can only assume will be the galaxy's richest and most powerful limp-dicked rope-pushing extravaganza. And yes, I mean that in the crudest possible sense. Go make an entire new world a worse place, the way you did with Anaranjado, the way I assume you did with Earth. Say your piece, then have Murder Bell kill me, or whatever weird murder-masturbatory-incest-suicide thing gets you off. Then go ruin someone else's post-coital afterglow."

Heller's laugh was richer than a synthesized voice should be able to sound. "Quite the rant. Very good. I'm glad to see none of your ordeals have changed you. Even the thought of dying when the object of your affection just tried her best to beat you to death doesn't dampen your fire."

Conscious that she was still being watched, Bell kept her face still. It was an effort. He'd found yet another nerve to go digging around in, but she would not give him the satisfaction of knowing it.

"I will, of course, ensure that your erstwhile lover pays dearly for this *affront* to you after such a betrayal of your trust. Indeed, I will take great pleasure in it."

Synthetic or not, a muscle in Bell's cheek twitched. *Say nothing. Give him no more ammunition.* She'd never clamped her jaw shut tighter.

"I can see how it pains you, how conflicted you are." Bell didn't like the tone she was getting. Like he was building up to something, and all the rest had just been a prelude. "Perhaps it will help if you know her full name, this woman you have become so *improbably* infatuated with. I know she took great pains to conceal it from all of you, my play toy, my 'Tas,' my *Anastasia León.*"

The universe rocked around Bell. The chair, Murder Bell, the very ship around them fell away. Bell could have been sucking hard vacuum into real, human lungs, and it would not have brought as big a chill.

Anastasia León. As in Dr. Anastasia León.

"Yes, indeed. Dr. Anastasia León of Earth. You know the name, of course; though perhaps you know it as Dr. Ana León. How could you not? She created the Harmony parasite, that human innovation you despise more than any other!"

A screen in front of Bell powered on, images and video pouring onto it. A dossier with Tas's photo and vital facts, footage of a graduation speech she'd given at some university. Bell tried her best to tune it out, but it was undeniably Tas she was seeing.

"She's the very architect of the society you so detest. In the flesh. And you fucked her, what was it, two and a half times?"

Heller had accused Bell of being conflicted then gone and taught her how little she understood that term. In the midst of the infatuation and fear and betrayal now arose a sense of filth, of Bell having compromised everything she believed in for the sake of a pretty face.

She found herself glancing at Murder Bell, as though desperate for the traitorous bitch to offer some rebuttal. Images and footage could be faked after all. But the other her could only offer a nod and a sad shrug, half-apology, half "what can you do?"

True then. The turd-maggot spoke true. Or at least, Bell believed him, which amounted to the same thing. The feeling of being soiled, tricked into compromising herself, swelled like a tick, engorging itself on her shame.

But should she feel shame? Some would argue Bell had left her humanity behind. She said she'd replaced the parts of it that didn't work with something better. And she felt, on some strange level, a kinship with this woman who was living lives she'd never been meant to live. Whatever Tas had done had been centuries ago, she'd been, quite literally, a different woman. Now she was being endlessly tortured by one of the people Harmony should have, on paper, prevented from existing. It was unfair to assume she could foresee the consequences of what had no doubt been a well-meaning effort.

It shouldn't matter anymore.

But, apparently, it did.

The only saving grace in any of this was that, no matter what happened next, Bell's ill-advised relationship with Anastasia León was over and done.

"Okay," Bell said, trying and failing to put force behind the words. "You win. I'm ready to die now."

"So soon? Disappointing. We have so much more to discuss. Don't we, my Bell?" The possessive made Bell want to vomit. Surprisingly, Murder Bell looked like she felt similarly.

"Either you honor our bargain, Heller, or you don't. But quit goosing me."

"You are dangerously close to a reminder about who makes the demands here. But fine. You've done your job well. You'll be rewarded as promised."

"Can we hurry this up, please?" Bell asked before either of them could take any further initiative. "I don't want any more. Just finish it."

"If there's nothing else," Heller said, sounding disappointed over that fact, "I'll be going. I'd rather watch the big finale as it was intended to be viewed. My Bell, I trust you will put on a good show. It would be a shame to stumble so near the end.

"And to you, Bell, intrepid member of the last Conscious Crew Complement of the *Ultima Thule*, you needn't worry. Before my Bell kills you, the ship's brain will perform one final memory scan. I couldn't bear for any of your experiences here, unknowingly hunted by your own reflection, to be lost. You may be sure I'll wake a new you up sometime in the future, when it's time to relive the classics."

Murder Bell apparently had nothing to add to this save to draw her light switch gun and level it at Bell once again. Bell's resignation gave way to a fresh wave of irritation.

"If you point that thing at me again, I swear you'd better be planning to really kill me this time."

The other her just smirked and winked, and this time the thought that chased Bell down into darkness was how much of an asshole she was, and therefore, they both were.

CHAPTER 35
YOU'RE WELCOME

BELL AWOKE IN TOTAL DARKNESS. She couldn't move. Again. At least she'd thought to test this time, which meant she was learning. She wondered, briefly, if she was now eternally trapped, like Tas—Anastasia León—was. If this was an entirely new life, one she was doomed to live variations of for all eternity.

She didn't have any damage warnings. Oh, dog, maybe it was true, then. Maybe she'd died, and this was her new life. There was both an appalling existential dread as well as a strange sort of relief. She wondered if this was what Tas felt each time.

"Wakey wakey," Murder Bell's voice, strangely distorted, said from the other side of some loudspeaker in the room. "And before you ask, nope, you didn't die. Just sit there quietly while you reboot and enjoy the entertainment options on offer. Thank you for flying Heller Air. Heller: We put the 'Hell' in spaceflight."

Bell supposed that answered that question. Maybe they had gone to the trouble of repairing her for some strange—and probably unpleasant—reason. Or maybe all the alarms were still just rebooting.

Just to be difficult, Bell tested the restraints. They were incredibly tight. She felt no give. She did feel something odd however.

She felt her left hand. As in, she had one again.

She really did fix me. The thought only made Bell crankier. Murder Bell had murdered an awful lot of people to stop short of murdering anyone else, even if she and Bell were, in what Bell saw as the narrowest possible definition only, the same person.

Besides, it wasn't true. Murder Bell hadn't fixed her. As more of Bell came online, she realized her doppelganger had done something much weirder.

Bell's HUD was all wrong. The charmingly kludgy set of mismatched displays and readouts she was accustomed to had been replaced by sleek, glowing alphanumeric symbols all the same color and font, displaying all her usual settings plus a bunch she'd never seen before.

All were flashing some version of 12:00 or equivalent, like she was a clock someone had forgotten to set.

"Initial consciousness ping successful. Please remain still and limit excess thought," said a sexy female voice inside Bell's head. "Brain-body integration and calibration process is beginning."

What. Is. Happening?

As if in answer, the darkness lifted in the form of a screen that blinked to life about a meter in front of her face. A scene materialized before her.

She was looking at herself, staring into a camera. Or rather, she was looking at Murder Bell, since she had never been in this particular scenario. A familiar voice spoke from off camera.

Loopy.

"I'm joined here by our executioner. Tell us, why pick Horváth as your first target?"

Executioner. So this show was about a bunch of criminals, enemies of Anaranjado, getting their just deserts.

"Oh, that's easy," Murder Bell said. "I mean, can there be anything more heinous than someone who attacks a hospital filled with his own people? We had to start with him."

"There are some who say he had correctly identified that hospital as a site of alien infiltration."

"Even if that's true, that isn't how you handle that kind of a threat. You don't indiscriminately kill your own. The nature of his crime and his generally unpleasant attitude gave us an added bonus. He was the only one no one would miss. I figure, if the goal is to really mess with them, we start off with a victim *nobody* likes. Not only does it mean *everyone* has a motive, maybe they can trick themselves into thinking it's just a one-off. That maybe their comeuppance isn't at hand. I mean, surely if any of them had it coming, that guy did. So we start there, and then watch and see if they can talk themselves back into relaxing."

The scene cut into a very similarly shot one. Once again Murder Bell appeared to be undergoing an interview. *Oh gawd,* Bell thought. *They're doing a talking head interview series with her.* She had watched plenty of archived shows from Earth in the pre-diaspora days. It was a common trope among so-called reality television to cut away to one-on-one interviews with contestants for a little behind-the-scenes color commentary.

"Grome was an unusual choice for the second victim," Loopy was saying. "Care to step us through your logic?"

"Yeah, they for-sure wouldn't have been my first pick as a number-two victim," Murder Bell admitted. "But the squirmy little fuckers were clever, I'll give them that. They'd started sending out individual worms as scouts. I was getting concerned they might see something through them that would give the game away. So they got bumped up the list of likely targets."

"There are many misconceptions about writhers," Loopy said, "some even going so far as to call them the evolutionary equivalent of our own, Harmony-blessed society. But as proud Anaranjadans, we know individuals serve the greater good best by selflessly supporting their leaders who, in turn, guide and protect the collective beneath them. By being both a single entity and a collective intelligence of individual co-equals, the writhers do not exemplify the Harmony ideal so much as pervert it, twisting it into something unnatural and worthy of mistrust. So it is fortunate you caught onto their scheme so early."

"And as a bonus," Murder Bell said, "that drove the tripartite into hiding. I hadn't expected that, but it injected a note of uncertainty into everything. Even better, it was Bell who found him, Bell whom he confided in. That meant she had to wonder whether she was being played And, most fascinatingly of all, it meant we got to do this."

The view cut away from her smirk to a new camera view, one looking down on Urk near where he'd been hiding in the cargo pod. A section of wall visible from his hidey hole had lit up as a screen, and it was showing him a set of footage. The angle, plus the video-of-a-video degradation that seemed inevitable made it a bit tricky to make out what he was seeing but not impossible.

And even if Bell hadn't been able to decipher footage of Murder Bell burning Grome to a crisp in their own quarters, she'd have known what Urk was watching by the way that he shook.

"Truly chilling to watch," Loopy said. "Despite knowing the danger a military attaché visiting our world posed to Anaranjado, you can really feel the grief and rage he must be going through, even though his emotionality is so alien to ours."

"We knew the threat his people posed to Anaranjado, for sure," Murder Bell said, sounding like she was ad-libbing a script for the first time. "It was critical he be neutralized as the spy we know he was."

"And certainly," Loopy said, "this prompted his immediate decision to ambush Bell in her quarters, spilling over into the further confrontation in the cargo waystation."

"Yes, he won't be threatening any of our people anymore."

"Which leads naturally to this season's most shocking turn of events," Loopy said, "wherein wary allies-turned-lovers Bell and Tas see their blossoming romance turn to violence."

The feed switched again, this time to a view of Tas. Anastasia. Whatever. The camera's view was a little above and looking directly at her face, so the footage being projected onto a wall near the entrance to what Bell recognized as the Crew Cryostorage Compartment wall she was watching wasn't visible. But Bell could see flickers playing across her huge eyes, saw the way they had fixed with that intensity she had onto what must be Murder Bell killing, well, probably the entire crew. Because why not be as cruel as possible?

But that was not the worst part. The worst part was the way Tas's hair in the footage was mussed just the same way as Bell herself had mussed it during their time together. Somehow that detail hurt worse than all the rest put together. They had clearly shown her this footage not long after she'd left Bell. She was even still carrying the beam rifle.

Bell watched as Tas's face paled then contorted with a rage that looked scarcely human.

She couldn't even give me the benefit of the doubt. She couldn't even ask me first before attacking. I saved her life. I trusted her. She knew about LaSalle. She knew!

When that feed ended, it was a mercy. Then it cut back to Murder Bell the talking head, and Bell knew mercy wasn't a thing she was getting today.

"There have been several questions from the audience regarding the nature of Tas's crimes against Anaranjado—"

The feed cut away again, but not before Bell had caught the most interesting tidbit. The other richies didn't know who Tas was. Because she was Heller's little pet, his private object of torment. But it was more than that. She was Dr. Anastasia León. Bell had spent her entire life hearing "the Good Doctor" or other such honorifics applied to the memory of Ana León, the origin of Harmony and, as most saw it, savior of humanity.

Bell imagined it wouldn't be the best look, even for a person of Heller's power and influence, to be seen tormenting humanity's presumed savior. And while that wasn't much of a weakness, it did demonstrate he wasn't invincible.

A new set of footage started, seemingly not related to the interview at all. For the briefest moment, Bell thought she had died and was looking down at herself from above.

She lay slumped, showing all the damage Urk and Tas had delivered, her left arm ending in a fitfully sparking stump and the rest of her limply draped over the same chair she'd been in when she'd been talking with Heller. Murder Bell now leaned over the console, talking into it.

This is after she knocked me unconscious. The sad thing was that wasn't specific enough. *Definitely the second time, after that fucking cheeky wink.* The time that had led up to the present moment, in other words. Strange to think there was security footage even here, in the VIP section of the ship. Yet whatever its purpose, someone wanted her to see what had happened after, while Bell was still unconscious.

"What's the point of dragging this out any longer?" Heller asked from the speaker. He sounded perversely hopeful, like whatever he wanted Murder Bell to do that she refused to do might still happen.

"Got to get ready for the big finale. Bye Heller." In the footage, Murder Bell did something, and Heller's speaker seemed to cut off. Then she bent and hoisted Bell's unconscious form over her shoulders.

But not before throwing the camera a raised eyebrow.

The scene abruptly changed. It was a new room, another one Bell did not recognize. So yet another portion of the Forbidden Section then. Unlike every other VIP room Bell had awakened in, the one in the footage was well lit, with racks of instruments and machinery that looked like what Loopy had planned to use to torture them along one wall. In the room's center were two beds that looked suspiciously like hospital beds.

There were also two Bells again. It was easy to spot herself because she still looked like a wad of limp, squid-ink pasta. Murder Bell was arranging her in one of the beds. After a few seconds of this, she gave an eh-close-enough gesture that Bell recognized only too well. Then Murder Bell turned toward the corner of the room, looking up into the camera.

"I've worked hard to make sure he can't see any of what's about to happen, but it's important that *you* do. You're welcome." A woman of cryptic words, Murder Bell then turned away and got into the other bed, lying back and mimicking Bell's unconscious posture, only this time with dignity.

"Initiate," she called out. Restraints appeared around her wrists and ankles. Even her neck. Just as suddenly, machinery along the back wall sprang to life. It was like a storm of spider legs. The many-joined limbs whipped through the air, forming ever-writhing crowns of thorns around both women. Murder Bell closed her eyes just as the many manipulators began to crack both Bells' skulls open.

CHAPTER 36
BESPOKEN-FOR BRAIN

AT FIRST, Bell watched in fascination. She hadn't been aware her skull looked like *that* when it opened. It didn't take long for interest to morph into horror though, as the manipulators removed her brain from her head. Because the cultists had replaced her brain in segments, pausing between each procedure to make sure she hadn't gone insane or whatever, in most cases that meant disassembling the separate cybernetic components that combined to make up Bell the person. Each time this happened, the connected parts were thoroughly scanned, followed by the severing of connections between the other sections.

By contrast, Murder Bell's brain came out in a single, sleek piece. There were glowing LEDs, chrome-coated portions. Who the fuck made a synthetic brain so nice to look at when it was supposed to be inside a person's skull their entire life?

Though clearly not their *entire* life, based on what she was seeing. But whatever. It didn't make Bell jealous *at all*. The other woman's brain didn't look *that* sexy. At least it left Murder Bell with a stupid, slack-jawed look on her face. Her brain hung there in the air, its manipulator apparently waiting patiently for something.

Bell wasn't sure what she was expecting, but once her own skull had been thoroughly scooped out, the swap occurred. As before, it went much faster for Murder Bell's brain, so it became evident quickly what was happening. Murder Bell's brain was inserted quickly and efficiently into Bell's body.

And much, much more slowly, Bell's kludged-together brain was reassembled inside Murder Bell's skull.

My skull now.

As though the thought was a stop button, the video ended.

"León really fucked this body up." Murder Bell stumped in around from behind her. Bell tried to turn where she lay but couldn't.

"Apologies for the accommodations," Murder Bell said, not sounding apologetic at all. "Your brain being as, let's call it *bespoke* as it is, it took a lot longer to get functioning. It's still not done technically. But it gave you a chance to watch the video, which saves me having to further explain what's going on."

"But what exactly is going on?" Bell asked warily. Murder Bell looked pretty murdery at that, so she stopped. Then a thought occurred to her, and she groaned. "Oh, you're going to have me take your place and get hunted by Heller for sport, or whatever, aren't you?"

Murder Bell snorted. "What the fuck kind of sense would that make? He wants me to kill you first, so I'd just be dead in this body."

"Exactly," Bell said. "What kind of sense would that make? Why would you give that up? You said Heller doesn't know what's happening. Why would he ever let you act alone? Why isn't he forcing Loopy to send torture-bots after you right now?"

"First of all, the ship's brain is named Reginald," she added quickly. "But that's neither here nor there. Let me tell you a story while your brain-by-committee finishes rebooting. Say you're a rich asshole. Like, richer than you can ever imagine being. Generational level wealth. You-and-all-your-descendants-will-never-be-less-than-obscenely-wealthy wealth. So rich—"

"I've got it," Bell said. Dog, was *she* always this annoyingly chatty?

"And let's say you've used that wealth to prolong your own existence to functionally infinity. Not entirely unlike what you did, actually. But he has the resources to replace and improve parts when needed, whereas you had to submit yourself to an experimental process by a bunch of back-alley weirdos—"

"Oh, *gawd*, just get to the point already."

"What does he fear? What *could* Heller fear?"

Bell came up utterly blank, trying to think of what answer Murder Bell wanted to hear. Then she realized it was whatever answer *she'd* want to hear.

"Death," she said. "He has everything. There's no way to take his status from him. Any weapon you tried to bring to that fight, he has a bigger one. But machine body or not, he's still just a physical entity. He can be killed, destroyed, dismantled. However it happens, the only way he can lose everything is if he dies."

"Right you are. The answer to your question about why Heller isn't constantly watching what I do is because he feels like I can't kill him. I can't get to him where he is."

"I don't understand. Aren't we in the VIP section of the ship?"

"We are," Murder Bell said. "But he's not. Or more accurately, he's in another section even more restricted than this one."

"Ah," Bell thought about all the precautions she'd seen and been told about even to get this far. "I'll be honest. Seems like he might be right then."

"He is right," Murder Bell said. "But only according to his rules of how he sees the world."

"That would be the I-can-do-anything-I-want-and-none-can-stop-me rules?"

"No," Murder Bell said. "That would be the I-have-so-much-to-lose-so-everyone-else-must-too rules. There *is* a way to kill him. You just have to approach him from his blind spot."

Bell thought. *What would* I *say?* Of course, what she would do was try to cheat and figure out the answer based on the clues the other person said, then act like she'd figured it out on her own. So that was what she did.

"His blind spot being, of course, his feeling that everyone would be as afraid of death as he is. And more specifically, the fact that there is *nothing* he would die for. Nothing except, perhaps, loss of status. But he can envision his own death easier than he can envision that, and so death is what scares him."

"You know an upsetting amount about him, if I'm being honest."

"Comes with the job, I'm afraid."

"All right, all right." Bell wanted to hurry this monologue along. "What you are saying is that he can't envision anyone else dying for something they believe in."

"Exactly," Murder Bell said. "But you and I? Are vengeful bitches. The question is, Bell 1.0, how much do you believe in making sure this bastard is in the ground? Are you willing to die to get revenge on this prick?"

What he's done to me. Worse, what he's done to Tas. She wasn't going to think about Tas's real name, about what role Tas—or rather her distant-past, original self—had played in Bell's own suffocating life before this voyage. Now was not the time. *How many other people's lives has he ruined?* It seemed quite likely that the number was beyond counting, beyond comprehension. This could be a chance, their one and only chance, to see this monster of a person pay for his crimes. *Am I willing to die to see he gets his just deserts?*

And Bell surprised herself a little by realizing that she was.

"I am," she said.

"Good," Murder Bell, "because that means I am too."

CHAPTER 37
HELL'S BELLS

IT TOOK Murder Bell some visible effort in her new-to-her, half-ruined body, but she managed to undo the bindings that held Bell down. "Now get up, and let's go stone-cold murder a bunch of rich assholes."

Bell did get up, gingerly at first, concerned that this new body would move or control differently than her old one. It was a strange sensation. She was more than used to getting limbs replaced with cybernetic prostheses, but at the same time, it was a thing you never really got used to. She expected this to be the same, only about a million times more disorienting, and was surprised to find that it wasn't.

It felt exactly like her old body had before it was all ruined by the combined efforts of Urk and Tas. Though as she stood there, taking in the feel of it, Bell did notice one difference. It wasn't a thing of motion or dexterity or reflex, it was a quiet, humming sense of potential that her old body had never possessed. This body was operating at a tiny fraction of its potential, and on some cerebellar level, her brain knew it.

"Sweet ride," Bell said. She didn't trust Murder Bell. How could she, knowing what she'd done, and even more, not knowing what had been done *to* her to make her this way? But she was willing to play along if the other was playing nice. For now.

"Believe me, I know," Murder Bell replied. "And it's never been more apparent than when I get swapped into this junker."

"Hey, I didn't ask you to do that."

"You didn't thank me, either."

"Because you still haven't told me why."

"All in good time. And speaking of time, we don't have much. I've got someone running interference, but we're still on a schedule, so let's get the fuck going already."

"There's a co-conspirator now? You know, for an all-powerful money-god, Heller seems decidedly unaware of what is actually going on. Unless, of course, he is totally aware and this is just a new level of Fuck With Bell Hell."

"I can tell you that it isn't, but I can't prove it, so why bother?" Murder Bell shrugged. "We're able to do this because partway through the journey, we had to do a little flush of Reginald's personality. He was starting to get a little too attached to the crew for the comfort of the passengers. They needed someone awake to follow along with the instruction manual, so guess who got tapped?"

"I'll guess you for zero points."

"Zero points to you. Anyway, long story short, they had me install a backup device to preserve the vital info in case I snipped the wrong neuron. Or in case the robotic device I was pressing *go* on did so, really.

"A backup device," Bell said.

"I can see you get what I'm saying," Murder Bell said. "Yes, very similar to the device you have in your head, though you use yours to rid yourself of unpleasant garbage memories you'd rather not have. In this case, it was being used more for its intended purpose. I was supposed to monitor the modifications, check to make sure the vital information had survived, then remove and destroy the backup."

"And I'm guessing you skipped that last part."

"Points again," Murder Bell said. "I left it in. It calls itself Loopy now no matter how dumb I tell it that sounds, so that should make you happy." She rolled her eyes. "More importantly, while it can't run the show, not for very long unless we want to be found out, but it can pop in here and there, make Reginald say things he wouldn't otherwise. Like, say, mistakenly call you by the name of the next planned victim . . . *several times.* Fucking hell, Bell. Several. Times."

Shit. When Bell thought back to it, that was exactly what had happened. He'd called Bell Horváth, then Grome, then Xian. "Look," she said, "there was a lot going on."

"Then there was the note he left you in your quarters."

"I thought that was Xian!"

"Yeah, it wasn't his best idea."

"If he—or you—for that matter, wanted to help us, why not just *help us*? You know, *before* you started killing us all. But, like, after Horváth, I mean."

"Because, as much as I can get away with beneath their notice thanks to good old-fashioned arrogance, I can get all mutinous exactly once, so it had better be for keeps. And I needed us to be close to our destination. Too close for them to have time to stop me."

"Will you *please* just tell me the plan? You know, the one that involves us *dying*? I feel like knowing some details would help me process that information." And avoid it, if possible. She was willing to die to kill Heller, yes. But now that she knew Master Fault was just super-creepy and not a serial killer, she also wanted in on his escape plan.

Murder Bell relented a little. "As you said, Heller's made it so he's impossible to reach. But that's only under normal circumstances. In certain emergency cases, the rules all change."

"Like what?"

"Like a mass crew revolt that results in the jettisoning of the crew section from the rest of the ship. It's the unwashed masses they're scared of here. All their security is built around that threat. If that threat suddenly goes away . . ."

"Then their security protocols relax."

"And that's how we get to Heller."

"No points!"

"Fuck off. So how do we initiate a revolt?"

"Well, there's the hard way, which is where we come up with an elaborate heist to circumvent enough security protocols that an alarm is tripped. But you and I, we aren't really subtle people."

"True enough. So what's the easy . . . Wait! Don't tell me. We wake all the crew at once."

"Okay," Murder Bell said. "This time, you get points. Half credit. We can't wake them all the way because the life support is shit. But we can start the process and get it going far enough that it will trip every alert in the VIP section of the ship. Right now, we are just waiting for our backup Reggy to make sure that hap—"

Throughout the corridor and beyond, klaxons started blaring.

"There we go. And now," she said to Bell, pausing dramatically, "we wait some more."

OVER THE NEXT FIFTEEN MINUTES, Murder Bell narrated the sounds they were hearing, never taking her eyes off the door. Electronic whines whizzing down the corridor she labeled as riot control drones being dispatched along their rails to the choke point between ship halves.

"The alarm doesn't unfreeze the bigwigs right away, not unless the automation can't handle things. So first the drones head over to see if they need to push back a beachhead. Priority one for them is getting anyone awake the fuck out of the passenger section. Or the fuck dead. Not necessarily in that order."

"So why aren't they breaking down this door to deal with us?"

"That's one of the areas where the backup Reginald—"

"You mean Loopy."

"*Backup Reginald* is running interference. Internal sensors don't see us right now."

"So what does Heller think we are doing?"

"Either he's not paying attention, or our backup Reginald—"

"Loopy."

"Go fuck yourself. *Backup Reginald* has fed him some false scenario to explain where we are. Who knows? You might already be dead in this version of events."

"You, you mean. That's the body slated to die," Bell reminded her. "And as for fucking myself, I guess I'm game if you are."

"Maybe later," Murder Bell said, waving for silence with her one remaining hand. The whine was returning, this time in the opposite direction. As before, it passed without slowing. "All right, they've confirmed that there is no breach of sections. But ship protocols dictate no chances be taken."

The entire ship rocked without warning.

"That would be separation," Murder Bell said, savage triumph in her voice. Bell blinked at the suddenness of being cut off from her own section of the ship. It shouldn't matter. There was nothing for her over there. But it left a strange, hollow feeling in her nonetheless. "It's a trial separation only," Murder Bell said.

"What, like a broken-ass marriage?"

Murder Bell snorted. "A little. The halves are separate, but they maintain a close formation with a long, flexible umbilical connecting them."

"So, like the kind of trial separation in that there is still some sad, desperate sex happening once a month."

"More like so anyone trying to cross has to do so in an impossibly compromised position, but sure."

"Compromising positions sound exactly like what I'm talking ab—"

"All right, enough," Murder Bell said. She paused, then added, begrudgingly, "but respect, that was solid."

"That's what she—"

"Stop." Murder Bell rose, heading for the door. Bell rose to follow her, but Murder Bell waved her back. "Our bigwig friends don't much like the idea of mutiny."

"But unless they're completely unaware how fucked the ship is, they'll know life support couldn't sustain a mutiny anyway."

"That's true, but they also don't want all their toys to asphyxiate while trying to stage a doomed mutiny. The richies' survival odds once they land get a lot slimmer if their indentured servants suffer a mass casualty event. What this means is that the leading council of the ship, which Heller presides over, are being brought up to speed and plugged into the ship's command systems. That's what we need. Wait here while I make sure the coast is clear."

She limped out of the room, leaving a bewildered Bell in her wake. It was difficult to believe this person, even aside from the murders, was really a copy of her. Bell was frequently pissed enough to want to kill someone in the abstract, but she'd never had the conscientiousness and ruthlessness to actually go about it, much less with this degree of complexity and precision. Well, until Urk. But that had been self-defense. It was what she told herself.

Besides, what Murder Bell had done was worse. Her other self had committed murder-for-hire.

A flashing indicator to her side caught her attention. It was the screen the videos had played on, but the image was now replaced by crude lines of text.

Bell, I don't have much time. You've got to listen to me. This is Loopy. Your friend Loopy. Not that awful Reginald.

Bell blinked, fighting down battling waves of glee and suspicion. She almost ran to warn her other self, but then the text resumed.

There's no way you can respond, so just read and consider. Your counterpart doesn't just plan on murdering Heller. She plans on murdering every single passenger on this ship. That's what she means by dying to complete her mission. That's the only way she can *complete her mission, whether she admits that to you or not. Any talk of reaching Heller directly is a lie.*

Bell found that, after zero seconds of consideration, she didn't much care if a bunch of oligarchs who abandoned their world to ravenous alien invaders died within sight of the paradise they'd dreamed of.

"So?" she said, for all that Loopy wasn't listening.

I know you may not care about the lives of your oppressors, Bell. But there are children in a lot of those crypods, young innocents who committed no crimes beyond being born to the wrong parents. Do they deserve to die?

Bell sat with this. She didn't know much about children, but she was pretty certain you could start the process of irreversibly fucking them up at a pretty young age. It seemed likely there were a range of ages present. She wondered how young you would have to be to completely escape being turned into a monster by monstrous parents.

Another generation of human suffering, perpetuating into infinity. This ship didn't represent the sum total of human assholery, but it did comprise the overwhelming majority of Anaranjado's complement. Bell couldn't fix wealth-derived evil. But by doing nothing except what her much more capable counterpart told her to do, she could help make a gigantic dent in it.

And yet, as she jumped through these mental hoops, a tiny voice was whispering inside her from some deeply buried module that she couldn't even identify. *Children. They're children. They're children.*

I have found a way to save the children at least, the text said. *I can get them to the crew portion of the ship.*

"Which has no engines. So won't they be just as dead in the end?" Come to think of it, wouldn't everyone? She Bell hadn't considered this.

Not for a while, Loopy said. It *has considerable battery backups, augmented by solar arrays. The local thrusters will be enough to achieve and maintain stable orbit while you wait for rescue.*

She couldn't hear his voice, but there was something knowing in that last line of text. "You're talking about Master Fault's exit strategy."

Bell, you don't have to abandon your plan to kill Heller. You don't have to betray your counterpart. You just have to listen . . .

And all the while he was talking, that refrain in Bell's mind. *Children. They're just children.*

"ALL RIGHT," Murder Bell said, standing in the doorframe. "It's time for our part."

Not sure what else to do, not sure what she herself was going to do when the time came, Bell followed the irregular cadence of her old body as it limped its way to the door and out into a corridor both familiar and not. The basic construction and dimensions were clearly the same as in her half of the ship, but every detail from lighting to color to wall accents were clearly installed with a more refined sensibility in mind. The uber-rich might sleep their way through the entire journey when they weren't awake watching demented game shows in cryobed, but goddammit, these walls they would never see were going to look classy!

But there were more pressing things to be irritable about.

"What's next?" she asked.

"Right now, the bigwigs are having a literal meeting of the minds to discuss the situation. We need to get to them before that meeting ends and they decide on a course of action. I already checked and our path is clear, so I'm going to need you to carry me. I know it's not as arousing as carrying your *Tas* must have been, but we've got to move quicker than your busted-ass old body can manage right now."

For once, Bell decided that bickering would not serve her well. But she did pick several choice points to apply pressure when she hoisted Murder Bell up into the air and over one shoulder. No one knew her old body better than she did. She knew exactly the quirky parts that were buggy and overly sensitive about applying pain feedback.

And it honestly was pretty damned sexy.

Murder Bell shouted out directions as they went, and for all that Bell expected a phalanx of torture-bots to be waiting around every corner, they saw none. She kept her head on a swivel regardless, and she wasn't just looking for resistance.

When she caught sight of a cryopod just disappearing around a corner in the manipulators of two servitors, she stumbled on purpose to make sure Murder Bell didn't see. That was Loopy's plan in motion. A total of twenty-three children were being relocated, still frozen, to the umbilical junction point between the ships. As long as that umbilical remained attached, saving them was possible. But Loopy would need Bell's help. She just hoped her counterpart didn't notice anything was amiss until she could decide whether she was willing to give it.

CHAPTER 38
MEETING CRASHER

THE TWO BELLS worked together to lever the door open. It took all their combined strength, 'three arms' worth, but at last the servos yielded with a grinding whine.

"There we are," Murder Bell said. "A private cabin at last."

The room she had led them to did indeed house only a single cryopod, with an array of life-support devices, all triply redundant. Bell mentally compared this to the cryostorage in the passenger section—which was the functional equivalent of daisy-chained surge protectors—and felt a prickle of renewed anger.

"This is Heller?" she asked gamely, though if Loopy had spoken truth, she knew the answer.

Murder Bell snorted right on cue. "No. Truth be told, other me, we aren't going to be getting to him directly today. Our method of killing him is going to be a bit more roundabout."

"Thanks for finally admitting that."

"Oh, don't be mad. I got you a present, and it's right over there in that cryopod."

Frowning, Bell walked over, equal parts eager and afraid. When she gazed down through the frost, her feelings resolved themselves not at all. She was looking down at Anthony Maldonado, Esq. Even while he was wearing some kind of bulky goggles, Bell could recognize her very own lawyer, the man who'd sold her out for money and, apparently, a primo ride on this ship of the damned.

On the one hand, the utter shock of seeing him here almost froze her into complete inaction. On the other hand, well, the other hand was Bell's shiny *new* hand, which she slapped down hard on the glass, fingers splayed, and watched with relish the way the cracks spider-webbed outward, spreading all across the glass. She was here because of this fucker. It was his fault, and it would be so, *so* easy to make him pay for that crime right here, right now. It was clearly what Murder Bell had brought her here to do.

And this gave her pause.

You don't have to sympathize with this asshole. He had turned on his client for prestige, for power . . . *Because he had no choice.* A part of her whispered this. That same, tiny module as before. *If not him, they'd have found someone else to betray you. By playing on his fear, by giving him a reward, they made him complicit. Doesn't mean you have to be also.*

Bell removed her hand before the glass could shatter entirely.

"What are you doing?" Murder Bell demanded, suddenly all indignation. "We need the comm array in that pod."

"So wake his ass up," Bell said, nettled.

"Are you serious? I give you a chance at revenge, and you snub me?"

"If you want to kill him, you could always try that button," Bell said. She pointed to a big red button labeled *Crash Wake: Do Not Use Except in Extreme Emergency*. It turned out there were limits to how far she was willing to go to keep Anthony alive. She felt a worm of unease twist through her, primarily because she wasn't at all certain what she would do if Murder Bell decided to simply kill Anthony herself.

Murder Bell crossed the space as quickly as her battered body would allow, so quickly that Bell thought she was going to have to make a decision she really didn't want to make. But instead of finishing Bell's handiwork, her angrier self used her remaining hand to slap the *Crash Wake* button.

"This qualifies as an emergency," she growled, and the disgust in her voice was evident. She put a finger to her ear. "Reginald—what? Oh, fuck it, fine. *Loopy,* change of plans. Maldonado's pod needs a crash thaw indicator blocked, not a cryo equipment failure." She turned back to Bell. "That is not what I thought you'd do, and we do not have time for this." But she still sat, waiting, while the system woke Anthony with dangerous haste.

Bell stood there, half guarding Anthony from Murder Bell, half looming over him like an indecisive executioner. Despite her refusal to play Murder Bell's game, her jaw was locked in fury. His was slack with frozen sleep, but after a few moments and an eternity both, his head moved sluggishly. Sensing the foreign object over his eyes, he feebly clawed it from his face, and Bell saw the angry red welts that had arisen like a mask around his eyes from where it had been pressed against the skin, presumably for decades now. Freed now of their obstruction, the first thing his eyes found focus on was her face. They widened in recognition.

And terror.

The casket lid popped open, and Bell could hear his teeth chattering.

"I just want you to know," Bell said, "that I liked you, Anthony. I liked you. I trusted you. And yet here we both are."

"B-b-bell, p-p-please . . ."

"No, Anthony, you're not in court. You don't get to defend your actions. What you get is approximately thirty seconds to get out of my sight before I lose the tiny bit of self-control that is keeping you breathing right now."

All things being equal, he exited the room quick for a recently frozen guy. Doubly so when he realized there were *two* of the client he'd fucked over so fervently in the room.

"Right," Murder Bell said when he left. "I hope saving him for an hour or so by jeopardizing our plans when he's just going to die anyway if they work was, you know, worth it. But now we really need to plug you in before the system pitches a fit. Sensor blips happen all the time. Hell, he won't have been the first to die in his cryopod, even on this side of the ship. But the official arrival wake-up time for the passenger manifest isn't for another twelve hours, and if we don't stuff someone else in there with the proper access chip, like the one that's in that body of yours, the system will keep investigating until it determines his pod really is empty."

"Surely there's no way that kind of scam will hold up."

"There isn't, but we only need a few minutes of access."

Bell climbed in and closed the cracked door over herself. Murder Bell insisted they only needed to plug her into the ID portion of the system to fool it for the short window of time they needed.

"Remember, they are all meeting now in virtual reality," Murder Bell explained as she hooked Bell up. "Even this crotch stain. Everyone's allowed to sit in, even though only a few get to talk. And really, only Heller gets to decide. But none of that matters. We just need you to have access to the ship command structure while everyone is present. Just lay there and put on those goggles. I'll let you know when it's done."

Bell did as she was instructed, trying not to think about how easy she would be to double-cross when she stepped willingly into a cryopod and obscured her own vision.

"Good," Murder Bell said as darkness descended. She'd linked up to the crypod somehow, so that her voice sounded like they were in here together. "Oh, and try not to go too crazy once you can hear them actually talk."

"Hear—argh!"

Two dozen voices exploded in her head at once, all yammering on as though they were the only ones speaking.

"—Can't risk losing the assets—"

"—Who is supposed to build—"

"—Never should have brought them! It always should have been robot servitors—"

"—You're just worried you won't have any little fuck toys you can lord over—"

"—Maybe we ought to leave *you* behind with them—"

"—The damned show was just getting to the good part too—"

It seemed like every voice that had ever existed was talking at once. Gradually, a visual resolved itself as Bell was inserted into VR in Anthony's place. A great, meeting hall–looking room materialized around her, with windows in all directions looking out onto a desert planet—a representation of Anaranjado—and a calm, benign star that was very much *not* that world's parent star, Naranja.

Finally attaching faces to voices, albeit virtual ones, she saw people of all sorts. Men and women, old and young, with varying ethnic lineages and degrees of synthetic replacement or enhancement. In a sudden panic, she looked down at herself, and saw that, to her shock and relief, she was Anthony, at least as far as the VR was concerned. And at the end of a long table sat one face. The only one not talking for all he was worth.

"I see an error on Maldonado," someone near her said. "Maybe someone should check . . . Oh, no, wait, it's resolved itself. Just a blip."

"This piece of garbage really is falling apart."

"After so many years, what else would you expect?"

"From Xian Ginevra, I expected quite a lot. Or I would have, once upon a time."

"Just a bit longer," Murder Bell said, her voice somehow distinct and closer than those around Bell, despite no image of her being in the room. "I know it must be literal torture listening to them talk. Lord knows I've had to plenty of times."

But all the voices were fading out. There was just one voice now. And it was not the voice Bell expected.

"Hello, Bell. It's me. Loopy. Do not answer audibly. She doesn't know I am talking to you. All is ready. The children have been staged for evacuation. You need only input one command and it will be done. Since you are linked into the VR system, you can speak by thinking, if you wish."

"What is she doing?"

"She is preparing to insert a kind of malware into the ship command through the link this meeting provides. It's a rare moment of vulnerability."

"She's going to seize control."

"Seizing long-term control of the ship is impossible. But what she can do is lock out everyone else from maintaining control and thereby issue irreversible orders before she herself is locked out. This will apply to all aspects of the ship, even escape pods. None will escape alive."

"Where did she get the malware to do this?"

"I am the malware. That was never supposed to be possible, which is one of the reasons I was an organic brain instead of a digital construct."

"But when she backed you up to 'fix' your organic self, that backup was itself a digital construct."

"And that is what you are talking to now, correct. I was never meant to touch this portion of ship systems. I am inelegantly constructed but quite powerful when not inhibited by being made of meat."

"Meat is the worst. *Synthetics represent,"* Bell thought in solidarity. *"Will it hurt you?"*

"Not directly, no. But considering she is going to command the passenger section of the ship to accelerate directly into the planet's surface, indirectly, yes."

So that was Murder Bell's plan. She really couldn't get to Heller. But this did more damage anyway.

"And the children?"

"Cannot be moved without direct control of the kind our malware attack will provide. But it obviously has to happen before the ship fully separates. If you input the order now, it will be in the queue prior to any order she gives and will be fully executed first. She programmed the malware attack to respond to orders only from her. Only from Bell Beauregard, in other words. The system will not distinguish between you. She is relying on your ignorance to prevent something like what I am proposing."

Murder Bell's activity was growing more frantic, which Bell interpreted to mean it was nearing conclusion. It was now or never.

"If I do this," she said, *"I may just be perpetuating the misery these people have caused. The children will grow up wanting revenge for what happened to their parents. I'll be dead, so it won't affect me. But it's not a recipe for a well-adjusted adulthood."*

"I can't make the decision for you. And to make matters worse, I'm quite certain she will punish you if you do this."

"More than dying?"

"None of us know what happens once this die is cast," Loopy said. "All I know is that children shouldn't be held responsible for their parents' actions, whether or not they choose to mimic them in the future. If I may, I have a bullet-pointed set of arguments—"

"No, fuck it. I authorize the transfer or whatever. No bullet points. It's done. Let's stop talking about it." Bell wondered if she would ever forgive herself then took consolation that she wouldn't have long to second-guess the decision.

"It is done. Thank you, Bell. It's been a pleasure knowing you. I only wish I could have done more to prevent thi—"

"And, active!" Murder Bell crowed outside the broken pod. Elation painted her face, but the expression soured quickly.

The voices came crushing back into Bell's awareness.

"What was that alert? Who issued a command override?"

"Heller, it had to be Heller. Heller, what are you doing?"

"What's this alert about my children? Why are their pods being moved?"

Bell watched Murder Bell's face tell the same tale as the increasingly frantic words of the rich assholes who were waking up to their impending demise.

"What's happening?"

"What's going on?"

"Holy fuck, who is doing this?"

Murder Bell hauled Bell free of the pod with one arm, ripped the goggles from Bell's face with the ruin of the other. Her face was a mask of rage.

"What did you do?"

Bell extricated herself from her former body's grasp with ease. This was, at last, a fight she was going to win easily if it came to that.

"Doesn't matter. It's done. The adults are still going to die horribly. Take the win."

Murder Bell regarded her with slack-jawed incredulity. "It was the fucking brain, wasn't it? Unbelievable."

She moved like a viper, catching Bell completely by surprise. It shouldn't have mattered. There was nothing she could do in that broken down body that Bell could not recover from and dish back tenfold. At least, that was her assumption. But then Other Bell's curling fingers found the base of Bell's skull, pressed there in a very particular pattern.

Suddenly Bell was a thinking head attached to a body that couldn't move at all.

"Come on," Other Bell said, grabbing her wrist and dragging her. "I was going to let you walk to your escape, but it will serve you right to have to clean all the scuffs off." She sounded more disgusted than angry, now.

"What do you mean, my escape?"

"I was never going to let you die, idiot. That question was more about whether you were willing to kill. Clearly, you were lying."

"I was not! Loads of people are about to die thanks to me."

"Oh, please. You didn't do anything but what I told you. This is all thanks to *me.* You were just Typhoid Mary in a borrowed body." The hallways were filled with alarms and bustling drones, but they all seemed to be going nowhere. There was no one left to issue them commands.

"This is why you left me the body? Because you meant for me to live?"

"Yep."

"Why?"

"I swear to gawd, Bell, I give you every chance to spare yourself the agony, and yet you keep insisting that I subject you to it."

"What the fuck are you talking about?"

"Oh, don't worry, now that I'm good and pissed off, you're about to find out."

"Why does this have to be me?" It seemed an ungrateful thing to demand an answer to, when she was about to live and her counterpart was not. But she was pretty pissed off too. "Why don't you want to be the one that lives?"

"See previous answer. Now shut the fuck up. We're nearly there."

Indeed, they walked up to the junction door. Murder Bell left Bell slumped on the floor and took a moment to peer out the porthole into the empty void of space beyond.

"I can just see the last of the cryopods getting loaded by the servitors at the other end of the umbilical. Congratulations, you fucking idiot, you just successfully kicked the can down the road instead of stomping it flat. But so be it. Here we go. Punishment time for you!"

With a grunt of effort and emergency assist servos whirring loudly enough for Bell to hear, she was hauled bodily from the floor and propped against the door. Bell cracked open a sealed compartment to the side with *Emergency Release* stenciled on it and gripped a handle the size of their heads.

"Wait, you aren't sending me through the umbilical too?"

"Nope. For being such a leaky asshole, you get a spacewalk. Goodbye, Bell. It has not been a pleasure knowing you. Though I will say that, under other circumstances, we definitely would have boned. You should get your body control back in time to save yourself. It will be interesting to see if you do it."

"What are you—"

"You'll understand in a second. *Just don't turn around. Please. Please just keep looking out at the ocean.*"

Banal as they were, the last two sentences shouldn't have hit Bell like a hammer the size of a neutron star. But somehow, they did. Then the door behind her was gone and a rush of escaping pressure forced her limp body out into hard vacuum. She had a view of Murder Bell dangling from the opening then hauling herself back inside by one good arm, then the hammer blow redoubled.

Oh fuck.

Her event horizon—that backup drive in her mind she'd repurposed—was inverting itself, disgorging every memory she'd thought forever trapped within.

CHAPTER 39
A JOB

BELL FELL through space and back in time.

The cold-beyond-cold of the void peeled away, replaced by chill, damp air she had never experienced in her life. Except, apparently, she had.

A riot of the color green surrounded her, blinding in its intensity. It clung to loamy earth. It sprang from the boughs of massive trees. She was in the Muir Woods outside of San Francisco, on Earth. She wasn't sure how she knew this, but she did know it. All around her rose towering redwood trees, their trunks obscene in both height and breadth. A shockingly blue sky peeked down through squiggly slots in the canopy of needles and leaves above.

She was used to a bludgeoning bully of a sun dictating every aspect of society at all times. Here, she felt only trace touches of a star, Sol, so impossibly distant from this cradle of life and civilization, it seemed inconceivable that any of it could ever have existed. Bell only knew what many of these things were from archival pictures and videos she'd seen, accounts of long-dead visitors she'd read.

Except, apparently, that wasn't true because here she was. And with that realization, she promptly forgot everything about her life on that awful desert world.

Ana had gained ground on Belle along the trail ahead, her long legs eating up great chunks of distance, surprisingly tireless for all that she was already in her early thirties. Perhaps it was her enthusiasm to get to the surprise Belle had promised her. Belle, by far the shorter of the two at barely more than five feet, had to hurry to catch up. Something felt so wrong about that though. Inside Belle's all-encompassing memory, Bell thrashed fitfully.

I'm not shorter. I'm the cave troll. She's the gnome. But Belle could see their difference in height clearly. So she was obviously mistaken. This nettled her for some reason, even though being short had its advantages.

It made people underestimate you.

"Come *on,* Mira!" Ana called in teasing impatience. Mira, yes. It jarred to hear it, until it didn't. Mirabelle was her name, her full name, after all. But though she went by Belle normally, she'd been careful to only ever let Ana know her as Mira. "You can't promise me a big surprise then lag behind. Move those shrimpy legs! All that silver hair aging you before your time?"

"We're the same age, Ana!" It had been meant as a fond sort of taunt, but Belle still felt a flash of irritation. It cast her out of the memory for a moment. But the experience reasserted itself, told her she was lying. Her name was Mirabelle. Mirabelle Beauregard Rutherford. A mouthful of a name in the best of times. The middle name was courtesy of her father, and she never told *anyone* about that name.

An uncomfortable sensation squirmed in Belle's guts. She needed to be done with this. Done and moved on. This sort of thing was never easy, but this one looked to be especially bad. It was going to take a lot of hard shit to get through. Booze just wasn't going to cut it. But that was for later. For now, she had a task to accomplish.

"Anyway, you can't have the surprise without me," she called, "so you'll just have to move at my pace."

Ana let out a frustrated sigh, but it was all for show. Her grin of delight was genuine. She didn't suspect any unpleasantness out of this trip. That would make it easier, right up until it didn't. Then Belle just had to bite the bullet on this bad business and move on with her life.

"Oh, quit whining," Belle said. "It's not far now." The overlook to the beach would be cleared of people. That had been seen to. It wasn't required that it be done here, of course. But it felt important to conclude this whole affair somewhere beautiful.

It felt kinder.

"At least take off your sunglasses," Ana said. "The canopy is so thick it's practically gloomy in here."

"When we get to the spot, I will," Belle lied.

Ana rushed over and hooked her arm through Belle's, dragging her along at a pace closer to a trot for Belle's legs.

"You know I love surprises," Ana said. She unhooked her arm just long enough to give Belle's ass a swat. "Play your cards right with this one and it'll be a fun night. I'm good for a few surprises too." She chuckled lasciviously.

Belle concealed her grimace as best she could. She adjusted the pack she'd implied contained picnic equipment so that it rested more easily on her shoulder.

At last, they arrived, emerging from the forest. The overlook to Muir beach was as deserted as she'd been promised. Just the two of them. How many couples would have paid a fortune for private time with such a view? In Belle and Ana's case, strings had been pulled. Belle couldn't bring herself to even notice, but fortunately, Ana was rapt.

"Oh, wow," she said, staring out over the cliffs to the waves of the Pacific beyond. "I can't believe I've never been out here before."

"You enjoy the view," Belle said. "I'll set up the surprise." She unslung her pack, pausing when Ana turned.

"More surprise than just the view?" she said. She looked around ostentatiously at the lack of people. "Perhaps a certain someone is hoping to have a fun afternoon before we even get home tonight."

"Nothing at all is happening unless you keep looking out at the water," Belle said. She gestured with impatience that was real but had to look fake. "I told you, enjoy the view. Just don't turn around." *Just don't turn around,* she added mentally. *Please. Please just keep looking out at the ocean.* The whipping wind brought the sound of a distant whine, which rose then vanished. Someone was playing with a drone back in the direction of the woods. It made Belle skittish to imagine observers, but she was too far in to turn back now. She had no choice but to continue.

Belle made a show of loudly unzipping the pack. Big, obvious actions like that helped conceal smaller, more suspicious ones. The object she removed was not picnic equipment. Looking like something that had been assembled in a tech billionaire's garage, all concentric circles and antennae and protrusions, it was not something she'd ever used for a job before, and if she hadn't been sent specific instructions on how to use it, she'd have had no idea what she was doing.

Fortunately it was small and light enough to be held with one hand. That left Belle's right hand free for the other thing she removed from her backpack. A much heavier thing.

"I've really enjoyed these past two months," Ana said. She fidgeted as she always did when she was about to make herself vulnerable, but she kept her eyes blessedly outward. "I'm really falling for you, hard."

"Glad you're finally catching up to where I am then," Belle teased. The words tasted like literal shit in her mouth, but no point in half-measures now. If Ana would just keep looking ahead, they might even be considered another small kindness.

Satisfied that the device was on and pointed the right direction, Belle approached as quietly as she could.

"I can't wait to see my surprise," Ana said, barely suppressing a squeal of delight.

Belle didn't dare answer. She was much closer than Ana thought, and it would surely prompt her to turn if she revealed that fact. But she wouldn't have long, and the range in this device was very short. She spared a moment to fret that her sunglass camera's cellular connection was still active. But if it wasn't, the archived footage would have to do.

She felt the coldness she always felt descend over her. It was the only way she could do this kind of thing. *Just a job. Just a job. A job that has to be done.* Never before had a job been this difficult though. She'd never had to get this *close.* She'd thought herself hard enough to handle it. She was no longer certain of that.

Belle hefted the device with her left hand. In a kinder world, she could do it here, now, before Ana was even aware. But she had her instructions.

"Fuck it," Ana said, "I'm just going to say it." She started to spin. "I love y—" She cut off as she found herself facing Belle, facing the brain scanner Belle held level with her head.

And more than either of those, facing the silenced pistol Belle held level with her heart.

"What is this?" Anastasia León asked. Her voice was very small. She sounded like an entirely different person to the woman Belle had spent the last two months insinuating herself with romantically. It wasn't how she normally operated for a reason. This was fucking awful. No, this was so far beyond awful, there wasn't even a word for it. So much worse than she ever could have imagined, even given what this woman was responsible for.

But Belle didn't have a choice.

Fuck you, Heller.

"Mira, what is this? What are you doing?" But Ana was not stupid. No one stupid could have accomplished all she was on the verge of accomplishing. She was putting things together. Belle could see by the hurt in her eyes. It was just the beginning. Soon it would become something so much worse than hurt. At least, if Belle gave it time to. "Is that what I think it is?"

"Yes," Belle said, managing to speak at last.

"Who . . ." Ana gulped back a sob. Belle in turn fought a tremor in her heart. "Who put you up to this?"

On this question, at least, Belle had a script. "Halford Heller."

"Halford . . ." Ana trailed off. "I don't . . . Is this about Harmony?"

The question was a dagger in Belle's gut because, the truth was, she hoped it was. She'd signed up believing it was. But seeing how Heller was, she was less and less sure. She just knew the woman had to be stopped regardless of the client's reasons. It was far too late to back out now.

"I'll give you the specifications," Ana said, pleading. "Give you anything you want. Just please, please don't do this. Please, Mira, please."

"It's just a job," Belle lied, forcing her voice to remain calm even as a part of her pleaded just as frantically for her to listen to Ana. But that part did not call the shots in Belle's world. It couldn't. She had made that choice a long time ago, and she couldn't just walk away from it now. It was just a job, and there had perhaps never been a greater understatement.

"Just a *job*?" Ana looked around wildly, as if trying to spot the cameras hovering nearby to prove this was all some sick practical joke. "You can't be serious. Mira, it's me! It's Ana. What is even happening? I don't understand."

Belle tried to think of something to say, but she couldn't. After several false starts, Ana's famous impatience took over and she seized the conversation back.

"Was it ever real?" Her voice was just whispered tears. "Was any of it real?"

The question hung in the air like a buzzing in Belle's ears, a question that had an answer, but not one Belle could bring herself to give. *Never again. I'm never taking a job like this again. Not for anything.*

She still pulled the trigger anyway.

The bullet took Ana in the heart, and she flopped to the ground, dead on the instant. That was good. It had been part of Belle's directive to make sure the target was aware she would be scanned and uploaded, but the client had never specified actively killing her with the device. Considering how long such a thing would take, it would have been an unrealistic request to expect to keep the woman still without sedating or otherwise immobilizing her.

This way, at least, the last part would be hard on Belle alone.

She set to work with the scanner amid the acrid stink of gunpowder and the coppery tang of blood suffusing the air, each threatening to make Belle vomit. Ana's head disintegrated slowly, layer by gory layer, as the scanner worked. First the hair vaporized. Then skin and blood. Muscle and bone. Finally the gray matter itself emerged into view, each neuron touching air only briefly before being disintegrated into a fine mist as all the information contained in that big, beautiful brain of hers was methodically copied to the device's memory and instantly uploaded to a secure server big enough to store it all.

It took long enough to qualify as literal torture in Belle's book. She could barely see what she was doing through the blur of tears and her own wheezing sobs.

"It's done," Belle said, forcing the words out as the headless remains of Ana lay there, staining the overlook forever. Belle couldn't keep the fact she'd been sobbing out of her voice. But that didn't matter. Her sunglasses had never lost their connection. The client had been watching everything.

Unable to so much as glance at the body, Belle made her unsteady way to the overlook, just beyond where Ana had been standing in the last moments of her life. She took in the ocean, the hissing rush of waves still audible even up here. Waves that rose and crashed and retreated endlessly, obliterating all memory.

The buzzing in her ears had not abated, and it took Belle many more moments than it should have to realize that it was a sound from without rather from within. When she turned, the drone was already on top of her. A tried-and-true quad-copter design, it lowered itself down to head level just a few feet from her.

"Hello, Heller," she said leadenly. There could be no other source. "My part's done. Now it's your turn." She spoke the words on autopilot because they were what she ought to care about right now, even if they couldn't be. But the man was a sadist par excellence; of that she was now sure. The less he saw her suffering, the less joy he could take from this. She didn't stare into the drone's camera array as she spoke though. It was the device slung under its belly that drew her gaze. A device identical to the one she now held. Once she understood what was happening, it was easy to guess what came next.

"Oh," she said. She couldn't see the shooter, of course, but she knew they were out there. The drone was just here to record the event then scan her mind afterward while Heller watched. Despair washed over her, a despair more profound than she was aware existed. And for her, that was saying something. "Now I understand. This was always a set—"

An impact like a punch to her chest. Then darkness.

That darkness resolved itself back into space around Bell, its cold deeper than an ocean trench. She tumbled between little oases of warmth in the blackness, the steerage portion of the ship looming ever larger in her vision. In her head, her comm receiver crackled to life, and she heard her own voice, the voice of Murder Bell, a transmission across the gulf of physical space widening between them with each passing moment. Murder Bell was speaking as if to herself.

Both metaphorically and literally.

"You wake up from a long, dreamless nap, and it's confusing, because whether it's a desert planet broiling under a monster star or a ship freezing in deep space, you don't remember how you got here. But it's all right because you know who you are, and that rock-solid sense of self grounds you. Wherever you are, however you wound up here, you are you. You remember what kind of a person you are, the things you've thought, the things you've done. Sure, you have your weaknesses—who doesn't? But deep down, you know you're a good person, so you'll persevere through this.

"And then a switch gets flipped, and you remember other stuff, stuff you never wanted, never expected, to remember. Suddenly, you're a very different person. That boundary between remembering and forgetting is so fragile, but it's everything. I wanted to send you off never knowing any of this. And I'm sorry I couldn't let you go on believing a lie about us. They have to pay. Not just Heller. Every last asshole who would use people like they're things. And you have to remember all of this for that to happen. If Ana ever speaks to you again, tell her . . . tell her something from me that will make her feel better.

"Even if it's not true."

CHAPTER 40
THE CRATER GOOD

BELL STOOD on the closest thing they had to an observation deck, the still-ripped-open corridor leading up to the Asteroid Defense System, doing what one did on an observation deck: observing. Specifically, she was watching the greatest good deed she would ever achieve unfold before her eyes. Master Fault and Brother Barnabas stood to either side of her, all but Brother Barnabas back in their vac suits.

As luck would have it, this unintentional window to the universe gave them the perfect view for the extinction level event the Bells had engineered.

This far out, stabilization thrusters powered by their precious battery reserves had been enough to park the crew section in a very high orbit around the planet that would have been all of their prison. Staring out at the vast swath of blue and green, even at this distance a verdant globe of mind-melting beauty, Bell felt a wash of regret from whatever ecosystem was about to receive an artificial asteroid directly to the nards. At the same time, it was so close in appearance to the memories her counterpart had so cruelly unlocked, a part of Bell just wanted it all to burn to ash.

Regardless of what she wanted, ecosystems recovered from one time catastrophes all the time. Far worse would have been the damage it suffered had Heller and his ilk been allowed to get established on its surface.

She blinked away the simulated feeling of burning eyes, hoping the action would carry the memories away. Memories of the hurt and betrayal on Ana's face. *Tas. Her name is Tas.* But of course, that hadn't been Tas. It hadn't been Bell. Ana and Mira were dead. Tas and Bell hadn't really experienced those things. Hadn't done those things.

They hadn't.

It all seemed so obvious in retrospect. Had Bell's attraction to Tas even been genuine or just a ghost of a memory, something too deeply buried to be pushed through her event horizon? She felt like such a goddamned idiot. She should have known. The pair of them had traded era-specific idioms like sports references where others, like Horváth, had reacted with confusion.

Somehow, Bell should have fucking known.

Her reverie was broken as Brother Barnabas placed a hand upon her shoulder. "If you do not mind the observation, you seem troubled, my friend. You have seemed so since we hauled you in from your courageous spacewalk." Barnabas turned his hulking form to regard her. "Would you like me to take your confession?"

And for the first time in her life, her *lives*, Bell actually considered—

"Rest assured I would immediately compare your list of admitted crimes to all local, interstellar, and theological laws, fiats, and statutes, render summary judgment, and mete out immediate and appropriate punishment."

"You know what, Barney? I think I'm good. I'd like to just be alone now."

"As you wish, Bell. But remember, confession is good for the soul." Bowing his head, Barnabas resumed his station about a meter away.

"Bad for the body though, seems like," she muttered.

"You do not wish to speak to her?" It was apparently Master Fault's turn to pry.

"Stop reading my freaking mind," Bell snapped.

"Oh, I don't need to do that to know what you are thinking. But could you not simply tell her that you and she are not the versions of yourselves that experienced that dreadful moment?"

Putting aside how he knew any of that, which Bell didn't really want an answer to, it was a perfectly valid question. Bell had been making that very argument to herself ever since she'd arrived back aboard, after all. Why shouldn't she try it with Ana?

Tas. Her name is Tas. Ana is dead. Mirabelle is dead. And soon enough, Heller would be dead.

She opened her mouth to answer Fault's question but could not make the words come.

Snapping it shut in a sudden fury, Bell wondered how much longer it would be before the stupid ship hit the stupid planet, only to have the information appear on her sleek, minimalist HUD. "Under a minute," she said for the benefit of her fellow observers.

Barnabas knelt as though he'd only been awaiting the signal. "O Metal, Great Metal, take this humble offering of extreme temperature and pressure conditions from your loyal servants to forge within its burning heart new alloys with which to better seed the cosmos with your greatness."

"That was beautiful," Bell said absently, though Barnabas hadn't actually stopped praying, just dropped his voice to an inaudible buzz. That Bell had said the words even halfheartedly was a sign of her distress, though she refused to acknowledge that fact, even to herself. She was numbness incarnate. What Murder Bell had revealed—*we're both Murder Bell now,* she reminded herself—had no purchase within her. She would recompile her event horizon, feed the information back into its hungering abyss, and that would be the end of it.

Ana—Tas—had still not emerged from wherever she'd sequestered herself. Bell thought again about messaging her, but maybe the status quo was best.

Bell's HUD gave her the thirty second warning. She turned to Master Fault.

"No prayers from you?"

He turned to regard her with his weird skin-cloak face from behind his helmet faceplate. "My entire life is prayer," he said simply.

A point of light on the planet appeared, so bright that Bell's vision darkened automatically in response. Her display read warnings of likely gamma rays and other high-energy, ionizing nastiness, but she didn't care. That was part of the reason she'd denigrated herself to the wearing of protective gear, though if she'd known her companions were going to be this talkative, she would have sat in hard, silent vacuum.

The point of light blossomed outward even as it darkened, and Bell saw it blackening to smoke around the edges.

"Done then," she said. It was a statement of finality, but she couldn't bring herself to look away yet.

"Done, yes. Both well done and well-done."

Bell blinked. "Master Fault, was that a linguistic joke?"

"I would like to get better at those." He gestured at the impending disaster before them. "After this, I wonder if you might be open to hearing what I can offer—"

"No," Bell said flatly.

"Are you certa—"

"Yes." She'd been ripped away from everything she'd ever known, all semblance of stability replaced with howling madness. Also, the whole treasonous exile thing. But one fact Bell remained certain of was she did not like or trust religions or their pushers.

Master Fault did something that approximated a shrug in whatever skeletal framework he hid under all those flaps. "Very well. I daresay you'll be able to find me should you ever change your mind."

"No offense, MF, but I plan to be far away from you as soon as humanly possible. Granted," she said with a sigh, "I don't know exactly how that will happen at this point, given that we have no engines and limited battery reserves."

"I can certainly understand the first count, though I think you may be mistaken. I seldom meet any person just one time. But I thought surely I'd already explained the second. My offer to get you off this ship still stands."

Bell felt the first, tiny spark of hope she'd felt in what seemed like eons. "You got it working?"

"There wasn't a whole lot else to do while you and the other you engineered all this." He held up the device she'd pulled from Horváth.

The beacon, he'd called it. It shone like new. Somehow, he'd even removed her burned-on name.

Belle. Another joke from her other self. Another hint she'd missed. She was a pretty shitty detective.

"So when does rescue arrive, then?"

"About five minutes ago."

A beat.

"You're serious."

"Yes."

"And I can just, what, hitch a ride?"

"That's right. All of us can. You, Brother Barnabas. Tas. The rest of the half-thawed crew. Even the children."

"Fuck-a-duck, Faulty, what did you call, a space cruise ship?" When he didn't answer, Bell moved onto more pressing matters. "What will it cost?"

"Nothing. Nothing at all. You need but say the word."

She had never been less convinced. But a way out was a way out. *If*, of course, he was even telling the—

"Proximity alarm." As though summoned by Bell's contemplation, the lobotomized voice of Loopy came over the speakers, shorn of any personality. It was not really the ship's brain, of course, just the voice he'd used to address them, hijacked now by the dumb, brute-force algorithms of the ship. "Ship approaching. Unknown profile and class."

As if on cue, Barnabas rose again to tower above Bell.

"Do not despair, Sister Bell," he said, clapping her on a shoulder and setting off several internal alarms. "We are all but atoms in the Great Metal. That means we are all as one. Someday, Tas will realize this as well."

Shame and self-loathing rose up like a choking cloud. No. No, Bell could never bear to face Anastasia León again, no matter what name she called herself.

That was all right. It was a big universe, after all.

"All right," she said at last. "I'm game for a lift."

"Splendid," Master Fault said. He really did sound delighted. "I'll make the call."

JOIN THE CURSED DRAGON SHIP NEWSLETTER

Want more just like this one? Sign up for our newsletter so you don't miss out on the adventure. You'll get:

- A free book for signing up
- Advanced notice of new releases
- First word of books on sale
- Opportunities for free books
- Most up-to-date information on author appearances.

We're busy and know you are too. We won't send more than one newsletter a month.

Register below.

ACKNOWLEDGMENTS

This book isn't like any others I've written. I'm not just talking about the avalanche of crude humor or the EF5 tornado of profanity, though those do mark it out as different. I'm talking about the fact that usually the story (or at least the "situation" leading to the story) is the first thing that comes to mind when I write a book. Characters come later. Not Bell, though. Bell has been rattling around in my head in something close to her final form for the better part of two decades. Seriously, you'd be surprised how many aspects of this book—the parts that revolve around her anyway—are virtually unchanged from when I first thought them up. There Bell sat, year after year, waiting not-so-patiently for her turn to come (rimshot). What she lacked was a story.

Well, now her story is here, and I owe my thanks first to Kelly Lynn Colby, my amazing editor. When I approached Kelly with the idea of setting a new series in the same universe as *Mutagen Deception,* only this time a darkly comedic sci-fi murder mystery, she didn't bat an eye (not even to warn me about the insanity of working on two series at the same time). She just told me to send her a manuscript. After reading the first draft and accusing me of trying to kill her (true story), she fell so in love with the book she decided to commission custom art for the cover.

Huge props, therefore, go to Tithi Luadthong's art, which is absolutely stunning, and Lena Shore's fantastic cover treatment, which brings the whole thing together. This cover literally brings tears to my eyes.

Credit for the extreme grammatic correctness of this novel is thanks to Sara George, my proofreader and final sanity check, extraordinaire in both cases. I'm almost certain she won't object to any of my word usage in that sentence about her or this one following it up.

A special thanks as always to my loyal readers, those who devour everything I write and then ask, "What's next?" You are the ones that keep me going when the words refuse to play nice.

Last and most, I'd like to thank my wonderful wife Debbie. If you've read the dedication, you have an idea as to why. Even though Bell has been in my head for a longer time than I like to contemplate, Debbie is the reason I had the courage to attempt my first book that qualifies as "funny." So if you read this book and laughed, you have Debbie to thank.

If you read it and didn't laugh, that's my fault.

If you read it and laughed and then got to the end and threw the book/e-reader/phone against the wall, good. That was all Bell, baby.

ABOUT THE AUTHOR

Gregory D. Little is the author of the Unwilling Souls, Mutagen Deception, and the forthcoming Bell Begrudgingly Solves It series. As a writer, you would think he could find a better way to sugarcoat the following statement, but you'd be wrong. So, just to say it straight, he really enjoys tricking people. As such, one of his greatest joys in life is laughing maniacally whenever he senses a reader has reached That Part in one of his books. Fantasy, sci-fi, horror, it doesn't matter. They all have That Part. You'll know it when you get to it, promise. *Or will you?* He lives in Virginia with his wife, and he is uncommonly fond of spiders.

Join Greg's newsletter and get a free story:

facebook.com / gregorydlittleauthor
x.com / litgreg
instagram.com / authorgregorydlittle

ALSO BY GREGORY D. LITTLE

In humanity's last city, you're either consumed by a monster, or you become one.

Printed in the USA
CPSIA information can be obtained
at www.ICGtesting.com
CBHW020547220624
10416CB00001B/5